A Little Ladykilling

A Little Ladykilling

by Victoria Webb

THE DIAL PRESS *NEW YORK*

Published by
The Dial Press
1 Dag Hammarskjold Plaza
New York, New York 10017

"The Man with the Blue Guitar" by Wallace Stevens.
© 1937 by Wallace Stevens, published by Alfred A. Knopf.
Quoted by permission.

Manufactured in the United States of America
Second Printing—1982

Design by *Paul Chevannes*

Library of Congress Cataloging in Publication Data
Webb, Victoria.
A little ladykilling.
I. Title.
PS3573.E199L5   813'.54   81-12626
ISBN 0-385-27413-0   AACR2

For Nicole, Nina, Lily, and Jessica

Chapter I

My fifteen-year-old Porsche was boosting along the Bayshore Freeway on the outskirts of Daly City. It's a flat industrial stretch: spools of cable, sections of pipe, and scrap heaps, with an occasional overpass ringed by gas and food emporiums. A good place to drive on radar, while thinking about recipes or clothes, or your next vacation. Up ahead I saw a slot developing between a bus and a Volkswagen. To reach it, I had to wriggle past a dinosaur from Detroit, a smoke-gray Chrysler with tinted windows. As I went by, I caught a flash in the sun. The rear door was opening, and something fluttered. I glanced into the side mirror.

What I saw was a life-size doll, tumbling over and over, then spinning from the impact of a bumper and flipping once, fast, under the wheels of a second vehicle. It was a moment or two before I grasped that the doll was human, and by that time I could see the cars behind trying to stand on their radiators, and I could hear the squall of rubber. For another second I was paralyzed. The tumbling of the loose-jointed body replayed in my mind like an unshakable dream image. Then I touched my own brakes and swerved to the shoulder, nearly clipping some farmer who was bungling along in an old pickup, oblivious to the world.

When I passed him again, trying to put the pedal through the floor, it was too late.

The Chrysler had vanished through the slot between the bug and the bus, and a station wagon had dropped

back to make it three in a row. I whammed past the row
of startled faces on the right wall of the bus, my outside
wheels spewing gravel. Traffic was moderate, staggered
through all three lanes. I stitched through the pattern,
the Porsche whining like a hornet. At an exit ramp a
quarter of a mile away I thought I saw a gray sedan peel
off. But the ramp bent to the right and disappeared behind buildings. By the time I got to the stoplight and could
see all three ways at the intersection there was no sign of
the Chrysler.

"P'lice depah'mun."

The voice was monumentally bored. A periodic blip informed me that the conversation was legally being re-
corded.

"I'd like to report a death. Possible murder."

"Yeah?" There was the barest flicker of interest.

"Yeah."

"Stay on the line, ma'am. Somebody be right with you."

Somebody was not right with me. Instead, there was a
sound along the wires like a million eggs frying. I stared
through the wall of my glass cubicle at a parking lot,
watching soundless doll-people get in and out of their cars.
An intuition told me that I was starting something I wasn't
going to like, and I half regretted the quick glance into
my rearview mirror.

"Hello, may I help you?" This voice was deeper and
had been through high school.

"I hope so. I'm trying to report a possible homicide."

There was a pause, while the eggs fried. "Would you
please give your location and . . . ?" There was another
brief pause. I could sense him rummaging through the
pages of the procedures manual. The one he carried between his ears. "I mean your name, location, and describe
the circumstances."

"My name is Stella Pike. I'm at the El Dorado exit off
the Bayshore. A Union Seventy-six station. I was on my
way to San Mateo and just past the Candlestick exit when

I saw somebody roll out of a car. The vehicles following me struck the person. I think it was a woman."

"Just a minute." There was a click and some fast electronic music. I shifted my weight. The sun was turning the glass booth into a passable sauna.

"Hello?"

"I'm still here."

"We've got a report coming in on this. It was an accident. One fatality. There are officers already at the scene. They're taking care of it."

"That's nice. But what if—"

"You say *fell* from a car? The patrolman indicates the subject ran in front of oncoming traffic. Did you strike the subject with your vehicle?"

There was a thread of stern attention in the voice now. I shut my eyes and used a couple of seconds to bank my rage for future use. "No, I did not strike the subject. I *saw* the subject—" I stopped. The recorder beeped a timely warning. "I caught a glimpse in the mirror. I believe she was tossed out of a gray Chrysler, late model, doing about sixty-five."

"Ah. Heavy traffic?"

It was all over. I knew by his intonation. Another dizzy broad. Too much cooking sherry. But he took my number and told me an investigator would call me back. I considered throwing a tantrum but dismissed the idea. It would only confirm his diagnosis. And I was feeling the numb weariness that follows a powerful hit of emotion. So I hung up and quickly dialed my boss, Alfred Garabedian, of Garabedian, Daugherty, and Bissel, Public Relations and Marketing Research, or How to Win Friends by Ripping Them Off.

"Where have you goddamn been?"

Gabby had a high, nasal voice with the kind of edge that could cut through fifty thousand fans cheering a touchdown run. I held the receiver a foot away.

"Witnessing a murder."

"*What?*"

"Gabby, you endanger the human eardrum. Very delicate mechanism. If you don't shout, I'll talk to you."

"What is goddamn going on?" He dropped a few decibels and put in a touch of manufactured concern.

"I think I saw somebody killed. I think I will go to the trouble of not forgetting it. In practical terms, I'm taking the day off."

"Stella, just tell me, sweetheart, what the hell is going on? Who got killed? Are you all right?"

"Fine, Gabby. Not killed. I don't know who. I just happened to see it. Or think I saw it. And I can't get it out of my head right now. Okay?"

Gabby was a first-class slave-driving dollar-squeezing sexist SOB, but his little bald head contained great shrewdness about the quirky mechanism we call the personality. He heard in my voice the traces of a real shock.

"Goddamn it, the Tyson and Allen people want their report today, but all right. You get some rest. I need you. Don't hell around."

"I don't hell around, Gabby."

"Not with me anyway."

"I'll call you in the morning. And thanks, boss. I really, *really* appreciate—"

"All right, all right. This is costing me money. I am hanging up. Good-bye." Click.

I smiled to myself and replaced the receiver. All you needed to handle Gabby was a quick burst of slightly damp gratitude. He couldn't stand sentiment himself, being in the business of selling it.

When I got back to the Porsche, which I had parked near the pump block, I heard a man talking to the attendant about the "accident." He was about fifty, soft around the middle, dressed in the salesman's standards—wide-check flairs and bright solid green jacket.

"Jeez, she was a mess. I tell you, man, if I hadn't been through Korea, I coulda been sick. Brains, blood, everything. And the guy in the Datsun that rear-ended the van was not in too good shape neither. I shit you not. Pardon me, lady."

I nodded and smiled. "It's all right. I don't speak French."

That was a lie, but it got a laugh. Already we were friends. "I was tellin' him about this horrible accident I seen back there. Woman run out on the freeway, and was she ever—"

"I know. I was there."

"Whaddya mean?" He had lost his smile. Upstaged. I hurried to restore our bond.

"That is, I saw the cars stacking up in my rearview mirror. What happened?"

"Well, I was just toolin' along, you know, on my run." He made expansive gestures. "And saw this terrific jam-up. I carry flares and a first-aid kit—my business you gotta . . . lot of traveling—so I stop and have a look. From what's left of the chick—lady—she was a Mexican lady—I can see she was hit several times. *Bad.* The people that got there first said she just ran right out on the pavement. Whammo."

"Really?" I put a fingernail under my chin.

"Yeah. I talked to this guy—Phillips was his name, I think, works for Crocker—and he ran over her leg before he could stop. Guy was white as a sheet. Even though she was sure as—I mean, for certain already dead. Said she just bounced right out in front of him."

I shook my head and tsked.

"Crazy people. Every loose nut in the country winds up on this coast. Continental tilt." While he laughed at his own joke, the attendant and I traded a quick look.

"I mean, did anyone see her *running?*"

He looked at me blankly. "Like I said, she just bounced out there. Ran? Who knows? Walked maybe. Or staggered. Somebody said you could smell tequila through the blood."

"Did you see her walking or just standing by the free-way?" I had dropped the pose of casual interest.

"Hey, what are you, a lawyer?" The man put up his hands, palms out. "I didn't see nothin', except one dead Mexican lady. Period. And my guess is you couldn't collect a dime on her."

"Just curious," I said. "Sorry."

The attendant rammed the press over a credit card and sales slip. With a flourish, the salesman recovered his plastic and filed it back in his wallet. "Not a dime," he repeated, and got into his station wagon. "She was loaded. Smashed. Hey, that's a joke." He laughed, but we didn't join him. "Too bad. Anyway, keep cool." He hit his horn and drove away.

"Thank you for watching my car," I said.

"Welcome, ma'am." The attendant was very black, and very beautiful, and gave me the kind of generous smile that let me know he thought I was one of the good things in life, too. "Come again."

"I probably will," I said, waved politely, and climbed back into the Porsche.

When I passed the scene of the collisions, things had gone back to what passes for normal: a scatter of bright glass fragments, the red spark of one flare still burning, a couple of black-and-white patrol cars on the shoulder. The cops lounged against their fenders, chatting. Traffic whizzed by. Somewhere in the city twisted junk and broken bodies were being unloaded for recycling or disposal. Sweet California.

Chapter II

I did not go home but to the Jolly Roger, a quiet bar on Clement Street where I often attempted to do my serious thinking. Danny looked up from washing a manhattan glass and grinned.

"Hello, sweet stuff. What's up? You quit already?"

I shook my head. He pointed questioningly at the Chivas Regal on the shelf, and I nodded.

"Fired?"

"Nope."

"Then to what honor does we owe this visit by your beautiful person?"

I watched the whiskey tumble into a boiling blast of soda.

"For an ungrammatical Irishman you make absolutely the best dollar drink this side of the Golden Gate."

"Don't change the subject, beautiful. How come you ain't at work, like normal people?"

"I got, as they say, a problem. But private, Danny. On this one I can't use your shrewd advice. Not yet anyway."

"Some guy?"

I laughed. "No such luck."

"All right. You know what I always say. If these other bozos don't know a beautiful lady when they see one, I do. I take you any day."

I smiled. "I'm keeping you in reserve, Danny. You're too sweet for every day."

His broad, homely face turned wistful. "Yeah. They always used to say that." He gave a little salute of dismissal and moved down the bar toward a couple of the steadies, who were already locking into their stools for a long day. I sipped the drink. It was like a draft of cold smoke. It reminded me of something. I glanced at the clock on the wall. Twelve thirty. Early, even for alcoholics.

The salesman at the service station had said the woman smelled of liquor. She was hit at around ten thirty, maybe eleven. It takes an hour or so to get looped. How many bars opened at nine o'clock? Or maybe she drank at home. Or maybe somebody poured a bottle over her before she was kicked out of the speeding automobile. Would anyone think of such a thing? I had suspicions.

My job with Garabedian, Daugherty, and Bissel encouraged suspicions, as well as a general cynicism about human frailty. I was what is euphemistically called a market research specialist. That is, a spy.

Market research specialists are hired to conduct what are known as depth interviews. In a depth interview, one appears to be asking questions for a harmless survey. In fact, one is probing for hidden attitudes, prejudices, anxieties—the kind of information that can be exploited for profit. An example: the Chamber of Commerce of a small city across the bay hired our firm to find out just how upset local businessmen would be at a rezoning of certain districts. The result of the rezoning would be a wave of low-income families. Federal funds, on the other hand, were available for "renewal" projects in such rezoned areas. Several members of the chamber, as it happened, were in the construction business.

So I put on a low-cut dress, spiked heels, and eye shadow and made the rounds: lunches and cocktails with mid-range executives and small owners, conducting a poll (I said) on something inane like "Whither Business in the Eighties?" After the completed questionnaire was stuffed in my briefcase, but just before he broke down on a third martini and lunged for my cleavage or launched the tale of his empty marriage, I would contrive to lead the client into a digression on matters of race and class. A few idle, leading questions, and I would know where your average floor manager stood on the issue of poor or dark-skinned neighbors. Usually he occupied a position just a little to the right of Mussolini.

A sordid business. There were times when I almost wished I were back modeling or even stewardessing. There, at least, hypocrisy was open, part of the job. The lechers leched in a ritualistic way; I could respond with smiles of saccharin and vitriol. But being a waitress six miles in the air was not very interesting. And there was a little extra challenge in the kind of mind burglary I was doing. Every so often I ran into a very sharp cookie who knew the game, too. The things I then found out about the human character were worth knowing. Also, I cultivated an observant habit of mind. I knew from listening to the salesman, for example, that the woman who was killed was Mexican, young, and drunk—or made to appear so. I also knew something even more valuable. I knew that probably everyone else at the scene had bought the theory of "accidental" death. The burden of proof. I had enough burdens already.

"Another?"

I looked up. Danny had very pale blue eyes with sad pouches under them and a road-map face that somehow combined utter cynicism and complete sympathy.

"I think not, Danny."

"Good. What's botherin' you? And if it ain't my business, say so."

I started to tell the truth and then thought better of it. However I phrased it, it would sound melodramatic. And there was always a chance that the unidentified lady had bolted from the car on her own, and the driver—husband, lover, boss?—had gotten scared and sped away. An odd sort of hit-and-run. Anyway, there was maybe a more personal and immediate issue.

"Do you think a person should ever mind another person's business?"

Danny considered the ceiling briefly, then the bar. The corner of his mouth lifted. "Nope."

"That's what I thought." I slid the empty glass into his big palm. "Good advice, Doctor. I think I'll take it." I stood up.

"Doctor should take his own medicine. See you later?"

"Tomorrow maybe. Ta-ta."

"Ta."

I went back to my apartment and ran a large tub of very hot water. Nested in the mounds of bubbles, I could finally get my mind off what I had seen on the freeway. Next to bars, bathtubs are my best environment for serious daydreaming.

What had been more or less on my mind for a few days was a young man named Webster, who had been rather badly shaken when I decided to call off our—up to that point—very casual relationship. Besides being filthy rich, Webster was pleasant and attentive and amorous—sometimes, in fact, quite unquenchable—but his solicitous ways wore thin after a few weeks. I had tried to keep things basic: the occasional dinner, movie, and bed. But Webster contrived flowers and phone calls at every opportunity. He even wrote me bad poetry. I saw he was getting in deeper than he knew and tried to cut things off neatly, but apparently I waited too long.

I sighed. The last time around, I had been on Webster's end of it. An actor, with a glorious command of the English tongue and a very small, hard heart, had put me through a bad couple of months. My work, however, had gone splendidly, as it often does when the rest of life is wretched. I had turned up some information on an estate sale that allowed a client to make a small fortune, and his gratitude was now safely in my savings account. Webster and I had talked around the edges of a trip to the Orient. The idea still had appeal for me. I knew they had wonderful hot baths in Japan. And tea. And jasmine. And white monkeys. And Toshiro Mifune.

The phone rang.

I grabbed a green silk robe and jammed my feet into a pair of clogs. I made it by the third ring.

"Yes?"

"Yeah, this Missuz Stella Pack?"

"Pike."

"What?"

"My name is Stella Pike. No 'missuz.' And I'm in the middle of my bath. Could you—"

"Yeah, well, this is Inspector Berrigan. You're the one called about the accident on the Bayshore?"

"That's right."

"Just what was it you wanted to report, ma'am?"

I realized I was going to have to start all over again, from scratch. If so, I intended to be comfortable.

"Would you mind holding for a moment?" I put the receiver on the coffee table and went back for a towel. Wrapped in the robe, with the towel for a turban, I felt better able to cope.

"I thought I saw a woman thrown from a gray sedan. A Chrysler, I think."

"Where was this, ma'am?"

"I gave all this information once."

"Just verifying, ma'am."

I stuffed a stray curl back under the towel in exasperation. "On the Bayshore. Near the Candlestick exit. About ten thirty this morning."

"Would you describe exactly—"

"I was proceeding south, doing about sixty-five. I had just passed the gray sedan when I saw the rear door on the driver's side open. Some clothing—something blue or perhaps violet—fluttered, and when I looked in the rear-view mirror, I saw a body on the roadway. The next car or two struck it."

"Do you feel the subject was already unconscious or dead?"

"I couldn't say. I'm telling you what I saw."

"You did not actually see the subject leaving the other automobile?" The voice, a low and solid one with a faint trace of some accent, had become flat and matter-of-fact; the robot tone indicated a mind no longer open.

"I don't know if I did or didn't. *Something* left that automobile. Would you mind if we referred to the person as a human being, instead of a subject?"

There was a brief pause.

"Sure. We think, Missuz Pike, that this human being ran into the road. Nobody else saw any gray sedan. A lot of people did see her being hit by oncoming cars. She hadn't been dead for more than ten minutes when the ambulance arrived. But we'll keep checking. Could I have your full name and address again?"

I sighed and recited it. "I suppose you discount the idea of murder?"

Again the pause. "We just go by the facts, lady. We get two, three corpses a day in here. We do what we can. We'll talk to this lady's family, see if we can locate anybody who saw her that morning. Get back to you if we need you. Thanks."

"Sure." We hung up. If I knew the bureaucratic mind, as I did, I had heard the final professional opinion on my theory of the case. *Forget it, sister.*

I began dressing, feeling pretty glum. The thin margin of cheer I could usually count on after a hot bath had already vanished. Danny was undoubtedly right. Minding one's own business was the first condition of a calm, well-balanced existence. Maybe I had misinterpreted what I saw. Could someone have thrown something—a wrapper or rag—at the exact moment when, behind me, the woman stumbled onto the asphalt? But if she had been walking on the shoulder of the freeway, I couldn't have missed her. The salesman had implied no one else had reported seeing her there either. She had come out of that gray Chrysler. I was sure of it. So? I tried telling myself I had done my best, reported things to the proper authorities, and so on. The trouble was, I had no faith in authorities. As I was mulling these matters over, I was selecting a wine-colored pantsuit, black silk blouse, and white scarf for the afternoon. Comfortable enough to walk or run in, but stylish enough to get me into offices.

I put my hair in a ponytail with a tortoiseshell and ivory

clip, gave my lips a touch of gloss, and dabbed a little perfume at ears and wrists. Then I stood in front of my full-length bedroom mirror and allowed myself a few seconds of vanity. At twenty-seven I didn't show a lot of wear. I still danced three times a week, walked the hills of San Francisco whenever possible, and was rather an ectomorph by nature anyway. It was a good body. Perhaps a little on the boyish side, but with some compact regions that only the very myopic could misinterpret. The face had perhaps too much bone. That used to get me modeling jobs, but I was not emaciated enough to meet the highest standards of the trade. I could pass for a flashy shopgirl looking for something better, a very low-key hooker, or an aspiring, trendy young professional. Gabby had once described the knack of spying—"research" is his term—as the ability to look like everybody else, only more so.

I had a vague plan for the afternoon. I would get the newspaper as soon as it hit the stands and find out the official version of the "accident." I could cruise the Bayshore once more. Perhaps I had missed a bush or embankment that could have screened the woman's approach. I would phone my ex-husband, who was a very sage lawyer, and make a date for a professional opinion. And that, I hoped, would be the end of it. Back to real life.

I winced and turned from the mirror to pick up my purse. *Stella,* I thought, *your life is too much with you, late and soon. You might have married Bill, the basketball ace. Or that tool-company executive who wanted to take you away from TWA. No bad dreams about rag dolls. No dubious skills of dissembling. Nothing on your mind but new drapes or pineapple cheesecake. Gag.*

It always sorted itself out the same way. I was born with a powerful yearning to know what was around the next bend. Or, as an analyst I once went to put it, I had an abnormally low boredom threshold. He tried to get me to knit.

I did a quick check on my purse: wallet, gloves, Kleenex, keys, hairbrush, nail file, hand mirror, checkbook, note pad, and a half dozen pens. I was equipped. I picked a wool blazer from a hook in the hall and was just closing the apartment door softly behind me when the phone rang again. I hesitated, tried to steel myself to ignore it, and failed. I left the door ajar and went to the phone.

"Hello?"

"This Missuz Pike?"

"*Stella* Pike, yes."

"Lieutenant Hand here. Calling about your report on the accident on the Bayshore? You the one?"

"I'm the one. But I'm afraid you're repeating yourself. I've given the information already."

"Yeah. We have your call in. But we'd like to talk to you some more. Would you describe—"

"Look, Lieutenant Hand, I don't mean to tell you how to run your department, but you just called me twenty minutes ago and I—"

"Who called?"

"Inspector Berrigan."

A pause. "No Inspector Berrigan on the force, ma'am. You don't mean Beeman? Sergeant Beeman?"

"Look, I spoke to an Inspector Berrigan. He took my name. And—" I stopped. All at once, with a quite substantial little jolt in my tummy, I understood. Because this time I heard the little beep again. In the earlier call there hadn't been any.

"You must be mistaken, ma'am. I'm in charge of this investigation. No Berrigan working for me. Hello? You still there?"

"I'm still here. Wondering who goes around pretending to be a cop. Do you have a badge number, Officer Hand?"

"Yes, I do." The voice was frigid. Before that it had been rather a nice voice, medium pitch and clean attack. "Seven-four-one-three."

"Good, seven-four-one-three. But rather than deal with any more mystery voices or numbers, I would like to present some testimony directly. If we can arrange that. Could we arrange that?"

"Lady, this is a routine accident report, except for some notion you have. We have eyewitness material on this accident, taken at the scene. If you have something concrete to add, I'd be happy to see you here at the Mission Street station tomorrow morning at ten. If you change your mind in the meantime—"

"Sorry, Lieutenant Hand. I'm afraid you're stuck with a dissenter. I'll be there at ten. I hope. Good-bye."

I hung up and stood for a moment, trying to stop my mind from racing over the implications of that elaborate fake call. And I had gone for it like a starved carp. Me, who was in the deep angling trade myself. There was a small sound behind me.

When I turned, there was a man standing just inside the open door. I jumped in spite of myself. Jumped in the direction of my middle dresser drawer.

"I di'n' mean to scare you, miss. I was passing in the hall and saw the door open. Maybe something wrong, I thought." He laughed soundlessly. His eyes were skating all around the room, probing, noting. He was a small man, compact, in an expensive blue suit that fitted him like a sheath. He was tanned, with a thin mustache and a twist of hair at the deep notch of his open collar. "Everything okay?" He took another step into the room.

"Fine." I took three steps, reaching the dresser and laying a hand on it in what I hoped was a natural gesture. I had done something very stupid. You never leave your door open in this city. Never, never, never. He lifted his foot to advance again. "That's far enough. I'm just on my way out. Going away for several weeks. If you will please—"

He started gliding forward and talking at the same time. "Maybe you need a ride? I can drop you off. I like—"

Out in the hall the elevator door opened, and I heard voices. His eyes slid away from my face, wary.

"Stop right there. Now get out of my apartment. I won't tell you again."

He looked at me for a couple of seconds, and I noticed a peculiarity of his eyes. They looked a lot like holes. He smiled broadly again. "Sure." He moved back to the door with a light, quick tread. "Have a good trip, miss." I heard the faint wheeze of his laugh just before the handle clicked shut.

My hand came out of the drawer with the little .32. I spun the cylinder to a live cartridge, released the safety, and then went to bolt the door.

Chapter III

"You're still cute." Frank dropped into the cushioned booth opposite me. "Can I pick you up?"

"I'm a little tired of that sort of thing and particularly not up to it today. All right?"

"All right. Only joshing." He looked at me quizzically. He was aptly named. Forthright, engaging, competent—everything the family lawyer should be. He was still cute, too. A trim thirty-four, gray at the temples, with eyes of Bunsen-burner blue. I remembered all of a sudden why I had married him. He listened. He waited now, big brown hands folded neatly on the table, ready to hear.

I pushed the newspaper around so he could see the item I had circled. It was only a few lines.

PEDESTRIAN CRUSHED ON FREEWAY

Rosa Esposito, 25, of 1731 Peralta Drive, was struck and killed by traffic on the Bayshore Freeway Tuesday morning. She was an employee of Start Over, the county rehabilitation program, but had not reported for work for several days, according to program officials.

Motorists said Esposito ran in front of oncoming cars. Police said an autopsy is being conducted to determine if the woman had been drinking.

"A friend?" Frank selected his expression of concern and comfort.

"No. I saw it happen. I thought she was pushed out of another car. Caught it out of the corner of my eye."

He gave a little humming grunt that I recognized as a

sign of real interest. The waitress had arrived, garbed—
or rather ungarbed—in North Beach flimsy, and he ordered a Gibson.

"Go on."

I told him everything I remembered: the opening door,
the flutter of clothing, the salesman's story, the call to the
police.

"They didn't seem overjoyed to hear from me. Then
somebody called back pretending to be a cop and suckered
me for my name and address. A couple of minutes later
a guy showed up at my apartment to case the place. A
creepy little person with holes for eyes."

The grunt again, louder. "How do you do it?"

"Get into these things? Gosh, Captain America, I was
just driving to work, minding my own business—"

"You know you always get flip when you're upset?"

I didn't have to answer that one because the waitress
flounced up with his drink.

"I'm wondering how they found out you called the police. And if they knew your number, they could have gotten your address without phoning."

"They wanted to know if I was home—and whether I
had changed my story."

"Ah." He nodded, combining the old uneasy apprecia-
tion for my deductions with the solider one of his first sip
of cold lightning. "You know—"

"I know. I should have been a lawyer."

We smiled at that old and slightly bitter joke.

"They were probably surprised I was sticking to my
theory. I guess I'm the cantankerous one in a hundred.
But there's obviously some kind of foul play, don't you
think?"

He didn't say anything for a while. He turned his glass
around a time or two, then looked away into a far corner
of the room.

"Drop it, Stella. That's my advice. I don't want you
hurt."

"I'm not involving you in this, Frank. I just want a

professional opinion." I put an edge into the statement, to make it easier for him. It didn't work.

"You already *have* involved me. I take responsibility for my own feelings." I tried to stare him down and lost. In the terminal stages of our marriage there had been a hard time when both of us pretended not to care anymore. We failed.

"Okay. But let's get it clear that you can stay out of all this. Your life is your own, remember?"

He smiled quickly, covering an old hurt. "I remember. Okay. So ask for the professional opinion, and let's get on with it."

"Suppose I go down to meet Lieutenant Hand—he's the *real* cop—and give testimony tomorrow. Suppose I keep hassling him, insisting on an investigation, go to the hearings, inquest, et cetera. What happens?"

"You say no one else can corroborate your story?"

"As far as I know. The man at the gas station was there in the midst of the pileup. He said nobody questioned the going explanation."

"And you yourself say it was a flutter, in peripheral vision." He sipped from his glass, and I caught a flicker of amusement in his eyes. "I could tear you apart in a cross-examination."

"You have, a time or two."

We both grinned.

"I take it you wouldn't hold out much hope."

"A little less than none. They'll treat you as a kooky female. They'll fill out the forms and put you through a deposition, but they won't do any real work on it."

"Suppose I do the work?"

"Sue Spade, private eye?"

I got mad. One of those sudden flashes from coals you thought were long cold. Frank always had a habit of treating any independent move of mine as an ironic aberration.

"You'd rather I joined you? Avoid too many questions about some lush who gets flattened one morning on an otherwise nice drive? No fat fees in that, are there, Frank?"

He went pale under his tan, and the face he hastily tried on—the impassive, detached expert handling a furious client—slipped badly.

"That wasn't fair, Stella."

"Neither were you. I am *not* Humphrey Bogart in skirts."

He sighed and motioned to the waitress with the empty glass. "Objection sustained. I apologize. This has gotten to you, hasn't it?"

"Well, it hasn't been one of my everyday days. I see a woman bashed to pieces in the morning, get sinister fake calls and strange men in my apartment in the afternoon, and my friends tell me I'm being unreasonable, if not foolish. A person could get discouraged."

He reached across the table and took my hand. "Christ. Then I start needling you. I'm sorry."

"It's all right. I like the challenge." As the waitress came up, I replaced his hand on the table. "And enough of that. I'm weak there, you know."

He bowed his head briefly, a sort of awkward, gentlemanly gesture that I always liked. "So am I. Onward then. I meant, there is something in all this you have to work out, no?"

"No. I was ready to drop it until the little visitor showed up. But now I'm curious. And cross-grained. The more people tell me to stay away from something, the more I get interested. And then the police were dealing with Rosa as a 'subject' or a 'fatality' and dealing with me as a bothersome screwball. I guess that sticks in my craw."

"I can see that. It isn't normal, but it's admirable."

"I don't give a damn about admiration. It's more that—" I stopped and tried to get a fix on the churn of feelings inside. "Maybe that they pushed too far too fast. *They.* It has to be *they.*"

Frank nodded. "What scares me is that man in your apartment. The fake call. For one thing it means there is an inside man with the police. You did say you called them immediately and didn't talk to anyone else? Had to be the police. Somebody in their computer network anyway."

"They must be very thorough."

"That also scares me. You see the problem. If you go to the police, they will know about it. As long as the cops treat you like a nut, you're probably safe. But if you gain credibility . . ." Neither of us felt particularly like completing the sentence.

"They, they, they." I quizzed Frank with a look.

"I don't do much in the way of homicide cases, love, but I have friends who do. They tell me that most violent crimes are traceable to domestic squabbles—son stabs dad because he can't have the car, husband shoots ex-wife for fooling around, and so on—and the rest has to do with dope."

"I doubt this is a family affair."

"That leaves dope. I can give you a possible hint. The attorney general has a core-sample investigation going on some of the state-funded drug rehabilitation programs. Like the one Rosa was employed in."

"What are they investigating?"

"I don't know. But I'll find out. I'd guess they're looking no further than misappropriation of funds for starters. But the funds in question can be rather large. For large sums, people get killed. I don't want—"

"Me either. I agree with Maurice Chevalier. Old age isn't so bad when you consider the alternative."

"I think it was Mark Twain. But why don't you take it to the attorney general's office or the state narcs?"

"It's an idea. But you know how agencies and bureaus are. . . ."

"I also know how you are." He smiled again, a little tightly.

"Meaning?"

"Meaning Stella trusts Stella, most of all. And you've left out one of your reasons. You like it."

I considered that one pretty carefully. "You're right."

I put down the last of my drink. "I am a born spy. And not for all the pineapple cheesecake in God's creation would I trade in my magnifying glass. Now, I've got a couple of hours of daylight left to snoop in." I stood up and hoisted my purse from the seat, conscious of the weight of the little snub-nosed revolver. "Call me?"

He unfolded from the booth. "Tonight. And about every twenty-four hours thereafter. I'll have information on the investigation, and I'd appreciate knowing where you are and what you—"

"I'll leave messages on your machine. I don't mean that to be sardonic. We've each got lives to lead. And thanks, friend. I mean it."

We shook hands. I had to withdraw mine first. He was feeling anxious and protective. And a little wistful.

"So long, Scotch."

Another old one. When we met, he told me I had eyes exactly the color of fine old Scotch. Later there was a remark about a soul of soda.

"So long, Frank."

Chapter IV

Peralta Drive was in the lower Mission District, on the seedy side of Market Street. It wound up out of the waterfront area, tawdry warehouses in a swarm of forklifts and tractor-trailers, along the slope of Potrero Hill, dipping down finally into one end of Noe Valley. The 1700 block was just at the base of the hill, a row of decayed frame buildings thrown up not long after the Great Earthquake. Most were cut into street-level and walk-up flats, and some had sheets of plywood over windows that had been broken. It was what is called a mixed neighborhood.

A shabby pickup half full of furniture was parked in front of the Esposito house, a paintless gray structure, but one of the few single-family dwellings on the block. The front door swung open, and a young Mexican emerged, carrying a stack of cardboard boxes. He reeled like a juggler down the walk and dumped the boxes into the pickup, then went back inside. He looked anything but grief-stricken. From a movement behind a curtain, I could see the neighbors on one side were also at home.

Reaching behind the seat of the Porsche, I came up with my trim calfskin briefcase. It was impressively official-looking, with a lock and name tag. It contained various questionnaires, mostly pointless, a clipboard, some previous "studies" done by Garabedian, Daugherty, and Bissel, and lots of pens. I took out a sheet of scratch paper, jotted down a few possible questions, and clipped the paper to the board. I checked myself quickly in the rearview mirror and pulled off the scarf. Too jazzy for a working girl.

The woman next door had a dirty baby on one hip, and from somewhere in the dim cave of the room behind her I heard another little kid in the process of destroying something. On a television screen people with blue-green faces were jabbering at each other. I disarmed her by telling her that I had nothing to sell and wasn't from the government. This was only a survey with no gimmicks. She was desperately happy for the interruption. She told me, in a voice that still had a little Appalachian blur, that she would be just tickled to answer any questions I might have. Probably it was years since anyone paid her as much attention as I was going to in the next ten minutes. I even offered to hold her baby while she warmed up the coffee pot.

When she brought the steaming cups, keeping the cracked one for herself, I positioned myself on a settee in the bay window to command a view of the pickup. Mrs. Goodman perched on a chair, poking alternately at her hair and the baby in her lap.

"What does your husband do, Mrs. Goodman?"

"My husband is a roofer, works off and on this season because of the rains. You married?"

"I was."

"Oh. I didn't mean—"

"It's all right."

"I guess you're supposed to be asking the questions. Hush, Lisa. This place is such a mess. Hard to keep anything clean, you know. . . ."

"Impossible with kids."

"What was this about again?" She laughed apologetically. "I mean, why is anybody interested in me, little old Billie Jo Goodman? Am I typical or something?" She prodded her hair.

"In a way. We're surveying shopping habits of family units in selected areas. You've been chosen by the computer." I smiled ingratiatingly. "Just routine questions. The Business Bureau wants to know what people typically buy." Billie Jo's eyes had strayed off to the little blue-green people who lived in the box. "How long have you lived at this address?"

"What? Oh. Two years."

And so on. I threw in filler questions on age and education as cover, then got to what I was after.

"How would you describe your neighborhood?"

Billie Jo looked blank for a moment, then flushed. "You mean . . . Well, I don't think it's a *slum,* if that's what you mean."

"Of course not," I said smoothly. "In general terms. Is there a lot of turnover, for example? It looks as if . . ." I switched my eyes toward the Esposito house. Through the curtains I could see the young man skidding a coffee table onto the bed of the pickup.

"Oh!" She jumped and the baby, who had nodded off, protested with a yowl. "Don't cry, Lisa. Nighty-nighty now." She gathered up the child and spoke rapidly to me over her bald head. "You know the most *awful* thing happened. Rosy—that's the woman who lived next door—Rosy Esposito, she was killed in an accident this morning. An awful accident. On the freeway."

"No!" I covered my mouth with three fingers. "How terrible! Did she have children? Is that her husband loading the truck?"

"Thank the Good Lord there were no kids. In fact, Rosy and Manuel—that was her husband—was separated. And a good thing, too." She gave me a meaningful glance, and I looked dutifully inquiring.

"They was coming and going at all hours. And shouting and slamming around and I don't know what all."

"You don't mean . . . ?" I looked shocked.

"Oh, yes. I'm sure he whupped her. I wouldn't never stand for it from Rob—that's my husband—he might be sour some days, but he—"

"Actually *beat* her!" I interrupted. "Did he drink?"

"Somebody did. You see bottles in their trash cans. But I think it was more Rosy. Don't blame her neither. Some people would probably think he was handsome. That kind of big guy with those white teeth and flashy clothes. Real dark—part Negro, I guess. But he wasn't friendly, you know? Cold, like. Eyes like old yellow marbles."

"Did he make her support him?"

"Well, now there's something real interesting." Billie Jo put her baby on the floor and stood up. "Can I get you another cup of coffee?" She looked at me, hungry and expectant. She knew she had me.

"Oh, yes." I swiftly tossed off a half cup of the tepid, bitter stuff. "This is so interesting."

When she sat down again, she leaned forward and dropped her voice, spacing out the sentences between sips of coffee.

"Both of them worked at a government office—something to do with getting people off drugs. But he had a real nice car. I was in their place once, borrowing a cup of brown sugar from Rosy—Lord, it's terrible to think she's dead now—and they had some real nice stuff in there. A water bed and stereo console and all. I think they had money from someplace else. Or he did anyway. Probably gambling or like that." Mrs. Goodman nodded wisely. "He wa'n't on the up-and-up. I could tell."

"Has her husband come back, then, to collect the things?" I nodded again toward the pickup.

Billie Jo shrugged. "Who knows? I haven't seen Manuel for six months. That ain't him out there. Probably one of his buddies. I expected Bennie, though."

"Bennie?"

"Her boyfriend. She was goin' out with this musician, a skinny little guy with glasses. He played at some nightclub across town, the King's something or other. He was a little weird, too. But kind of nice."

"A musician."

"Rosy was sure going from one extreme to another. Poor kid. She was real quiet. Originally from South America, you know. And the women there are supposed to be quiet. We don't know how lucky we are. Here in California, I mean."

Billie didn't know where the man lived or his last name, only that he played at the King's something or other. I asked her another cover question and wound up with a request for secrecy. Business Bureau policy and so on. Mrs. Goodman promised to tell no one but Mr. Goodman. I doubted this claim to self-restraint, but a wobbly promise was better than none. Then I waved bye-bye to the children and thanked Billie Jo. She had fattened the file on Rosa Esposito a good deal.

By the time I left her house the moving man was slamming shut the tailgate on a jumble of cabinets, boxes, lampstands, and cushions. I poised on the curb, briefcase under arm, and smiled brightly at him. The smile was perhaps a little empty because I was repeating the truck's license number to myself a few times, to burn it in, but even so, his response was on the chill side of uninterested.

"Moving?" I volunteered cheerily. Not a flicker. I made a mistake then. I couldn't control the impulse to jar him a little. "How nice to inherit everything so *quickly*."

He examined me then with the merest shred of attention. "No Inglish," he said, and hoisted himself into the cab. I stepped off the curb and was halfway across the street when he spoke again. A soft and insinuating voice, just audible, the last word punctuated by the racket of the engine catching.

"And mind your own fucking business, *gringuita*."

Chapter V

The Yellow Pages yielded a tavern called the King's Table. It was across town, not far from Fisherman's Wharf, but away from the busy strip directly on the water. I took the Bayshore North and for once did not weave through the afternoon traffic with my usual sense of sport. I sensed that things were moving too fast, and I wanted to spend the next few minutes watching San Francisco turn beautiful in the gathering darkness. By day it was a quaint city, despite the naked spires of progress. A city of brick edges and brass fittings. The cable cars and swooping bridges and aromatic coffeehouses were what decorated the travel brochures, but San Francisco was most ravishing in late evening, at the moment just beyond the exposure limit of the tourist camera. The bay went inky blue, and in the east, the Berkeley hills were black heaps against a sky of violet. Carpets of lights were spread around the headlands, and on the most magic nights, a bank of fog moved through the Golden Gate and between the hills, leaving the tops of the bridge pilings and skyscrapers afloat above a downy white sea.

Every year a few more of the old landmarks were erased. High rises had spiked the horizon until Coit Tower was dwarfed, and suburban boxes marched in rows over the Peninsula hills. But on evenings when the fog rolled in and the moon ballooned up over the bay to scatter silver on the water, we forgot all that, or forgave it, delighted simply to be witness to the queen's beauty. We forgot about our boring jobs, tangled loves, or uncertain futures. Such glory of velvet dark and jeweled light always promised better, a twist out of a fairy tale. And I had a theory that the belief in such things—romance if you like—had a way of confirming itself. People did come to San Francisco to gamble on dreams, which had a way of coming true here.

They also, I reflected a moment later, taking the Marina exit, could turn into nightmares more lurid than most. Maybe Rosa Esposito had come to the city of flowers full of hope, too. What had driven her to that ramshackle flat and the man with marbles for eyes? Something, I was fairly sure, more powerful and sinister than hope gone stale.

The King's Table was tucked between Al's Liquor Store and the Saratoga Hotel. It was a small sign in Gothic lettering above a red door. Not a neighborhood bar, I judged, after one glance into the lobby of the Saratoga. Two old men dozed on the sagging furniture, with a solitary fake palm tree and an ashtray for company. I pushed through the red door and found myself in a little world of amber lights, polished wood, and ongoing conversations. The decor was Disneyland British—a few gargoyles and hanging tapestries bearing coats of arms. There was a small bandstand at the rear of the place and a postage-stamp dance floor. I went to a table near the bandstand and ordered a glass of white wine. It might be hours before the music showed up, and Scotch is a little dangerous to nurse.

The number of customers was surprising. So was their diversity. Along the bar was the usual row of serious juicers, mostly men in their late twenties or early thirties, dressed in fashionable suits and groovy ties. They had twenty-five-dollar hair jobs, and there were a lot of spiked mustaches and trimmed beards. But here and there was a workingman, open-collared and red-nosed, and at least two of those ladies who paint over the cracks, throw up a screen of cigarette smoke, and belt them down all day long.

I could see a couple of the groovies sneaking glances, sniggering, ordering another round to gain courage to make the usual offer. The problem for a single lady in a bar is the same one that confronts a tourist in a Moroccan medina. If you accept a guide early, you're stuck with him. On the other hand, he will keep the other hustlers at bay. I had already decided I didn't have the energy to fence with some half-looped ad exec when a man came from behind a curtain in the back of the room and began fooling with the amps and microphones.

I ordered another glass of wine and settled in to observe. The man disappeared again behind the curtain, then reappeared, carrying cardboard cases. He opened them and began assembling a drum set. A black man in a tan suit and blood-red tie, he moved with an indifferent grace, tapping and tuning. Except for one flick of the eyes, he ignored the customers. The curtain swung again, and an upright cadaver shuffled in. He was white—too white— with wrinkles so deep they looked like knife cuts, and great blue parabolas beneath his eyes. I had a vague memory of seeing the elongated face on the back of a record jacket in somebody's collection of oldies, but I couldn't attach a name to it. Except for his hands, he could have been one of the derelicts dozing in the hotel lobby next door.

He sat at the piano, a baby grand so scuffed and stained I hadn't even seen it against the wall. The hands flexed and then glided over the keys like pale spiders. With no sense of intrusion, the music was just there, as if it had always been there. I could recognize no particular melody, only music threading through the jumble of conversation as naturally as a breeze through leaves.

The next one through the curtain was surely Bennie. He was skinny, with horn-rimmed glasses, a rumpled suit, and the nervous, dodging walk of a Methedrine man. The bass he was lugging was much larger than he was. Unhurried, he fitted a few notes around the wandering stream of the piano, adjusted a couple of pegs, nodded at the drummer, and all at once they took off. Again, it wasn't obtrusive. What happened was a function not of volume, but of intensity. The music was materializing swiftly, overshadowing the voices in the room.

I hadn't heard jazz in a long time, belonging as I did to the rock generation. In my bubble gum years it was the Beatles who pressed my button, and I didn't listen to anything more serious until I ran into Frank. The seven years between us were an eon of musical time. He had grown up with Getz, Mulligan, Kenton, and late Brubeck, and when we were in the new couple's stage of show and tell, he made me listen to hours of it. It got to me finally, and the memory of all that rode back to me on the magic carpet these gentlemen were weaving. They started with "Cottage for Sale," but that melody vanished into elegant improvisations. The piano and bass began to cross-stitch little scat phrases, while the drummer put down a solid bottom and added embellishments with brushes and cymbal.

My toes began to work a little, then my fingertips on the tabletop. The duet grew too complicated, so the piano shifted to big, chiming chords, and a little dissonance, and the bass embarked on a long romp. By this time they were aboard the A train, picking up drive. Bennie went up and down the neck of the instrument like a monkey, the strings thwacking away. But the sound was gorilla-sized—agile as King Kong bounding down the chain of the Himalayas.

At first sight I had wondered what Rosa found in him. Now I understood. I knew the feeling myself. It was the reason musicians, however homely, never lack lovers. I didn't see a skinny four-eyes anymore; I saw only his hands, supple and powerful, stroking and darting, drawing out of old wood and worn gut a vibrant, fascinating sound. The warm swirl inside was the result of imagining my body in place of the bass, a medium for all that articulated energy.

The cadaver on piano wound it up. The heavy blocks of chord shattered into notes as pure as ice. The A train went down a long tunnel, and we came out the other side, singing in the rain. Blue skies, nothin' but blue skies, broke through then, and next a shuffle of other old swing tunes, too fast for me to sort them out. Finally the drums and bass joined to make a kind of formal, benign commentary on the whole thing, something crystal and mathematical yet flashing with high spirits.

Suddenly it was over, and there was a moment of absolute silence before the patter of applause. Jazz buffs do not stomp and holler, but there were respectful "yeahs" and a couple of whistles. The piano player looked once around the room, and I saw the slightest of smiles bend his mouth. Then they went at it again. It was a good hour, while my wine glass stood half full on the table in front of me, before they broke the set, this time to a storm of clapping. The piano player mumbled something into the microphone about the powder room. Everyone laughed, and they all lounged out through the curtain.

They drifted back, one by one, sometime later. When Bennie passed, I said his name casually, just loud enough for him to hear. He gave me a swift once-over and veered to my table. He sat down without being asked.

"Sure. What can I do for you?"

"Talk to me."

"Love to." He slipped a cigarette case out of his side pocket and offered me one. I didn't want anything to impede our fellowship, so I took one, and he lit it for me. We mingled smoke over the little round table. I smiled, and he smiled back. But his eyes remained opaque.

"You're a beautiful chick. You got style. Some class. But I never seen you here before. Beautiful chick shows up, knows my name, wants to talk—I get curious. So back to square one. What can I do for you?"

The suggestive nuance was gone, and the question had an edge.

"Your music did a lot for me. It moved."

"Thanks. Before you bother with any more of that, what's your name?"

"Wilma Rogers. A friend of Rosa's."

The opaque eyes held mine for a long moment. "You

lie good, whoever you are. Thing is, I got two more sets. Then maybe catch something to eat at Wo's. Little action afterward would be nice. But I can't use this bullshit. So you want to tell me what you want, Wilma, or do we say bye-bye right now?" He talked in bursts, with a slight undercurrent of hysteria. He stubbed out the cigarette and put his palms flat on the table, ready to push himself out of the chair.

"Do a lot of your girl friends wind up dead? Thought I should know before our relationship went any further." I smiled sweetly at him over the rim of the wineglass. "And I would like it to go a little further."

He started to get up, thought better of it, then slumped back in the chair. His eyes took on a little depth. "She got hit by a car. The fuzz says so, too. You tryin' to say I had something to do with it? Who the hell are you anyway?"

"I guess you could call me a posthumous friend."

"A what?"

"Skip that. I have certain uncertainties about the accident that was supposed to have happened to Rosa. I'm curious to know whether anybody shares them."

"Like what uncertainties? You a lady cop?"

"I'll make you a deal. I answer a question, you answer a question too."

"Deal."

"I'm not a lady cop. But I happened to have caught a glimpse of something out of the ordinary on the freeway this morning. You think it was out of the ordinary?"

"Does it matter what we think?"

"I thought the deal was answers, not new questions."

He shook out another cigarette, lit it, and drew deeply. The look he gave me was shrewd and speculative. "A little out of the ordinary. Rosa drank, but she could always find the door. My turn. How come you are so interested?"

I sighed. A lot of people seemed to find my ways abnormal. My boss, my bartender, my ex-husband, small-time jazzmen. I decided more or less on the spur of the moment that I could use cover.

"Let's say I'm a free-lance investigator. And a possible speculator. Do you think Manuel had something to do with it?"

"Manuel had something to do with everything that ever happened to Rosa." Bennie's mouth tightened. "She was his thing for a long, long time."

"Until you?"

He shrugged. "Until she'd had enough. I happened to come along at about that time. Few months ago. It was no big deal. Nobody'd been nice to her for years, that's all. She was grateful."

"How did you meet?"

"Nice try." He grinned at me, for the first time without suspicion. "Now how did you know about Manuel?"

"Neighbor. So how did you meet? Here at the club?"

Bennie shook his head. "You are something, question lady, you know that? No. On a ferryboat is where we met. A couple of tourists, like. And you know, boats makes me think of deep water. That's where you're at, baby, and I want to—" His eyes flicked over my head, and he nodded. I glanced around and saw the cadaver ambling back toward the bandstand. I also glimpsed, at the far end of the bar, a face I had seen before.

"Gotta do it." He stood up quickly. "Anyway, I want to give you a little advice. Go back to shore, and stay away from the cops. Okay? You got it?"

"Not altogether. I haven't run out of questions."

He shrugged. "I've run out of answers."

I watched him disappear behind the curtain. Then I gestured in an offhand way to the waiter. When he brought the glass of wine, I gave him the napkin I had scribbled on.

"Give this to Bennie?" I asked. He gave the weary smile of the waiter who has carried a thousand such billets-doux and headed for the back room. Leaving the wine, I gathered up my purse, slid out of my chair, and walked toward a doorway labeled "Rest Rooms." I hoped that it was a nonchalant walk and that my eyes strayed quite naturally past the corner of the bar where I had seen the familiar face.

The rest rooms adjoined a corridor that had another service door at the far end. It was unlocked, and I eased through into a small storage area full of brooms, mops, and cans of floor wax. There was a narrow window on the far wall, and through it I could see into an alley, a pit of dark air. I popped the catch, swung the window aside, and peered out. The pavement was no more than eight feet below me. I had wriggled through and was gripping the sill, toes jammed in a niche between the bricks outside, when the door opened and a busboy wearing a dirty apron stepped into the room. He froze when he saw my face in the window. We both were trying to think of something to say, but I got there first.

"Geronimo," I said brightly, and let go.

Chapter VI

I hit the ground already moving at a lope. It would take the watchful little man twenty minutes to figure out that I wasn't coming back, and I wanted to be inside my apartment door by then. Of course, he had managed once already to get into the building, but that was in the daytime. Security was better at night. There was a patrol car in the neighborhood until six o'clock in the morning. I could double-lock my door, put the .32 under my pillow, and get a decent night's sleep.

When I reached the end of the alley, I stopped short. There was, I realized, a measure of self-deception in my arguments. A decent night's sleep no longer appeared to be a reasonable possibility. I had known that when I recognized the dark, mustachioed face in the crowd at the bar. My little visitor with the soundless laugh was not the sort of man to encourage sweet dreams. Either he had followed me all day, or he was also keeping track of Bennie. Either way, he knew now that my hint of a long trip elsewhere was a bluff and that I was hanging around Rosa's boyfriend. He also knew where I lived.

I wondered where *he* lived. I remembered some awful James Fenimore Cooper novel I had been assigned in college. The hero—Bumpkin, or whatever his name was— outfoxed the Injuns by circling around and following them. It might work. At least I would know the enemy's whereabouts. If he staked out my apartment, I would call Frank, or my friend Alice if she was at home, and arrange temporary lodgings. I remembered then that Frank had said he would phone me tonight. A twinge of familiar guilt and anger came and went. I had, after all, a pretty fair excuse for a minor attack of the dependencies.

I took the Porsche and circled the block until I found a parking space a few doors away from the entrance to the King's Table and on the opposite side of the street. There was fairly steady traffic. Pairs of car lights, diamond and ruby, receded in glittering necklaces up Russian Hill. The moonlight stamped shadows as sharp and black as print. I could see a few couples, leaning on each other as they strolled the sidewalks, and one or two old Chinese men in too-large suits—as much a city landmark as the Ferry Building. I slipped into a reverie, remembering a starry-eyed youngster on the arm of a successful lawyer, both good and stoned and crazy with new love, on their way to a play, late supper of crab and a tangy sauterne, and then each other. I caught myself sighing and stopped the little movie inside. I was old enough to know self-pity when it moved in.

Then the door I was watching swung open and the man came out, moving at a heel-snapping pace. I waited until he was a dozen strides from the corner and started the engine. When he turned left and vanished behind the building, I eased quickly into the stream of traffic and pulled up to the light. I was lucky and hit it red. I let the Porsche creep like a fat little cat over the pedestrian walkway and saw the man opening the door of a new Mustang, black or very dark blue. The car was headed away from me, fortunately, so I flicked on my turn signal and prayed for the light to hold until he was out of his parking slot.

I had to feign a stalled engine and take a few angry honks to adjust the timing, but then I was on his tail, hanging back to leave a couple of cars between us, feeling rather proud of myself. And somewhat safer. He was erratic and not very good, burning too much rubber and not looking far enough ahead to figure the pattern of lights and traffic. I had no trouble floating in his wake across town, down familiar streets at the base of Twin Peaks, to the quiet little section I live in, on the border of

Noe Valley and Dolores Park. Traffic had thinned until I was a full block behind, squeezing through the intersections a split second ahead of the signal change, hoping no cycle cop was lurking nearby.

When we reached my street, he cruised my apartment twice and then parked directly across from it. I live on the top floor of a large, comfortable three-story building that was once a small and not very ostentatious embassy. My blinds were drawn, and I had left a night-light burning. The man would watch the windows, hoping to catch shadows from movement within the room. I had pulled into a driveway near the intersection and doused my lights but left the motor running. I had a couple of options. I could try waiting him out, taking the risk that when he broke off the stakeout, there would still be enough traffic to cover me while I tailed him home. Or I could drive to Frank's, give him the Mustang's license number, and have him run a check on it in the morning. And take the risk of reopening some doors between us that I would rather keep shut tight. I sighed, turned the key, and the engine gave a little cat sneeze and quit.

The situation didn't come clear after five or ten minutes of inner debate, so I knew I was too tired to think. Then it solved itself. The Mustang's headlamps came on, and it moved slowly away from the curb. I hesitated, my fingers fiddling again with the ignition key. Then a pair of fog lights flicked on and off from another parked vehicle. The silhouette looked like that of a pickup. When the Mustang had passed, the pickup swung out and headed toward me. I slid down in the front seat and put my hand inside my purse until I felt the cold lump of steel in my palm.

The pickup racketed by, the hole in its muffler just a little louder than the sound of my own heart. Indecision was a lucky response. I must have become very important to have deserved a double tail. And I was lucky, to begin with, that the man in the truck hadn't seen me dogging the Mustang. Now, I thought as I sat up again, if I was triply lucky, I would manage to control my breathing before I reached Frank's apartment so I would be able to explain calmly what I had been doing until two o'clock in the morning.

I was triply lucky. Even though I was still a little shaky, Frank was in what was for him a state of distraction. He had warm milk on the back burner, a somewhat dehydrated BLT in the oven, and so much control working on his voice that I could hardly hear him.

"Adjust the volume, Frank." I took off the scarf and dropped it on my coat before sinking into the soft leather of a chair he had pulled in front of the fireplace.

"I said, do you want something to eat first?"

"First? What's second?"

He wheeled around at his kitchen door and strode back across the room to my chair. He took me by the shoulders and pulled me up a little, not roughly, but firmly.

"Stella," he said, "I've been sitting here for nearly six hours, imagining a lot of unpleasant things that could happen to you. I want to help, you know that, but my nerves won't take a lot of witty fencing right now. Okay?"

"Sure," I said. "Feed me, Frank, and then we'll talk." He gave me a one-sided smile and lowered me back into the chair. I felt a little guilty at being so breezy, but a little sad, too, that he hadn't seen that it was a mask for exhaustion and my own bad case of nerves. In a moment he was back with the BLT and hot cocoa, and I discovered that I was famished. By the time I downed the last crust there was a snifter of Courvoisier at my elbow, to match the one Frank balanced on his knee. He was sitting with his back against the fireplace, his face sculpted in deep shadow by the flames.

"Mmmmm." I took in deeply the aroma of the brandy. "You have no idea how nice this is."

"Maybe some idea. I can see it in your face. You look like a cat in a creamery."

"Should have seen me an hour ago. More like a cat in a rainstorm."

He laughed softly. "You've got me begging. Tell it."

I did, quickly and flatly. When I was finished, I waited, but Frank said nothing.

"So I've got two license numbers for you to check out and a strong hunch that Mr. Esposito is a dope dealer of some kind and possibly a jealous maniac."

I waited some more, but Frank said nothing. The fire had gone to coals, and I couldn't read his face in the shadows.

"Can you do that for me?"

"I can."

"But you don't want to."

"That's right."

"Okay." I put the snifter down and reached for my purse. "I'll get it on my own."

"Stella." He moved so rapidly I was startled and put up my hands. His face bumped into them and forced them apart so that my arms were partly around his neck. His mouth, so close, was tense with a strain I hadn't seen before, even in the worst period of our breakup. He looked, for an instant, almost old.

"I want you to drop it. Now. Don't check anything out. Take a couple of weeks off from work, and let me take you to Maui."

I was too surprised to answer. He cupped my face in his big hands and kissed me. He was very good at that, Frank was. For a couple of seconds I didn't have my bearings and kissed back, but then I pulled away and pried his hands from my cheeks.

"Whoa, now, my good friend. You remember, we decided to be good friends?" I pushed on the lapels of his dressing gown with my palms, lightly, and he sat back on his heels. "And I think I heard you say not so long ago that you wanted to help?"

"I do. I am. I want you out of this thing. I don't like the way it's going."

"What's different now? From this afternoon?"

He looked away for a moment, then dropped his head to stare between his feet. "I've got some news I haven't told you."

"Ah?" I leaned forward now and put one finger under his chin to bring his head up. "So you thought you'd make your play first, and if it worked, you wouldn't have to tell me at all. So?" He gave me the little one-sided smile again. "Frank, Frank, you trick yourself sometimes. So tell me. What's the scary news?"

He turned toward the fire and spoke rapidly, professionally.

"I managed to get through to the attorney general for a few minutes. Mostly because we went to the same high school for young snobs. There is an investigation going on, and it is at a very delicate stage. A state assemblyman or two may be involved. Those are big fish. And dangerous fish."

There was a pause, with no other sound but the fire hissing. I waited, and finally he went on.

"Little fish like Rosa Esposito can be swallowed up. But for the moment nothing will be done about it. Otherwise, the big fish will get away."

"Very interesting parable. Do we have here old Zen lawyer proverb, one big fee better than many little fish?"

"That's enough, Stella." He had swiveled around and had the tight-mouthed, squint-eyed expression I knew so well as his bluff for rage.

"No, it isn't. Not nearly enough. I need to know, right now, if you are professionally involved in the case. Representing the fishermen, for example?"

"Stella!"

"That's not an answer."

"I am not directly involved in the case. Absolutely."

I thought that one over for a minute and then smiled. "Not directly. So. You know, Frank, I learned a very important lesson from you: You can always trust a lawyer. To trick you fairly. Tell me what that really means—'not directly.'"

We traded another of those long looks that exes know well, the kind that starts out in defiance and rancor and goes through nostalgia to end up in a little ironic affection.

"Christ," he said finally. "I'm glad you went into some-

thing else. And I wish you'd stay in commercial snooping.
But you won't, I can see that now. All right." He stood
up and walked to the glass wall to look out over the city.
His voice came to me a little muffled by the partly drawn
drapes. "Indirectly I have an interest in this business. The
State Crime Commission, as you may know, intends to
appoint some special investigators. It's a choice opportunity. The evidence is that the biggest bust in California
history is shaping up, and the guy who gets the goods will
make himself a reputation that could be ridden very far;
at least to the U.S. attorney general's staff."

"The *guy*?"

"Okay, okay, *person*."

"You knew all this before?"

"All right. I wasn't altogether straight with you. I don't
apologize for being ambitious, but I don't wear it on my
shirtfront either. I've got an eye on that job—like every
other lawyer in town—and I've been doing some homework." He turned and came back to lean against the fireplace. "That's it."

"Uh-huh."

"What do you mean?"

"You know what you look like?"

"What?" He looked puzzled and a little pained.

"Like one of those ads in the supermarket magazines
for the successful drinker of fine whiskey in his high-rise
lair. Dead giveaway. Come off it, Frank. What's in the
homework?"

"Merciless." He looked at me in feigned compassion.
"Absolutely merciless. Okay. You want the lecture?"

"Sure. You know I love it." I curled my feet under me
in the chair. Frank was an excellent lecturer and almost
always ended up saying more than he intended to.

"I'll give you a general outline to start with. California,
as you perhaps know, is the narcotics capital of the
world—one effect of the Vietnam War—because it makes
both the South American connection and the Far East
connection. New York and Miami probably see more her-

oin, but coke is the current hottest stock, and most of that, as well as most Colombian grass, moves through L.A. to the rest of the country."

"We have always been leaders."

Frank winced. "At any rate, the drug traffic is heavy in this state—in every sense of the word—and as I told you, a big share of police work, especially homicide investigation, is connected with that traffic. There are also some interesting local twists to the business. In New York the Italians and the blacks handle most of the trade; here you've also got a much more complicated picture."

"Democracy, too."

He gave me a severe look and hurried on. "The main problem is to tag the big operators. A few years back, in the sixties, when the dealers were moving out of the ghettos and into the youth market, handling several new products, it was easier to make big busts. Guys like Owsley and Super Fly cornered the markets, and when you had them, the whole operation collapsed. Temporarily anyway. But nowadays there are a lot of people in the game, and sometimes you find an elderly British gentleman with a Hong Kong passport funneling stuff to a Mexican used car dealer who retails to a petty hoodlum in North Beach with aspirations to be a *capo.*"

"I catch on, Frank. Let's get to the assemblymen and skip the British gentleman."

"A lecture you bought, a lecture you get. Now, a year or so back two things became apparent. First, a whole lot of fresh stuff—both coke and smack of very high quality—began hitting the streets. There was a new big fish in the pond. Then it became clear that the law enforcement apparatus had been infiltrated. Leads evaporated. Witnesses disappeared, once even under police surveillance. Some evidence confiscated in one of our few successful raids vanished from the safe in the Hall of Justice. The underworld, as they used to call it, seemed to know every move the narcotics people made."

"A leak, they called it."

"Right. And it hasn't been plugged yet. That's why it's no surprise that you found the little man in your room right after you telephoned the police. So much for the overall outline. We move now to the specific case of Rosa Esposito."

"One question, Doctor. We are to assume that these two developments are connected? The new stuff on the street and the leak?"

"That's the thinking in the state prosecutor's office. But none of that is really their concern. Law enforcement people are jealous over their spheres of influence, and dope is mostly a matter handled by feds and local cops. The state got into the act because of another twist. In the last few years California has invented a number of rehabilitation programs for addicts: Methadone, Peer Counseling, Start Over, Outpatient Workforce, a ranch in Sonoma, and a sailboat in the bay. One result is another labyrinthine bureaucracy, and it's a bureaucracy that employs a lot of ex-junkies, by definition. Now—"

"I can see it coming. The state prosecutor has reason to believe that some of these agencies are a cover for dope deals."

"Quick."

"In particular, they suspect Manuel. Employed by a Start Over rehabilitation center."

Frank gave me his keep-coming-you're-a-good-student smile.

"So Manuel was dealing—I had that one figured out already—and Rosa found out about it and wanted to spill the story or blow the whistle or whatever your favorite cliché is, and they killed her."

"But we doubt that Rosa was innocent of the operation. I do have reason to believe that she didn't know about the inside man or men—"

"Persons."

"—persons in the police apparatus and tried to make some kind of contact with the narc squad. We don't know her motive."

"What about the assemblymen?"

"Ah." Frank looked again out the glass wall at the bright jewels of the city scattered through the night. "Well. I can't say anything definite about that. No names yet. But if you think about the police department infiltration, the use of state agencies as covers, the well-oiled international exchanges involved . . ."

"All right. I can check the voting records on appropriations for the rehabilitation programs or see who drafted the legislation in the first place."

"Look," Frank said, advancing on me again, "you know you could help me with this thing. Work part time on the legal staff if the appointment comes through. It takes a lot of people—what they used to call a task force—and it's slow, but it's a lot more efficient and safer than going it alone. These people don't fool around. They'd kill you, Stella. Before lunch." He was sitting on the arm of my chair, one arm along the back, gazing down on me intently. "I wouldn't like that. At all."

"Me either." I ducked under his chin and stood up. "At the moment there is some danger I might pass on from exhaustion. Point me toward the bedroom. The guest bedroom. I'll be able to talk like a human person in the morning."

"You won't give it up then?"

"Nope."

"Stella, for the love of Christ!" He stood, his face heating up. "This is no game for—"

"For a woman? Oops, Frank. You *know* that's the wrong tack. It's not a game either, you see. That's what's wrong with all your crime commissions and special investigations and grand juries and all the rest of it. They're in a game. And the name of the game is what they call visibility. That means, 'Look at me,' the Defender of Justice, the Fearless Fighter of Malfeasance, the Peace Officer, Matt Dillon, Dick Tracy, Top Gun, yattatayattata. It's just the other side of the coin from the mobsters. Their organization is built the same way—everybody trying to be Mr. Big, the

Death Father, Mr. Most Wanted. Your jobs depend on
each other. You *need* each other, to keep the game going.
If it were TV, with fake blood and a few wrecked cars, it
would be okay. But people like Rosa get caught in between. They're the pawns. They put them in boxes and
stick them in the ground, and the game goes right on. So
I'm not interested in forwarding your investigation, Frank.
I'm interested in getting the bastards who pushed that
lady out of the car."

There was a pause, and he swallowed. "All right, Stella.
Let's call it off. A truce. I'll put you in touch with what
information I get. I'll check out the licenses for you. But
you let me know every move of yours. And be careful."

"It's a deal. Thanks for the lecture. It helped. Now,
I've got an appointment with Lieutenant Hand tomorrow,
so . . ."

"Through the archway there. First door to your left.
Bathroom's right across."

I walked over and kissed him quickly.

"Nighty-night, ex."

Chapter VII

On my way to the Mission precinct station the next morning I thought about how to handle Lieutenant Hand. I was still in the wine-colored pantsuit I'd worn the night before, and I looked a little too frayed to pass as a cool professional. If Frank knew the lieutenant, there was a chance he'd alerted him to brush me off gently. I didn't put it past Frank to make a quick call to identify his "distraught" ex-wife. For two reasons: to make sure I ran into more discouragement, and to make known to the inside man, if he was eavesdropping, that the little lady had an important lawyer to watch over her.

It angered me to think that my security was still a function of my former husband's position, but there was a secret pocket of relief in the irritation. I didn't like being followed or having unannounced visitors either. I decided my best tactic would be to do the part of a kook. Women have immense kook power when they want to use it. A rising pitch in the voice, the roll of an eye, a flexing of claws—it can clear a room faster than a sackful of rattlers. In this case, I had in mind getting Lieutenant Hand out of his lair onto some neutral ground and throwing a little scare into all the game players who were anxious to match their investigation to an election timetable. The possibility that a loud and inaccurate female might get the story out first would stimulate the good lieutenant, I hoped, to a reluctant cooperation.

I was not, however, prepared for Lieutenant Hand. A sergeant took me through the concrete chambers of the station to a dingy little office. Behind the door, at a desk that his size made small, was a Great Stone-faced Indian.

That phrase I made up later. If I am honest, I have to report I noticed first that he was handsome, if stern, in a way that made a sudden, slight hollow in my solar plexus. He had straight black hair, an impressive hawk nose, and fine planes of bone throughout. The eyes he moved from the papers in front of him were dark amber, unblinking.

"Stella Pike?"

I nodded. He motioned slightly with his hand to a chair before the desk and looked once at the sergeant, who left. I didn't sit down.

"You have some information on Mrs. Esposito's death?"

I shook my head.

He frowned. "I understood from your call . . ."

I shook my head again and put a finger to my lips.

"Not here."

He moved his hand again, impatient. "It's all right. You may speak freely."

"I can't talk here. Do you realize people are not safe in this city anymore? I mean, *really not safe!*" I began to pace back and forth a little. "Mr. Hand, something has got to be done."

I was getting through the stone face, which began to show cracks of alarm. "Look, Mrs. Pike," he said rapidly, and pushed back his chair, "why don't you sit down for a moment and I'll get us some coffee?"

"There are murderers running around on the highways, Mr. Hand. And people pretending to be policemen. We can't talk here."

"Mrs. Pike, just *sit down*." He had his hands flat on the desk top now.

"Why? You're about to stand up yourself, aren't you?" I said innocently, and then strode to the door and threw it open. In the larger room outside, a few clerks turned from typewriters and file cabinets, startled. "We might as well tell everyone," I called out into the room. "You may as well all know about Rosa Esposito. She—"

The lieutenant's large hand at my elbow moved me effortlessly aside, and with one foot he snapped the door shut.

"Mrs. Pike—" He kept the hand firm on my arm. The stone had definitely warmed up.

"Not here." I advanced the volume a little. "*Not* here."

"Okay." He swept a light overcoat from a hanger and guided me to a second door at the back of the office. "Not here."

We went by a counter manned by a surprised cop, then through a locked steel door with a glass observation window to a parking lot outside. We got into a rather dusty Nova with no extras, aside from the long scorpion tail of the radio transmitter.

"I thought I would get to ride in a real police car," I said.

He drove with a sure, steady force, just at the border of legality. Under the hood, clearly, there were some extras.

"You're a fake," he said, without looking at me.

"I beg your pardon."

"I doubt that, too. Now just what is it you have to say?"

"Lieutenant Hand," I said, putting as much ice as I could into my voice, "I am not doing this to amuse myself. I think I saw a murder committed. I have been followed by people I do not particularly care to cultivate. Furthermore, I think people in your organization have abused the information I have tried to give. Coffee would be available at that diner on your left. And since I have not been able to change clothes or water my plants or collect my mail for two days, I am not in a mood to waste more time. There is a parking space." I pointed somewhat imperiously, being quite carried away now in my kook role, and to my surprise he laughed.

"A good fake, I might add." He looked quite different when he smiled. The amber eyes took on heat. He opened the door for me with exaggerated politeness, and we stepped into the diner and took a booth at the rear.

After the coffee arrived, he left his cup untouched and regarded me steadily. I tried to outwait him, and then, at the same instant, we both grinned.

"I give you credit for figuring out that our security isn't perfect."

"Thanks."

"But why do you trust me?"

"I don't. Yet. That will depend on what kind of help I get."

"What kind of help do you need?"

It was a difficult request because it stirred up some possible responses that had nothing to do with the investigation. And I wasn't quick enough in answering to pretend that I took the question as entirely innocent. He smiled again.

I started over. "Let me ask you a couple of questions. Why is the police department interested in Rosa Esposito if she died in an accident?"

"I'm not the police department. I'm an officer on the homicide squad, and you turn in a report that claims you saw a murder committed." He shrugged. "It's my job."

"Second question. Did Rosa make contact with the police before she was killed? And by the way, it makes me nervous to be stared at constantly, Lieutenant Hand."

"Sorry." He didn't move his eyes from my face.

"No, you're not."

"You're right. I'm not. My name is Jack. Jack Bad Hand."

"Okay." I took a deep breath, trying to get rid of the hollow place. "Stella. But not right now, okay? I want to get things straight about Rosa first. You probably wonder why. I can't explain it. I just never saw anybody killed and swept up and forgotten, all inside an hour."

He nodded. "You didn't have to explain it to me. And the answer to question two is yes. She did. I take it you know about the state attorney's investigation?"

"I know of it. Not much about it. I'd like to hear more."

"At the moment it's a lot of rumor. We don't know each other well enough to allow me to speculate on rumors. But this much I do know. The last decent bust we made—I was part of it because a street dealer who agreed to plea-bargain got offed before the trial—involved three people who had worked for the state."

"In the rehabilitation program?"

"Right."

"Was Manuel Esposito one of them?"

Hand shook his head and gave me what I categorize as the pale grimace of admiration. "We've got nothing on him. He's been straight since he got out of the joint. And if you're going to ask where he was at eleven yesterday morning, I can tell you he was at work. Twenty people, including a security guard with a fifteen-year service record, saw him there. He's clean."

I smiled broadly. "What makes you think, Jack, that this accident was really a murder?"

He laughed out loud. A big, easy laugh through very white, very wide teeth. "I asked first."

"So you did. Have you by any chance driven the section of the Bayshore where the subject was found?"

"I have. I get the point. It isn't a likely place to stroll. And in all the eyewitness accounts that were filed, nobody claims *for certain* that they saw her on her feet before she was struck."

"If she had been, I would have seen her myself. A reeling drunk at roadside on a weekday morning? Hard to miss. And I have a habit of noticing things when I drive."

"I saw that."

We sat for a while, doodling with our cups. I shut my eyes then because the talk about the freeway had brought back a replay of the little nightmare I had seen in my rearview mirror.

"What's the matter?"

"I was just thinking about Rosa."

His eyes snapped to my face. "I didn't know you knew her."

"Oh, I didn't really. I've just thought about her. Married to some creep, strange country, getting it—that way."

"Maybe she asked for it."

"What makes you say that?" I flared a little. "Who asks to be hit by a truck?"

"I mean, she probably wasn't innocent of what Manuel

was up to—assuming he was up to something—and she worked in the same program."

"So what else was she to do? She hardly knew the language."

"She had another job."

"Oh?" It was my turn to be alert.

"Nothing connected to Manuel. She worked for an import store sometimes."

"Importing what?"

"Stuff from the south. Ponchos, skirts, huaraches."

"She was from down there?"

"Yeah, Peru."

I opened my mouth to protest surprise, but Hand was ahead of me.

"We checked out the firm. Very respectable. Customs went over them with a microscope. The stuff wasn't coming in that way."

"Very thorough." I pouted a little. "I thought maybe I would have a little job to do there. I like shopping anyway. What's the name of the firm?"

"Cordilleras Imports. Run by Alvin Zwicky, of the San Francisco family. Sugar, real estate, and Far East shipping."

"I've heard of them. Far East shipping. Well."

"Well what?"

"Just thinking about what a friend said to me. About California as a place where many roads cross. In certain trades."

"Umm." Lieutenant Hand had lost the thread of the conversation. He moved his empty cup around a little in its saucer. I noticed he was looking at my hands. I held them up and turned them around.

"Just hands."

"Umm. You don't play the piano."

"How do you know?"

"Piano players keep their fingernails short."

"Ah. Of course. Dumb of me." I wasn't really aware of an intention to take the lieutenant's hand, but he extended it in such a way that it was natural to do so. I frowned and began an inspection, but it was not very thorough.

"Well, you don't smoke. And you don't do a lot of rough work. And you are left-handed. By the way, how did you get the name?" I made a slight and not very convincing effort to release the hand.

"From my great-grandfather. He was a Hunkpapa Sioux. When he was a boy, he had some fingers blown off by a Crow scout."

"Oh." I couldn't think of anything appropriate to say.

"But my other half was shanty Irish, and we've been off the reservation for fifteen years. So you don't have to worry."

"I'm not worried."

"How about you?"

"I'm all white mongrel. Born in South San Francisco. Brought up to love money and leisure. But I turned into a meddler."

He smiled a little. "I gather. You know"—he shifted a little in his seat—"if you really want to help with this case . . ."

"Yes?" I cocked my head and began to smile but not with amusement. I had a hunch about what was coming.

He was examining my expression with care. "You know what I'm going to say, don't you?"

"I think so."

"And the answer is no."

"Not exactly."

"What?"

I released his hand and reached for my purse. "I'm not giving up, Lieutenant. I might have, actually, if so many bright young men were not so anxious to discourage me. But I must say you are the first to see the danger of heaping coals on the fire, or whatever the saying is."

"I'm not anxious to put out the fire," he said, "just keep it from burning you."

"I can take care of myself."

"Then why did you come to see me?"

"I thought we might help each other."

"All right. I'm telling you how you can help. By laying off right now, at least for a few days. I think the case is worth investigating, and I think it's possible you may be a very valuable witness, but I can't spring a man right now to tail you, and I can't do it myself. Give us a chance. You say you were followed. Can you give me a description of the man?"

"Sure. Also his license number." I fished around in my purse for the slip of paper with the numbers on it. The little revolver clanked against the edge of the table. Lieutenant Hand tugged the leather flap aside and glanced inside.

"Do you have a license to carry that?"

I jerked the purse away from him. "Do I get my one phone call right now?"

We locked eyes in a long look. Fire and ice. Back and forth.

"Forget it."

"I might." I found the slip, took a pen and copied the license number quickly on a napkin, added my friend Alice's phone number and address, then handed the napkin to him. "I'll lay off for two days. I've got a job I have to go to once in a while anyway. You can reach me at that number. I'll expect to hear from you by the weekend."

"You will." He was back to being Stone Face. We left the café, having paid separate checks, and on the way back to the station, I described the little man with the noiseless laugh. Otherwise, we exchanged exactly three more words.

"Next time," he said, letting me out of the car.

"Maybe," I answered.

Alice Talbot, my best friend, worked at a branch library in the Sunset District. She lived nearby, in a ground-floor flat with a neurotic sheep dog named Baudelaire. When I called her and told her why I wanted a place to crash for a few days, she wasn't at all nervous. In fact, the notion that I might be followed turned her on. Like a lot of librarians with degrees in English literature, she read nothing anymore but trashy stories of love and death.

"It's not like that, Alice. The man was an utter creep. One look, and I started carrying a gun."

"Oh, yum. You want to shoot him?"

I sighed. "No, Alice. Look, I'm going to swing by my apartment and pick up some clothes. And I've got to check in at the office. We could rendezvous at your place around six thirty?"

"Great. God, I'm so excited. *A murder.* I'll mix margaritas."

"Yeah. Listen, Alice, even if you don't know what we might be in for, I do, and I'm grateful."

"Well, you listen to my life story enough." She coughed.

"Who is it this time?" I tried to sound genuinely interested.

"An actor."

"An actor. Alice, you had an actor two years ago. It took the sheriff to get rid of him, if I remember correctly."

"Eric is *entirely* different."

"Eric? My God. But let's not start now. I'll see you tonight, okay?"

"Okay."

I left the phone booth feeling as if I had lived in one for the past twenty-four hours. Not only the real glass coffin, but a figurative one too. Since the man in the Mustang had entered my life, I had uncontrollable urges to look behind me, and even an empty sidewalk seemed sinister. I felt safe only in the Porsche. I relaxed on the freeway, except for the little stretch where Rosa had become a broken doll. Seeing it again, I knew there was no conceivable way I could have avoided spotting someone walking there. But I also realized how fast life is on the asphalt and how unaware of it most drivers are. They stare straight ahead, stoned on speed, until the taillights rush at them or a great bank of yellow warning blinkers jars them out of their trance. It was a good place to manufacture an accident. Very little would be left of the evidence.

When I stepped into the cool turquoise cave of the office, Gabby beckoned me from the open door of his inner chamber. I nodded to whichever of my cohorts happened to look up from a desk and registered, in their expressions, curiosity, and a touch of awe. The rumor of violent death had obviously made the rounds.

"I am losing my mind," Gabby began, picking up a batch of papers from the heap on his desk and slamming them down again. "The Tyson people called again this morning. 'Where is she?' I ask. Nobody knows. You have to do this, I know. But we cannot go on this way. I need you." His voice took on a whine, and his round, bald head tossed like a Ping-Pong ball going over rapids.

"Easy, Gabby, easy." I threw out both arms expansively. "Look at this, Gabby. A successful business. Dacron wall to wall, gold thread in the drapes, typewriters that look like the control panels in a moon shot—what more can you ask for?" Gabby was one of those men, often short and ugly men, who need constant reassurance. Nothing calmed him quicker than talk of success and money.

"Yes, yes." His head stopped bouncing for a moment, but then he looked darkly at the corners of the room. "But the month is bad. We need a shot in the butt. This woman—what happened? You're all right?"

"I'm fine. She's dead. Listen, bubbe, I've got to ask you—no, no, don't say anything yet—for some favors. The truth is I've run into some trouble. I can't tell you about it yet, but I need some help. *Really* need it. Because it's real trouble. Have you ever done any work for Zwicky, the sugar and real estate people?"

The expression of deep concern Gabby had assumed vanished immediately into his familiar look of narrow calculation. "Yeah. They were in that group of realtors that had us run the study of Chinatown."

"How about an import firm, Cordilleras? Alvin Zwicky runs it."

"Lemme think. Wait. No." He shook his head. "We did do something on Cost Plus once. They had an employee problem. But Cordyhairus—what the hell is that, I never heard of. Why?"

"I want to talk to them and make it look like business. Suppose I con them into an employee-attitudes study like the one you did for Cost Plus. That would make up for my being pretty scarce for a couple of weeks?"

"A couple of *weeks!*" Gabby said something clearly obscene in Armenian and reached for the edge of the desk with an unsteady hand.

"Don't run that act on me, Gab. I know you can spare me. I'll work all afternoon on the Tyson thing, and you've got nothing really hot for me after that. And I will land something with Zwicky. I promise."

"Listen." He leveled a crooked little finger at me. "You—"

"I can't, I've got to get busy. Money flies, you know. Why are we loafing?"

I left him, the finger still extended and his mouth open, and made my way cheerily to my desk. I was glad, for once, that there was a stack of forms and a list of urgent calls to make. It felt good to be a normal employee for a few hours. Even if it was a dangerous illusion.

Chapter VIII

I betrayed Jack Bad Hand, and made a terrible mistake, on my way to Alice's after work. I was looking over our old account with the realtor's association, to see who represented the Zwicky interests, when I found myself humming "Bernie's Tune," one of the numbers the trio had done at the King's Tavern. "Bernie" to "Bennie" was an obvious play, and when I remembered the way he looked, hunched over the bass, lost in the music, I had a sudden impulse to talk to him again. There was something in that look I trusted and wanted to know more about. Whatever Rosa had been to him, I was willing to bet he hadn't hurt her. But I had also sensed, when I traded questions with him in the bar, that he was protecting her still, hiding something.

It took only a casual call to the tavern to get his address. I became, temporarily, a clerk at a music store. A gentleman had left a package on the counter. In chatting with him, I had learned where he was employed. Was there a short, slim, bespectacled young musician there, and could we forward his package . . . ? Wearily the gravel-voiced bartender interrupted me to tell me Bennie lived in the Haight District, the former psychedelic slum that was gradually being transformed into a toney residential neighborhood. It was more or less on my way to Alice's, so I left the office early, hoping to get in an hour or so of talk with Bennie, in more comfortable circumstances.

The number I had corresponded to the one on a rambling gray house. There was a tricycle on the front steps, however, and some kind of mandala made of macrame and seashells hanging in the window. Along one side of the house there was a narrow path of broken concrete screened by a high hedge. It ended in a rickety gate that bore a small sign: EAT ART. That sounded more like Bennie than tricycles or seashells, and as I neared the gate, I could hear a stereo playing what sounded like Stan Kenton at close to full volume.

I pushed open the gate and found myself in one of those hidden courtyards that lurk behind a lot of old San Francisco houses. There was a little cottage at the rear almost swallowed in wisteria and bougainvillaea, and the yard was a mass of unkempt ferns, roses, and Japanese plums. The cottage lacked paint, and there were a couple of splintered lawn chairs collapsing into the vegetation, but it was still very pleasant, much more so than I had expected. The music was loud enough to vibrate the glass panes in the door, I noticed, as I punched the button. I could hear no chime within, so after a decent interval I pushed on the door, and it swung open.

Sparse but comfortable. A fat, old-fashioned sofa and chair, one good Persian rug, a few cheap prints. The bass was parked in a corner next to a cabinet stuffed with sheet music and topped by a few bottles and an ice bucket. The music was thundering out of a huge walnut stereo cabinet, obviously the most valuable piece of furniture in the house. Its top was propped open, and I could see a stack of records on the spindle of the turntable. Through an archway a kitchen glared white under a bare bulb. Another door to my left was ajar, and I could see the corner of a bed and a patch of dappled light coming through the window. I went to the door and nudged it open. Bennie was sitting in a leather chair with his back to me, looking out the window at the leaves dancing in the sky. One foot was parked on a small table in front of him. The sock had lost its elastic band and drooped around his skinny ankle.

I cleared my throat. "You're home," I said brightly, stepping around the chair. "I hope you don't mind—"

Bennie didn't mind. His eyes were wide open, like the shutter of a broken camera. His mouth was open slightly, too, and a bit of drool strung down to a dark patch on his shirtfront. One hand was tangled in his fly, as if he had started to rip away his clothes. The sleeve on his other arm was rolled up, and sticking in the colorless flesh were a little glass tube and a pink balloon of rubber.

My throat tightened against a thud of acid from my wrenched stomach. Something about the hands, one frozen into a claw, the other loose and shapeless, made me avert my eyes. A night before those hands had shaped beautiful sounds. They had been deformed by death, made ugly in their stillness.

I don't know how long I stood there, working to control my breathing. I remember that I took note of the little envelope, with a spill of white powder on the open flap, the spoon with its discolored bottom, and the burned matchsticks. I saw also a month-old issue of *Newsweek* and a heavy square book with the title *Ancient Kingdom of the Sun.* Then I didn't notice anything but the silence. The record had ended. I heard the arm click back, and the next disc dropped.

It hit me then that somebody, maybe Bennie and maybe not, had put on that stack of records. And if there were several still on the spindle, that meant that only two or three had been played. Less than an hour. Less than an hour ago Bennie was probably alive. I jumped when a piano and sax boomed the chords of the first cut on the new side. Brubeck and Desmond. "Time Out." But there wasn't any time-out for me, I knew. I turned and walked, leaning stiffly, as if I had to face a cold wind, out of the room, out of the house, back down the path to the street.

I did not think. My body moved out of its habit. I did not really see either. What I remember next is trying to get my ignition key into the door lock. As I did so I became aware of a car engine, a low burble of exhaust, beside me. Then a hand closed on my elbow. When I jerked around, there were two of them, one on each side of me, and they began to laugh uproariously and shout in my ears. One was the little man with the pencil mustache and black holes for eyes; the other was the driver of the pickup in front of the Esposito home. I tried a scream, but shock had already taken most of the breath out of me. Down the street I could see a lady getting out of a station wagon with a bag of groceries, and a group of school kids dawdling along. They looked our way and grinned. The two funny men were moving me toward the car, whose back door was open. It was a big car. A Chrysler. I was badly crowded in this threesome. My feet were not in constant contact with the asphalt, so my efforts to run may have looked like a kind of prancing. The lady, on her way to the front door, gave us one disgusted glance over a carton of eggs.

"Now I give you a ride, baby," the man in the suit said, between his loud and mechanical bursts of sound. He took one of his hands away and placed it on the roof of the Chrysler for leverage. That gave me a little room, and I managed to get my fingers under the flap of my handbag.

The younger man, still in jeans and dirty T-shirt, slid his hand to the back of my neck and pointed my head toward the dark cavern of the back seat. "Get the fuck in," he said, and dug his thumb behind my ear.

The other leaned toward me, still grinning wide, the holes of his eyes only inches away from my face. "Get in, baby."

I got the gun clear of the purse, and though I could move my arm only from the elbow down, he was so near I managed to put the barrel on his mustache, its mouth at his nostril, as if to demonstrate an unusual new spray device for clogged sinuses.

"I'm going to blow your head off . . ." I whispered hoarsely. At last something flickered in his eyes, above the frozen grin. The laughter stopped as if someone had jerked the plug on an audience-response generator.

"*La puta,*" snarled the young man, and his hands fluttered away from me. I rotated the revolver slowly so that the stubby barrel rested lightly on the end of the little man's nose.

I had forgotten about the car, which of course had a driver—though from my angle I could see nothing but a hand on the wheel, like a pale, dead fish through the tinted glass. Now the car surged ahead, and the young man gave a choked cry and lunged after the door handle. My eyes shifted a little, involuntarily, and the man in front of me moved. I squeezed the trigger, hard. Nothing happened. The man's face floated away from me, and I swung the revolver to follow it, the muscles in my hand rigid with strain. As in a slow-motion sequence in a film, I saw them falling into the car as it pulled away, arms and legs splayed out, the door gaping open until, halfway down the block, it clapped shut.

When they were gone around the corner, I brought the .32 in close and inspected it, like a rare and strange flower found in my hand upon waking from a dream.

Ah, the safety. Of course, of course. I remembered then. When I first acquired the weapon, when the whole city was jittery about the Golden Dragon massacre, the salesman had stressed over and over the dangers of accidental discharge. So I learned to lock the mechanism in place with my thumb. My body, still operating on radar from the shock of seeing Bennie's corpse, had automatically made its accustomed movements. The trigger finger obeyed my will; my thumb—a stubby little agent of the unconscious—canceled the message.

With something between horror and exhilaration, I slipped the revolver back into my purse. I had tried, despite a complete lack of experience, to kill someone. Had I thought of it, I would have slipped the safety and the hammer would have fallen, the percussion cap would have ignited the powder, and the small teardrop of lead would have made its way through a man's skull, emptying it of all evil intent. It would have been messy at such close range, and I was relieved not to have to deal with that.

On the other hand, I felt a new confidence, based, I suppose, on the simple knowledge that I could do it if I had to. I hoped I wouldn't have to. But if I knew myself as well as I thought I did, I would have strict orders ready for that thumb next time.

When I managed to get into my car, I drove to Alice's with the persnickety care of an octogenarian in a Model A. Because my automatic pilot had definitely quit. The rush-hour traffic crawled through the up-and-down streets of the city, so by the time I rang the buzzer to the flat— sending Baudelaire into paroxysms of mock ferocity—I was more or less steady.

"Shush, stupid." Alice dragged the door open with one hand, while Baudelaire yelped from the other. She shook the dog's collar, and he subsided into growls. When I stepped inside, he shrank behind his mistress.

"You look tremendous." Alice embraced me, and we pecked each other ritually. "A little pale and narrow, but I like. Sort of Jane Fonda as Camille. Come into the kitchen. I'm making pasta, and the margaritas are in the freezer." I followed Alice's athletic stride down the hallway, noticing that she had gone to Turkish pants of deep indigo while maintaining her faded blue work shirt with the sleeves rolled up.

Alice was one of those deceptive types: She wore horn-rimmed spectacles and a severe suit at the library, but if men observed closely what was inside this costume, they started coming around, checking out more books than they were ever likely to read. "A sleeper," the term is, and in Alice's case it had a sometimes unfortunate appropriateness. Though shrewd and able with words, and a walking secondhand store of rare information, she had trouble controlling certain primal urges and was usually taken advantage of. Much of her time away from the job was spent either dodging passes or falling for them with a dangerous enthusiasm.

When the margaritas were poured, in proper glasses with a hoarfrost of salt on the rim, Alice propped a fist under her cheek and looked at me with a little sheen of wetness in her myopic green eyes.

"Oh, Stella, I don't know where to start. This thing has me going around like a washing machine stuck in full cycle."

"The actor?"

"Yeah." She sighed and sipped her drink. "I've been belting these down every night for a week trying to attain clairvoyance, but it doesn't work. I know I should stay away from him. The life they lead, you know, in the theater. But great God, Stella, he's"—she sighed even more deeply—"a wonderful bastard. You know. I can't stay away from the type."

I nodded. "I know."

"So it's all up in the air, as usual. You know, the last time—" She stopped and blinked.

"I remember. The broker."

"But what am I going on for? Good Lord, Stella. You've been finding strange men in your apartment and investigating murders, and I don't know what. How've you been?"

I gazed into Alice's wide and sympathetic eyes, and all at once I started to laugh. I laughed until the tears ran down and dropped from my chin, while Alice fluttered around the kitchen in alarm, asking if I wanted water or aspirin.

"It's all right," I got out finally. "Don't mind me. I've had an unusual week. You go ahead with the pasta, and let me use the phone."

I left her rolling out the dough and glancing at me nervously, took the margarita, and went in to lie on the queen-size bed and dial a number on the Princess phone that was hand-painted in a zebra pattern. Alice had a sense of humor.

The clerk who answered had asthma.

"Homicide detail," he wheezed.

"I have a message for Lieutenant Hand. Tell him to call the nonpiano player. Now. From a safe phone."

"Who is this?"

"Just tell him that. The nonpiano player. Outside line."

"*What?*"

"*Non*-piano player. Right away."

"Just one—"

I hung up.

The bedroom was cool and dark. Alice had slightly unorthodox tastes. The bedspread and drapes were harem purple, and there was an ornate brass candelabrum on a nightstand, with long black candles in the sockets. But these touches, like the zebra telephone, were comforting. Evidence of harmless eccentricity that I found restful. I drifted back over the day. The tentative alliance with Jack Bad Hand was the only anchor I had to cling to.

I began to realize something else, too. Until this afternoon I'd kept open the option of dropping the whole thing. Frank's argument had some force. There were people who drew salaries for this sort of thing; they had secretaries and expense accounts, and contacts with the underworld, and cars with radios, and obedient thumbs. I thought that I could convince them to seek out Rosa Esposito's killers, so I could return to my normal harmless life. But things had gone too far for that now. Frank had indicated that the professionals were going to play along for the moment, until they thought the big fish were in the net. In the meantime, I was one of the minnows that were serving as bait. In fact, I was the chief minnow because I was the only one who had witnessed the murder.

The phone jangled me out of my reverie.

"Can you help me?" I said into the receiver.

"If you need a hand."

"That's very good. A Hand. I may need both of them. I have just seen my second body."

"What?" His voice had sharpened.

"One of Rosa's friends. A musician named Bennie. He's dead. I left him about thirty minutes ago, in a cottage at the rear of Two-forty-seven Oak, just off Haight."

"What do you mean, you left him? What the hell were you doing there anyway?"

I felt oddly the way I had twenty years ago, when my

mother found a cache of books I wasn't supposed to be old enough to read. "I'm sorry, Jack. I shouldn't have. I guess. But I did find something, didn't I?"

"Goddamn it. You—oh, forget it. Dead how?"

"There was a needle in his arm."

"Hot shot."

"What?"

"Strychnine. Listen, have you told anyone else?"

"No." I thought of the absurdity of my conversation with Alice. I hadn't told her because it was hard enough for me to believe what I had seen. "No, but I think the word is out. Coming out of there, I picked up an escort."

There was a pause. "Stella, spare me jokes right now, okay?"

"Okay. I'm sorry. I was rattled, and I get smartass when that happens. The little man who showed up in my flat, and another hood I saw moving furniture from Rosa's. The two of them tried to give me a little joyride—in a Chrysler just like the one I saw her shoved out of."

There was an extended pause. When he finally spoke, Jack Hand's voice had gone to pure stone.

"Tried?"

"I shooed them off. With that gun I don't have a license for."

"They'll kill you. They have to now. For the sake of their pride, if nothing else."

It was my turn to pause. It was one thing to think the worst and another thing to hear someone state it flatly.

"I suppose they'll try."

"You suppose. Jesus Christ, Stella, do you see what you've gotten yourself into?"

"You know, I'll tell you something. I'm getting very tired of listening to people who seem to think it's *my* fault a band of creeps is running around pushing people out of speeding cars or sticking needles in them, or whatever. If we're going to go through that again, I'm hanging up. I've reported the crime, Lieutenant Hand, and you can take it from there." I poised one finger over the button of the receiver cradle, ready to sever the conversation.

"Okay. Go ahead. Hang up."

I didn't. The finger wobbled a little, just touched the button, and then retreated. After a while he spoke again. Some humanity had crept back into his voice.

"Okay. Let's drop that line of discussion. You're in it, up to your neck, and that's that. No use beating it to death."

"I'd prefer another phrase."

"Right. Sorry." I could hear the smile in his voice. "The priority now is to keep you alive. I want you to stay where you are—at this address you gave me—and I'll be over as soon as I deal with Bennie. Don't let anyone else through the door. I've turned up a couple of interesting things to talk about."

"I've got no urge to roam around. I'll be here. That's a double promise. Shall I save a plate for you? Alice is making rigatoni."

With a surprising reserve and tone of propriety, he answered, "If you are certain I won't be disturbing you."

"A small disturbance might be good for one."

"Yes. It might. You know something?"

"What?"

"You've got guts. But I like you anyway."

"I don't know what to say."

"Good. I'll see you in a couple of hours. So long."

I lay there musing for a few minutes after hanging up. *Guts* but *I like you anyway. But.* What should I tell him? *You're honest, tough, smart, bigoted, and twice my size,* but *you attract me anyway? You're hard as a stone, but that's what I need right now?* Men. I sighed and sat up to fumble after my shoes. If you didn't bore them, you scared them. Or—I sighed again—you ended up having to fool them.

Chapter IX

Alice and I waded into the pasta, green salad, and French bread, jabbering between bites about life, fate, new fabrics, and my murder.

"It's not really mine," I remonstrated. "I think I have found a trustworthy detective to take responsibility for it. He's coming around to discuss the case tonight."

"Oh?" Alice gave me a keen, speculative look. "Well, fabulous. I plan to be at Eric's right after dinner. So make yourselves at home." She grinned. "How positively *necromantic* to meet somebody this way. Tell me about him."

"Oh, no," I began. "It's not—"

"Don't kid me, Stella. I know you. What's he like?"

"I see it is useless to try to derail a one-track mind. There *are* other things in the world, Alice."

"Most of them boring. So tell me."

"He's half Sioux and half Irish. Can be considered handsome, in a stern sort of way. Honest, I think."

"An *Indian.* Interesting, interesting. He can trace the killer by the broken twigs."

"You're off base. He's a hip Indian."

"I'll bet." Alice rolled her eyes.

"Anyway"—I frowned—"it's very useful to have a large and alert friend right now."

"Useful. Don't get carried away, Stella."

"I think you could be useful, too."

"Tell."

"Check the *Assembly Record* and find out who set up Start Over, what committee keeps it going."

"Easy."

"I also need a book. *Ancient Kingdom of the Sun* by Hof-glauben or Von Gaugen or something. A German."

"For a detective you're not much on names."

"There was a corpse in the way. I couldn't see the whole page."

"What corpse?" Alice had just moved dessert between us. Her eyes grew wide, and she reached for a strawberry, then dipped it in sour cream.

I told her about Bennie.

"So I'm not taking up archaeology. It just might give a clue."

"God, Stella. Sure I'll get you the book. God." She was popping one strawberry after another. "You have a talent for finding dead bodies."

"You have a talent for being late." I glanced pointedly at the clock on the wall.

"Ouch. Right."

Alice slipped hurriedly into her night costume and departed in a receding roll of thunder from her sports car. I took a glass of cold white wine into the living room and picked out a book to while away the hours. I selected a chair near the fireplace, away from the bay windows and the double-locked front door. Already I was acquiring the habits of a fugitive and becoming accustomed to an odd vacuum of expectation under my ribs, a feeling that something unpleasant—yet obscurely exciting—was coming sooner or later.

Alice's library had a front of tomes by writers like Kier-kegaard and Sartre and Jung, covering a main stock of much-thumbed paperback novels and a few volumes of poetry. I didn't feel I had the resources to embark on an investigation of the ultimate nature of reality, even with white wine for a chaser, and too many of the paperbacks had titles like *The Hooker and The Hangman* or *Terror on Fifth Street.* So I wound up with poetry, which I approach somewhat like those chips of beef jerky that Danny sells in his bar. Small bites that take a lot of chewing but last you for many hours.

It was an anthology of modern stuff. Modern apparently meant recently deceased. A few of the contributors I had heard of. Wallace Stevens I remembered because his titles were always funnier than his poems. The poems weren't bad either, but my teachers in college were fond of inflicting them on us as "examples of contemporary sensibility." By the time they were through festooning the lines with a claptrap of symbols and allusions and biographical anecdotes, I didn't understand them at all. I turned a page, and my eye caught and held on a pair of lines.

> Morning is not sun,
> It is this posture of the nerves.

I didn't bother to read the rest of the poem around this terse statement. It sufficed. It expressed what I feared my mornings were going to be like from now on. The little .32 would be under my pillow, and every car that whispered by on the street below would trouble my sleep. When the day began, I would be poised and wary. No more dawdling over coffee and the *Chronicle*. No more late-evening strolls through Dolores Park to the coffee-houses in Noe Valley. That single idle glance into my rearview mirror had altered the set of my spine, given me the tense attitude of the hunter—and the hunted.

Outside, a car pulled into the driveway. Without thinking much about it, I slid to the window, took the little revolver out of my purse, and edged the curtain aside to peer out. It was Hand. He unfolded out of the front seat, shut the car door gently, and patted his coat. I grinned, knowing he was checking a shoulder holster. His swift scan of the front of the building stopped at the crack of light where I stood. With the barrel of the gun, I pushed the curtain wider yet, so he could see my face. I stuck my tongue out at him, and he shook his head and bounded up the porch stairs.

When I unlocked the door, he stepped in quickly and nodded at the .32 still in my hand.

"Loaded?"

"You bet."

"You're guilty of a violation of California Penal Code, Section one-two-oh-three-one. Put it back in your purse where I can't see it, and we can add a count on Section One-two-oh-two-five." He looked exhausted and worried, but he tried a game grin. "You must be dangerous."

"So disarm me."

We each took a step then and clapped together like magnets. I hadn't realized how much pent-up need had accumulated. It was the same for Jack. There is, as everyone knows, a certain current that passes between certain people: a current of liquid fire galvanizing hands and lips first and then erupting in the loins. There is no explaining it and—in my experience—not much use in fighting it. I don't suppose it was very proper—it being our first date, so to speak—but propriety had not recently been playing a significant part in my life anyway. What we said, or murmured or gasped, whenever our mouths unstuck for a breath, I don't remember.

I don't remember anything, actually, except for the ease with which his large hands cupped my bottom and lifted me away from earth. When I started registering things consciously again, we were on the purple bedspread, without any clothes, looking at each other with stupefied expressions. I watched my own hand move lightly over Jack's chest, over strands and sheets of muscle that made a surface like dented copper.

"Well."

"Well."

We laughed simultaneously. A small, embarrassed laugh.

"A pleasure to meet you again," I said.

"Indeed."

We looked at each other for a while the way people without clothes do.

"I think," I said, "we should postpone discussion."

He smiled. I smiled back. We got vertical and tidy and returned to the living room, where I poured us both stiff drinks. There was an awkward silence. He gave me a little salute with the glass.

"Only a postponement."

"Agreed."

"Ready?"

"Sure." I settled into the couch. "Let's go."

"The worst of it first. It wasn't strychnine. Your friend Bennie was hit with enough pure horse to kill a football team, and there is no way we could manage a murder charge. It looks like a clear case of OD. To treat it otherwise would tip off the inside man. Same thing with Rosa. The blood tests showed she was drunk to the point of passing out. A couple of the witnesses on the scene said they 'thought' they saw her stagger onto the roadway. I had an excuse for going over the autopsy report because of your objection, but if I persist, they'll get suspicious—if they aren't already—that we are working together. My best chance to find whoever it is who leaks this stuff is to pretend I'm dropping the investigation because I think you're batty."

"Hence," I said with as cool a laugh as I could muster, "leaving me a lonely and defenseless psychotic."

"That was my original idea. I thought they might try to scare you a little. Then, if you pretended to give up the whole thing, they'd leave you alone."

"They scared me all right." I mentioned the attempted abduction but left out the matter of my recalcitrant thumb. I pretended that I only had to wave the gun to drive them off.

Hand was frowning, giving me a steady stare. "I suppose you know you can get hurt bad that way. Bad."

"Maybe even hurt dead."

"I've thought some more about that. I doubt that they will kill you. Yet."

"Oh?" I threaded a note of petulance into my voice. "Have I lost status since you called this afternoon?"

"No. But I filed a report on your testimony, to keep the case open in my office. It wouldn't look good to take out the only dissenting witness. Besides, you're a white lady, ex-wife of an influential attorney."

"So Frank talked to you."

Hand didn't speak or nod. He waited.

"I'd like to know what he's told you."

"Not much. He said to take care of you."

"I doubt that he expected such thorough care."

Hand didn't flinch. "I didn't expect it either."

"Nor I." I unwound from the couch and went to replenish our drinks. After I filled his glass, I kissed him lightly. "Very thorough."

"We're postponing, I thought."

"Right. Sorry." I sat back down.

"Anyway, I don't think you're in danger of running into anything worse than a broken arm or nose or maybe some fingers or a faceful of acid."

"How considerate of them."

"Oh, they'd *like* to kill you, I imagine. It's just not advantageous."

"These impersonal pronouns give me the creeps. Do you have any names to substitute?"

Hand sipped his drink. "Nothing I can prove."

"Oh, come on, Jack. Surely we have established the base for a little confidence. I won't tell."

"All I know for certain is that the names are likely to turn out to be very familiar and very big. That's why Frank is interested. As you know, in this state the attorney general's office has often been the trampoline that gets you into the governor's mansion. And whoever is chief prosecutor in this business will have an excellent chance of being the next man on the trampoline."

"That's Frank. He lacks an upper limit."

"He's not alone. That's what makes the matter so tricky. You know about the rehabilitation programs?"

"A little. Newspaper knowledge."

"And how do you figure the Espositos' connection to them?"

I took a deep breath. "All sheer speculation, Officer.

But here goes. I get the impression that some of the funds allocated to the programs wound up in the pockets of people who put them to rather unusual uses. I remember reading somewhere that one of these programs made a point of hiring ex-junkies. On the AA principle: A reformed sinner is the best preacher. A noble principle, but dangerous if the reformation doesn't go deep enough.

"I also know that the methadone program, for example, actually deals dope—legal, medicinal dope, of course—and so there's a mechanism for shipping and handling and dispensing drugs, maintained and protected by the state. Isn't it just the most perfect cover ever invented for a narcotics racket? Especially if the people who pass the laws that set up such programs are willing to take a little grease. Why, the taxpayers' dimes and dollars could be purchasing coke and smack for our criminals without any need for private capital. It's socialism. That's maybe what's wrong with it."

"You have an odd sense of humor. But you get a lot out of the newspapers. More than most people. That's pretty much how I figure it. But there are some other twists. The counties where these rehab centers are located enjoy having a few million injected—so to speak—into the community economy. Also, some of the bills that authorize the programs are general mental health legislation, and a lot of politicians argue that the baby mustn't be thrown out with the bathwater. So there's some resistance in Sacramento to the whole investigation. Another irony is that the taxpayers aren't really out any cash—the funds may be used to float dope deals, but they always put back the seed money."

"So where's the crime?"

"Misappropriation of funds is the only charge that might stick at the moment. And the auditors are having problems finding the laundry. It will be extremely difficult to connect a murder or narc rap to this outfit. They're careful."

"Why would it be hard? You have the body."

"Multiplicity of motives." He ticked them off on his fingers. "Manuel—jealous estranged husband. Or anybody else in the vehicle could claim she was drunk and jumped, so they got scared and left the scene. That's abetting a suicide or maybe hit-and-run. Involuntary manslaughter at most. They'd pay off somebody to take a light rap like that. With a good lawyer, maybe he'd walk."

"Walk?"

"Get acquitted."

"Oh." I smiled at him. "It will take me a while to learn the vocabulary. What about Bennie?"

"Impossible to tell homicide from an OD. When a street pusher wants to get rid of a junkie, he can pass him a bindle of pure stuff. If the junkie is used to smack that has been stepped on—cut—he'll shoot up with his normal hit and go out."

"Was Bennie using regularly?"

"Hard to tell. He had tracks, all right. The autopsy might turn up something else. But it's hard for me to justify investigating dead dopers." Hand shrugged. "Hierarchical society. Even among corpses."

"You're saying nobody is really interested then."

"That's about it. No relatives have turned up so far. Nobody has connected the deaths to the investigation of misusing funds. Nobody cares." Hand smiled thinly. "You'd be surprised how many people would shrug and say, 'What's one more of those people?' "

"A week ago, I might have too."

"We've got nothing except for a prior address. I ran it down, and it's a hippie house in Berkeley. Man by the name of Eliot holds the lease. You might check it out—less threatening than I would be." He took a slip of paper from his wallet and handed it to me.

"What about hole-eyes and his friend? Any luck tracing them?"

"The Mustang belongs to somebody named Guillermo Gutierez, who was born in Bogotá. May or may not be the man who was following you. The pickup—" Jack grinned, without much humor. "Guess."

"I give up."

"Rosa."

I nodded. "Like you said. They seem to be careful."

"I may have got something on the Chrysler."

"But—" I intercepted an expression of what was probably as close as Jack ever got to glee. "Okay, Old Brokentwig, how did you do it?"

"Pretty elementary. I was looking over the readout on stolen cars for the last couple of months. A Chrysler— any luxury car, in fact—is a very poor choice for auto theft. They're easy to spot, hard to unload, and they usually belong to people who put a lot of heat on us to find them. So I noticed that one of those big boats was listed, a model like the one you say you saw Rosa fall out of."

I leaned forward. "You caught them, or . . ." Hand shook his head. "Ah. So who did it belong to?"

"It was a company car. Registered to Cordilleras Imports."

I sat back. "Bingo."

We looked at each other for a while.

"Could be coincidence." Hand emptied his drink.

"Sure. Could be."

We were grinning at each other like a couple of sharks.

Chapter X

The postponement was rescinded finally, and Jack did not glide out the door until nearly 4:00 A.M. Before that happened, we agreed on a rough working plan. My part of it was to worm my way into Cordilleras and try to find out what, if anything, connected Zwicky enterprises, Rosa, and Bennie's former landlord. My partner was going to concentrate on locating the leak in police security and look for an underworld contact who might drop some hints about the rehabilitation programs in our county. We were to check with each other every day and sometimes, it was understood, at night. There was a lot unsaid between us. And we both knew it might never get said either. Still, it was very nice. Not the sort of thing I generally rush into, and there were twinges of wait-I'm-not-that-kind-of-girl, but for the moment it was doing a lot for my metabolism.

Morning was sun after all, not a posture of nerves, when I eased into the parking lot in front of the import store. Cordilleras was one of four firms in a big, remodeled warehouse on Bay Street. An architect had done a lot with redwood and glass, and a landscaper had matched it with ivy and ferns and a couple of tiny courtyards where some urban pigeons were strutting stagily about.

The receptionist, Darlene Jaspers according to her little nameplate, was thin and middle-aged, with uninhabited eyes and a tense mouth. She was dressed like the pigeons, in gray and starch white, and looked at me the way one of them might regard a piece of popcorn that had been in the gutter too long.

"May I help you?" She didn't mean it. She looked down to feed her pet typewriter another slice of white paper.

"Tell Alvin Zwicky the lady from Garabedian, Daugherty, and Bissel is here. Stella Pike."

"Who?" She was adjusting a margin, punching one corner of the tight mouth between her teeth.

"Never mind, I'll tell him myself." I was beyond her desk and had a hand on the door to the inner office before her head snapped up and she was ready to take me seriously.

"You can't—" she squawked, but it was too late. I was inside, standing on a huge blaze of color, surrounded by hideous carved faces, feathered lances and clubs, and great disks of intricately worked metal. At the far end of the room, against a glass wall full of bare sky, was a desk with a man behind it.

Alvin Zwicky was a man who had been around money all his life. The charcoal suit had a fine pinstripe of smoke gray to match the shade of his full head of hair; there was a glint of gold at his cuffs and on the big, knotted fingers; the skin of his face was tanned and stretched tight over the skull. Everything about him had the kind of care and precision that money by itself won't buy. It takes two or three generations to achieve that grade of polish.

"What is it?" His eyes, a blue shading to tarnished silver, were not polite.

"It's a great opportunity," I said, striding across the brilliant carpet. "You can be happier, Darlene Jaspers will be happier—so will your other employees—you'll have more time off, and you'll save money besides."

I parked my briefcase on one corner of his desk and flipped it open. "I'm Stella Pike, from Garabedian, Daugherty, and Bissel. The people who understand people. We're—"

Not very gently he reached across the desk and pushed the flap of my briefcase closed.

"Miss," he said, and the pale blue eyes were at my face like flames, "I don't appreciate your approach. You do not have an appointment. If you will please step out—"

"You will. Believe me you will." I opened the case again and took out a couple of our most impressive fake studies.

I was doing what in my trade is called walking on water.
If you move fast enough, you may not sink. "We can show
you what your closest associates are *really* thinking. What's
really going on in your organization." I winked at him.

A burn appeared underneath his tan. He moved aside
the folders with one finger. "That's quite enough. I must
ask you—"

"You know, Mr. Zwicky, there are people who wonder
if you really are in business. That is, in the business you
say you are in."

The burn faded into a hint of ash.

"What in the world are you talking about?"

With a little laugh I sat down in the contoured leather
chair beside his desk. "I thought you'd never ask. It will
take a little explaining, but I assure you it's worth your
time. Would you mind if I smoked one of those Balkan
Sobranies?"

There was a considerable pause. A couple of decades.
Finally, somewhere a long way on the other side of the
silver-blue eyes, a shadow moved. He smiled briefly and
pushed the tin toward me. "Please."

I took a cigarette, tapped it on the desk, and hung it
from my lower lip. He snapped the desk lighter for me,
and we regarded each other over the flame. When there
was a curtain of smoke between us, I smiled back.

"Thank you. I should apologize for being so forward.
But you are an extremely difficult man to reach."

"You seem to have managed."

"Not very politely, I'm afraid. I am sorry."

He flashed a grin suddenly. "I'm afraid I don't quite
believe you, Miss Pike. You may even be a little proud of
yourself. Not very many people have gotten around Darlene. But now that you are here—as you certainly are—I
would appreciate your getting to the point." He glanced at
a small, flat gold watch. "I have an engagement in fifteen
minutes." He turned on his patina of professional cor-
diality. Coming through it was a cold, shrewd stare. "What
is it you want? Really?"

I almost told him. *I want to know if you run dope, Mr.*

Zwicky. And have people killed. But I didn't say it out loud. The hesitation would be enough to let him know he couldn't be sure of me, and uncertainty would keep him listening.

"Well." I aimed a jet of smoke at one of the snarling wooden faces on the wall. "In fifteen minutes it will be difficult. But I'll try." I took one of the reports in hand and flipped a few pages into it. "Actually we worked for you once before. You're a partner in a real estate firm— Best Buildings—and we did an employee profile on that firm for the Realtors' Association in '77. See? Here. Now, although the results of that study were available in very inexpensive printout, the association says that Best Buildings never even requested a follow-up. Even though every other firm that undertook the EP study and complied with our recommendations reported substantial savings at the next quarterly production accounting. Now—"

"We are no longer connected with real estate ventures. It was a temporary sideline, an experiment." Zwicky glanced again at his watch.

I sliced under one column of figures with my fingernail. "Of course. The point is you didn't look at the results of the experiment. And it didn't cost you anything. Or very little."

He leaned back in his padded swivel chair of burnt orange and regarded the city through the glass wall. "So. You conclude that Alvin Zwicky doesn't care if a business makes money or not. Is that it?"

"I didn't say that."

"What, exactly, did you say, Miss Pike?"

I gave him my most sparkle-toothed smile. "Call me Stella?"

The smile he returned was on the thin side. "Fine. What, exactly, did you say, Stella?"

I took another drag on the cigarette, feeling very glad that I was not on the other side of the table from Zwicky in a stock war. "I said people might get the idea your businesses weren't serious. If somebody gives you an opportunity to boost earnings and you pass it up . . ." I shrugged. "Anyway, a friend of mine—a writer—has been interested in what she calls the Playboy Merchants. The scions of old families in San Francisco who undertake business as a hobby or as a social accomplishment. Companies like charter boat lines or foreign consulting firms. Or import stores. Businesses that involve travel, some excitement . . ." I trailed off.

"And?" He was watching me the way a snake watches a baby bird teetering on the edge of its nest.

"Well," I said, as ingenuously as I could, "I told her she couldn't jump to conclusions about you. That I had just gotten the job of doing employee profiles and that I'd find out if you really were interested in running an import company properly. It's my job anyway. If you're not . . ."

The bird lifted one claw and lurched. The snake glided forward.

"If not?"

"She might want to feature you in *Western Ways.*" The magazine was a large one that practiced a very popular blend of muckraking and gossip. If I remembered rightly, it had been among the first to print the rumor of shenanigans in the state's drug rehabilitation programs.

"I wonder if it occurred to your friend that I might not wish to be 'featured'?"

"Oh, of course." I laughed airily. "The way she sees it, the Playboy Businessman won't collaborate because he's a little ashamed of not making money. So she has to *dig.*"

For the first time I saw Zwicky wince. A bare flicker at the corner of the mouth. "I believe I am beginning to get the picture," he said evenly. "You are practicing what I believe is a kind of blackmail."

"Alvin!" I sat up straight and widened my eyes. "Really. That isn't fair. There is a vast difference between extortion and a little sales pressure. This is a very straight proposition. We do the profile, cost-free, and if you show a profit increase at the end of the quarter, we collect a commission. That's it. Plain and simple."

"Tell me something, Stella." He leaned forward and

put an elbow on the desk, his face so near I got a whiff of the pinewoods cologne he used. "What is it *you* want? Plain and simple."

I was ready for that one. "I want to be vice-president of Garabedian, Daugherty, and Bissel. Making three times what I am now." I put all the sincerity I could muster behind my look and voice. It wasn't hard because there was a little truth in the statement.

We locked eyes for a long moment. Then he sat back and nodded. I stubbed out the cigarette.

"I see. You are remarkably persistent, Stella. Impressive. I'm interested. What is an employee profile?"

"We do depth interviews of your key staff. With that information we can compile a kind of psychological X ray of the firm. You can see the tensions that won't surface at a staff meeting, the combinations of people that won't work."

"We're quite a contented little family here at Cordilleras."

I almost laughed but caught myself. The nasty little pigeon outside the door—listening, I assumed, on the intercom—and Zwicky with his office full of cannibal artifacts were not my idea of domestic tranquillity.

"A lot of corporations think that. We usually show them they're kidding themselves."

Zwicky glanced at the bound folders on the desk. "So you file a report. Is that it?"

"Generally we have a few counseling sessions with the top people in the company. Make some recommendations." I picked up the folders and snapped them into my briefcase. "The reports alone don't mean much."

"Do you know anything about the import business, Stella?" Zwicky gestured slightly with one hand, indicating the trophies on the walls.

"No. But I expect to learn."

He smiled, like an uncle. "You are very confident. I am beginning to wonder if I should offer you the vice-presidency of Cordilleras and have done with it. In any case"

—he examined his watch with more attention—"I am sure that I prefer an employee profile to a feature article in a magazine. You will discover that I am not a playboy, but a real merchant." He stood up and extended his hand. "You may proceed. I shall send out a memo alerting the staff to expect you."

I shook his hand. It was smooth, well muscled. "Thanks. I'll try to stay out of the way. This is an immense help to my work."

"Happy to oblige. How soon will you begin?"

"A day or two."

We were moving toward the door. He opened it for me and nodded at Darlene. "It's fine. Miss Pike will be in and out for a few days, doing some work for us. She will need your cooperation."

"Of course, Mr. Zwicky." She pecked at me once with her eyes. "In every way." We smiled icily at each other.

Chapter XI

A flight of wooden stairs, paintless and warped, led me to the back door of the second-story flat. The house was one of those Berkeley Victorians that had somehow escaped restoration. The redwood shingles had weathered to a dull silver, and speckles of moss survived there, nourished by the morning fogs. The leaded glass of the narrow high windows stretched or shrank the reflected trees and cars. My face, when I tried to peer in, came back as a Modigliani version of Countess Dracula. I knocked.

I had already turned to go when I heard feet shuffling somewhere inside, drawing nearer. The feet stopped behind the door. I waited.

"Yeah?" The voice sounded a long way off, like somebody whispering at the far end of a tunnel.

"Hello-o-o. Anybody home?"

"No. Nobody home."

I waited again and heard what I thought might be a giggle.

"Good," I said, dropping the good cheer. "Then I'll come in and wait. Maybe the owner of this fleatrap will show up. Mr. Eliot. You know? Bennie told me about him." I turned the handle and pushed. The door was locked. I heard a rattling from inside, and then it swung open.

The man standing there was dressed only in faded jeans and an undershirt, both soiled. He had red hair in an Afro that nearly filled the doorway. It didn't seem right for a man to have hair like a burning bush. The face under the hair was gaunt. Eyes too far back in the skull, and lips too thin to cover the teeth.

"Bennie's dead."

He started to close the door, so I put a hand on the doorjamb.

"You know who killed him?"

He jerked the door then, but I was ready for that and got my foot braced against it in time.

"Hey, look." I lifted empty palms. "I'm not here to hassle you. I heard you were a friend of his. So okay. Me too."

He looked at me long and hard and finally released the door handle and stepped back.

"All right. So come in. It's not a fleatrap. It's an ashram. Take off your shoes."

I came in and shook off my modest platforms beside a set of battered moccasins and an old-fashioned pair of leather thong sandals. The floors held a scattering of worn rugs and grass mats, while the walls were mostly bare, except for some Sierra Club blowups of alpine flowers and a couple of reproductions of Tibetan tapestries. The kinds that are all arms and legs and dragon eyes, intertwined in a suggestive way.

I followed Herb Eliot into a main room, which was furnished more elaborately. That is, there were a few cushions, a couple of Pres-to-logs smoldering in the little fireplace, and some kind of altar, made of a wooden box, a short plank, an incense burner, and a photograph of a man with a white beard, illuminated by a stub of candle.

Herb bowed in front of the photograph and then fell down on one of the cushions. He indicated that I should do the same. I nodded at the bearded man and sat down.

"He's enlightened," Herb said softly. "The Most High, and all, but a very accessible guy." *Chinrupa Bainjii,* I read under the picture. "You know he likes Cheerios and grass?"

I looked properly charmed.

"Totally human."

"I would not be surprised. Quite a good-looking old gentleman, too."

"Three wives. Two American. Chinrupa doesn't believe in asceticism and self-denial and all that destructive bullshit." He opened a little brass box and took out a folder of cigarette papers, with which he began expertly to roll a joint. "He's totally modern, in one way, and totally more ancient at the same time. Dig?"

"*Plus ça change.*"

"What?"

"I mean, the old and the new are all the same, in one way. . . ."

"But in another way—"

"Right," I interrupted vigorously. "We've got to keep moving all the same. Which is why I'm here." I launched the first of the guesses I planned to make. "I understand you moved on from the scene you and Bennie were in. The political stuff?"

He nipped off one twisted end of the joint and slid it between his thin lips. "You a cop?"

"I'm mainly a friend of Bennie's."

"That's not saying you're *not* a cop."

"Okay. I'm not a cop." I sighed wearily. "Anyway, that stuff is ancient history now. The movement. Weathermen and Panthers. It seems like a million years ago."

"Oh, man." Herb leaned over and lit the joint from Chinrupa's candle. He sucked in a lungful and then held the cigarette out to me. Not wanting to destroy the mood, I accepted it and inhaled a modest toke.

"Ancient history is right. But we were totally into it at the time. Bennie ever tell you?" He took another hit but kept a steady, keen gaze on my face.

"Not much. He was kind of cagey about all that. But I knew he was involved in Latin American groups. His girl friend, too."

"Which girl friend?"

"Rosa."

He shook the great nest of hair and shrugged. He didn't know.

A bead curtain separating us from an adjoining room parted, and the owner of the thong sandals came in. She was about my age, pretty but extremely pale; she wore only a kind of sheet gathered around her and pinned somehow.

Having just lit a king-size cigarette, she left it in her mouth and talked around it. "You the one he's balling?"

I shook my head. "Never saw him until just now. I'm a friend of Bennie's. Or was. He's dead."

"Heavy." She looked at Eliot.

He lifted his shoulders, then sucked again on the joint. "Did you know him?"

She shook her head and sat cross-legged on the floor. "You into Chinrupa?"

I shook my head. Eliot passed her the joint.

"Dawn," he said.

"How do you do. I'm Stella."

There was a quiet period while the two of them smoked and looked at the bare walls and I fidgeted. Then Eliot spoke again.

"You don't like grass, do you?"

"Sometimes."

"You're not into Chinrupa." Dawn focused on me again. "So what are you here for?"

"Bennie," I said. "I was a friend of Bennie's."

"Oh, yeah." Eliot sat up. "What do you want to know? Bennie—he could play the shit out of a bass."

"I know. But you met him doing political things, right? During the war."

"Yeah, right. He was into that for a while. But when the war fizzled, he shifted over to other stuff. The crop-workers and all that."

"*La Raza?*"

"Yeah, I guess. Something with Mexicans or South American dictators or like that."

"You remember any names?"

Eliot squinted through the veils of smoke. I waited.

"Spozo? Pozito?"

"Esposito?"

"Hey, yeah. That sounds right. You know him?"

"No." I was sincere. "I don't think I want to. What do you know about him?"

"*Nada.*" Eliot thought some more. "Some other guy, Gutterez or something—"

"Gutierez?"

"Yeah, maybe. He was around a couple of times. Short guy, built square. One of those little-bitty mustaches."

"Right. Him I know. What was he seeing Bennie about?"

Eliot shrugged again. I was fighting a rising irritation that felt as if it might turn slightly hysterical. Getting information out of these two was like trying to fill a canteen from a fogbank. Then Dawn came through.

"He deals."

"Who?" Eliot looked at her with surprise.

"The Gut. I know the little creep."

We both were looking at her now. She enjoyed it.

"How do you know he does?"

She ignored me and looked very hard at Eliot. "Is she a cop?"

I cut in before he had time to shrug again. "No, I am not a cop. You want me to get stoned to prove it? Look, I have a real strong suspicion that Gutierez had something to do with Bennie's death, and with another homicide too—Esposito's wife. I'm trying to get enough credibility to bring the facts to the right people. That's all." I gestured at the smiling man with the white beard. "If the tenets of Chinrupa don't allow for catching killers by telling the truth, fine, I'd better go." I reached for my purse.

"Easy." She took a fistful of the sheet and hoisted it higher on her body. A vague gesture of pride. "I've left all of that for good. I don't want to get jerked back into it by no cop."

I nodded. "No chance. I've already forgotten your name. I just want the information."

She smiled and for a moment looked the way she probably had a long time ago, before the Gut and Chinrupa, too. There was a likable person back there.

"I was heavy into junk for a long time. After I dropped out of the phony university. A lot of kicks, I thought. I did a lot of drugs—a lot of people, too—and wound up on the heavy stuff. Begging, screwing, finally stealing to get it." She stopped and looked down. We looked away, and then she went on. "I was getting my bindles from a lot of guys, all kinds of guys. Chinese, Latino, some baby-faced college types—they were the worst. I ran into the Gut a couple of times and heard him talked about. Also a guy named Alejandro and a Manuel."

"That's Esposito. Most likely. What was their story?"

She twisted uncomfortably inside the sheet. "Well—I can't say for sure. They weren't dealing directly to the junkies; they were distributors. But once I talked to this guy about doing some pushing myself—I didn't because that scene is too heavy—but he told me that you could get the stuff already cut and weighed from some state office. You dig? They had an *office* somewhere."

"You don't remember hearing an address?"

She shook her head. "That's about it. When I backed out of it, the guy made it real clear he didn't want to see me around anymore. About that time I kicked it and haven't been back on it since." She straightened up proudly. "Except once. Eliot left."

"I came back," Eliot said dreamily. "Chinrupa told me to."

They looked at each other fondly. I could see it was time to leave.

"Thanks," I said, getting up and nodding to all of them, even Chinrupa. "You've been a help. And like I said, I never remember names."

"Yeah, gee." Eliot managed to get to his feet. "Nice talkin' to you. Ever want to drop in, fine with us. Maybe you can catch a community night. Meet the Master." He winked.

"Maybe," I said. "But I don't think I'm ready yet. Too much bad karma to burn off right now."

"I dig." He grinned and gave the great bush of hair a toss. We shook hands, and I started for the door.

"Oh, one thing." Dawn looked at me again with innocence from a former life. "I remember the Gut thought he was a great lover. But he was a real creep. So keep your back to the wall."

"I will. He's not really my type." I smiled and waved and left, wondering if the next time I met him, I would get another opportunity to blow the great lover's head off.

It was nearly four, and I had had enough for the day. The toke or two at the ashram had also weakened my resolve. I wanted to beat the Bay Bridge traffic and collapse into Alice's bubble bath, then call Hand and reconnect the circuitry we had discovered together. A person in my situation needs that kind of direct, physical reassurance, I decided. A moment later I wondered whether our situations create our need or the other way around. And a moment after that I didn't even care.

Chapter XII

When I got back to the apartment, Alice was delivering a crab soufflé from the oven, and her actor was sprawled on the couch, watching Dan Rather warily.

"Stella, you're still alive." Alice motioned at the man with the soufflé. "That's him. The bastard I love." She ducked back into the kitchen.

The man looked away from some scene of a street littered with crumpled bodies. He had tousled blond hair and cool, insolent eyes. One of those classic ski-resort types: handsome, athletic, completely untrustworthy. This one was also good at mind reading.

"You don't trust me," he said, with the beginning of a smile. "You suspect my intentions are not honorable."

"I hope not. Alice would be terribly disappointed."

He laughed. Teeth very white and even.

"Truce." I put out a hand, and he took it with a grin. "Eric, I presume."

"Right. You are, of course, Pike, the well-known investigator."

"Body finder," Alice corrected, jubilant in the doorway. "My God, it's thrilling, isn't it? Let's have the soufflé while we get grisly." She swept us into her dining nook, where candles reflected a soft glow from glasses of sauterne and a tureen of white sauce.

"Die." Eric picked up the serving knife and plunged it into the fluffy ring of eggs and crab meat. "Die, arthropod."

It went that way through dinner. I liked Eric in spite of his impossible good looks. For an actor he was modest, but with a devastating gift for mockery. By the time fresh fruit and coffee arrived we had reached a level of confidence and insult that normally requires weeks. I sighed at the first strawberry and turned to Alice.

"Enough of this decadence. Now a little business. What hath the librarian brought?"

She left and came back carrying a monstrous book with faded yellow binding and a note pad. The table shook when she dropped the book in front of us.

"Doctor von Gaugen's little contribution to the achievement of human knowledge. Good luck."

"You'll sleep soundly." Eric ran a finger over the stack of pages. "It makes me yawn to look at it."

"Maybe it has an index," I said hopefully. "Anyway, that's the lonely task of the scholar. What about the *Assembly Records*?"

Alice flipped open the note pad and propped it against the fruit bowl.

"You want the best first?"

"Always have."

"A Chicano named Francisco Ugarte and a honky ex-used car dealer named Hugh Drummond, both in the State Assembly, sponsored the legislation that set up the original drug rehabilitation program. They argue for an increase in the appropriation every year, but that's standard procedure. Drummond has friends in the racetrack crowd. Ugarte was a street kid—he's only thirty-four now—and was once on the fringes of the radical political groups in the barrio."

"Promising. Go on."

"Now about the Start Over thing. It was designed to treat addicts right off the street and use ex-addicts as counselors and even administrators. This was Drummond's baby, but he had help from a hotshot organizer and PR type borrowed from Ugarte's staff, guy named Johnny Caswell. The program's been running for three years. Last year, when appropriation time came up, a subcommittee run by Mike Flannigan put the program through a severe X ray.

"The subcommittee's report expresses concern over the amount of time spent in 'confidential client interviews.' They wanted to know what the state was paying for behind the closed doors. Also, bookkeeping was very sloppy—nothing missing, but a lot of shifting around of accounts for no apparent reason.

"Ugarte and Drummond blustered at first, then got real cooperative. A lot of the staff were trotted through a hearing to explain the benefits of what they were doing. One of those giving testimony was an M. Esposito."

"Pay dirt."

"I hope so." Alice waited, watching me over the top of her notebook.

"More?"

"Well, you didn't ask for this, but you might be interested. I looked at the list of affiliations and memberships that every assemblyman has to file, by law. The Shit List they call it in Sacramento. Ugarte and Drummond and Zwicky are all on the board of the Trade Commission. The Trade Commission's report for last year is mostly about their aggressive campaign to establish business contacts in South America, particularly Peru."

"Alice," I said, and came around the table to squeeze her shoulders, "you are wasting your time as a librarian. You should work for the Washington *Post*. A genius. And my best friend. And a doll. And—"

"Stop." Eric held up one hand. "She must learn humility."

"Shut up, Eric. I like it. I'm too young for humility."

I grinned at Eric over the top of Alice's head. "Anyway, you deserve a rest. Talk to your slave there, and I'll put on some more coffee."

I went to the kitchen and ground fresh beans, replaced the filter, and poured through another pot of hot water. When I brought the coffee back to the table, Alice and Eric were intently discussing my motives for mingling with criminals.

"She is not a crusader," Alice insisted. "Crusaders have causes and faith and all of that. She's just troublesome."

She smiled triumphantly and held out her cup. "Like I am."

"You don't take chances with your life just for the sake of causing mischief. Unless you are unbalanced." Eric turned to me. "Are you unbalanced?"

I filled his cup, then my own, and sat down before I tried to answer.

"I don't know." I looked at them a little dubiously. "Am I among the unbalanced here?"

"Definitely." Eric grinned. "We may speak openly."

"I don't understand quite how I got into it. Maybe because everybody kept telling me to stay out. Present company excepted." I nodded at Alice. "There are the thrill seekers of the world."

"Anyway"—Alice waved a cigarette before she lit it— "you *are* in it, so let's go on. What's next? How do we proceed?"

"I have been doing more dodging than figuring. Trying to locate somebody in Cordilleras Imports who will talk. The boss either likes me or is afraid of me because he hasn't tried to interfere. Total cooperation is the policy so far."

"But, my dear"—Alice stared at me in myopic earnestness—"you've got to have some kind of strategy."

"How about survival?"

"That's not enough."

Eric nodded. "You ought to know what you're after. I mean, you must know already, up to a point."

"Sure. Up to a point. I see a lady get killed, and a lot of people seem anxious for me to forget what I saw. That makes me curious. Maybe it's a simple tale of junkies and jealousy. What happens every day. But I don't think so. I think our taxes have been buying a lot of heroin and cocaine, and the rehabilitation centers have distributed it, and the profits have gone to certain people whose reputations would suffer a lot at the slightest hint of such a scandal. And quite possibly Alvin Zwicky is one of those certain people, whose job is transporting the stuff."

"Possibly, possibly. But couldn't it be somebody else in his organization, using the company without his knowledge?"

"Could be. There was something odd in his manner. Almost as if he *wanted* me to find out a little but couldn't bring himself to tell me." I thought again of the nameless shadow that had passed swiftly behind Zwicky's eyes.

Alice sipped coffee, looking at me through the veil of steam rising from her cup. "Sordid matters like dope and murder would not go well with his role of Pacific Heights *bon vivant*."

I remembered a company manager who had hired Garabedian's Goons to improve "bookkeeping procedures" when he already knew very deep down that the unauthorized hand in the till belonged to his own daughter. It was an outside possibility that Zwicky had had an attack of conscience—or fear—because he had let things go too far.

"What about this guy Bennie?" Alice asked.

"I haven't figured that one out. What bothers me is that he died just a day after we met."

"They thought he might tell you something?"

"Not unlikely."

There was a silence. Alice frowned and got up to secure a bottle of cognac and a tray of glasses from the sideboard. Eric lit a cigarette and began to meditate intently on its smoldering tip.

"Did I say something wrong?"

They looked at each other, then at me. Eric shifted in his chair and dragged on the cigarette. "If you can bear a worn cliché . . . Doesn't that put you next on the list?"

Before I could answer, the door chimes sounded. I was on my feet and moving a shade too fast. Alice grinned. I abandoned my attempt to be sedate and, after a quick look through the curtain, threw the door wide.

Hand looked like a happy man struggling unsuccessfully to appear impassive. We tottered for a half second and then fell against each other hard. The current flowed, strong and sweet, while we muttered things that neither of us heard. Finally there was a discreet cough and clink of glass behind us, and we pulled apart.

"Alice, Eric, this is Lieutenant Jack Hand."

"Well," Alice said, and looked at me with approval.

Everyone shook hands and mumbled the things one mumbles, while I poured Hand a glass of cognac. There was an awkward pause while we looked at each other expectantly.

"You first," I said.

Hand glanced swiftly at Eric.

"It's all right," I said. "They know, and I trust them."

He put down the glass and smiled a little one-sided smile. "Tell me what they know."

I ran through it—told him about Bennie's old friend, the rehabilitation programs, and the Trade Commission—referring to the notes Alice had made. "So," I wound up, "a couple of big targets have surfaced. Ugarte and Drummond and Zwicky all have connections. Or maybe I should say there are implications of connections. For the moment I've got Zwicky to work on. And he's not objecting."

Hand looked puzzled.

"He could have thrown me out if he had really wanted to. I got a funny hunch that he might want me to hang around. Maybe to throw a scare into his partners."

The lieutenant nodded. "The car. He hadn't figured they were going to use it for a hit. Now he's scared."

"That bothers me." Eric looked around the table. "Why would they risk using a company car? Even with the dodge of reporting it stolen first?"

"They just may have screwed up there. It wasn't a smart move. I suppose they didn't have time to steal a car off the street. Maybe Rosa had threatened to spill the whole thing or was trying to blackmail herself a bigger cut, and they had to move fast. They were afraid to use a car registered to anybody in the ring, in case it was spotted and traced, so they rigged the steal. The Chrysler is on the books as a company vehicle, and the theft was reported by the chauffeur. Chances are good he thought it *was* stolen."

"But why have they held on to it?" I asked.

"It's an albatross. Luxury cars are hard to unload. Now they know that it was spotted, they'll get rid of it."

"How?" Alice was wide-eyed. "A Chrysler?"

Hand grinned. "Donate it to a museum."

"Be serious."

"All right. They'll find a chop shop and take it apart and haul the pieces to wrecking yards or scrap them. It may be already gone. Drummond used to be in that business."

Eric whistled admiringly. "You would make a very good criminal."

"Thanks. I respect the good ones."

"Now how about you?" I waved at the stack of papers in front of me. "All we've got is hints. Possibilities. Nothing so concrete as an automobile."

"I've been working on Bennie. What you got on the political angle fits with what I know. For a while we had people working on political groups. They didn't do much but compile lists, but one of the lists had Bennie's name and Rosa's, too. From what I could gather, he was in it because she was. The group was collecting money, staging benefits for guerrillas in South America. When they developed contacts with the organizations in the prisons—Soledad, Folsom, and San Quentin—the thing fell apart. Dope came into it then."

Eric had been absorbed in the story, but now he blinked and cleared his throat. "Speaking of which, I don't want to disrupt a business meeting, but would anybody mind?" He slid a little metal box out of his pocket and popped its lid. A half dozen slender and perfectly rolled joints and a small box of wax matches lay inside. He and Hand locked eyes for a moment. "I understand you're in homicide?"

"My God, I hope so." Alice's eyes were wide and curious again.

Hand smiled and shrugged. "I hadn't intended to disrupt a party."

Alice sighed. "Your hostess is relieved. I know a judge who does, and several public defenders. But I didn't know the cops did."

"Sometimes that's where the judges get it." Hand took the joint from Eric and drew smoke, then handed it to me.

I was looking at Eric in admiration. He had wanted to remove a trace of doubt or reserve he had picked up in Hand. It worked. Crime creates trust.

"A lot of cops do this?" I asked.

"A lot of cops."

"Harder stuff, too?"

"Sometimes." Hand was looking over my head, thinking about somehing far away. "That may be where our leak is." Then he began to speak rapidly, as if giving a report we had asked for. "One theory is that the only difference between cops and crooks is that the cops are dumber, so they need the advantage of legality. Another theory, the one I subscribe to, is that in this advanced stage of our social development, very few people give a shit about much beyond survival."

"And if you have to get high to survive, you get high?" Eric was contemplating his little box. "So why are you a cop?"

"I can stand it all except for the freaks who get high on killing people and the politicians who protect them." Hand looked swiftly at me.

"That's what it comes down to." I took the joint again. I was getting stoned in cold waves. "They shouldn't push people out of cars."

It was quiet for a few minutes, and then Hand went back to his rapid report.

"Anyway, the political business. Revolutionaries and dopers got hooked up in the sixties, in a loose sort of way. In the prison system the connections got tighter, and it was hard to tell whether people were offed for burning somebody or for being the wrong kind of communist.

Either way I was seeing a lot of bodies. And after a while I got the distinct impression that my superiors were not interested in finding out where they came from. So I moved underground. It used to be out of conviction. Now I think it's to stay alive."

"It's a natural transition," I said. "I'm getting there. So the men in blue are not our allies."

"Not necessarily. A few. I know them. But it's better to assume there aren't any allies. Just us."

There was a silence around the table.

"Us." Eric was looking at Alice, who was gazing into a candle flame. "Okay. I don't know what I could do. But if you think of anything, man . . ."

"Thanks." Hand considered for a moment. "There might be. You're an actor, you say?"

Alice stood up. "We're going out," she said briskly. She had gone a little pale. "For a nightcap, and doubtless more. I'll be at Eric's. The number is in the book by the phone."

"Thanks for the drink," Hand said, "and the information. It's good."

We got up, too, and saw them out the door. I envied them. Kids again, out for fun.

I navigated back to the couch in the front room with some care. Eric's grass was quite good. I had the impression that I was not walking but flying over the rug in a soundless helicopter. Already I had decided to be very careful tonight. And tomorrow night. And the night after that.

I sank down on the couch. Hand stood in front of me, smiling.

"How do you feel?"

"Tired. High. Possibly confused."

"Not defused?"

"Oh, no." I stretched up my arms. But he didn't move. "You are?"

He shook his head. "I just want to stand here and admire you."

"Wait. I'll find my pedestal."

"Not that. You do good work. You figure people."

"Like Eric?"

"Like Eric."

"It was smart of him to pull out his stash. Smart of you to sample it."

He grinned. "People who have something on each other have to trust each other. He knew that."

"Do you . . . ?"

"No. Not much." He tossed his head as if at something behind him. "In the service I smoked a lot, and then I was married to a woman who loved the stuff. But you know, you can lose your edge."

"Or get very edgy."

"Yeah. That, too." He nudged one leg between my knees. "I have other interests."

"Interests?"

"All right. Fascinations."

"Better. Maybe we balance. I'm the sort that gets edgy. Or used to. Things have changed."

"I noticed that. Not everybody can eat strawberries and smoke dope after trying to shoot somebody."

"It just takes some care."

Hand put his fingers on my cheek. "Having fun with care."

"Anything with care."

He pulled me up then, and I stood on his toes to be walked into the bedroom. We fumbled dreamily at straps and laces and buttons until the hungry bodies were free. For an instant we stood a little apart, my hands cool on his big, flat chest, enjoying the jolts of anticipation going back and forth between us.

"You like this," he murmured absently.

"Oh, yes, I do, I do."

"No, not this. I mean this whole shot."

I cocked my head and tried to read his eyes, but they were gone in shadow.

"I mean what you meant by living on the edge. You like that, don't you?"

I thought for a moment, and what he meant came in on me like a train. I took a deep, shuddering breath.

"Yeah. I like it. It's part of this, too, you know."

"I know."

We fell over then into the bed, like Romeo and Juliet machine-gunned.

Chapter XIII

I woke up in an empty bed. Hand had left me a note shaped into a little cone like a tepee. It set our next meeting three days hence, specified the times for phone calls, and closed with what qualified for him as an outburst of verbal passion:

lv
Jack

I smiled, crumpled up the tepee, and tossed it in the wastebasket. It was very nice, for a change, to know a man who didn't go in for a lot of postcoital blather about "it" and "us."

Alice had apparently gone directly to work from Eric's, so I fed Baudelaire and gave him a pat. He took it grudgingly, probably feeling that matters had taken a turn for the worse since I had moved in. I downed a glass of orange juice with a couple of cold croissants from the bread box and dressed quickly in a pantsuit of brushed denim. It was a clear, breezy day, the fog well offshore, so I decided to walk to Russian Hill and catch the cable car to Columbus.

The city was at its best, the high rises sharp against the blue sky, the air fresh with a dash of salt, gulls flapping over the rooftops. On the cable car I squeezed myself onto one of the running boards, so I could grasp the vertical rail and hang out over the street, letting the wind take my hair and getting an unobstructed view of the shoppers passing by. I had a head delightfully empty and managed to keep it that way during the five-block ride to the Cordilleras office.

Darlene the Dragon brought me back to things with a snap. Her mouth the size of a button, she informed me that she ever so much regretted that my interviews for the day would have to be called off. A large shipment was going out on short notice, and people were ever so busy, working against deadlines. Mr. Zwicky was sure I would understand. Unfortunately Mr. Zwicky was not in and was not expected. Of course, in a day or two everything would be back to normal, and I would receive their fullest cooperation. Before this last word was out of her mouth, she was typing again.

I purred my deep concern for the problem, my respect for deadlines, and my sincere hope that Alvin was not ill. There was indeed a problem, because I had ever so much to do, too, and had set aside today especially to make good progress in the profile. Profiles tended to blur if they weren't fixed rapidly. Perhaps a beautiful compromise was possible. Come to think of it, it was a wonderful idea: I would simple float around—out of the way, of course—and get a feel for the work that was going on. No head-to-head interviews; that was only part of the picture anyway. Just observation and a little question here and there. Sure. It was amazing how people of goodwill could work these things out. She had been such a help.

Darlene left off pecking and looked at me with a sugary hatred. She picked up a pencil to point at me. Now her mouth reminded me of one of those tiny, heart-shaped cinnamon drops, bright red, that used to burn our tongues when we were kids.

"I'm afraid that won't be possible, Miss Pike. We are *terribly* busy."

"Oh, Darlene, don't say 'can't.' " I leaned over and put the tip of my finger lightly on those shrunken scarlet lips. "We won't tell anybody, and everything will be just peachy." I straightened up and gave her a big smile. Physical contact was more than Darlene could readily handle. She was stricken, and the pen drooped in her hand, forgotten. I made it out the door before she managed to get her breath. It may have been coincidence that the interviews I had scheduled for the day included one with Consuelo Palacios, Rosa's replacement, but I doubted it.

On my way to the shipping and receiving division, I dropped by the custodian's office. Custodians are generally among the best-informed people in a company. They see the garbage, for one thing, and people are remarkably thoughtless about what they throw away. Bottles, roaches, and the residue of carnal acts, for example. Cyrus, the import firm's floor sweeper, was a wizened old gentleman whose shuffling deference probably masked a mean gossip. I found him in his cubicle full of buckets and brooms, pushed back in a chair listening to a Giants' game and smoking a Marlboro.

" 'lo, little lady," he said, and indicated with a tilt of his chin the one other available chair.

"I hate to interrupt, but . . . you're Cyrus, aren't you? Let me introduce myself. I'm—"

"I know. You wanna ask questions."

"Why, that's right. Do you mind?"

"Shoot. I don't guarantee I got any answers." He eased his chair back to the floor and turned the radio down imperceptibly. "Forgitful, you know. Old age."

"Most of it is worth forgetting."

His face split, revealing a row of yellow snags. "Ain't it the truth? So anyways, what questions you got?"

"There's a lot of coming and going in this place. People in and out all the time. I wondered if that created a problem for you. Do they make a lot of trash, boxes, that sort of thing?" I smiled encouragingly, pencil poised over my little pad.

He squinted at me through the gray threads of smoke unraveling from the cigarette. "Now you don't have to go through all that, little lady. I see where you're aimin'. You want to know who those people was, don't you?"

"Cy, you ought to tell fortunes. How did you know that?"

"Figured it out the first time I heard about you. You go clear 'round Robin Hood's barn to find somethin' out. You're one of them efficiency experts, ain't you? Lookin' for the trouble between people in this outfit?" He puffed gleefully on the cigarette, his eyes narrowed and bright.

"Bingo." I held up my hands in a sign of surrender. "You got me."

"Well, let's get right to it then. I'll tell you where the trouble is, all right. That little bitch up there in the front office. Jaspers." He jerked a hand at the ceiling. "She's your problem." He sat back to wait.

"What do you mean? I can see Darlene is perhaps . . . difficult . . . but—"

"Difficult!" Cyrus hooted. "*Difficult!* She's goddamn impossible. She runs this whole shebang, you know."

"No, I didn't know. I thought Mr. Zwicky—"

"Alvin Zwicky don't know diddly about the details of this operation. He just signs the checks. Only thing he keeps hold of is the advertisin'. That's part of the comin' and goin' you was talkin' about."

I looked intensely curious, and Cyrus licked his lips.

"A couple of young fellers, prissy little bastards with mean eyes, kind that wears them little booties and ties as big as a man's hand. They're in and out of here all the time, comin' from the ad company. And sometimes an old guy, tall and gray-haired."

"Mr. Zwicky never mentioned his interest in advertising." I looked thoughtful. "I wonder—"

"Never was interested in it before, neither, until about two years ago. They used to just phone in the sales and special shipments and stuff to the newspapers, and that was it. Simple. Then all of a sudden these guys come in, and we get color pictures and the Andes and all that. But just once in a while. I don't see much work comin' out of it, for all the movin' around."

"What was the ad agency?"

"Baxter and Ferguson, or McFergus, or somethin'."

It was Baker and Ferguson, on Sansome Street. I knew the firm. Small, aggressive, and trendy. It had made its reputation selling peek-a-boo jeans in the last days of the hard rock concerts. Not a likely partner for the distinguished name of Zwicky.

"Anyways, Darlene don't have nothin' to say about that. Everything else, you go through her. You know, she's got a list of every goddamn washrag and mop handle in his place, and if I lose one, she's got to hear about it. She sent a memo around onct askin' people to use the paper cups at least twice." He fixed me with a triumphant glare. "Now do you see?"

I got up hurriedly before he could get his second wind. "I certainly do, Cy, and I thank you for putting me on to it." I winked. "Just between us, now."

"You betcha." He showed his yellow fangs again.

I went out and down the hall to the shipping and receiving department. Mostly there were packing cases and tables of goods, with shredded paper and Styrofoam chips on the floor. Two or three clerks were at work cataloguing and inspecting. In the back was the Product Acquisition and Control office. Consuelo ran this operation now: the expert appraisal of pottery, textiles, and jewelry.

When I tapped, there was a brief rustle within, and then the door opened far enough to reveal a thin dark face under tightly waved black hair.

"What is it?" Her eyes went over me, impatient but observant.

I wrapped my fingers casually around the jamb, so she couldn't shut the door without amputating them. "Hi. I know you're very busy, but I've got just a question or two. Cordilleras is doing an employee profile, you know, and—"

The opening narrowed perceptibly. "That's been called off. I'm busy. Talk to—"

"I have. It's on again. Really, I won't interrupt what you're doing. What are you doing, by the way? I know it's very important to the firm. Can I see?"

There was a pause, and Consuelo said something in Spanish under her breath. It did not sound like something nice. But then the door came open all the way.

I stepped inside and got a better look at Consuelo. She was small and quick, yet impassive. Swift reflexes and cold blood, I thought. A lizard.

"What do you want?"

There was nothing in the little room but a desk, a long table covered with colorful woven fabrics, a few boxes, and a hot plate with a pot on it.

"How lovely!" I passed a hand lightly over one of the pieces of fabric, some kind of large poncho with intricate embroidery on it. "Is this one a good one?"

"Not particularly."

"Why?"

Consuelo's eyes were black and opaque. My question hung in the air for an uncomfortable time.

"I think I told you I was busy. Now what do you want?"

I confronted what our trainee handbooks called a Difficult Subject and what we termed among ourselves a Hard Ass.

The recommended counterstrategy is known as the Firm Approach.

"Look, we're all busy. I don't like this shit much more than you do. But can't we be more or less human? For starters, just tell me what you're doing in this rat coop." I walked over to the hot plate. "You got any cups?"

There was another pause, but shorter this time. "In the left-hand drawer. No, the *left.*"

I didn't misunderstand. But all I found out was that Consuelo was a secret M&M's freak. "You want some too?"

"No. But help yourself."

The sarcasm in her invitation would have curdled an angel's milk. I poured myself a half cup of coffee I really didn't want and turned back to the Difficult Subject. "Cheers."

Consuelo stalked to the table and began flipping over corners of cloth. "I'm checking for flaws. Patches. Pieces that have been added to or chemically treated." She sounded weary. "These are mantas from Pisaq, a market town in the highlands. Mostly they are only fair quality— the good stuff is hard to get these days, and Pisaq is too well known. We've got to move farther back. Now here"— she jerked the cloth from the middle of the stack—"here is a rather good one."

I looked at the square of tightly woven wool, done mostly in dark reds, with black bordering and trim. "Just looks older and raggedier."

She didn't bother to look at me. "It's at least a hundred and fifty years old. The stitching is—fantastic. Look at this row of little vicuñas." She pointed to a series of figures on one border. "Every one of them is matched with the condors in the next column, so that the background makes a design too. Can you see it?"

I looked, and all at once a row of warriors materialized in the spaces between figures. "Yeah. That's something. What about the rest?"

She flipped further into the stack. "Here's a patch job. You see the seam?" She held the cloth up against the light.

"So there is." I was clearly going to make headway as an attentive pupil. "Who buys this stuff for the firm?"

Consuelo replaced the cloth in the stack. "I buy some. Mr. Zwicky used to. We make fewer trips now."

"How come?"

"The system is pretty well set up to run on its own." She turned to a ledger on the table and picked up a pencil beside it. I noticed that all the entries were made in a precise hand. "We travel only to look at large lots of new stuff. You'll have to excuse me. I've got to get this batch out now."

"Sure. Don't mind me. I'll just look through these and be on my way." I moved around the table, fingering the goods. Consuelo went back to work as if I were not even there. She was a cool one and clearly knew her business. There was a chance I had it wrong. Maybe she was an experienced buyer of legal merchandise, brought in to take over Rosa's official job and no more. *The system is pretty well set up to run on its own.*

Toward the bottom of the stack I ran across three mantas of fine weave, made of thread of different colors. The detail and craftsmanship looked extraordinary to me.

"These," I said. "Incredible. They must be valuable."

Consuelo glanced away from the ledger, and the pencil in her hand stopped moving. "Don't take them out," she said evenly. "They are fragile. And yes, they are valuable. Worth the rest of the stack."

"Where are they from?"

"From a convent in Tingo María. We pick them up in Lima. Nuns lose their eyesight making them."

"They're exquisite. What do the different colors mean? And these bumpy fringes? I've never seen lace like this."

"It isn't lace. It's fine tapestry. Modeled on originals from tombs at Parapas." She dropped the pencil on the ledger and straightened up to give me a long, hard look. "I'd appreciate it if you'd let me finish my work. I'm not up to giving classes right now." Her unblinking lizard eyes followed me as I strolled over to put the cup on the counter by the pot.

"What's the hurry?"

I heard her breath go in and out once, slowly. Then she gave me a swift, tight smile. "I've got to catch a plane in two days."

"Oh?" I beamed back at her. "How nice. Buying trip?"

"That's right."

"Peru, Bolivia, maybe Colombia?" I knew what I needed to know for the moment. Why Darlene had tried to postpone the interview for two days. Consuelo would then have been eight thousand miles away.

"That's right." Consuelo's voice had become a soft hiss.

"You lucky girl. A vacation. Wish I could join you. But"—I waved my hand at the building around us—"so much to cover. So many little corners. Like this one." I stepped to the door and opened it. "Send a card," I said over my shoulder. "We'll miss you."

Chapter XIV

For maybe an hour I wandered around, finding nothing of particular interest. Then, from the second-story window of an office where a couple of clerks were sticking labels on things, I saw Zwicky's limousine parked at the back of the building. I put away my notebook and made my way back to the front desk. Darlene was still in her perch, busy with pencils and clips. She allowed me one glance. I stopped in front of her and leaned on the desk top.

"Darlene," I said, "I'd like to see Alvin."

"Mr. Zwicky isn't—"

"Oh yes he is. I'd like to see him. Now."

She thought about it for a moment, then punched the intercom savagely.

"Mr. Zwicky? Miss Pike is here."

After a pause I heard Zwicky's voice. "Yes. Of course. Send her in."

The wooden masks on the walls were still leering. Zwicky was uncharacteristically informal. He wore a loose-knit sport shirt and golf slacks. For sixty or so, he looked rather trim. Money slenderizes some people.

"Stella," he said, advancing with a manner one might deem cordial, "how are you and what can I do for you?"

"I'm fine. You can tell me about a couple of things. The advertising budget for a start."

He had me by the hand and was leading me to the guest chair. "Well, as such we really have no advertising. Cigarette?"

"Thank you." After the ritual of waiting for him to snap

the lighter and picking a shred or two of tobacco from my tongue, I settled back in the chair to drum my fingers on its arm and regard him archly.

"No advertising?"

"That is, on the budget. You see, the trust that manages my affairs has several investments which do employ a firm for advertising. As a kind of side benefit they do a few things for us. A nominal fee." He strolled about behind the mahogany plain of his desk. "Why does this interest you?"

"A couple of people mentioned that the B and F people drop in on you. You personally. I wondered if that was some aspect of the business I was overlooking."

He laughed as one laughs at the innocent questions of a child. "It's really nothing. Clarence Ferguson is an old friend of our family. We stay in touch this way. We team up to do a little fund raising."

"Political?"

"And public service."

"I see. What sorts of investments does the Zwicky trust have?"

"Oh, we dabble in sugar, have a small trucking line, a few ships—TransPac Orient—a confection business— you've heard of TopTorts probably—and own a little property. I assure you it is not the tentacled monster of capitalism."

"Just a squid?"

"You might say."

We fenced with our eyes for a while. He was doing a very good job of impersonating a man at leisure who had dropped by the office unannounced to take care of some trifle.

"So the sugar goes in the TopTorts, and the trucks and ships carry it all over the globe, and your old friends do the advertising."

He laughed again. "You really ought to be running a business, Stella. You have the touch."

"No, thanks. It takes more than touch."

"Not really." Zwicky did another impersonation, the overgrown boy. "Look at me."

"I have been. You told me a week ago you didn't belong with the playboys in town, but I frankly can't see how Cordilleras fits into the squid. It doesn't relate to the rest of your enterprises, and if it doesn't lose money, it doesn't make a hell of a lot either."

"Stella," he said gently, "money is—I know you've heard this before, but perhaps not from someone worth fifty-seven million—money is not really everything."

I laughed a mouthful of smoke at him, and he came around the table to sit on the arm of my chair.

"You know, you are really a very remarkable woman."

His arm brushed my shoulder and stayed. Although it took something out of my midsection, I leaned into the pressure just a little. "How very sweet and old-fashioned of you, Alvin. Some people think I'm a bitch."

"Some people don't mind that."

He was starting the lean down for my mouth when I contrived to brush glowing ash onto his leg and utter a cry of surprise.

"Stupid of me. I'm sorry."

He was brushing the sparks with one hand and fumbling after my neck with the other, so I stood up.

"I hope I didn't ruin those slacks."

"No, no. Look here, Stella, I'm a man who—"

"Wastes no time. I know. But I mustn't be too distracted from my job after all." I gave him an encouraging smile. "The reason for Cordilleras still interests me. I gather you at one time did a good deal of the buying yourself?"

He stood up and moved away from the chair. "Sit down. I shall not risk being branded again. Yes, I was very fond of travel. That was, you see, the reason, if it comes to that. Travel and an interest in those beautiful, lost people who built Tiahuanaco and Chan Chan and Chavín and all the rest. If that makes me a playboy—but see here, I made myself a rule: My passions must pay for themselves. And in ten years I think you will find we show a modest profit."

He sat on the edge of his desk, striking a pose of ease and restrained triumph.

"That's a very good line. Passions must pay for themselves."

"Sometimes passion even turns a nice profit, you know."

I looked away, not wanting to follow that lead. "But what happened? Consuelo seems to be doing the traveling now. Day after tomorrow, in fact. You're not tempted to go anymore?"

I was observing from the corner of one eye Zwicky's alligator hide loafers. I had learned in my trade that men get nervous with their feet, women with their hands. You watch the extremities for signs of uncertainty or fear. When I mentioned Consuelo's trip, the polished toe bounced a couple of times.

"There is no temptation in going to the same place every year. Once in a while I get out to scout new markets, places I haven't been."

"But it's rather an important part of the business, isn't it? The foreign connection?"

He laughed indulgently. "You make it sound like a new movie about spies and smuggling."

"Really?" I laughed too. "Have you ever been tempted to smuggle anything, Alvin?" I looked at him with eyes as wide and curious and innocent as I could make them. The shoe tip was working steadily now at some invisible treadle that would spin the next lie. I glanced at the masks and clubs on the walls. "Like this valuable art, for example."

He manufactured a laugh of considerable gusto. "Oh, not really. Once a little vase that I simply couldn't do without. An ingenious piece of Mochica pornography. But nothing exciting like gold or cocaine."

I let that last word, "cocaine," hang there between us for a time. "Pity." I sighed. "It sounds exciting. Anyway, I am interested in Consuelo's side of the business. Does she operate all alone in South America?"

"Not at all. There is an office for the assistance of

American business firms in Lima, and several small companies use it. There is a full-time staff—"

"Courtesy of the Trade Commission?"

His eyes slashed once across my face, but he said nothing.

"How fascinating. I envy Consuelo."

"You've spoken to her?" The bouncing toe stopped.

"Yes. In spite of Darlene. Luckily, it seems. She's leaving for Lima soon."

"An excellent buyer. Her work is the one skilled job that none of us can do. Selecting and pricing and watching for an overlooked treasure. Darlene tries to protect her." He smiled ruefully. "You are the first person to be more than a match for Darlene."

"She keeps me fully awake, too. Between her and Consuelo the place does seem to be pretty much under control. But I'd rather have Consuelo's job."

"You like travel?"

"Yeah. It's one of my strong likes."

"The others?"

He was still working to turn things that way. I decided to reinforce my image as an unprincipled grasper.

"Money. Liberty. The sybaritic pleasures." There was a silence. He was waiting. "Men who can help me get those things."

He leaned forward a little and licked his lips. "I think I have already said Stella is a remarkable woman. And fascinating. I might add that one of the most fascinating things about her is that I cannot tell when she is lying." The boy had vanished. A hard, shrewd man was here now.

"And you like that, or you don't like it?"

"Both." He had bolted his eyes to my face. "Why don't you tell me what this little game is about?"

"What little game?" My fingers had begun a drumroll on the chair arm again. I stopped them with an effort, remembering my own rule, and tried recrossing my legs. That didn't distract Alvin.

"Don't play dumb. You're not convincing. This profile study is a fake. You're a smart, very able professional.

Your boss wouldn't offer you for free. The idea is yours."

"So what do you have against a woman with ideas of her own?"

"I want to know just what the ideas are. Here you arrive, an attorney's ex-wife, trying to blackmail me into giving you access to my people and files, fishing around in your interviews for information about my business contacts and habits, dropping hints that your services—your complex services—might be available for a price. Just what the hell are you after?"

He was good, very good. It took all my strength to keep my fingers and my eyes still. I thought very fast and decided to pretend to know a lot of things I didn't.

"All right, Alvin." I gave him a wry, one-sided smile. "The tale about my friend on the magazine was partly true. Journalists in this town have a nose for catastrophe, and the word is out that a lot of rather influential people are teetering like Humpty-Dumpty these days. Scandal, in a word, is right around the corner. Now you mention my former husband." I closed my eyes and took a couple of breaths, as if quelling some old trouble. "He wants to be attorney general someday, and he needs a couple of good scandals in government to put him there. The finger of suspicion, as they call it, has swung in recent weeks toward a few of your friends. I remembered that our firm once did a little job for you, so I looked up the file. That's when I discovered you never even applied for the results of a survey you paid for. A few questions around town led me to believe this operation wasn't a serious one at all. Cordilleras could be a grease money laundry. I didn't know."

"So you're here to nail me." It was a gentle, perfectly flat statement.

"Whoa, Alvin. You misinterpret. Frankly I didn't know what I would do with any information I came up with. If it was worth my while to forget it, I'd forget it. It would, you see, give me a certain pleasure to foil Frank's plan to be a big shot."

"And if you decided not to forget it?"

"I'd have the satisfaction of making him a big shot my-self."

Alvin smiled. "I'm sure he would be grateful."

"Materially."

He nodded. "So you covered yourself both ways. Ad-mirable." He examined me like a rare new species of life. "You are quite a woman. Completely captivating and completely untrustworthy. Probably you have heard the term 'bitch goddess'?"

"Sure. I went to school. But flattery will not move me."

He laughed, for the first time with genuine pleasure. "And you think I am a likely suspect for political scandal?"

"I think something like that. Maybe Consuelo hauls dollars around two continents until all their nasty associ-ations are washed away."

Some light that was not quite mirth came and went swiftly in Zwicky's eyes.

"I would like to be a dashing figure from the demi-monde of international finance, Stella, but I'm afraid I have to disappoint you. And your ex-husband. I'm quite an ordinary sort of person. We are all here at Cordilleras pretty ordinary hardworking people. And I think I can prove it."

"Living pretty regular lives?"

"Yes, I would say so." He moved smoothly toward me, one hand reaching for my elbow. I let him guide me to-ward the door. "You know I have a surprise for you—if you still suspect us of dark deeds in our foreign connec-tion—"

"Dying pretty regular deaths?"

The hand left my elbow. "What?"

"Rosa. She died a pretty regular death, Alvin?"

He touched his temple quickly. "Rosa. Rosa Esposito. One of our best employees. A very tragic thing. But— how did you know of her accident?" He wrinkled his brow carefully.

"I saw her die."

Good as he was, Zwicky did not quite have his balance

this time. He didn't lose color or tighten his jaw, but there was a split-second absence of expression in his face, a blank of real shock, gone as swiftly as one missing frame in a movie. They hadn't told him that.

"Good Lord. How horrible. I understand—" He stopped.

"Yes?"

His eyes kept slicing back and forth across my face. With an effort he went on. "An accident. Terrible." He swallowed. "Wasn't it?"

"Yes, it was terrible. Or did you mean wasn't it an accident?"

"No, that is . . . Of course it was an accident."

I smiled. "Of course." There was an awkward pause. "Anyway, you were speaking of proof of your regularity? And surprises. I like surprises." I leaned toward him a bit.

He appeared to think hard for a moment. "All right. It's true that our acquisition trips are important. And perhaps there are procedures in that area we could improve. So—" he beamed and touched my arm again "—why don't we go along with Consuelo? You can see our operation in Lima, talk to our people there. A week at Cordilleras's expense and no strings attached."

It was my turn to be off guard. Zwicky saw it and chuckled. His fingers dug into my arm, and he moved nearer; I could smell his lotion, an overripe citrus. "You said you like travel."

"I do." I let his lips brush my temple. I was stalling for time to think. If I turned the offer down, it would remove all doubt about my intentions; I couldn't pose anymore as an opportunist, a free-lancer. Zwicky would know I was not interested in him or his money. But if I accepted . . .

He was mouthing my ear. "O-h-h. You're making it very hard to concentrate, Alvin." I pushed him a little away, in what I hoped was a coy gesture. "A very attractive offer. But I do have a job and friends and the like."

Even as I said it, I knew it sounded unconvincing. "It

would take a little doing. Might I have a day to think about it?" He looked at me intently. It still wasn't enough.

"Make the reservations anyway, just in case." I kissed him. His lips were smooth and stiff as paper, the hands ravenous on my back.

Chapter XV

By the time I walked back to the apartment my brain was at a rolling boil. It would be crazy to run off to Peru. I was by no means sure of Zwicky's motives. Maybe he fell for my pose, and maybe not. He could want me as far as possible from the scene of the action. Or he might still want to throw a scare into partners who had been leaning on him.

Then again, maybe it wasn't so crazy. It was possible Zwicky was another one who liked to ride the edge. He and Consuelo could try to run a shipment of goods right under my nose. If I didn't catch them, that was proof of innocence. If I did, Zwicky could offer a deal: I would already be incriminated by the trip, a co-runner of whatever they were running, so why not join the organization and take a piece of the pie? Either solution would be less risky than trying to get rid of me the old-fashioned way.

Maybe I thought too much. I needed Hand to help me figure it out. I sat on the bed and tried to reach him on the zebra phone, but he wasn't at headquarters. I got my suitcase out of the closet, opened it on the bed, then made an aimless trip to the kitchen for a glass of water I didn't need. To go or not to go. Stay or not to stay. I went back to the suitcase and the phone. To keep the option open, I realized I had to take some preliminary steps. Like call Gabby.

"Yeah, who is it?"

"What telephone tact, boss. It's one of your exploited wage slaves."

"Stell! Christ in his heaven! What is this going to Peru?

Why don't you quit and have done? To you three years means nothing. I trained—"

"Whoa, Gabby. Don't shout." Zwicky was keeping me off guard. I knew by the whine in my employer's voice that he'd already been bought.

"How much is he paying you, and just exactly what did you tell him?"

"You speak in riddles. What the hell do you say?"

"Don't bullshit me, Gabby. How much and what did you tell him?"

"I don't have to—"

"Gabby?"

"You are overdue one week already, so I charged him for two total, and I don't say nothing. Zero. You were out to drum up business, no more. So what the hell is going on? Who is this Swizzle?"

"Zwicky. That is absolutely all you said?"

"All absolutely. Maybe I say you are not bad-looking. For a joke."

"Hilarious. Look, Gabby, maybe I'll go to Peru for a week, and maybe not."

"You crazy? I paid already. You're going."

"Zwicky paid. I heard you."

"No difference. Immaterial. Anyway, I got all the inconvenience."

"Now listen. Whether I go or not, you keep your mouth shut. Where I am you don't know. It might be my life. Money, to you."

"Christ." He sounded genuinely upset. "Why do you put me through this?"

"Because I love you, Gabby. Especially when you are in torment. So long."

Next, I called Baker and Ferguson and went through two receptionists before I got to the man who handled spot commercials for political campaigns. I told him I was a graduate student in sociology interested in the impact of television on voting patterns. I needed to see some figures on Nielsen ratings for the past couple of years. He didn't have much time. I said I would only have to know which candidates Baker and Ferguson had done ads for. He named five people. Two were city supervisors. Three were state assemblymen. Francisco Ugarte and Hugh Drummond were two of the three.

I thanked him profusely. I was a strong supporter of Assemblyman Drummond's. Happened to know a member of his staff. Johnny Caswell. Public relations. The man on the other end of the line chuckled. He knew Cas. Very well. In fact, Cas was no longer with Drummond but was also a B and F man, with a very sweet assignment. He was overseas, the lucky so-and-so. Selling peekaboos to the natives.

"Fantastic. Where?"

"Lima. He loves it."

"Too much. Listen, tell him hello from Darlene."

"Sure. Listen, talk to you later."

"I doubt it. I think this is good-bye forever."

"What?"

I hung up and got busy filling the suitcase. Jeans, three white blouses, a T-shirt, socks and undies, a blue dress with cream weskit, one evening outfit, a sweater, and my toilet kit. I took the .32 from my handbag and dismantled it as Frank had taught me to do. The chamber went in the toilet kit; the barrel, in a tampon case. The wooden handle I stuck in my coat pocket.

I needed to get traveler's checks and pick up my passport at my own apartment, so I left the suitcase open for last-minute additions. Or for quick unpacking, in case I decided the whole idea was preposterous. Then I went out to warm up the Porsche. I wanted to visit Peralta Street and talk once more to Billie Jo Goodman. She was the sort of abandoned mine that would always yield a few nuggets if you could stand the digging.

I didn't stay long in my own apartment. It had the dank and musty atmosphere of a funeral parlor, and I didn't care for the association. I threw out some withered flowers from a vase on the dining-room table and briefly inspected the contents of my refrigerator, which had produced some remarkable cultures. I washed the lone coffee-stained cup in the sink. Then I took my passport and a necklace and two pairs of earrings and left.

At the bank I withdrew a thousand in traveler's checks, a greater part of my worldly substance, and headed back to the Mission. The old frame house still leaned behind its palm trees, but the Esposito place next door looked empty, cleaned out. The bit of yard before the sagging steps was cluttered with paper scraps and bent cans. I began to think maybe I was wasting my time, but another interview more or less wouldn't matter much in my career.

I took my briefcase from the back seat and rapped on the front door. Inside, I could hear the muffled metallic voices from the television, the bursts of programmed laughter. After a second and louder knock I heard feet, heavy and slow. The door opened, and I faced a squat lump of a man in blue work clothes.

"We don't need none," he said after one pointed look at the briefcase, and began to shut the door again.

"Is Billie Jo home? You must be her husband. My name is Stella Pike." I extended my hand quickly. He had to remove his grip on the doorknob to shake it. He didn't look as if he enjoyed shaking hands with young women. "Billie's helping me with a little survey," I said helpfully.

"I said we don't need none." He kept his thick body in the doorway.

"I'm not selling anything, Mr. Goodman. Really. Not a thing."

He turned his head. "Billie?" A burst of studio laughter replied. *"Billie!"*

"Yeah, what?"

"Some woman here to see you."

In a moment Billie appeared in the hallway behind her husband, one of her children hanging on her skirt. I noted that it was the same skirt she had worn the first time "some woman" had come to see her.

"Oh, hi!" Her dough-white face took on a flush and

she gave an embarrassed little laugh. "Miz Pike. Rob, this is who I told you about, the lady doin' the study. Miz Pike, this is Rob. Don't mind him. Git out'n the way, Rob, and let Miz Pike come in. I'll git you some coffee."

With little shoves and waves she cleared her family from my path, and I found myself back in the living room on the soiled settee, drinking another cup of flat, barely warm coffee, listening to neighborhood lore. On my lap was an employee profile form, and periodically I stabbed it with the felt-tip pen in my hand. This gesture seemed to act as a goad on Billie; each time I made it she heroically strove for a new topic. Rob remained sunk in an over-stuffed chair, glowering at the little luminous rectangle on the table. Billie had insisted on turning the volume down, so the waves of hilarity were now distant. Periodically one of the little Goodmans ran howling through the room or peered at me suspiciously from a doorway. Finally we got to the Espositos, and Billie took to the subject with gusto.

"Like I told you, they fought a lot. Some people do that, and it's healthy, like Rob and me, ain't that so, Rob? But not the way they did it. Not that he marked her, but he made her feel real bad, you know."

I shook my read disapprovingly.

"Worst thing a body can do, make another precious soul so unhappy."

"Isn't it the truth?"

"I always say, don't I, Rob?"

Rob grunted and closed his eyes.

"But he got what he deserved when she died. He didn't feel so uppity then. Those people, you know, they can be the nicest happy-go-lucky people, and the uppitiest people in the whole world. You know what I mean? Especially when they git ahold of a little money. . . . He come over after you left, you know, just humble as anything, apologizing all over the place, feelin' sorry he'd been so mean to Rosa."

"Really?" I put the felt-tip aside.

"You bet. But I didn't trust the snake anyways. He was incinderating things. Wanting to know all about Rosa's boyfriend, the musical fella I told you about—"

"Bennie?"

"That's the one, and about her comings and goings with him. That's right. The woman was hardly in her grave, mind you, and here he was prying into her personal matters."

"Billie," Rob said warningly.

"I don't care. Rob thinks I gossip. But he was a snake. They was separated. None of his business."

"Billie." Rob's eyes looked dull and opaque as the eyes of some prehistoric fish. "Quit talkin'."

"Mr. Goodman, as you know, this is only a survey, and we absolutely do not use names. Privacy is protected always." I gave him the most winning smile I could muster. "And we are very interested in the composition of this neighborhood. The Espositos seem to have been rather different from most neighbors, that's all. Did you know them, by the way?"

The dull eyes rolled back and forth between his wife, me, and the television set.

"He was a nigger." Rob shook his head. "She wa'n't. You got to expect fights."

"Did you see him very much?"

"Livin' next door. Bound to see him. But he run off six months ago, and then wa'n't but three days ago he come back. Askin', like she done told you." He jerked his head at his wife.

"Thought we might know about her money or her pots and clothes and things." Billie sniffed in disgust. "We sure ain't much for knowin' about money, Rob and me."

Rob hit her with the fisheyes. "We get by."

"He thought she give it to Bennie. They was in some kind of club together. One of those clubs to defend somebody or git them out of jail or—"

"Com'nists," Rob said, and shook his head again. "And niggers."

"More coffee?" Billie scooped her smallest from the

floor and, before I could answer, placed the baby in my arms. "You watch the kid a sec, and I'll get you some nice and hot."

She left the room, and I sat regarding the bald little being on my knee. The head, like a knout of pale rubber on a stick of a neck, swiveled unsteadily to regard me. Large, empty, watery eyes seemed neither pleased nor disappointed at what they saw, and the pink hole of a mouth was similarly expressionless. I looked at Rob, but he had returned his attention to the television, where now a great crowd of people were singing about some cans they held aloft in their hands.

"You're a cute little thing," I said rather unconvincingly. Outside an engine raced and died.

"Sugar or cream? I forget," Billie shouted from the rear of the house.

"Straight," I shouted back.

"Well, speak of the devil. A coincidence, Lord. Why don't you talk to Mr. Esposito yourself? He just pulled in."

I was paralyzed, listening to the window slide open, then to Billie's voice, now false and high, calling, "Manuel! Oh, Manuel! Can you come in a sec? Got somebody to meet you." I stood up, fighting panic, the baby dangling from my arms. Billie appeared in the doorway again with two cups of steaming coffee and a malicious little smile.

"He's comin' in," she hissed. "Now you'll see."

She put down the coffee, and I handed her the baby.

"Lovely child," I said, and had time for one breath before Manuel stepped into the room.

He was very dark, wide from the front and flat as a blade in profile. The face was hollow-cheeked, sullen, quite handsome. He smiled, but his yellow eyes remained bright and mad as a goat's. Everything I had expected was confirmed. He was bad, bad, bad.

"Manuel, this here is Miz Pike, the survey lady. She's doing a study of this neighborhood for a real big company." Billie stood between us, like a referee giving the fighters instructions before the bell. "Miz Pike, this is

Manuel. Used to live next door. Like I told you. *Formerly.*"

The goat's eyes looked at me. All of me. Slowly. "Yeah," he said finally.

I managed to nod and keep my own eyes steady.

"Miz Pike and me was just atalkin' about things around here, like the comp-o-sition of the block and all, and I just thought maybe she'd have a few questions for *you.*" Billie stepped back a little and signaled me with her eyebrows.

Manuel was capable of looking unutterably, lewdly insolent without moving a muscle. I was having trouble unsticking my mind from the yellow eyes and the odor of extreme cruelty he gave off. Just before I drew a breath to ask him a pointless question, he turned his back on me.

"How you doin', Mr. Rob?" he said tonelessly.

"Cain't complain," Rob answered without looking up.

"You ain't seen none of my wife's friends hangin' 'round in recent days. No packages?"

"Ain't seen nothin'. Like we said."

"Right." He stared for a few moments at the flickering screen. "Shee-ut," he said then, and turned suddenly back to me. "You thought up your questions, Miz Survey Lady? Important Company Survey Lady? You gonna git my name in the papers? Comp-o-zishun of This Important Neighborhood?" He gave me a sudden and evil smile, and as he talked, he jived toward me, swiveling his hips and cocking his legs like a dancer. When he was a couple of feet away, this fluid movement stopped, and he was still, tense and poised as a drawn knife.

"That wouldn't be much," I said evenly. "You've had your name in the papers before."

"Think so? You seen it?"

"As a matter of fact, I have. The story about your wife's accident. Too bad."

"Yeah, too bad." Manuel grinned again. "She boozed too much. Killer booze it was, Miz Survey Lady. Stay away from that. You don't look like no boozer." He went over me again with his eyes.

"Anybody can get hit by a car."

"That's so, ain't it? Anybody."

"Understand you had been separated from your wife."

Manuel flicked one glance at Billie. "Yeah. We was split. That part of your important survey?"

"Yeah, it is. And race, I notice your name is Spanish. You don't look Spanish."

"Yeah?" Manuel seemed amused. "What do I look?"

"You look black. Chicago or Detroit." That was a wild guess, but I saw Manuel hesitate for a split second. Then he laughed.

"*¡Eh, carrajo! Hay negros de abajo también, chica.*"

"*Verdad. Pero no hablan inglés como tú.*"

It is wonderful how an unused language rushes back when the need is desperate. One quick sentence was about all I was good for, but it was enough to take the smile from Manuel's face.

"Well, you put in your important study that there is one nigger on this block who got some Spanish in him." Manuel leaned his face very close to mine. "My mama was half Puerto Rican, and my daddy was an African man, a big ol' African man. His ancestors used to cook up missionaries."

"I should think they would make thin soup. You ought to stick to importers or people in politics."

We stared at each other for so long that Billie finally spoke. Her voice was small and awed.

"Would anybody like to sit down?" she whispered.

"No, this lady got to get on with her survey." Manuel also spoke softly. The yellow eyes had begun to glow with a new level of madness, some incandescent compound of desire and vengeance. "She got important work to do. And I do, too. Yes, I do." He made a sweeping gesture toward the door, and I took a step toward it, as if hypnotized.

"Oh, Billie," I said then. "Walk to the car with me. I've got a little form for you. You can fill it out and mail it in."

Billie looked dubious. She was dimly aware that new tides were running, rather deeper and more dangerous than she had imagined. On impulse I snatched the baby from the couch.

"Come on. We'll all go." I marched out the front door, Billie scurrying after. I threw a glance over my shoulder when I reached the curb, but Manuel had given up on the porch. He stood carelessly there, then stuck a cigarette in his mouth and lit it, watching without appearing to watch.

I rummaged around in the Porsche and found an old questionnaire on purchasing habits. Billie clutched it in one arm and received her progeny with the other. The two of them regarded me with round, wondering eyes.

"Lord," Billie said. "The both of you talk funny."

"I'm sorry, Billie. I'm afraid I don't get along very well with some of your neighbors. But I have to ask you one more question."

Billie looked away. "Well—"

"Look. Rosa did leave something with you, didn't she?" She looked shocked. "Nothin'. Nothin' worth anything."

"Of course not. I'm sure it was only a memento."

"Just an old shawl and a little box of some kind of wood that smells real sweet. I've seen that box for sale for seven ninety-nine. They was just between friends. None of *his* business. Nor Rob's either." Her jaw set. Billie had some steel under that bread-dough complexion.

"Certainly. Someday I'd like to see them, okay?" I was already behind the wheel, turning over the engine.

"Well." Billie looked over her shoulder. Manuel was still on the porch, smoking. "Some morning. When Rob ain't around. I enjoy talkin' to you, Miz Pike. Though, like I said, you do talk funny sometimes, you know."

"I know I do, Billie. You take care of the little one now." I smiled and waved and left the curb, the tires barking a little on the asphalt in what I hoped was a discreet burst of speed. But in the rearview mirror, as I rounded the corner, I saw Manuel still motionless, watching, on the porch.

Chapter XVI

On the dining-room table at the apartment there was a note from Alice. She planned to spend the evening with Eric again, so I could make my own dinner, and Frank had rung twice, leaving a number for my return call. The note ended with a mention of my open suitcase on the bed and the simple question "Where are you going?" It was a question that struck deeper than I wanted to probe at the moment.

I called Frank, and we made quick arrangements to meet at the Jolly Roger in an hour. He sounded tense and distant. He was letting me know I had been out of touch too long to suit him. He wasn't going to like what I had to tell him either. The protective instinct in him was indistinguishable from the possessive, and both would go sour when I notified him of my new options.

I went into the bathroom and sent hot water tumbling into the tub. When I had stripped off my clothes, I found the thick volume in the yellow cover and took Professor von Gaugen with me into the bubbles and steam. He didn't seem to mind; the little black ant columns of print marched inexorably across the pages. I learned some novel, if irrelevant, things: that the entire populace of Peru had paid tribute to the Incas, that the Spaniards melted down most of the artwork in gold, that these brilliant stonemasons did not have the wheel, did not even have a written language.

Then, finally, I discovered something useful. There were maps. All the styles of valuable art were identified: Chavín, Nazca, Moche, and so on. A topographical color index showed the distribution of arable lands, now and throughout history. The interesting thing was that Tingo María, the northern city where Zwicky and Consuelo bought fabrics in a nunnery, was of no importance on these maps. It wasn't marked with one of the little symbols indicating a ruin, an artistic craft center, or an ancient culture. It was hundreds of kilometers from any of the sites of past civilizations. Its purpose was summed up this way:

> The provincial capital of Tingo María is largely a trading post where products of the jungle, especially coca and hides, are exchanged for weapons, tools, and rum. It is ideally situated to control this semi-legal traffic, being connected by road and air to the coastal cities, and by the adjoining river drainages (Marañon and Ucayali) to the Amazon basin and hence to the Atlantic Ocean.

I slammed shut the book and threw it on a clothes hamper. The famous shawls of Tingo María could be a cover, a very elaborate and convincing cover for travel to the area where the original suppliers of coca leaf did a thriving trade. It began to look as if there were good reasons to tag along on the trip. At least I had some idea of what to watch for.

I got out of the tub and put together a street outfit of jeans, a fitted leather jacket, and Frye boots. The fog had moved in again and gave signs of becoming a fine rain, so I slipped into a raincoat for the walk.

When I came into the blue cave of the bar, Danny flicked his rag toward the booths on the far wall. His road-map wrinkles shifted into an expression of noncommittal sadness. "Back there," he said. "I'll pour it and bring it to you. Good luck."

"It's not what you think, Danny. Sheer business. I'm still available."

He brightened a little and winked. "Me too."

Frank stood up to greet me. Not an auspicious sign. He wore a thick English sweater over his carefully faded jeans and suede boots. His lips were quick and tight on my mouth.

"Very formal," I said, dropping into the booth.

"I feel like I'm being offered a rare interview."

I let that one go. "What's up with the investigation? Any of the big fish ready for frying?"

Frank set down firmly the glass he had just picked up. "Stella, I haven't heard a word from you for days. I think we'd better start with what's been happening with you. If you don't mind."

I shrugged. "All right. What do you want to know?"

"Where you've been. What you've seen."

"I've been working at a place called Cordilleras Imports. Alvin Zwicky runs it. Rosa used to work there. Looks promising."

"How so?"

"Zwicky has connections with a lot of people. Assemblymen for example. Assemblymen active in supporting drug rehabilitation programs."

"Interesting." Frank did not, however, look terribly interested. Danny arrived then with my Scotch and soda, put it down swiftly, and left.

"That's about it," I said.

"Is it?" Frank was regarding me steadily. The cross-examination.

"There is another body, of course. I suppose you know that."

"The musician?"

"Yeah. Apparently listed as an overdose or suicide. But Jack thinks otherwise."

"Jack?"

So that was it. I looked at Frank wearily. "Yes," I said. "Jack."

"I see."

There was a frosty silence, while I sipped my drink and waited, fighting off irritation and the groundless guilt that produced it.

"Can we go on?"

Frank bowed. "Of course."

"So they've killed two people and might very well do it again. I think it's time for you fearless lawmen to make some kind of move. You might start with some fellows named Ugarte, Drummond, and Ferguson."

Frank opened his mouth, closed it, opened it again, and left it that way a rather long time before he thought of something to say. "What is this?" He gestured at me. "How the hell did you get . . . such completely—"

"Ah." I grinned at him and rolled my glass just under my chin. "Got hold of a nerve, did I? Thought you had the story all to yourself?"

"What story? A pipe dream? What leads you to the remarkable conclusion that Hugh Drummond has something to do with this?"

"Let's start with Ugarte. That's easier. He's one of the sponsors of the original legislation establishing the street programs that Manuel Esposito worked in and has voted to increase their appropriation every year. He's straight from the barrio: young, tough, smart, and greedy. Before he went into the system, he fooled around with the Venceremos Brigade, the revolutionaries. That gives him connections with the political movements in the state prisons, which is where Manuel worked to build an organization and groom his employees. You think it's preposterous, Frank, that this guy is a suspect?" I looked at him with genuine curiosity.

"Of course, it isn't *preposterous*. I'm not a dolt, Stella. Ugarte was, and still is for some people, a prime suspect, for the self-evident reasons you have just enumerated. But I assure you the state auditor's office went over him with a microscope. He's clean. No campaign fund hanky-panky, no unexplained sudden wealth, no hidden vices."

"Okay. Maybe on paper he's clean. But who is his collaborator on the rehabilitation bills? Drummond. A used-car king. Very handy in getting rid of vehicles used in crimes. A Chrysler fitting the description of the one I saw Rosa fall out of was stolen the day before the murder and has since disappeared. You know where it was stolen? Cordilleras. Zwicky's own car."

Frank gave a small hoot. "Farfetched, Stella. Really. They would have to be bungling amateurs."

"Or scared. Now, to make this association a little less farfetched, we'll take a look at the advertising firm of Baker and Ferguson. Baker may be a respectable fellow, but Ferguson does Zwicky's advertising, sits on the Trade Commission with him and Ugarte and Drummond, and handles television ads for the election campaigns of both of them. An aide of Drummond's, Johnny Caswell, moved to Ferguson's company after helping fend off the auditor's investigation. Before *that* he worked for Ugarte."

Frank was studying the grain of the wood on the surface of the table. Finally he looked up with a rueful smile.

"All right, Stella. I'll be honest. I'm jealous. That's very nice work. I didn't know about Caswell. Baker and Ferguson may be completely innocent, but the lead is definitely promising." He raised his drink. "You're a champ."

I clicked my glass against his. "Nice that you think so."

"Anyway, it will take a few weeks to check things out— carefully. You can go back to your previous existence, and all this will be, as they say, a bad dream." He smiled encouragingly.

"A vacation will do me good." I turned and motioned to Danny. "Don't you think?"

"You bet. You've earned it. That jaunt to Hawaii—"

"Actually I had something else in mind, Frank. Not that I didn't always enjoy the Islands with you. But I'm going to Peru. I think."

"Peru?" Frank's mouth came undone again. He watched blankly as Danny put down the fresh drinks on the table.

"Yes. While you are doing that careful checking, I thought I would poke around at the source. I mean, the little cans of white powder come from somewhere down there, don't they, Frank?"

He worked a little with his mouth. "Stella, you . . . that's so . . ."

"Crazy? Ah, well. I hardly know anymore. Anyway, I'll probably be gone a week, Frank. You can expect a couple of postcards of the principal monuments."

His hand shot across the table and clamped onto my wrist. "You can't be that mad. You've done something really substantial here, with that Ferguson lead. Now leave it alone." He was talking hoarsely, through his teeth.

"Hands off, Frank."

His grip tightened. "I can't let you do it. Who are you going with?"

"Zwicky. It's probably an attempted bribe. Let go, Frank."

"Zwicky!" His tan had taken on a definite shade of red. "A notorious—"

I lifted the glass of Scotch and soda and balanced it on my palm. "Take your hands off me, Frank, or I'll let you have this right on the button. That's a nice shirt. You don't want to ruin it. I mean it."

After a moment his fingers loosened, and I pulled away and placed my glass neatly on the napkin. Then I took my purse and stood up. "You seem very concerned, my love. Too concerned. Maybe more than my welfare is involved. Maybe you would hate to have somebody else crack this open?" I didn't really expect an answer, and I didn't get one. Frank was concentrating again on the tabletop, a new ridge of muscle along his jaw. "I'll wait a little longer, Frank. But you'd better not count on my returning to what you call my normal existence. I wouldn't, even if I could."

On the way out I stopped at the bar and dropped a five in front of Danny. "Set him up with one more," I said. "He needs it."

Chapter XVII

The rain puddles preoccupied me on the walk back to Alice's, and I suppose for that reason I didn't see the man in the car at the curb. Nor did I hear him get out of the car and walk toward me while I fiddled with my keys at the door. I smelled him first: an odor of stale cigars and something vaguely medicinal, like witch hazel or menthol. I glanced up quickly, and there he was, just behind me, an ugly little man in a plastic raincoat and a battered hat. He stood motionless, quite close to me, drops falling from the hatbrim like a bead curtain. The curtain did not obscure the bulbous nose and the shaving rash above his collar.

I slid my hand into my purse, remembered the pistol wasn't there, grabbed a felt-tip pen instead, and jabbed it against the side of the bag.

"Touch me, and I'll put little holes in you and tell them you tried to assault me. Step back."

He didn't move. A strange, one-sided smile appeared behind the slow, steady fall of raindrops.

"Maybe you're hard-of-hearing. I'm not kidding, you know."

He shuffled sideways, and the smile went away. "Take it easy." He had a voice like pebbles falling into a tin plate. "You wouldn't look too good, shooting a police officer."

I stared into his muddy eyes for a time, but he didn't blink.

"I'm not kidding either. My name is Dryer. Harry Dryer. Friend of Jack Hand's. Put the gun away, lady. Please."

"Show me some ID. Slowly."

He sighed and with exaggerated care produced a leather folder. It opened to reveal a seal and a yellowed card with a picture. Harold Dryer. Lieutenant. Homicide. The picture was definitely the little man. Few people are that ugly.

"Okay?" He put the folder away and nodded at the bulge in my purse. I retracted the pen but kept my hand inside.

"Okay. So you're a friend of Jack's. Where is he?"

"People call me Stump." He looked out at the street. "Can we step inside?"

Something I didn't like moved suddenly in my heart. "What's this about? Where is Jack?"

He looked back at me, at my hand knotted around the key ring. I saw it in his eyes, and a cannonball took away the whole middle of my being.

Stump let out his breath and took another. "He's dead."

I thought maybe I would just stay there, in the slow rain, for the rest of time. I didn't move, and the little man didn't either. The tires in the street hissed by, and water gurgled in the gutter.

"You okay?" He stepped forward and put forth a hesitant hand.

"I'll be all right." I stared stupidly at the keys in my hand. "Open it, go ahead."

He took the keys and unlocked the door. He waited on the threshold, while I turned and looked out into the rain for a little while.

Finally I turned back and stepped inside. Mechanically I reassured Baudelaire and pointed Stump to a chair. I undid the belt of my coat and sat on another chair opposite him. With his hat off he revealed a fringe of rusty hair around a knobby pink skull. The mud-gray eyes had a softer look in the lamplight.

"It was probably a setup," he said. "I've been out with Jack before. He don't make a lot of mistakes. Somebody told him there was a big tip, a big break, and he went for it. I figure it had to do with what you two were working out."

There was a hint of a question in his last remark. He waited.

"Maybe we'll get to that," I said. "Go on."

He shrugged. "A girl working in one of those fast chicken-fry places went out with some trash. She opened the top of a Dumpster, and there was a foot sticking out. They killed him with one shot in the head, up close. A thirty-eight. Probably his. We'll know tomorrow. Carried him in the back of a car, pulled into the rear of this place, and stuffed him in the Dumpster. It's in a back alley. No traffic—the fog for cover. Nobody saw anything." Stump took a deep breath and looked down at the little hat that he had twisted into a damp lump. "He was covered with grease and broken glass. The dirty sons of bitches."

Neither of us spoke for a time. There were only silent riptides of grief.

"So you think he was killed because of our case. What did he tell you about it?"

"Not much. Jack said a week or so ago that he was looking into this woman who got hit by a car. Both of us have been careful because we got a fink somewhere in our system. Dope money can buy damn near anybody in this town. The day you came to the Mission Street precinct—I saw you leave with Jack—he came back and spent the whole afternoon checking stolen car readouts. I knew the two of you were onto something."

"We were. And Jack said it was likely the fink knew, too."

"Yeah. Only I ain't so sure he's in my office. We got computers now, you know. Some guy in Sacramento can ask the goddamned things for our daily reports and get them."

I nodded. It was reasonable. I had done a little of that kind of technological snooping myself. It went through my mind that certain security personnel in an assemblyman's office might have access to the right machines.

"This whole thing is going to end up in Sacramento anyway, sooner or later," Stump said, and I detected rage running deep in his voice.

"How's that?"

"Shit, lady, you know how this deal runs. You know about the auditors digging into the Start Over program, right? Sure you do. I put that much together. The funds for those programs are juice for our local dealers, the way I figure. And some of the profit goes back to the capitol to pay off the guys who set up those programs."

"Seems to be common knowledge. My ex-husband says the same thing."

"Pike?"

"Yes. Know him?"

Stump shook his head. "Nope. Just that they say he's trying to make a name. Nail Ugarte. Some talk that he might be chosen as chief prosecutor for a special investigation."

"It makes me curious. If everybody knows what's going on, why doesn't somebody do something?"

Stump looked at me with jaded amusement. "On the street everybody knows. On the witness stand nobody knows."

"They're that strong?"

He laughed. "They got maybe three hundred members in the joint and that many more running loose. Guys with advanced degrees in knives and pipes and bike chains, smuggling shit in and out of the toughest prisons in the world. Before they get out, a guy from Start Over comes in—they got the right to talk to the cons—and gives them the rap. They play the rehabilitation game, get assigned a job as a 'counselor' in a rehab center. Sometimes they get promised a room there. All they got to do is make dependable pushers out of the other addicts that show up to get cured. Everything is safe—the honchos even got offices of their own, cars from the motor pool, credit cards on the airlines. They got *salaries,* for Christ's sake."

"Guys like Manuel."

"Right. It works on the privilege and terror system. If any one guy gets busted—which ain't likely since they got such perfect cover—he keeps his mouth shut. If he gets sent up, they take good care of him in the slammer. He can deal dope in there, too, and the organization will handle his affairs at home. Make sure the kids are fed, keep an eye on the old lady. If he screws up, gives out any information to the wrong people, they will take care of him in there, too. Prison hits are never solved." Stump looked depressed. "It's one hell of a system. Better than ours."

"So how do we get back to Sacramento?"

He sighed and rubbed his pink scalp. "That ain't my specialty. Politics. But it looks damned funny when those butterbrains in the Assembly keep sending money to that pack of rats. Somehow part of the loose cash must get back to them. I thought that was your angle, maybe?"

I thought for a while. He was entitled to know what my angle was, I supposed. "I've poked around a little. For one thing, getting the goods into this country requires some international connection. Passports, customs, and so forth. Likewise, to get clean money to an assemblyman requires some fast financial shuffling. That means there are middlemen—aides, consultants, business associates. I've got my eye on a couple of local companies for that job."

Stump looked at me, cool and speculative. "You done this kind of work before?"

"More or less."

"You must be good. Jack didn't fool with anybody who wasn't."

"That would go for you, too."

He looked pleased for the first time. It didn't last long. "Anyway, however good you are, they can nail your ass. So you need all the help you can get."

"Maybe you do, too."

Stump allowed himself a very small smile. "Don't give anything away, do you? Yeah. Maybe I do. If I mess with this deal. So how can you help me?"

"I didn't say I could help you. But when I run across something, I'll check it out with you."

"You mean you're going on with this?"

"Sure."

He shook his head. "Most people wouldn't fool with these people for a suitcaseful of money. You—" He stopped, catching the expression on my face. "All right. You want to find yourself dead in a trash can, that's your business. I'm dumb enough to stay on it, too." He looked at me in his muddy, phlegmatic way, waiting.

"Fine. Tell me what we're looking for. I'm told that eventually things culminate in a grand jury investigation. So what sort of evidence counts?"

Stump pawed inside his plastic coat. "You mind cigars?"

"Not good ones."

He produced a stubby black torpedo, bit off the end, and lit it with a wooden match scraped on the edge of Alice's coffee table.

"Names. Dates. Conversations," he said, with a puff of dense white smoke for each word. "Stuff you can present to the jury to convince them you got a criminal case. Usually it ain't that hard. I'll tell you a simple fact. Keep track of almost anybody—your aunt Betsy—and you'll get something on them. It's an illegal life. For everybody. A little chiseling on the taxes. Little on the side with the baby-sitter. Taking the company car fishing. Once you turn up a little thing, you just keep going. Crooks got to keep a record of some kind, just like any business. They got to communicate with each other." He rolled the cigar in his mouth. Probably he didn't often get the chance to lecture, and he enjoyed it.

"The outfit you're after seems to have a real good code. The feds monitored the Start Over phone lines for months and kept taps on Ugarte's office and home. They've tailed Manuel and his buddies. Nothing. But somehow they've got to know when the stuff is coming in, and how much of it there is, and what it costs. The job is to intercept that information. We don't know how they pass it. Until we do, we can't bust them."

"Whether or not you find the right phone to tap, seems to me the stuff has to move from down there to up here. Have you got any idea how they move it across the border? What do the customs people do anyway?"

"They do all they can. I've worked with the border people in San Diego. You got to realize there are too many bags and bales and flatcars to check. But I've got one hunch."

"Like?"

"Like I don't think they go for big shipments—thirty, forty, fifty kilos. I think they move a steady ten or twenty every month or two. Just the way it shows up on the street makes me think so."

"So what do the customs people look for?"

"Another little-known fact. A lot of it is intuitive. The best inspector I ever knew refused to listen to tips or even look at documents. He just looked at people. He could smell fear the way a dog sniffs out raw meat. He'd joke with a guy, watch how he swung his luggage onto the table, flirt with his wife. And he seldom missed a cold hit."

"A what?"

"A cold hit. An arrest without any advance suspicion. Pure intuition."

"Sounds like palm reading." I stared through the swirls of smoke between us. "Anyway, it hasn't worked for this bunch."

Stump grunted. "They're very cool, very smooth. Or else we're not looking in the right places."

"How about import firms, commercial operations?"

"They get a regular check. A thorough check. If it's equipment, the border people X-ray it, dismantle it, weigh it, taste it."

"I'm a little green at this. What quantities are we talking? Pounds and dollars?"

"For coke figure about fifty thousand a pound, a hundred a kilo. That's street value—and they control it right to the user. Ten kilos is around a million. For heroin a little less."

"So what's your theory?"

He frowned. "Don't have any. Theories cause trouble. I'm just surprised the border people haven't noticed somebody making too many trips or getting nervous. When you've got three kilos of junk in your suitcase or strapped to your crotch, it's real hard to be natural, no matter how tough you are."

"I can imagine. Well, thanks for the instruction. I'm going to do a little traveling myself, and it will come in handy." I stood up and shook off the raincoat, which had left a little ring of water around the chair.

Stump got up too, and straightened out the twisted hat. "Traveling?"

"Yeah. I'm following one of the leads to Lima." I was a little surprised that the statement came so easily. Apparently I had made up my mind.

"You think that's smart?"

"No. But it isn't any smarter to stay here. If I don't go, it's likely they'll be certain Jack and I were working closely. So far I think they haven't been sure. They believe I might be for sale. That may be what's keeping me alive."

"You think you can stay that way in Peru?" He flopped the hat back over his knob of a head. "You're crazy."

"Probably. But I've got more than that to worry about." I felt a wave of numb exhaustion pass over me. "It's been a tough week."

"Yeah." Stump contemplated me. "I bet. I'm sorry. I didn't mean what I said about you winding up dead. I wouldn't like that." He fidgeted for a moment, then plunged a hand into his coat and produced a card. "Good luck. Call me at the number on the back if you need to."

"I will. Thanks." We shook hands, and I opened the door for him. Night had come sweeping in with the rain, and car lights were shattering in the pools in the street. He halted on the bottom step and looked back at me.

"We'll get them," he said. "The dirty sons of bitches." He turned and walked away, not seeing my lifted hand.

Chapter XVIII

I mixed myself a drink and sat for a long time in the living room. One shaded lamp burned in a corner. There was no sound but the tires outside on wet pavement and an occasional whine or thump of the tail from Baudelaire, dreaming some dog drama. I was waiting for the liquor to take hold and give me some relief from the fight to keep my mind clear of memories, of the terrible image of Jack in the Dumpster, of the surges of wild rage. Again and again I caught myself moving my thumb, tripping the imaginary safety on the little revolver, firing point-blank into the mocking face of Gutierez or Manuel. And finally there was a big chill wind of despair.

I had begun with righteous anger over the glimpse of murder in my rearview mirror. A woman I didn't even know. Step by step, death was getting closer. I met Bennie, heard the magic of his fingers when they made music. Then I saw him twisted and empty-eyed while one of his own records played a song he couldn't hear. Jack—big and smart and tough—came along, and for a week we ran off the dynamo of work and love. Now he was gone too. Stump said there were hundreds against us. Working for the state. Protected by powerful people. They drove around in taxpayer-funded vehicles, killing those who interfered.

Me, it appeared, they would rather buy. I wondered about that. Maybe the theory was that women can be bought. Or they didn't think I was much of a threat. At the moment I didn't either. I had a sudden, deep pang of doubt. Doubt and something else, some combination of revulsion and fascination. The thought took form, blunt and ugly. What was I worth? Tens, maybe hundreds of thousands. I couldn't beat them anyway. I could become Frank's office girl, feeding a little imagination into the machine he was building to take himself to the top. He would make it worth my while. Or I could play with Zwicky and reach an understanding. We wouldn't even have to mention the vulgar facts. Just take the money and keep my mouth shut.

It was becoming clear. If I stayed, I would wind up collaborating in what Frank called an investigation, what I called playing politics. If I went with Zwicky, I ran a risk of getting enmeshed in the operation I was supposed to be working to destroy. And Zwicky would put the pressure on, skillfully, subtly, but powerfully. He wanted me, but he also wanted my allegiance. The tapping foot, the strained casualness, the sudden offer told me a lot. He wanted a partner, an alliance against those who had gotten him into deep waters.

I looked at the half-empty glass. My knuckles were white around it. Where could I throw it? I looked vaguely around the room. Then the telephone rang.

I let it go four times, then put the glass on the coffee table and went to the bedroom to pick up the receiver. I waited, listening to the open line. It sounded like a booth on the street.

"Hello? Stella? Are you there?"

For a second or two I couldn't trace the boyish, slightly breathy voice. Then I remembered. Webster. The young broker who wrote such abysmal poems to me. A century ago.

"I'm here."

"Stella, my God! I've tried—what has been going on anyway?—I've tried everything to reach you. Your office won't say a word. You're never at your apartment. I know what you said. Maybe it is over. But I can't stop thinking—"

"Webster, please. I'm not well right now. You are a very nice person. A wonderful person. The whole thing was nice. But things have been very . . . turbulent . . . these last weeks."

"Only three weeks, Stella."

It was true. Though incredible. Three weeks ago I was dating a nice young San Francisco junior financier. Watching movies and eating crab Louis.

"An eternity sometimes, Webster. Look, how did you know I was here?"

"I ran into Alice and her boyfriend at the theater. I asked her where you were, and I could tell she was lying to me. So I guessed maybe you might be staying with her. I haven't been able to sleep, Stella. Or do a decent portfolio. Maybe we can't go back to what we had before, but—"

"Webster, you are a lovable man. And rich. San Francisco is full of beautiful young women who hunt nightly for someone just like you. Surely—" I stopped because I had an idea. An idea that went beyond mere warmth and giddiness.

"Stella? Are you all right?"

"Yes. I think so. Talking to you, I was a little, well, overwhelmed, Webster. There was a lot between us. You're right about that."

"Yes! There really was. Ah, Stella! I hoped you would understand what I was trying to say."

I could picture Webster on the edge of his expensive contoured leather chair. He was probably calling from his office because he lived in it most of the time. The beautifully trimmed black mustache would be quivering; the helmet of hair, coiffed and blow-dried at the best salon in the city, would be in romantic disarray; his big brown boy's eyes would be glistening. I hated myself for what I was going to do and admired myself even more for the genius of it.

"It's not just the old feeling, Webster. There's something different."

"What?" The word was charged with a cavalier's eagerness.

"I'm in trouble, Webster. I need your help."

"Stella"—his voice was as warm and big and manly as a John Ford movie—"I would do anything for you."

"I hope so, Webster. Because I want you to go to Peru with me."

"Of course." There wasn't even a pause. "That's a terrific idea. We'll wind up with a cruise to the Galápagos or maybe fly over to Rio—"

"Wait a minute, Webster. It's more complicated, much more complicated than that. I can't explain it over the phone. You will have to be a kind of guardian or bodyguard rather than a . . . travel companion. But I've got to explain it in person. Can we meet now?"

"I can't believe this! I thought you wouldn't see me, and now—" He had to pause to master himself. "I'll be there in fifteen minutes. I remember where Alice lives. I want so much—"

"I know, Webster. I look forward to seeing you, too. Fifteen minutes, okay? So long."

I hung up and went back to my drink. It would help matters if I didn't change, didn't even brush my hair, left the half-empty bottle and glass on the table. Distraught damsel. The qualms came again. I had a terrible ability to use situations and people. A strength and a curse. Webster was actually quite a wonderful person. He was expert at making money and generous about sharing it, and his indefatigable good spirits and inexhaustible affection were good for me. For a time. After Frank, I had gone through the usual period of vengeful promiscuity, a series of very forgettable men. Then Webster had come along to throw himself at my feet, and I took advantage of it, enjoying a few months of stability and very good wines. But I had known, from the beginning, that we weren't written in the stars, and finally I couldn't stand stringing him along.

But scruples were for people who did not plan voyages to strange continents with dangerous escorts. I would be able to tell Webster part of the truth. I was scared, and I needed help. A kind of investigation, I would say, a fact-

finding junket. But I couldn't trust the people I was
working with. I needed a real and true friend to tag along
and unobtrusively chaperon. This friend would have to
play the role of a thick-skinned and overattentive former
admirer, met by chance at the airport. A part Webster
was by no means ill-equipped to play.

There was a beautiful symmetry in the plan. Webster
and Zwicky would keep each other at bay, and I would
have a means of applying counterpressure. Webster knew
his way around San Francisco society and was himself used
to money, so he would not be cowed or tongue-tied. He
also had boundless energy, so I might be able to turn over
some of the work of surveillance to him. I poured myself
another drink, fighting the qualms that I knew were going
to be with me for a while. Webster was so easy to take for
a ride. He even wanted to go. And I had to do it. But I
knew I would end up feeling like a bitch anyway.

The sight of him, standing flat-footed with his arms
spread wide, grinning like an idiot in the rain, nearly
broke my resolve. I buried my face in his shoulder to keep
my eyes from running and then pushed him back.

"I'm glad to see you, Webster." I didn't have to fake
that.

"Stella!" He walked around me, a 360-degree tour.
"You look terrific!"

"I do?" I gave him a wan smile, and he took another
look, registering the bottle and glass.

"No, I guess . . ." He looked confused. "You said it
was a tough three weeks?"

I looked into the wide, sympathetic brown eyes, and I
knew there was no way I could tell Webster anything like
the whole truth. Murder, drugs, guns. He wouldn't be
able to talk to me for three days. So I got busy fabricating
a story that might do.

"So most of all, it has to look accidental, and you have
to stick to us all the time. Otherwise, my virtue, as well as
a big account, may be sacrificed." I patted his hand, while

he furrowed his brow thoughtfully. The story seemed to convince him. I had explained that a certain firm had called me to ask for a probe of Cordilleras's operations. If they were sound, the firm was interested in buying the company. But there were rumors of smuggling. I had volunteered an employee profile study as a means of worming my way into the company and had found myself besieged by the owner and cornered into a junket to South America. A golden opportunity to observe Zwicky's maneuvers as an import buyer, but at the risk of being finessed into bed.

"So I keep the situation muddled," Webster said, slowly.

"Yes. All right. I even have a certain talent for it."

"Don't think of yourself that way. This is an acting job."

"Right. The thing is, Stella, I don't understand why this has upset you so much. I mean, you do this kind of side-stepping all the time." He smiled ruefully. "Don't you?"

"This trip isn't the only problem. I've . . . I've also lost someone close to me." I lifted a hand quickly. "I don't want to talk about it. In fact, I don't want to talk anymore at all. Let's pour a drink and kiss good night. We've got a plane to catch tomorrow evening."

He was on his feet instantly to get himself a glass and pour the shots. "To the spies," he said with earnest good cheer, and we clinked glasses. "Bon voyage."

I sighed. It was going to be wonderful to have an ally. Wonderful for all of me except my conscience. I downed the Scotch, set the glass down, and kissed Webster wholesomely.

"Now get some sleep, and call me tomorrow at ten so we can work out the schedule." I laid a finger on his lips to inhibit the confession of devotion that I knew was rumbling to be born. "We'll talk about us later."

I sent him back out into the rain, eyes a little mournful, but basically happy.

Chapter XIX

After a quiet breakfast with Alice and Baudelaire I took a taxi to the airport. At the last minute I put Von Gaugen in my handbag. It would add to my disguise as an earnest tourist, and it proved a useful conversation piece in the ticket line. In the lobby Zwicky and Consuelo and I traded the usual travelers' talk, effusive and awkward. He wore a smile of paternal enthusiasm, and she was managing a degree of charm at least appropriate to airports. They had a porter in tow, with a cartful of baggage.

Our fellow passengers were mostly student adventurers with backpacks, then a sprinkling of sleek businessmen, and finally a troop of elderly Peruvian ladies, painted and hung with ornaments. There isn't much to say while waiting in line, except how boring it is to wait in line, so we kept Von Gaugen propped open and Consuelo and Zwicky talked learnedly about pots and fabrics for my benefit. It was the perfect moment for Webster to arrive.

We hugged each other soundly, with just the right amount of self-consciousness when we unglued. I introduced him to Zwicky, with a naughty lowering of my eyes, and then to Consuelo, who I was gratified to see could not chill Webster with her lizard look.

"Wow, great. You brought a book. And you are importers? I could learn a lot. Stella here has always been a great teacher." Webster grinned his irrepressible grin.

"Surely," Zwicky murmured.

Consuelo only looked at us, one after the other. "That's terrific, running into you like this. We haven't talked in"— Webster cocked his head and heaved a major sigh—"ages and ages."

"Ah, going to be in Lima long, Webster?" Zwicky moved a protective hand to my elbow and edged me another space closer in line.

"A week or two." Webster moved with us and put his hand on my other elbow. "It'll be great having company. Listen, you've got to have dinner with me tomorrow night. All of you."

"Ah . . ."

"I'd love to, Webster. So much." I turned to Zwicky and gave him a bright little smile. "Let's."

And so it went, through the brief wait until first-class passengers were seated, the tucking-in ceremony carried out by an obsequious steward, and the takeoff. Webster and I chatted, until I could sense Zwicky falling below a certain threshold of gloom, at which point I turned things enough his way to warrant rebirth of distant hope. Consuelo had retreated into a savage silence behind a week-old *Time* magazine. We were into our second drink before I thought the situation too dangerous to press further. I managed to unplug Webster and retire myself into Von Gaugen. Zwicky was staring vacantly at the inflight movie, and Webster promptly fell asleep.

When I woke, Von Gaugen had slid to the floor and bore a heelprint from Webster's brogan. He was still out, and so was everyone else. The sky was pale gray through the little plastic porthole, and inside, all was calm, no sound but the hum and click of the lights and the distant whisper of the engines. Below I could see a surface of cloud, a darker gray with a violet tinge, mottled and textured in piles and dips, tufts and open patches. When the east began to grow hot and metallic, I realized that I wasn't looking at cloud but at the jungle, a great sweep of it under the silver wing, stretching hundreds of miles to the horizon.

"Freshen up?"

A voice of molten plastic. The steward held out to me a little tray of foil packets. One was open to reveal a folded paper towel, steaming slightly, giving off an odor of phony lemon. I shook my head.

"You might try me with coffee in ten minutes."

He bowed as if I had given him a rabbit punch in the solar plexus and left. I dug into my handbag for my own towel and soap, makeup, and fingernail kit and picked my way over the sprawling bodies to the rest room. When I emerged, the steward was ready with a small Thermos of coffee. It was not bad, hot and aromatic.

"Breakfast in an hour," the steward volunteered. "Lima in two."

I sighed and glanced down at the jungle again. I felt flaming bridges dropping behind me. We were going to be a very tight little foursome. I gazed at my companions, trying to guess at their dreams. Zwicky's age showed in sleep, the skin draping into folds around his chin, eyelids sunk in shadow. There was something cruel about the mouth, but also something vulnerable, a slight pursing of the lips. Maybe only the potential for doubt. Consuelo looked pretty much the same, only with her eyes closed. I knew how she would wake up, her lids snapping open, perfectly alert but motionless. Webster snored a little, mouth slightly ajar, his hair looking much better mussed. He looked blissful, at home in an invisible nest of green bills and social connections.

The coffee was gone. Beyond the curtain I could hear a stewardess opening little doors and rattling plastic trays, and a rumble of conversation had begun in the tourist section. The sun balanced on one rim of the world now, and on the other edge a range of snow-covered peaks had sketched itself, pink in the new light. The elderly Peruvian lady in our cabin woke up then and squawked out some appeal in Spanish. Consuelo's eyes were all at once open, as I had predicted, and Zwicky stretched and turned uneasily. Webster yawned, smiled to himself, and settled back.

I returned Consuelo's fixed stare. We didn't smile.

"Sleep well?"

She glanced at Zwicky, then at the Peruvian lady across the aisle, then back to me. "Your friend," she said just loudly enough for me to hear. "Get rid of him."

"He doesn't have a parachute."

"You're funny, aren't you? Comedian."

"I can see you're amused. Sorry, I don't get rid of my friends. Like some people."

Zwicky mumbled something and sat up, rubbing a thumbnail across one eyelid. He composed a vague smile. "Good morning, all."

"Good morning, Alvin," said Consuelo, but her look didn't flinch from my face.

Zwicky threw back his cuff and examined his wrist. "My goodness. How soon?"

The steward swept the curtain aside and pushed a cart loaded with trays into our cabin.

"One hour. *Buenos días, señores y señoritas. Bienvenidos a Perú.*" He popped the bright steel cover from a dish and smiled at us through the cloud of steam that escaped.

Chapter XX

In the rush of deplaning, passing through customs, and piling ourselves and our bags into a taxi, Webster stuck to us like a burr. Then in the lobby of the Hotel Bolívar he stood at Zwicky's elbow as we signed in, so there was no choice but to get four singles. Webster's room was on the same floor, only two doors away from mine. Zwicky was having trouble controlling a grimace of irritation and alarm, and Consuelo had been driven into an icy fury, so I complained of fatigue and proposed that we all retire to our rooms to rest. Everyone seemed ready for a truce, so we agreed not to disturb each other until around six, when we would meet in the hotel bar for pisco sours before dinner.

I didn't have any intention of abiding by my own recommendation. I phoned Webster a few seconds after our doors closed and told him to stand watch on our companions while I did some scouting in the city. For one thing, I wanted to find out a little more than Von Gaugen could tell me about the goods Cordilleras was handling, what they were worth and where they came from. And there was no use fooling myself: I was a tourist, too, and anxious to get the savor of the place.

At the desk I got directions to a museum of native arts and crafts but declined to have a cab summoned. I like traveling on public transportation systems—buses, converted trucks, rickshaws, mules. Lima, the clerk told me proudly, was famous for its buses, painted different colors to symbolize the various quarters of the city they serviced. I was to take a big yellow one across the main boulevards to the port district of Callao.

It was crowded. The passengers were working people, vacant-eyed and heavy with fatigue. I was squeezed into the aisle and had barely adjusted to the pressure and some powerful odors when a small man with a large paper sack in his arms climbed rather rudely over and through the packed bodies, trying to reach a seat that had just become empty. The bus lurched as we swerved toward a stop, and other passengers crowded toward the doors. The man was having trouble controlling his sack, rattling just under my nose, and he was mumbling apologies.

It struck me swiftly that he was a decoy, and in that same instant I heard a sharp command behind me, then a firm voice in English. "Your pouch, madam."

I turned and faced a large, spectacled man, bald except for two tufts of gray hair over his ears. He was holding a sullen youth in a Windbreaker tightly by the arm. A very rapid and profane exchange was going on between them, with several bystanders joining in.

Things began to flutter to the floor. I recognized them as my gas and electric bill—somehow I'd forgotten to pay it before leaving—a boarding pass, and a couple of pencils.

"Your pouch." The man blinked behind his spectacles. "Cut."

I turned over my bag and found a long, straight slit along one edge. My compact, some loose letters, and a roll of mints were about to slide out. I clutched the opening and with my other hand rummaged inside while the controversy went on around me. My combination wallet and passport case was gone.

By this time the driver was on his way down the aisle, but before he reached us, one of the bystanders uttered an exclamation and produced the leather case from among the columns of surrounding legs.

"*De usted, señorita?*" the driver asked, and I nodded. He consulted the photograph inside the passport, nodded pompously, then handed the wallet to me. The twenty in soles was gone, but the traveler's checks were still in the inner compartment. The sullen youth had begun righ-

teous declamations, but the driver steered him—not un-
gently, I thought—to the door.

"Good fortune," the man beside me said. "These rats
are very quick." When he smiled and blinked, the oversize
glasses and tufts of gray hair made him look like an owl.
"You are first time in Peru?"

"A lamb, we say. And nearly shorn. I owe you a great
debt, Señor . . ."

"Torres. Alberto Torres. I am pleased to make your
acquaintance, madam." We shook hands as the bus got
under way again. "I regret your inconvenience. My countrymen, you know, many are very poor. . . ." He lifted
his shoulders in a gesture that expressed both humor and
exasperation.

"Quite all right. In my country they put the knife directly between your ribs. Cruder but often effective."

He smiled, then touched my handbag. "This you must
repair. And not carry in it your funds and passports. You
see how they work. The man with the paper bag—"

"I figured it out, a little late. He distracts me while the
kid cuts the purse and takes the wallet. Two of them."

"Three." He laughed, almost proudly. "The man
who picked up your—wallet, you say?—also dropped it
there."

"So. The kid passed it to him in case someone fouled
things up."

"*Foul?*" Alberto looked puzzled. "It is a bird?"

"No. 'Foul' means to louse—I mean to ruin, spoil, make
a mess."

"I see." He blinked judiciously. "I thought it was a ref-
erence to myself. Many think I am an owl. You find the
resembling?"

"Oh, yes." I grinned. "But you see very well in the daytime, too."

Alberto closed his hand into a fist and held it out. He
wore a large silver ring with a dark stone carved in the
shape of an owl's face. "My good luck," he said. "My sign.
As Minerva, you know?"

"Wise messenger," I ventured, with dim memories of a college class in Greek literature.

"So it is!" He struck the fist lightly against his lapel. "You are not a tourist?"

"Not exactly."

"Yes." Alberto looked down politely with a slight smile. "We are coming to my stop. I live in Miraflores—the place of what you call the bohemian life—and I would be pleased to invite you to my home for a coffee."

I hesitated, and he added, "My mother is there, too. No worry. Madam . . . ?"

"Pike. Stella Pike. I hate to trouble you, but if I might ask you a few questions with the coffee?"

He gave a little bow. "It is to be my pleasure. I serve you."

Alberto's apartment was small and clean, on a quiet street with a walled courtyard in front, where a pair of dwarf peach trees were flowering. Every inch of wall was covered with bookcases. Many of the volumes were leather-bound, the pages yellow with age, and in spaces between rows of books there were pots painted with distinctive red and black figures, patterns I recognized from Von Gaugen. Also a number of owls, done in iron and wood as well as ceramics.

His mother was a gnarled brown woman with heavy perfume, very red lipstick, and a sweet smile. By the time she served us the pungent black coffee I had learned that Alberto was a psychiatrist working in a government clinic, the author of several professional papers, and an amateur student of archaeology. He had done advanced work in Germany and had traveled extensively in Europe. So for a while we talked about the Rijksmuseum and the Tiergarten, Danish cafés and English weather. Then we began a discussion of Peruvian crime.

Contraband, he said, was the economic lifeblood of his country. People smuggled everything: chain saws, medical instruments, automobiles, gold, drugs, and books. If I strolled this evening around the Plaza San Martín, or on the Avenida Abancay, or even in Miraflores, I would see the *ambulantes,* the sidewalk merchants, selling everything conceivable to passersby. The government placed very high import duties on all manufactured articles not produced in the country, Alberto remarked, in order to keep the prices high on the goods the generals were smuggling in themselves. Only last week customs officials had opened some crates consigned to the minister of health—the boxes were marked as medical supplies—and inside were color television sets. Sixty-seven of them.

"A way of life." Alberto sighed and poured himself another cup of coffee. "I myself have managed to peddle a few books to the Japanese, who wish to build up their libraries and have much money these days."

I looked interested.

"You wonder that a man would market knowledge? Sell his birthpiece—what is it? Birthright, yes—when we need these things here?"

"It doesn't seem your style."

"No. It isn't. But if I did not do it, the booksellers would do it instead. One must live. Besides"—he spoke with a sudden bitterness down at his cup—"if you could see the Medical School of San Marcos, where I did my studies, once the finest university in all South America—a rathole now. Even the grounds are dust, the palms dying, windows broken. . . ."

We were quiet for a while. I went on.

"How do you do it?"

"Smuggle the books? It is easy. The customs people care little for books anyway. Or art. The important thing is the carrier. He or she must look normal, act normal. I am a psychologist, I know, so I make the right selection."

"How about drugs? That's the big money, isn't it?"

"The big money? Ah, yes. What a marvelous expression!" He blinked with owlish delight. "Very big money. But very dangerous. People will try anything. Fools. Last year one of your citizens—a young man from a college—swallowed a toy, a kind of rubber sack—what do you call it?"

"Balloon?"

"Yes, balloon—and it burst inside him, and the cocaine killed him. Or last month in Colombia two people were caught when they tried to take a large amount—big, big money—over the border inside a dead child. Sewed up inside a dead girl in a coffin. Their daughter, they said." He grimaced. "Rats."

I had a sudden vision of Zwicky asleep on the plane, his mouth slightly agape. I wondered whether there was among his dark dreams one of myself in a box, my innards stuffed with white powder.

"What is it?" He was looking at me hard.

"Nothing. That's just so . . ."

"Yes. But you are interested in this subject?"

"In passing. You are a good psychologist. Yes, I'm interested." I glanced around the room. "Will you take me on a tour of your little museum?"

Alberto got to his feet and bowed. "I am honored."

"So far everything I've learned comes from a book. Von Gaugen's *Ancient Kingdom.*"

Alberto made a gesture of dismissal. "Germans. Everything collected, and everything dull. I assure you Von Gaugen did not understand the spirit of Moche art. Now here . . ." He stepped to a shelf and picked up a small pot. "You see the two bottles put together, one handle. The faces. There is no better."

I examined the pot with two spouts, a handle bridging them. The bas-relief faces decorating it were sharply individual: one caught in mid-laugh, the eyes squeezed shut; the other sly, bemused. The glaze was good, and the colors soft but true. "It's beautiful. How old?"

"About five centuries after Jesus."

"Why the two spouts?"

"One whistles when the other pours."

"Very nice. Would it still work? That is, could one carry things in it?"

"Things?" Alberto regarded me for a moment, smiling. "Not drinks, but things?"

"Could you?"

His head turned from me to the pot, and with a large, slow blink he assumed his own mask. "You mean with something hidden inside?"

I laughed. "I suppose I mean that."

He shook his head. "One would not do this. It would break easily, and it is already priceless."

We moved on, past the pots to a collection of small gold figurines, then to a cabinet full of tapestries. They were of all sizes and conditions, from scraps faded and eaten by time to bedspread-sized swatches of cloth with vivid and intricate patterns.

"Cotton," Alberto said, "endures. Better than llama and alpaca. And it takes the dye well. Look at this." He indicated a square of material, an indigo background into which were woven gray, maroon, and sulfur emblems—stylized birds, llamas, and leopards.

"Beautiful. Where from?"

"From the coast. Nazca graves."

"What are they worth?"

"Not the big money. In ancient Peru everybody was weaving—Nazca, Moche, Chimu—everybody. The best are from Parapas, where the mummies come from."

I ran my finger along the edge of the glass case, admiring the fabric's rich design. "How much, in dollars?"

Alberto shrugged. "A few hundreds."

"What about the stuff from Tingo María?"

"What stuff?"

"Don't they produce copies of these old patterns there? At a convent?"

"Perhaps. But Tingo María—" He frowned. "A sewer place. Woodcutters, poor Indians, *regatones.* Cocaine. Criminals. Next to Pucallpa the worst. Now here is a fine example—"

"Really?" I put my hand on his arm. "I know an American who comes ten thousand miles to buy cloth from Tingo María."

Alberto blinked again, then laughed. "He is a fool, or a *traficante.* See over here, señorita, the quipus."

He was pointing to a small case full of knotted cords of different colors.

"Decorations? Interesting. But this American is not a fool. If he is a smuggler—"

"Not decorations. This is Inca writing."

"Wait a minute. According to the unimaginative German, the Incas couldn't write."

"This was their writing. The quipus. The colors mean something, and the kinds of knots, and the spaces between. All their economics and messages—the weights, measures, times of delivery, and so forth—were by quipus. Anyway, you Americans say—no?—not to believe everything you read in the funny papers?" He laughed and folded his hand over mine. "You are a sensational student, Señorita Stella. Now we should take soup with my mother and discuss this American *traficante*. This is on your mind, no?"

I grinned and moved toward the table with him, arm in arm. "Señor Owl is a good professor and a very smart bird. And I'll bet his mother makes excellent soup."

Chapter XXI

It was excellent. *Sopa de mariscos,* full of bits of clam and crab and scallops in a thick white cream sauce. As she served us, Mamacita mentioned politely that she could not help overhearing us speak of Tingo María. A foul den of thieves that the Virgin must preserve us from. There was nothing of value there except the Convent of Santa María Magdalena, where they made fine imitations of the old fabrics. Their work was for export to my country, *verdad?* and the profits were supposed to be for the relief of orphans. Here she shrugged and gave me a shrewd look.

Alberto struck his forehead with the heel of one hand. "*Carajo!* Yes, of course. Santa María Magdalena. You were right, Señorita Stella."

"But they are not always good, the sisters." Mamacita scowled.

I looked inquiringly at Alberto. "The nuns have a reputation for independence," he said. "Once they got themselves in great trouble for helping guerrillas. In the time of Ché.

"In those days," he said mournfully, and tapped a silver spoon against the thin china cup so that it rang a note of regret, "the forces of change had many friends in the church. The fathers and the sisters were ready to fight, side by side, with the people. Now"—he sighed—"the people do not know where to turn."

"And if they did know?"

"Ah, then." Alberto looked pleased and struck the cup again, harder. "Then we might hope for some fast change."

"Revolution?"

"*Cómo no?* It happened before."

"You do have experience with that down here. We've only had one little one up north. A long time ago."

"Perhaps you will have some more. By example."

"Perhaps." I smiled. "But revolutions are expensive, *verdad?* No wonder the guerrillas need help from the church."

"The church is not so rich. Not the big money. There are many poor to take care of."

"So where could the money come from?"

Alberto hunched forward and blinked rapidly. "The cocaine, it is said."

"For a revolution?" I deliberately gave my eyebrows the altitude of disbelief.

"Why not? It must come from somewhere."

"I thought drugs were a filthy capitalist habit, or a plot to fry the people's brains, or—"

"Fry brains?" It was Alberto's turn to look incredulous.

"An expression. So you're telling me a revolutionary party would risk dealing drugs to pay for guns?" When Alberto nodded, a piece of the pattern I had been working on fell into place.

"But to sell drugs to gringos is a difference," he went on. "This helps destroy the Yankees, and our revolutionary young men say you are our enemy because you give the generals money."

"Instead of giving the radicals money."

"Yes. You have it. But of course, the generals also sell cocaine. They get the money both ways. It is not, as you say, the free enterprise."

"But big money."

"Yes. Very big money."

"Interesting."

"May I ask a small question? Why do you find these things interesting? The usual tourist does not interest herself in these things."

"It's very complicated. In my country there are people

like your generals, and your radicals, and also people who simply want big money and will do anything to get it."

Alberto nodded sharply. "*Ratas.* They are here, too."

"Then there are other people—ordinary people—who get involved with the rats, and so the rats use them, frighten them, even kill them."

Alberto shrugged. "Perhaps the world is now everywhere the same. So?"

"Have you ever seen people killed?"

We stared at each other over soup now cold.

"I see." Alberto spoke softly. "You have decided to—how does it go?—take things in your hands. That is very brave. I salute you." He turned and said something to his mother. She rose swiftly, went to a sideboard, and came back with a decanter and two small crystal glasses. When she had poured us each an inch of the liquor, a warm gold with the odor of fruit, Alberto rang his glass against mine.

"*Buena suerte,*" he said. "Success in your investigation. You will catch this *traficante.* Should you need a friend, I am here, and I ask no more questions."

We drank, and I rose to take my leave. Mamacita gave me a long embrace, blessed me, and handed me my purse. While we were talking, she had stitched up the cut. In the courtyard, heavy with the scent of roses and bougainvillaea, I convinced Alberto to let me find my own taxi. I did so by holding his round, mournful face in my hands and promising to see him again, sometime, somewhere. We kissed, honorably but with feeling, and I stepped out the door.

"Good-bye, beautiful student," he called.

"Good-bye, owl." I waved and walked away fast.

It was five forty-five when I returned to my room. I showered and changed into the light blue cotton dress and white weskit, then went to the bar. I took a table and ordered the World's Finest Pisco Sour, as the menu forthrightly put it. The Bolívar was an elegant old hotel that had seen better days. The carpets were frayed, and the brass chandeliers had not seen polish in a good while, but the waiter who delivered the drink was cool and crisp in his white jacket, and the pisco was of generous proportions, made with fresh limes and a real egg. In a far corner of the room a group of French tourists quacked away intently, discussing from what I could gather socialism and Inca culture.

Zwicky glided through the entrance and gave me a wave and a bright smile. White duck pants, huaraches, a turquoise silk shirt, and a beige twill jacket. He carried a small leather notebook in his hand.

"Very sporty."

"You look fresh, too. Glowing, I might say."

"Anticipation is good for the complexion."

"But you have already sampled a little of the city?" He watched me behind his smile.

"Once out the door, it was hard to go back. I wandered a little around the plaza. Took a quick bus ride."

"Enterprising." The waiter arrived with Zwicky's pisco. "What did you see?"

"Much bigger and dirtier than San Francisco. It's trying very hard to be modern. The clothes on some of the women downtown would make a Pacific Heights debutante jealous. I didn't see any sign of the kind of thing Cordilleras deals in."

"There are a few markets. Out by the airport. But we prefer to buy in the highlands, close to the source. We will be going there in a day or two. You will like it, I feel certain."

"I like high country."

We smiled a little at each other, enough to extend the metaphor for a moment.

"Altitudes frighten some people."

"They shouldn't climb."

"Or if they do, they shouldn't fall."

Another smile.

I nodded at the notebook. "What's the plan?"

Zwicky sipped his drink, eyes closed. "Excellent. The gum arabic makes the difference, I think. Many bars use only sugar. We should drink a number of these, Stella, because where we are going there are few such luxuries." He set down the glass and flipped open the leather cover of the notebook. "Tomorrow I have an appointment or two here in Lima. Business quite boring and routine. I'll drop in on our representative here and visit the embassy. You need not suffer through that. Perhaps you and your . . . friend . . . can try the museums or—"

"You forget I'm officially working, too. I'll earn my money. Count me in. I like talking about money."

Zwicky seemed about to say something, then changed his mind. "Very well. Perhaps you will make your usual clever suggestions and astonish me even more. The day after we shall take a flight to Huaraz, spend an afternoon at the ruins, and go on to Tingo María." After a moment's hesitation he reached across the table and took my hand. "Do you understand what this trip is about?"

His eyes were nearly closed. Again I saw how the line of his jaw was not kind, how the strain around his mouth kept twisting his smile a wrong way. Something heavy and ugly sat on his heart, and he needed help to get rid of it.

"Not yet. Tell me."

"It's about the future. My future. And yours. If we make the right choice—"

Fortunately I didn't have to think up a comeback for these breathy suggestions. Webster and Consuelo appeared through the archway at the entrance and advanced toward us. They looked like opposing delegates to a cease-fire conference and probably hadn't exchanged a word during a long elevator ride and hike across the lobby. They joined us, ordered their drinks, and then the sparring began.

As obtuse as Webster might pretend to be, there was no avoiding the ice in Zwicky's manner. Whenever Webster broached the subject of our itinerary, he got pointedly evasive answers. I tried to fill the long silences with empty chatter, but Consuelo's cool, speculative looks warned me that our act was wearing thin.

Finally, in desperation, Webster asked, "What are you really here for, you guys? Don't you want to go *somewhere*, in particular?"

"One of my reasons for travel," Zwicky said in his quiet, murderous, chairman-of-the-board voice, "is to escape my countrymen."

Webster gave me a desperate tap with the toe of his brogan underneath the table. I excused myself, and in the ladies' room I wrote on the inside of a match cover: "Split now. Huaraz tomorrow night. Then Tingo María." When I got back to the table, Webster had flushed a light rose and there was dead silence.

"Well," I said with inane brightness, "have we run out of things to say, and is it time to eat?" I sat down too hurriedly and lost a sandal. "Drat." I reached under the table, poked at the sandal, and slid the matchbook down the side of Webster's shoe. "Can't seem to stay fully clad. Anyway, have we worked out plans for dinner?"

Consuelo examined me. "Have we?"

"We could eat here," Zwicky said, "or we might go out."

Webster was shifting uncomfortably in his chair. I didn't even see him take out the matchbook and flip it open.

"I'm a little tired," he said. "Maybe I can join you later. Talk about old times." He grinned wanly.

"Of course." Zwicky got to his feet. "I hope you enjoy your stay. You didn't mention your own plans. Cuzco and Machu Picchu, of course?" He allowed himself an expansive gesture. "So much cooler."

Webster nodded, shaking hands with Consuelo. "I've seen 'em before. Actually I don't mind staying here for a bit."

Zwicky and Consuelo and I smiled at each other, for rather different reasons. Webster was masterful, I thought with surprise.

"Yeah, I'll hang around here tomorrow with you guys. Then take off for the mountains. Been thinking, actually, about Huaraz."

I didn't dare look at Zwicky, though I would have enjoyed seeing his smile congeal.

"Oh," I said. There was a considerable pause. "That's great, Web. We'll probably see you there." I tried to make it a noncommittal remark and added a little sigh for good measure.

"Hey, you guys are going, too? Fantastic. I'll skip tonight then. Catch you for dinner in old Huaraz. Hey, great!" He bathed us in a loud laugh of adolescent enthusiasm and strode away, waving.

I looked up at Zwicky wryly. "Yeah, great."

He swore softly, and for a moment I thought the fury in his eyes was meant for me. Then he got control of himself again and managed a bitter, short laugh.

"He is a remarkable person, isn't he, in his way?" he said, and we went to our chilly dinner.

Chapter XXII

The next morning we toured the city in a private car with driver. We swung in a long arc along the hills for a look at the slums, a crazy patchwork of mud-daubed sticks and galvanized roofing crowned by spindles of television antennas. The *ambulantes* Alberto had mentioned occupied the sidewalks and curbs. Women in broad black skirts and cheap cotton shawls stood guard over their wares: crockery, plastic buckets, ball-point pens, bars of soap, and kitchen knives. Men in rags squatted over heaps of auto parts, files, wrenches, combs, and cigarette lighters. We kept the windows rolled up and the air conditioner going, but the roar of engines, the honks and cries and dust beat like a surf against our thin bubble of glass and metal. Zwicky watched impassively, as if he were at the zoo, while Consuelo stared at the strip of pale sky visible over the rooftops. Webster practiced his lugubrious Spanish on the driver.

"A developing country," Zwicky said finally. "And this is one of the more prosperous."

"Interesting," I said. I wondered if he toured this section of the city often and what that would mean.

"I've seen enough," Webster announced. "It breaks my heart."

Consuelo stared a hole in the back of his head, and Zwicky spoke to the driver.

We returned on the Avenida Abancay to the city center and then took Arequipa. Zwicky pointed out the old vice-regent's palace, the Italian cultural center, and the quaint houses of Jesús María. The architecture here was spare and elegant, the yellowed stone and gravel walks reminding me of Versailles, but the grounds were a pale, baked green where the flowers seemed to burst like flame from the dry foliage. The limousine parked before a stone wall with ornate iron gates, behind which I could see a low building almost buried in violent purple blossoms. A small bronze plaque identified the place as the Inter-American Business Institute.

The beautiful woman behind the desk inside had the cold, remote features of a stone goddess. She greeted us in good, if stiff, English and ushered us directly into an inner office. There a man in a sport coat and flowered shirt advanced on us with a wide grin.

"Al! Terrific to see you. And Connie! Whaddya say?" He clapped Zwicky on the shoulder and gave Consuelo a movie embrace. Then he nodded at Webster and seized my hand. "I don't know this one, but I'd sure like to." His eyebrows went up suggestively.

"This is Stella Pike. Of Garabedian, Daugherty, and Bissel of San Francisco. She's doing some public relations for us. And, uh—"

"Webster."

"—her friend, Webster."

"Terrific. Listen, I'll get Ada to get us some snacks. Get down to serious drinking later." He poked his head out the door and made the order in rapid and idiomatic Spanish. A bilingual Babbitt. Then he waved us through open French doors to a small shaded patio, where we took chairs around a glass table.

"So how's it going, Al, in the city of Saint Francis?" He grabbed his knees with large hands and tilted forward to grin hungrily at us.

"We're managing," Zwicky said. "The mayor doesn't seem as interested in the Tourist Bureau as we might like, but we have four conventions coming in for June. The fog and the cable cars and bridges still work."

"Oh, boy. How I miss it sometimes. Just that cool salt air." He nodded enthusiastically at Webster. "Know what I mean?"

Webster started to agree, but Zwicky interrupted. "Terry, we're doing all our business today so we can spend the rest of the week on the road. Hate to rush you, but can we . . . ?"

"You bet. Hey, here's the starting fluid."

Ada set down the tray and poured the cold coffee concentrate from a small glass decanter, then added hot water from a plastic Thermos pitcher.

"Well, I've got some bad news first. The duty on the art stuff is going up as of the first of next month. A fat twenty-two percent. González promised me three months ago it wasn't gonna happen. *Caramba!* You can't trust 'em."

Zwicky frowned, but it looked like a token expression. Consuelo had taken out a small pad and was doing some figuring.

"A discount for large lots?"

"Minimal. What we might do is ship everything you can lay your hands on right away, before the shift."

She nodded, and the pencil flicked across the page. "We'll have to raise prices at least fifteen percent on everything, or thirty on duty items, to cover a *subida* like that."

"Obviously." Zwicky sounded testy. "Now what about the rest?"

"Well, you probably want to know how your line is moving here. Not bad. For some reason you're selling more candy in the summer. Maybe to tourists, who recognize the brand. The figures for the quarter and the schedules for the contest winners Cas has for you." He bounced up and went through the office again. We could hear a mutter of conversation with Ada.

While he was gone, we watched a hummingbird appear and disappear in the air around the purple blossoms. So far none of this was distinguishable from the boring world of business as I knew it. That Terry might be speaking in metaphors, and "candy" might in fact be cocaine or heroin, seemed to me incredible. He did not have the air of one who had experience with metaphors.

Terry returned with a folder stuffed with papers and laid it on the glass table before us. Zwicky began flipping through the material. I noticed pictures and what looked like personnel forms. The people in the pictures were sitting around the wreckage of a banquet or smiling arm in arm in an airport lobby.

"Al, some of these winners are really from hicksville. How does your man come up with them?" Terry selected one of the photographs and showed it around the table. A middle-aged couple, he paunchy and scant-haired, she plump and frilly, grinned cheek to cheek into the camera. They were holding a large gold-plated llama mounted on a ceremonial plaque of some kind.

Zwicky shrugged. "I don't have anything to do with the selection. Ferguson's people arrange the contest and the trips. With Cas."

"Well, he sure has middle America by the short hairs. Some of them have never been out of the sticks. But the papers here have picked up on that angle a couple of times, so we've got a few freebies out of the deal. Sales here, like I said, are moving better all the time." He slipped out a foldout chart that showed the usual climbing black line.

I couldn't restrain a yawn.

Zwicky smiled indulgently. "Consuelo, why don't you show Stella some of the things in the back? She needs excitement."

"I'm fine. This is all fascinating," I lied. "What is this contest about?"

"TopTorts," Terry said brightly, as if this explained everything. "I mean, everybody knows the Zwicky name in the sugar business and now in modern confections, too. Especially entertainment foods."

"Entertainment foods?" I tried not to wince.

"Sure. You know, desserts, luxury snacks, party favors. TopTorts is the name of our line of special European-style pastries, mostly frozen. To move the products in some areas—especially the Midwest—we launched an ad campaign featuring a contest. First prize is a two-week all-expense trip to Peru."

"Wow." Webster was also stifling a yawn. "What do they have to do to win?"

"Send us a cake recipe and a family picture with rights for use in our advertising. All there is to it." Terry flourished one hand in Zwicky's direction. "One of Al's great ideas."

"Actually it was the ad people," Zwicky said quickly, and shifted in his chair. "But I'm sure Stella is hoping for something more engaging than cake recipes. Really, my dear, you ought to have a look at some of the goods we'll be taking back with us."

Consuelo had buttoned up her little pad and pencil and was already on her feet, waiting with an indecipherable smile. The discussion of entertainment foods was definitely not entertaining. I decided to let Webster keep track of the cakes so I could have another look at the shawls and pots.

We left the men to admire their graphs and passed down a corridor to a storage area at the back. It was stacked from floor to ceiling with fabrics and pots and wood carvings, some of them tagged and folded, others in a heap. On one shelf was a row of the gold-plated llamas, their nameplates blank. Consuelo appeared to be all business. She put me to work reading the dates and prices on a stack of mantas while she wrote them down. Then we did the same for a few pots.

Consuelo didn't look up. As far as I could tell, she was simply a competent clerk. If this whole operation was a cover, it was a very good one. So far I had noticed only one faint shadow of irregularity.

"Buying more this trip?"

"Possibly."

"If the duty is going up soon, wouldn't it make sense to buy all you can and ship them now?"

"If things are available."

"Most of the good stuff I believe you said came from around Cuzco—Pisaq and Andamarca?"

Finally she looked up at me. A steady, cold look. "You catch on fast. Tell me one thing. If you plan on selling yourself to the owner, why do you bother with the details of the business? Or do you count on running the company, too?"

"Well, well," I said, and put down the pot I had in my hands. "That's very refreshing. Honesty deserves an answer. I pay attention to the business so I can figure out what kind of business it is. Anyway, I've been told by reputable sources that this business runs itself. I'm beginning to believe it. Now suppose you answer a little question for me, Consuelo. Import taxes are going up soon; you admit the smart thing is to buy heavily now. The goods are south of us. Our plan is to head north—Tingo María. What's in Tingo María, Consuelo? What grows there in the high jungle?"

I had gotten up and moved to the table where her notebook lay open. Her face had contracted. "Did Rosa make trips to Tingo María? Buying trips? Now me, I'm selling myself, you said. Buying and selling, that's what it's all about, isn't it, Consuelo?" I leaned over the table, jabbing at the book with my finger. "What did you sell yourself for? A few lousy pieces of cloth? Or did you buy into something a little more profitable?"

Our noses were not more than six inches apart now, but Consuelo didn't give ground. Suddenly she drew back and struck at me with the pencil. I caught her wrist, and the point stopped, trembling, just above my cheekbone.

"You don't want to start that," I said. "I don't think the boss would like it."

The force went out of her as quickly as it had come, and the pencil rattled to the floor. An invisible sheath dropped over her eyes, turning them to dull stones.

"I don't have to do it," she whispered, as if to herself. "I don't have to do it. They'll take care of you. All of you."

"All of us?" I was genuinely surprised. "All of who?"

"You dirty cops. *Putas.* Killers."

She talked like someone in a trance, as if I weren't there anymore.

"A cop? You think I'm a cop?"

Maybe the surprise in my voice broke through to her. "You put people in prison, you think they won't bother you. You can keep them down. But the people won't be kept down. *La Raza,* it will be free someday." All at once her eyes took on life again, and there were tears in them that spilled out onto her face.

I stepped back. She wasn't faking. The hate burned in her clear and hot. "The people," I said. "You mean Latinos, Hispanics, Chicanos—"

"Spics, greasers—go ahead, *gringuita,* say them! Yes! Those are my people!" She was on her feet, moving toward me. Her words were not loud but came fast and hard as bullets. *"Peruanas como Rosa también!* The people you have cheated and enslaved and oppressed, the—"

"Wait a minute. Who, Consuelo, *who* are you talking about?"

She stared at me a moment and then went on. "My husband, Luis, I am talking about. And my brother. Beaten to death in Los Angeles in the barrio. Luis in prison. Where you cops put him, because he tries to fight for his people the best way he can."

"Just hold on, and tell me something, Consuelo. If you think the *blancos* are oppressing you, how come you work for this company? Peddle these ponchos? How come?"

She was panting with the effort to control herself, to recover her reptilian malice. "Because Alvin is different."

"Why? He helps you smuggle stuff to your husband so he can get high in jail?"

I thought she was going to try to hit me again, but she stopped with her claws drawn back. She gasped a couple of times and then spit at me. "Bitch," she said, so softly now I could barely hear her. "You think you know things, but you don't. Alvin is trying to save my people, give them a chance. You are trying to kill them."

I got a handkerchief from the pocket of the weskit and daubed away the spittle on my collar. "Consuelo," I said slowly and carefully, "Rosa believed all that shit, too."

There was a pause, no sound in the room except her shallow, rapid breathing. Then the door sprang open.

"Hey, c'mon out, you two! Cas and the TopTorts winners are here. Gonna have a drink. Whaddaya say?" Terry flung an arm around both of us and moved us through the door, his eyebrows wagging and fingers administering friendly pinches. I got one swift glance at Consuelo before the shield dropped over her face again, and what I saw there was a flicker of something new. Something that might have been fear and doubt.

Chapter XXIII

The winners surrounded Zwicky in the patio, the man gesturing at him with a long, crooked forefinger while his wife blocked access to the door with her considerable bulk. To one side stood a small, fattish man with not much hair or chin and fast, impenetrable eyes. Terry swept us into the center of this group, trumpeting introductions.

"Connie and Stella . . . Johnny Caswell, and our TopTorts winners. This is Chester Cooper and his wife, Millie, from Ainsworth, Kansas. They're here for two whole weeks, all expenses paid. How about that?" Terry stepped back, as from an exhibit at a state fair.

"Never believed it," Chester announced, and his pale blue eyes grew a little moist. "You coulda knocked me over with a feather." He shook his head and craned toward us to inspect us more closely. The blue suit he wore was a double-breasted style at least thirty years old. A tie as wide as his face displayed a flock of green ducks progressing through a purplish sky. "I was pullin' the gears on my loader," he continued, and leveled the gnarled finger at me, "and let me tell you in Ainsworth in August that is mighty hot work. *Mighty* hot." He paused, and his long, creased face took on a bemused look, as if the heat had reached all the way from Kansas across months to interrupt his thought.

"They don't dispute it, Chester," his wife observed crisply. "Nobody in their right mind would want to be in Ainsworth in August."

"And here she come," Chester resumed his narrative,

"just aflyin' over the field, apron blowin' all hell, west and crooked, yellin', 'We won! Chester, we won!' " He looked at his feet, then at the ceiling. "Lord."

"I did get excited," Millie said, and allowed herself a kind of giggling sigh. "Peru! Why, land o' Goshen!"

"A surprise, right? A terrific surprise." Terry nodded at all of us around the room, his grin fixed.

"You bet," the little fat man said.

"Oh, my Lord." Millie waved one hand that dismissed all possible unbelievers. "Those Incas."

"Engineers," said Chester fiercely. "You better believe those folks were engineers."

"You don't say?" Webster managed an expression of interest.

I caught Zwicky's eye, and he gave me a wan smile and tilted his chin toward the door.

"We are surely forever and ever grateful to Mr. Zwicky and the Top Torts people—and Mr. Caswell here—for this lovely trip," said Millie, and I heard coming through that voice all the inexhaustible benevolence of my own great aunts and grandmothers, the earth-warm, broad-as-the-plains friendliness of rural America a generation ago. "How are you folks enjoyin' it all?" she went on, turning her smile to me.

"Wonderful," I said. "But this is only my second day."

"You're gonna love it," Millie said with a confident shake of her three chins. "You wait until you see Match-you Pitch-you and all the stones there. You won't hardly believe your own eyes."

"I do look forward to it." I edged a little toward the door, now open to reveal our driver in the hallway.

"When are you folks headed back?" Millie called after us. "We've only got one week left. Sure hate to go back to Ainsworth, don't we, Chester? But we sure do appreciate it, Mr. Zwicky."

"Yessir-e-e-e-bob!" shouted Chester, and stabbed us out the door with his finger. "Surely do!"

* * *

Three of us made it into the hall outside: myself, Zwicky, and Caswell. We followed the driver to the car. Webster had to stick with Consuelo, who evidently would return to finish her inventory. When we were moving through afternoon traffic, I decided to try shifting to the offensive. Caswell's appraising glances had been all over me from the moment Consuelo and I entered the room, an indication that Zwicky hadn't had time to tell him how I did or didn't fit in with the enterprise. So far I hadn't had many opportunities to strike a first blow.

"You can go ahead and talk," I said to Caswell. "I'm familiar with the operation."

He exchanged a look with Zwicky, who cleared his throat and touched my arm. "Stella is a remarkable person. She doesn't know the details of the business yet, but has a surprising grasp of general matters."

I rewarded him with an inflammatory little smile and then turned back to Caswell. "Alvin doesn't even grasp what a grasp I have," I said, and then added as if it were an afterthought, "I don't want to be slow. I saw what happened to Rosa."

He may have been small and fat, but Caswell was not easily jarred. "Indeed? That must have been disturbing." He didn't sound particularly interested in the topic. "Do you plan to take on partners, Alvin, without telling us? That's not really fair to your employees." He spoke in a quiet voice, with a slight rasp in it. Zwicky had gone a little pale, and I felt his hand on my arm, squeezing hard.

"We haven't discussed partnership much," I went on in a tone that all of us knew was ironic. "I haven't been introduced yet to all the mysteries of the firm. Only recently, for example, I learned that we're actively supporting some unfortunate people in prison. Not many American corporations can show sympathy for both the Chester Millers and the Manuel Espositos of the world."

Zwicky's fingers convulsed around my arm, and Caswell stared at me hard, with no particular expression. His face looked like a small, dead moon.

"What kind of contribution do Baker and Ferguson make to these admirable causes?" I asked archly. "Free TopTorts for good behavior?"

Caswell ignored me and looked fixedly at Zwicky. "I don't think it's a good idea," he said. "Not without discussing the matter with us."

"I know what I'm doing," Zwicky said tightly.

"Really, Cas—may I call you Cas?—I'm interested in your part of the business. Just what do you do? Since you've given up politics." I met his gaze, and without the slightest change of expression, using only some radiation from his eyes, the little fat man let me know how very much he didn't like me.

"We do ads here with local firms to sell American goods. I handle Alvin's account, which includes the TopTorts contest and some of the paper work involved in shipping for Cordilleras. Very routine, I assure you."

"Perhaps there are other compensations."

"Like what?"

"An exciting country, don't you think? Government scandals, art treasures, smuggling, unexplored jungles, and all that?"

His eyes slid away. He didn't like games very much. "Drop me at the Plaza Brasil," he said evenly. "I don't think you need me right now. We'll go over the few items we have to discuss some other time. Before you leave. Pleased to have met you, Stella." He gave me his soft little hand for a second.

"The pleasure is all mine," I said. "I'm sure we'll meet again."

The car drew up at the curb, and he got out. Before he slammed the door, Zwicky leaned toward him and spoke.

"Don't worry, Cas. Everything is still in the discussion stage."

"I hope so." He gave me a brief, enigmatic smile and closed the door carefully. The car pulled away, and neither of us looked back.

We rode in silence for a while. When I heard Zwicky take a deeper breath, preparing to say something, I spoke quickly.

"I tried to move too fast. I'm sorry." I looked down and twisted my hands for a few moments, then put my fingers lightly on his knee. "Please forgive me."

He hesitated, then shook his head. "Too fast for me to quite understand you. What is this business about prisoners? And Esposito?"

I decided to gamble. I slid my fingers along his sleeve to his shoulder, from there to his jaw, where I let my hand rest as gently as a spider. "Alvin, please don't. I know about it. What I don't know is why you do it. I was fishing, that's all. And I shouldn't have been."

He turned his head slightly and began to nibble my fingertips. I closed my eyes, hoping that this would be taken as a sign of mild ecstasy instead of the disgust it was.

"You must be careful with Cas," he murmured.

"Even you?"

"He is not my employee."

"Ferguson's? I thought you and Ferguson were friends." His tongue was in my palm, and I barely controlled a shudder.

He laughed to himself. "It is a complicated friendship."

"Aren't they all?" I took my hand away and turned to look out the window at the buildings flashing by.

"Do you think this one is?"

"I do. It's complicated when we keep dealing in these dark hints. I'd like to know what Ferguson has on you. And what that has to do with ex-cons like Esposito."

"It's the other way around."

"He owes you?" I turned to look him in the eye again. "And that's a problem?"

"In a sense." Zwicky sighed. "Debts may be canceled many ways."

"Another dark hint. Tell you what." I swung around to bump my knees against his. "Remember the kid's game of trying to guess somebody's secret and the person with the secret just says 'warmer' or 'colder'? Let's give it a try. Now you and Ferguson are old friends, go to the same clubs, know a lot of people in common?"

"Lukewarm." Zwicky's smile widened.

"Naturally then, when he went into advertising, he came to you looking for an account—Coastway Sugar, Coastway Freight, TransPac-Orient, TopTorts, Cordilleras—that's a lot of business. An annual advertising budget of, say, half a million?"

"Still warm."

"You gave him the account. After a few years, things going well for both of you, you found yourselves together on the top story of Northern California society. Meeting political figures, entertainers, big spenders. It's an exciting life. Also an expensive life."

"Warmer."

"Also, you have to do favors. Ferguson wants a place on the Trade Commission. You help. First obligation."

"Warmer."

"Second obligation. A program for the rehabilitation of released convicts and their families. Ferguson asks you to help out. You hire Rosa."

"Hot." Zwicky's smile waned a little.

"She works hard, does a good job. Lots of activity at Cordilleras. Extra shipments, lots of travel. Then a payoff. Ferguson does your advertising for next to nothing, organizes the TopTorts contest, maybe makes contributions in your name to political campaigns. You begin to wonder if the payoff isn't too big for the service you provide. You ask for an explanation. Ferguson replies with still more goodies. And you take them."

Zwicky wasn't smiling at all now. It was merely an ugly twist of the mouth.

"Then Rosa has an accident. And you find out her husband works for the Start Over program, which has come under investigation. You find out also that a car stolen from Cordilleras may have been involved in the accident."

"Very hot." Zwicky was barely audible.

"You have a talk with Ferguson, maybe a couple of politicians too. Like Francisco Ugarte and Hugh Drummond. You don't like what they tell you. They say you have already taken a lot of favors, maybe some cash, and it would be wise not to ask too many questions yet—especially if an investigation is brewing—so you promote Consuelo, who also has a man in stir, and things go back to normal. But you're scared. You just might need somebody to talk to. Somebody like the ex-wife of the man who will wind up as head of the investigation."

The car had pulled up at the curb in front of the Hotel Bolívar. From its layers of gray stone a flock of pigeons scattered. I dropped the girlish manner and looked at Zwicky with a little savage satisfaction, hiding only the acid revulsion I felt whenever I thought of Jack Hand.

He gripped the door handle and took a long, unsteady breath.

"White-hot," he said. "You are a white-hot lady."

And you, I thought, *are the Emperor of Ice Cream.*

But I didn't say that. I said, "Thank you, Alvin," and smiled demurely.

In the hallway in front of my room he pulled me to him, hurried and feverish. "Stella, I had no choice but to remain aloof," he breathed into my hair. "My family's name means something in San Francisco."

I kept my stomach quiet and managed to whisper, "Of course."

"When you approached me with your threat of an unpleasant journalist friend, I had to listen." He slid his hand to the back of my neck. "But that is not the only reason."

I dodged his mouth and with my cheek against his spoke rapidly. "But what about the prison connection and the Start Over program? You must have noticed that both Rosa and Consuelo—"

"Certainly. It was just a small return favor, I thought. They told me those of us at the top ought to set an example."

"A small favor." I played with a small smile. "But greatly appreciated. Did you wonder . . . ?"

"I was advised not to wonder. It is often good advice."

"True."

"For you, too, Stella. The old saying: What you don't know can't hurt you."

"Sure." His hands were busy at my back and hips. I was thinking of the truth of opposites: Knowledge can kill you. Rosa and Hand confirmed it. "Look, our friends are coming back soon." I pushed him away gently.

"Yes, I—"

"There will be time."

He looked suddenly tired and shrunken beneath the health-club tan. "Tonight Consuelo and I must confer about our buying strategy. We'll take dinner in our rooms. We leave early tomorrow, so I think I shall turn in afterward. Perhaps you and your friend—"

"I'll keep Webster amused. And ship him off tonight."

"Good night then."

"Good night." I kissed him lightly, but his fever had evaporated. He had withdrawn somewhere deep inside himself. There was suddenly a silence and a distance between us. I had the feeling that one of us had said too much. I wasn't sure which one.

Chapter XXIV

I handed Webster a glass of cold white wine from the carafe I had ordered from room service. He took it gratefully and collapsed on the bed. For once he looked like a man who has done what is called an honest day's work.

"This is harder than I thought."

"They have been quite nasty."

"He gives me the creeps, with those white eyes, and *her* . . ." He jerked his head at the room down the hall. "All the charm of a cobra."

I patted his knee. "You're doing a marvelous job. You have the hide of a rhino. But all the same I'm afraid Consuelo suspects something. It might be better if you flew ahead to Huaraz tonight. It will give them a little breathing space, and maybe they'll get careless."

"I need a break myself. I'm tired of being insulted." He placed his glass against his temple. "And of counting pots."

"That's all?"

"We stayed in the storeroom. All she did was fool with shawls and ponchos."

"Did anything come back to the hotel?"

"A couple of sample pieces. But no sign of anything illegal. Maybe your information is wrong."

"So far it looks like a legitimate business. But there are some leads."

"Like what?"

"I found out I'm dealing with a couple of contradictory motives. Greed and patriotism. That guy Caswell represents the greed. Consuelo wants to see heads roll."

Webster frowned. "I can't follow you. Maybe—"

"No," I said. "If I tried to tell you, in a hundred words or less, you might find the role hard to play. And you're doing it just right."

"Whatever you want." Webster saluted me with his glass. His eyes were warm, brown, ingenuous. "I'll do it."

I smiled at him and felt terrible inside.

"You are a dear man, Webster. I know this isn't the trip you had in mind."

"It's all right." He took my hand and kissed it. "I love you."

"Webster—"

"I know." He stood up and looked at me ruefully. "And we're both tired. You get some sleep. I'll keep watch in case they go out since I've got to pack and catch a ride to the airport anyway." He paused at the door. "Can I send up anything for you?"

"No, thanks." I patted the cover of Von Gaugen, on my beside stand. "I've got a heavy sedative here. I'll see you tomorrow afternoon in Huaraz."

"Right."

When he was gone, I tried to concentrate on a few paragraphs about the Chavín cultures whose ruined monuments were near Huaraz. The fierce, cat-headed gods of these extinct people were a mystery. It was thought that priests made human sacrifices to them. Perhaps for rain. Or to prevent earthquake. Or for fun. But my mind kept drifting from these speculations to my own mysteries. To what strange gods had Rosa, Bennie, and Jack Hand sacrificed themselves? And was I the next offering?

Then I turned to the question of strategy. Did I have a strategy? A tacked-together, make-it-up-as-you-go affair, it seemed. Tease Zwicky, needle Consuelo, soothe Webster, and pray for scraps of information that would indicate the next course of action. Stella Quixote. But I wasn't dealing with windmills; the opposition was murderous. To counterbalance that unsettling thought, I recalled the couple from Kansas, and imagined how nice it would be to stroll among the old stones with no concern but to snap photos for the folks back home. In the soft haze of such fantasies I fell finally sound asleep.

The bedside phone burred at a little after sunup. Zwicky was unctuous, considerate, very awake. We were to be at the airport in an hour and a half. Consuelo was already ordering us a continental breakfast in the restaurant below, and a taxi would be waiting as soon as we had eaten. He sounded easy, sunny, careless. There wasn't a trace of that pinched, harried tone of the previous day.

At breakfast Consuelo, too, was almost gay. She gave me a sour twist of the lips that could pass for a smile and even asked after my health. She and Zwicky traded theories about what was the matter with me. Jet lag. The shift in climate. An unfamiliar diet. Zwicky glanced at his watch and clucked sympathetically. He hoped my digestion wouldn't suffer, but we had to hurry. Something was definitely behind all this flattering attention, but I had no idea what it could be. The doorman swept us into a cab while I was still picking crumbs off my lapel, and at the airport Zwicky sent a porter through the line with our bags while he flashed tickets at the counter clerk. I could see a thousand-sole bill peeking out of the ticket envelope. He got back our baggage stubs and boarding passes in record time.

I didn't get it until we were crowding through the gate to the tarmac and the waiting plane. I happened to glimpse another passenger's ticket, opened for inspection by the stewardess at the bottom of the loading ramp. "Lima–Tingo María, Tingo María-Lima," it read.

"Hey," I said.

Zwicky and Consuelo glanced back at me. "Hurry, my love," Zwicky said, and reached for my elbow.

"What happened to Huaraz?" I stumbled along after them, like a drunk.

"Didn't we tell you?" Zwicky looked surprised. "Consuelo, didn't you—"

"No. *¡Dios mío!* When could I say anything? I thought you—"

We were inside the plane now, picking our three-in-a-row seats with bright blue coverlets.

"Ah, my dear"—Zwicky briefly touched his temples with the thumb and middle finger of one hand—"we were so hasty this morning and decided only last night—"

"To skip Huaraz." I was working at my face to give it the right blend of bewilderment and disappointment. I cranked up the eyebrows, puckered the mouth, as a puppeteer adjusted his doll. "Oh, dear, poor Webster will be unhinged. Wondering what became of us."

"I doubt it. Would you like the window seat?"

I shook my head. "Aisle." From now on I intended to try to stay between the two of them and the door. It had been simple. A phone call, a quick change of reservations, a hurried breakfast, and Webster was eliminated, at least until I could get in a long-distance call. Even then it would take him a couple of days to reach me.

"I hope you're not too upset?" Zwicky was smooth, solicitous, perhaps very faintly triumphant. After all, his rival was unhorsed, the maiden at his mercy. "Frankly, I found Webster just a little—"

"He *is* my friend." I gave Zwicky a smile with a sliver of ice in it. "I know his faults."

"Of course. I didn't mean—"

"Never mind. I'll get in touch with Webster." I pulled Von Gaugen from my handbag and opened him on my lap. "It's quite all right," I added, turning a page with a snap. Zwicky started to say something that turned into a cough. I did not look up, and when his hand touched my shoulder, I went rigid until he took it away. I intended to play the miffed coquette for as long as possible. For the next few days I had to get around Zwicky without Webster to run interference. But I couldn't sulk in my room. We were on this trip to make a deal, and I had to stay close enough to the action to figure out how it was going to be made.

I allowed myself to thaw a little when the plane cleared Lima and began its climb over the Andes. The Pacific side of the mountains was barren as the moon, cleft and wrinkled, with here and there a dark outthrust of rock. Then in a steep rush the earth became a line of peaks jagged as shark teeth. We cleared these and rode above the pale greens and ochers of a central valley, beyond which loomed another range of mountains, these shrouded in snow and knife-edged against the blue sky.

"Our namesakes," Zwicky observed. "The *Cordilleras— Blanca y Negra.*"

"Very nice." I gave him a slight, cool smile. "A lot to live up to."

"We try."

He looked at me, the silver-blue eyes moist with longing and apology, but I didn't pursue the point. The plane was bounding through turbulence over the white spires, and we held on in silence until it steadied and then tilted downward. The eastern slopes of the Andes were a dark, luminous green. The jungle climbed high into the rocks, almost to the hem of the snowcap, then swept down over rugged hill land, where I could see a pair of rivers, looping and twisting like great brown snakes.

All at once, in a drop and sharp turn, we were below the green ridges, flying in a canyon, and the landing gear went down. I could see small patches of cleared land, some thatched huts, and the mirror flash of a metal roof. Then a whole group of buildings went by, surrounded by torn earth and fallen trees and crisscrossing roads that made a dense patchwork of cropland. The tires barked on the runway, we rocked uneasily a moment, and then the backthrust hit and we were turning, lumbering toward the airport.

"Welcome to the selva," Zwicky said, and Consuelo laughed.

The airport was new, glass and concrete with plastic trim, but like others I had seen in various corners of the world, it was no match for its environment. Walking across the pitted tarmac, where spears of green burst through the larger cracks, I saw at my feet what appeared to be the foreleg of an animal. Huge, iridescent flies swarmed over it. A group of men in rags leaned against one wall of the building. The warm air carried a rich blend of blossoms, gasoline, and excrement. Inside, a couple of fans roared from their perches on the wall. A soldier with a submachine gun looped on his arm dozed by the door.

When we had retrieved our luggage, one of the men in rags detached himself from the wall outside and shuffled toward us. "Taxi," he said, and wrenched my bag from my hand. One of his eyes was shrunken and fogged over, the other red-rimmed but clear. A hard knot the size of a golf ball jutted from his brown jaw. We followed him to a cluster of dilapidated automobiles in the muddy lot that fronted the airport. He opened the doors of a vehicle that I guessed was a Plymouth perhaps twenty years old, though it had undergone radical changes since then. The seats inside used to belong to a bus and were now bolted to makeshift wooden mounts on the floor.

"Transportation is not so well developed out here," Zwicky said, and settled himself gingerly in the seat. "Life is cruder. We must get to the hotel and slip into something cool."

"If this thing moves, that's all that counts."

Consuelo gave the driver an address for the Hotel Turístico. He picked up a jangle of wires from the floor and with a shower of sparks twisted a pair of them around the steering column. The engine hacked and blatted for a few moments, then settled into an uneven but sustained thunder. We lurched away and down the rutted, puddle-flecked road.

"The hotel is quite nice," Zwicky shouted into my ear. "Quite modern."

I nodded, but the racket was too much for conversation. We went through a grove of vine-draped trees, then fields of banana, their sprays of huge, floppy green leaves brushing the car top. We passed shacks of bamboo and palm frond surrounded by pigs, chickens, and naked brown children. The shacks huddled closer and closer together. Larger structures of adobe or concrete block appeared, some of them festooned with garish signs: COCA-COLA, CERVEZA, RESTAURANTE. Our driver reached into a cotton bag on the floorboard and produced a pinch of dried dark green leaves, which he stuffed under his lip and worked into the knot on his cheek. From a little bottle on the dash he removed a sliver of wood and daubed a dark resin in the same place.

"Coca," Zwicky said matter-of-factly. When he smiled, the sun lines bunched at the corners of his eyes, leaving only an unreadable silver glint. "Would you care to try it?"

"Perhaps later. It kills the appetite, they say, and I'm starved. Legal here, isn't it?"

"Yes," Consuelo said. "It is legal. The people need it." There was something hard in her tone, but without the malice I had gotten used to.

"Because they don't have enough to eat."

She looked at me without expression. "That's correct."

"Fortunately we'll be at the edge of town," Zwicky said. "It's rather dirty and loud in there. This is a rather quaint quarter here. Our hotel is just beyond the corner."

The Hotel Turístico was a Formica and concrete monster, with a thin skirmish line of fleshy roses and lilies between itself and the surrounding dung heaps and chicken yards and cornfields. Through a wrought-iron gate I could see the blue curve of a pool and a patio furnished with dining tables covered with white cloth. The lobby smelled like Lysol and overripe bananas, and the clerk's mustache was trimmed to a ruler-straight edge. The place was clearly deluxe for Tingo María, an island of grotesque, air-conditioned sterility in a sea of rank life.

I had already steeled myself to bunk with Zwicky. The headache routine wouldn't be credible; I had been finessed out of my chaperon; it seemed unwise to risk offending him and arousing suspicion. So we took a suite, and Consuelo a large single. I feigned pleasure at being put up in the most elegant quarters available.

"Far beneath San Francisco standards, I'm afraid."
Zwicky looked at me sharply. "But you really don't mind?"

"I like having a lot of space. If the mattress is hard and
the mosquito netting works, I don't care." I did my best
to put a touch of reserve behind my coy look. "Now what's
our schedule?"

"Consuelo has some things to do at the convent," Zwicky
said smoothly. Behind the bellboy we entered the rooms,
tiled and painted in revolting pastels, furnished with
polyester bedspreads and plastic lampshades. "We can relax. I'll order a brunch later on and—"

"Oh, I'd love to see the tapestries at the convent!" I
tossed my suitcase on the middle of the bed and snapped
it open. "I'll go with her." I began taking out clothes,
careful not to look at him. "We can relax this evening,
no? It's all old hat to you, but for me . . ." I turned,
keeping a pair of shoes in my hand as a buffer, and gave
him a swift kiss on the chin. "A brave new world."

My Prospero looked nonplussed and muttered something about my energy.

"Oh, I'll collapse by nine o'clock." I gestured with the
shoes. "Could you tell Consuelo to wait for me while I
hop in the shower?" I retreated to the bathroom and, just
before turning on the taps, heard the door click open and
shut. I was over the first hurdle.

Chapter XXV

After the shower I dressed quickly in lightweight jeans and one of the white blouses, put two silver hoops through my ears, assembled the .32, loaded it, and packed the gun along with my notebook, passport, and wallet in the bottom of my handbag. I slung the bag over my shoulder and stepped out the door.

From the veranda I could see over a courtyard to the other rooms facing the pool. Consuelo was already on her way, swinging the room key in one hand, a large woven shopping bag in the other. Zwicky had probably told her to leave fast, figuring on making up some excuse to explain his failure to deliver my message. I hailed her and watched her freeze for a moment, then turn slowly around. She had composed an expression of surprise.

"I'm tagging along," I said, "to watch the actual business of Cordilleras Imports."

"You may find it not very interesting."

"Then again I might. Buying and selling always arouse me."

One of the taxi drivers intercepted us at the curb. His ragged shirt had no buttons, and I could see the rivulets of sweat forking down his flat brown chest. He conducted us to a battered Toyota, and Consuelo gave him the name of the convent.

"*Sí,*" he crooned enthusiastically, "*las hermanas santas. Muy amables.*" He ground the machine into gear, and we swung out into the street, dodging a mud-splattered pig and a group of Indian women with great bundles on their shoulders.

"The Convent of Santa María Magdalena seems to have quite a reputation."

Staring out her side window, Consuelo did not respond. But I could see her face dimly reflected in the glass. A blank face. Hypnotized. For a while we jounced along. The driver turned on his radio, and an agonized baritone blasted forth a story of jilted love and revenge. The traffic of pushcarts and rattletrap delivery trucks began to thicken.

"I have heard that the good sisters sometimes dabble in politics."

Still, she did not turn, but her reflection congealed into a mask of caution and distaste.

"Have you?"

"Yeah. Took a hand in a little guerrilla activity a few years back."

"Everyone here is in politics."

"I'm talking about revolution."

She came around then and tried for a few seconds to stare me down. "You don't even know what a revolution is," she said acidly. "But someday maybe you will find out." She laughed. "I would like to be there when you learn."

"You still think I'm a cop, don't you?"

"You have to be. Either a cop or a whore."

"My, that doesn't give a girl a lot of range in her choice of careers. I suppose one could hope to work up to judge or madam."

"Always so funny. Maybe you are both, a whore who works for the police. Or maybe you work for yourself. If you can't marry Alvin, you will blackmail him, is that it?"

"Sure, that's it."

Consuelo was trembling with the suppressed urge to dig my eyes out with her fingernails. While he swerved through the traffic, the driver kept glancing in his rear-view mirror. If he didn't know English, he knew the intonations of violence. We had skirted the downtown area, a few attractive old mansions with red tile roofs and gardens, surrounded by new concrete and glass beehives, and were winding up a hillside.

"Now that we've got that settled, maybe you can tell me what I am supposed to be blackmailing Alvin for."

She went back to staring through the window, where now again we could see cornfields and thatched huts. We passed a man riding a burro.

"I wonder," I said as if thinking aloud, "what kind of car Manuel Esposito drives. Now Alvin had a gray Chrysler, until it was stolen. Probably air-conditioned. Of course, your modern revolutionary has a lot of downtown errands. But doesn't it get hard, Consuelo, to tell the true believers from the moneygrubbers?"

She spoke into the glass, so the words were a little muffled. "You know what I hate about you? Your kind? You think because people do not always live up to the ideals they will die for, you can make fun of them. You are the worst, because you believe in nothing."

It was a considerable speech, and I was impressed. There was also a defensive note in it that interested me.

"All right, Consuelo. Maybe I've been too flip. But you haven't encouraged much straight talk. I'll tell you what surprises me about you. You talk about the people here and Alvin and Manuel and your husband and the revolution as if they were all part of the same ideal. All equally honorable. But I don't see any difference between your honorable ideal and the system we've got—rotten as it may be. Some of you are rich and getting richer; others are poor or in jail or both. Oh, yes, and some of you are dead. Like Rosa."

"Rosa died in an accident."

"Bullshit."

That brought her head around again. Her eyes were black fire.

"I saw it."

"I don't believe you."

"And Bennie. You think that was an accident, too? And my friend Lieutenant Hand?"

"So you are a cop."

"No, I'm not a cop. I wish you would get that idea out of your head. You didn't answer the question."

"Bennie was a junkie. I don't know anything about any lieutenant."

"He had an accident, too. He ran in front of a bullet and then jumped in a garbage bin behind a chicken-fry drive-in. People who fool around with your ideal system seem to be accident-prone."

The taxi had taken a side road, narrow and rutted, and now wheeled into a large yard before a group of buildings, mostly brick with galvanized metal roofing. A thin iron cross topped the largest building, which also had Roman arches over the entrance and windows. The grounds were well kept, with roses, rhododendrons, and birds-of-paradise in plots and bordering the paths. Quick and silent as ghosts, a few gowned figures moved along the paths.

Consuelo seized her shopping bag and clutched it to her breast. Defensive again. I noticed an edge of woven cloth protruding from the bag. "You should think about that yourself," she said softly. "All those accidents."

"So should you. Did you ever wonder what would happen if you started to disagree with the ideal? Like Rosa did?"

That was a shot in the dark, but it struck something. Getting out of the taxi, Consuelo appeared pensive beneath her hostility. I got a sidelong, speculative look as we marched up the main path. Behind us the taxi driver settled down in his seat and lit a cigarette.

In the foyer underneath a picture of the Virgin with glowing heart exposed we were intercepted by an Indian girl in a novice's gray gown. She brightened at Consuelo's nod of recognition. We were ushered into an adjoining office, where a small, plump woman rose from behind a desk with an exclamation. She and Consuelo clasped hands and began the rapid twitters that are exchanged between old friends. Mother Lefebre had skin as solid and yeasty as fresh dough and gray eyes, empty and clear from decades of contemplating bare walls and candles. I was curtly introduced as a traveling colleague and "associate" of Señor Zwicky's.

"We are pleased to have you with us," the good mother

said in her soft trill. Her English bore a heavy accent. I guessed northern France or Belgium.

"I look forward to visiting your studios. Everyone has heard of the fine needlework of the María Magdalena Convent," I lied earnestly.

"Oh, my dear, the sisters are at prayer still this morning. We have only a few assistants working today."

I glanced at Consuelo.

"We have our accounts to do. And completed work to review," Consuelo said smoothly, showing her teeth. "I warned you it would bore you."

"Oh, yes. I am so sorry it is so dull. At least we shall have some coffee." Mother Lefebre picked up a small silver bell from her desk and tinkled it.

Immediately the door opened, and the Indian girl stood at the threshold.

"I permit myself one indulgence." Mother Lefebre cast down her eyes in repentance. "I have European coffee, very strong. Would you like milk or the sugar?"

"Negro. I have the same weakness."

"Tres cafés. Uno con leche." The Indian girl nodded and shut the door swiftly and gently.

I thought it was interesting that the good mother knew how Consuelo took her coffee. In the course of the next hour I saw more of that familiarity. I listened to a pair of shrewd bargainers going through routines they both knew very well, a complex blend of flattery, feigned disappointment, innuendo, and sudden, bold proposal. Mother Lefebre had heard of the impending rise in import duties and foresaw an attempt to whittle down the wholesale price to compensate for the increase. She was ready with a counterproposal of bulk purchase, paid in advance, to justify the discount.

I was drawing a blank again. I knew enough about the workings of business—any business—to be sure that this act was not devised for my benefit. Whatever else Cordilleras might be up to, it was running an import trade and running it hard, as far as I could see. When Consuelo looked at me, it was with a smirk of triumph. The good mother glanced at me only to be sure I had a full cup and to apologize for the dreariness of all this talk of prices. Once she said something of more interest.

"We are so grateful to Señor Zwicky for his support," she murmured, and rolled her eyes heavenward for a moment.

There was a little pause, and I moved quickly to keep the topic open. "You must be," I said. "He must help in many ways."

"Oh, yes. The building fund. The program for orphans. He is such a kind man!"

Consuelo cleared her throat and tried to derail us, but I didn't let her.

"Is he helpful with—the work with the people?"

Mother Lefebre looked swiftly at Consuelo, whose face was still except for a tiny movement of the jaw.

"Oh, I'm sorry to bring up such things," I gushed, and leaned forward to capture the good mother's attention again. "I know you're busy and this is not the time. But your work with the people is very important. Dangerous, I know. We admire you."

"Thank you, señorita." She flushed and looked at me, Consuelo, and the Virgin on the wall. "We—"

"We have other work to do here now," Consuelo interrupted. "Let's leave these purchases for now and look at what's done." She stood up, uncoiling like a spring.

"Of course." Mother Lefebre looked relieved and hurried us through the door.

As we made our way though a courtyard full of blossoms, she chattered on about the convent and her charges. It was a couple of centuries old, although it had been inactive at times for long periods. Its purpose was to bring young Indian girls into the order, educate them, and send them back into the villages as teachers, nurses, and mission aides. To help pay their expenses, they had recruited some highland craftswomen to train the novices to weave expert copies of traditional mantas, ponchos, and tapestries, which were then sold to tourists or importers.

"We were so lucky to find artists who had knowledge

of these rare old things," Mother Lefebre said, ushering us into a cool, spacious room with high windows. There were several looms with half-finished work on them, sprouting many-colored threads, and tables heaped with fabrics or fluffy hills of raw cotton. In one corner three old brown women did not look up from their task when we entered. "Consuelo knows all the patterns from the coast and from the south—Bolivia—and Rosa taught us so much from the central region."

"Rosa worked here?" I watched Consuelo, who seemed not to hear or care if she heard, drift on toward the three old women.

"Yes. She was so good with us. Señor Zwicky hired her to help him in the United States. But she came back often. It was so sad, what happened." She looked at me with her blank, pure eyes. "God's will be done. Did you know her?"

"Very briefly." I saw once more the film clip of the rag doll under the wheels.

"A wonderful, sweet person." The good mother sighed and turned to the largest loom. "It is unfortunate that our workers are today at prayers and studies. They could explain to you."

"It's all right," I said. In the corner I could see Consuelo bending down beside one of the seated women. She took one of the pieces of cloth from her own bag and spread it out on the woman's lap. I moved closer and could hear them conversing in a tongue full of rushing consonants and singsong vowels.

"Quechua," Mother Lefebre said proudly. "The language of the ancient Incas. Many of our girls speak it."

The Indian woman was very old, and when she lifted her head to answer Consuelo, I saw that she was blind. Her pupils had fogged over, white dots in the black iris, negative-image eyes, sunk deep in a face wrinkled and hard as a knuckle. She sat upright, like a dead branch rising from the black pool of her skirt spread on the floor. Like the taxi driver, she had a small, hard lump on her jaw. As she talked with Consuelo, her twisted, clawlike hands rummaged in the piles of woven cloth heaped around her.

"We feed them and watch over them, and they help by doing what they can. Repairing some old pieces, adding fringes."

I nodded sympathetically. The old woman cocked her head like a bird toward us. "How can she tell the colors apart?"

"By smell. She knows all the dyes and even combinations of them. She can match them that way as closely as you or I with our sight."

"Remarkable."

Consuelo threw me a glance, an opaque smile, then said something to the old woman, who nodded and gave a hoarse chuckle. They went back to fondling the stack of goods. At the side of the room there was an open entrance to the grounds outside, and now through this archway a man stepped. He was short but very sturdy, leaning only slightly beneath the immense sack on his shoulder. The quick black eyes touched all of us and dwelt longest on me.

"*Venga,* José," Mother Lefebre said with a peremptory wave toward the old women. He padded on bare feet across the room and dropped the sack beside Consuelo.

"He comes from the jungle. A *chuncho,* as they used to be called. But he is civilized now and brings in a little work from the villages along the river, where our girls have taught the women how to weave in our style."

As the man unpacked his goods, the blind woman seized each item and tugged at it with her claws, sniffed it, and grunted. Certain pieces she passed to Consuelo, who examined their texture intently. The man squatted on his heels, watching impassively.

"These are quite good, these three," she called to Mother Lefebre. "I'll take them as samples." She stuffed the mantas into her bag and touched the old woman on the shoulder, uttering a few phrases that had the ring of a farewell. "The others are like these?"

"Oh, yes. They are doing better and better work."

Consuelo nodded. "Then I don't see why we couldn't buy them in bulk. But I must talk to Señor Zwicky first."

"Of course. Will he be coming to visit, too?" Mother Lefebre sounded wistful.

"I believe so." Consuelo looked at me then, her eyes hard and mocking. "If his other interests allow him time."

"We should be so happy. All of you must come back when we are working."

"We will send an order in any case. Shall we go?"

I hesitated a moment. So that was it. The Tingo María connection. A sweet old nun and Indians as silent as stones, trading hand-done fabrics. A few thousand dollars' worth of honest business. "All right," I said. "You win."

Consuelo smiled. She looked happy in her contempt. We exchanged farewells and promises with the good mother and returned to our taxi driver, who was trying to bend his yawn into a smile. He slammed the doors on us, waved at the convent, crossed himself, and fired up the engine. On our return down the driveway I glanced back once and saw the little white boat of the good mother's hat sailing along the path to the main entrance. Then a hedge cut off that view, and the somber, quiet buildings and wide lawns and flower plots dissolved in our dust.

Chapter XXVI

"It wasn't so boring. I didn't know, for example, that Alvin was such a philanthropist. How much does he give, Consuelo? To the cause?"

"It isn't my business."

"Come on, Consuelo. That's why you're in this deal, isn't it? For the poor and downtrodden?"

Consuelo continued to stare coldly out the car window at the banana trees shuttering by. I got a handful of her hair and jerked, not hard, but enough to bring her around and startle her out of the various masks she used.

"Listen, I'm trying to save you some trouble. You don't have to tell me anyway. A million soles, more or less?" She tried to twist away, but I kept the fistful of thick black hair, and she had to look at me. "That's fifty grand, Consuelo. A lousy fifty grand, in dollars. Sure it's a lot here, but do you think Zwicky or Ferguson or Caswell or Drummond give a good goddamn about the orphans? Fifty grand is nothing, Consuelo. It's ratshit. How much do you think they keep?"

We stared at each other for a long time. In her liquid black eyes I saw a lot of things: hate, curiosity, doubt, fear. I took away my hand and tried a friendly smile. "And I know you are also doing a straight job, and doing it well. You seem to know your stuff." I nodded at her basket.

She smiled enigmatically. "You would be surprised to know how much I know."

"Surprise me."

"That isn't my job. Anyway, Alvin has done much more than support an orphanage."

"Sure. He hired you—and Rosa—and maybe other convicts and relatives of convicts. He's contributed to certain campaign funds, for assemblymen who drafted the Start Over program. But he doesn't even know exactly why, does he? That *is* your job, isn't it? Keeping him ignorant but useful?"

She swayed a little, bumping the window. Again her fingers dug into the sack and pulled it to her. "And your job," she whispered finally, "what is your job, Stella? You say you are not a cop. You say you are not a whore after Alvin's money. Just what are you then?"

It was a hard question. I tried another smile, a shrug. "I don't expect you to believe me, but how about a concerned citizen?"

She looked at me hard for a long moment. Then her eyes went dull, and her mouth shriveled a little. She turned away.

"All right," I said. "I guess I also like poking around."

She didn't answer, and I knew I had lost another opportunity. I still hadn't the dimmest notion of how Consuelo contributed to the system of transforming the bales of green leaf into white powder in the briefcases of Start Over counselors. So far Cordilleras had tended strictly to business, and my hopes for finding dungeons in Tingo María knee-deep in cocaine were apparently misguided.

On the edge of town Consuelo gave the driver directions to the Chifa Martín. We were to meet Zwicky there for lunch if we were early, she said. We found the café on a narrow, dusty street, where vultures hopped in the gutter like sparrows and emaciated dogs skulked in doorways. But inside, the Martín aspired to some degree of elegance. The tablecloths were white, if not clean, and a fake pagoda over the bar and some paper lanterns gave it an Oriental veneer. There was a partition dividing the dining room from the bar. When I stepped behind it, I saw that two tables were occupied. Four Japanese businessmen hunched together in earnest discussion, and at the other table, between two men, one of them in uniform, sat Zwicky. I caught something in his expression when he looked up and saw us—something hunted, frightened, and resentful—and then the other man turned around.

It was Gutierez. His white, even teeth were exposed in a wide smile, and the black holes of his eyes contained something that glittered. He was on his feet, greeting us in Spanish, motioning the waiter, fixing my arm in the little spring trap of his hand. Zwicky looked at Consuelo as we took our seats, and the look was numb and blank. We were introduced to the chief of police of Tingo María, a man with a comfortable paunch and a huge, glossy mustache. His gray uniform had a grease spot or two on the lapel. He held my hand for a long time after pressing it damply with his mustache, while Gutierez grinned like a hyena.

They were so glad we had come at this moment, this precise moment, as they were explaining to Señor Zwicky the new regulations concerning the registration of commercial travelers. A few forms, a few questions, a waiting period. For Señor Zwicky and Señorita Palacios, already registered under the old system, there was no problem. But for myself—ah, that was a little bit different. The *capitán* would appreciate my visit to the station, to his private office. There we could do this paper work, and Señor Gutierez, a longtime friend and well-respected international businessman here, would assist me. It was good fortune, was it not?

Zwicky interrupted sharply. "We must return tomorrow to Lima. There is some last-minute business. Señorita Pike is my guest. She—"

"But of course! She is the guest of our whole country." The *capitán* struck Zwicky on the shoulder with his thick hand. "Do not worry. We shall take very good care. I shall show her our city. And then, what luck! My good friend Gutierez is going to Lima in two days, three days, something like that, and he can escort her. Eh?" He nodded at Gutierez, who, without taking his eyes off Zwicky, clamped my arm again in his hand trap.

"Most surely. To travel with such a beautiful woman—

I would be delighted." He laughed his silent laughter. He was positively convulsed.

"Surely we can arrange these papers in a few hours," Zwicky protested. There was a fine sheen of moisture on his brow, which I noticed had begun to lose its tan. "Perhaps there is a fee we could pay, and with a letter from you . . ." He gave the *capitán* a meaningful look.

Gutierez and the *capitán* laughed uproariously. A wonderful joke. The fat hand swatted Zwicky again on the shoulder, a little harder.

A waiter slid piscos before Consuelo and me. They looked pale and flat. When Consuelo looked at me, her eyes had gone reptilian again, but there was a faint flicker of something else: a warning.

"These regulations." The *capitán* made an ugly noise with his lips. "I detest them as much as you do, Señor Zwicky. A man of honor. A great patron of our convent. A man of wealth. I know you are all these things. But the law is the law." He sighed and, seizing my hand, planted another wet, furry kiss on my knuckles. "This fine lady even. We must investigate, to satisfy Lima, you understand. So many *traficantes* these days. So much drugs." He laughed, and Gutierez joined in. "I know she is not a *traficante*—ridiculous!—but if they find out in Lima that I have not registered her—*a-i-e-e-e, carajo*—they will skin me alive!"

"*Capitán*," Zwicky said in the measured, metallic tone that he used in board meetings, the voice of money and influence, "you will find that they will be even more upset in Lima if you detain Señorita Pike. My embassy will be informed, and the ambassador, as you know, is a very close friend of General Morales, who I believe is the commander of the Policía de Investigación. He will not be pleased to know that our trip has been interfered with." Even in Spanish Zwicky was impressive. He delivered his threat in the quiet, direct way of a man describing market conditions. He was trying to give the impression that a mere inconvenience to himself would be a very grave misfortune for the *capitán*. But the thread of desperation underneath his calm was still noticeable.

"Señor Zwicky exaggerates," Gutierez hissed, leaning across the table and digging his fingers into my arm. "And as he knows, General Morales has many friends. I do not think he will be disturbed. Besides, the trip could be lengthened a little, perhaps?" He glanced at Consuelo. "Are you in such a hurry?"

Consuelo had drawn the basket to her knees, one hand thrust into its depths. Her eyelids lowered, and she seemed to be concentrating. She looked like—what did she look like? I groped for the right word. A warm pressure grew in my midsection. Reading. Like someone reading. Braille. Of course. The idea flowered hot in my brain at last. It was a rush of pure joy at seeing how they did it and of rage at my stupidity.

Maybe if I were blind, like the old Indian woman who wove the information about the coca and how much of it there was and what it cost into the fringes of the shawls. The quipus. Rosa had read them. Consuelo was reading them right now. Because Gutierez wanted to know how soon the shipment would be made. The *chuncho*'s cargo.

Later she would knot her own messages into the cloth: when the stuff would leave Lima, how much of it was ready, where it would go. And from the States she could make orders by sending a single poncho. Air express could have information in Caswell's hands in a few hours. A cablegram of cloth. It was so neat and so simple and so obvious. Find the information and how they pass it, Stump had said, they have to have records. They did. In an unwritten language five centuries old.

Consuelo's eyes opened. "We must be in Lima in three days," she said tonelessly. "Or we can do no business."

"You see?" Gutierez grinned. "Plenty of time. Go tomorrow. We shall take care of Señorita Pike. In a day or two, when the registration is done, I shall bring her back to you. Such a being, though, it is tempting to keep her here forever." He rocked back and forth in the silent wind of his laughter. The *capitán* guffawed, too, and both of them went over and over me with their eyes, raping and looting.

"So it is all settled then?" The *capitán* slapped Zwicky on the shoulder and leaned so close to me that I could feel the heat from his face. "Señorita Pike, you shall be my honored guest. At my own villa by the river."

"Delighted," I said. "Very interesting. But I would like to get my luggage from the hotel."

"I send the driver." The *capitán* snapped a finger, and a man in green fatigues carrying a submachine gun stepped from behind the partition.

"I'll have to go," I said, and got up quickly. "My things are not packed."

"Just a minute!" Zwicky gave me a look that was both stricken and angry. "Stella, they can't do this. Caswell said nothing to me. I—"

"It's such an overwhelming invitation, Alvin." I nodded at the soldier with the gun. "A hospitality not to be denied. If you aren't careful, we'll all three be staying here. Maybe a long time." I didn't have to fake the bitter smile I gave him.

"Get your things," the *capitán* said with a magnanimous wave. "We shall order your lunch. *A la criolla.*"

"I'll take these shawls back for you," I said, and tugged the basket away from Consuelo's side.

"Oh, no!" Her voice was sharp, too loud. The *capitán* looked at her curiously. He didn't know.

I tugged harder. "No trouble," I went on casually. "In the *capitán*'s car."

She opened her mouth, panic in her eyes, and then released her grip, and the basket swung against my leg. She was staring hard at me. I smiled back innocently. "Just put them in my room on the bed." Her voice was carefully indifferent.

Gutierez rose behind me like a cobra swaying to music. "I shall go with you," he said. His eyes were like gun barrels and swung from my face to the basket. Zwicky stared at the untouched drink in front of him.

"Fine." I clutched my handbag under my arm and strode for the door, maneuvering the soldier to a position at my side where I swung the basket. I didn't look back.

When the black Buick was moving swiftly through the streets, traffic scattering respectfully out of its way, Gutierez turned to me and ran one finger along my thigh, from knee to hip.

"You are a smart *gringuita*," he said in English. "Why do you get yourself in such trouble? You have such legs." The finger ran down again to my knee, and then it was two fingers. In the rearview mirror I saw the driver's eyes flick over us and narrow in amusement.

"Maybe I like to meet new people." The muscles of my leg grew tense in spite of an effort to keep myself easy. "Find out who's running things."

"Or who has the money? *Puta*." He moved three fingers to the inside of my thigh. "Whore." He spoke dreamily, his voice soft and hoarse. I recalled the hippie girl in Berkeley. A lady-killer, she had said. In every sense of the word.

"Too bad." His voice had gone suddenly flat. He took his hand away. The Buick nosed into the driveway of the Hotel Turístico. The soldier got out and opened the door for us, the automatic pointed nonchalantly at our knees.

"*Espere*," Gutierez said to him, and took hold of my elbow. We walked that way, stiff as an old married couple, to the lobby. The room clerk slid my key out onto the counter, his mustache thin and perfect above an expressionless mouth.

Gutierez took the key, and as he did so, I stepped away from him and slid my handbag from my shoulder and wrapped its strap around my wrist. At the bottom of the bag I could see the little bulge of the revolver. When he turned from the desk, I walked across the lobby ahead of him, onto the patio and along the motionless turquoise oblong of the pool. The door of one of the ground-floor rooms was open, and a maid's cart was parked outside, mop handles jutting into the air. Otherwise, the courtyard was deserted.

Behind me I could hear Gutierez's heels snap on the tiles as he quickened his step, and glancing at the ground, I saw his shadow extend a hand to grasp my elbow. I took one extra-long stride and then pivoted on the ball of my foot, bringing the handbag around in a long arc. The gun at the bottom of the bag, swinging at the end of the strap and my extended arm, had a good deal of momentum when it collided with the side of his head. The sound was like a hammer pounding a piece of wet wood.

He stumbled, tried to get his feet under him, and stepped out into the water. I watched him disappear into the blossom of foam, and when he came up, pawing at the rim the pool, his voice strangled and small, hair plastered over eyes squeezed tight with pain, I swung the bag again. The gun caught him solidly on the temple, and when he went down this time, he didn't come up for a while. When he did, it was only a black cap of hair, with a pink haze in the water around it.

I walked on, fast, past the last apartment and through the grounds to the fence that marked the Turístico's boundary. There was a gate in it, and I let myself through. I heard the scream before I closed the latch and looking back, I could see the maid standing above a strip of blue water, poking at it with a mop, her mouth round with terror.

Chapter XXVII

On the other side of the fence from the spacious lawns and barbed shrubs of the hotel was a meandering muddy track overhung with ragged green. A couple of huts crouched at its edge. In the bare, beaten earth around these huts a few chickens pecked at imaginary tidbits, and a pig lay inert under a cloud of flies. There wasn't a human being in sight, and the maid's screams already sounded dull and distant in the dense, warm breath that came from the land.

I set off at a sort of sedate run in the direction of town. If I was lucky, the driver would go inside to help pull Gutierez out of the pool and try to resurrect him, so it would be a few minutes at least before he could get back to the restaurant. After that, every cop and soldier in town would be looking for me, and I was about as incognito as Karl Marx at a DAR convention. They would have the airport blockaded first, and the bus and taxi terminals. They would expect me to take the basket of shawls and run for Lima.

There was one alternative. I had seen on Von Gaugen's map that the river near Tingo María was part of the Marañón system but bent very near the net of streams that fed into the Ucayali, the major tributary of the Amazon. If I could get into that net, I might reach Pucallpa and fly from there. Pucallpa was, I gathered from my reading, the largest, smelliest, most corrupt port on the continent. It had a harbor where freighters docked after steaming three thousand miles up the Amazon, and one could arrange passage of some kind to anywhere. For a price.

Thinking about money led me to make a quick inventory of my kit for this journey. I had the little gun, my makeup, the clothes on my back, a passport, and a few hundred dollars—mostly in traveler's checks, which I guessed would be worthless where I was heading. And the shawls. It occurred to me suddenly that except for my last-minute tug-of-war with Consuelo, there was no reason for her to suspect that I knew what I had. As I walked, I poked through the contents of the basket and saw that only three of the pieces bore knotted fringes like those Alberto had shown me in the museum. These I stuffed in my handbag along with two decoys, and the others I scattered on the road. Then I pushed the basket into the mud with my foot and kicked it a couple of times. There was a chance they would believe I had thrown the whole batch away and would spend some time looking for the missing shawls.

I had an idea where the restaurant was, so I skirted that part of town and kept to the hovels at its border. Brown faces stared at me from doorways, and a time or two a small band of children and dogs yapped after me for a few yards, but no one accosted me. Somewhere at the other side of town, probably on the main road to the airport, I heard a siren. So far, so good.

The river, when I reached it, looked big and brown and mean. A cluster of shacks and two or three long, rambling sheds perched on the bank, and a rickety wooden dock extended a little way into the stream. The current was strong, and here and there on the surface I could see a roiling of the water, a sudden bulge like a muscle flexing, that left a scum of dirty foam in its wake. A few boats butted against the dock as if fretting to be swept away, but the dugout canoes were drawn up on the muddy bank, amid old gasoline drums, derelict hulls, and flapping vultures. A few men stood or squatted in front of the shacks or on a platform before one of the sheds, where a door was open and I could see a heap of sacks that probably were the source of the coffee smell that invaded the general atmosphere of mud and rot. They watched me as if I were some kind of animal creeping up on them.

I couldn't pretend to be anything but what I was: a *gringuita* with more money than they would see in years, in my denim tourist costume, offering to engage them in some kind of utter insanity. I spoke to the one who wore a wristwatch and exposed a gold tooth when he smiled. I was interested in transport downriver, I said. And possible portage to the Ucayali. Immediately. They stared at me, then at one another. I could pay, I said. Well. They remained utterly silent. The man looked at his watch.

"Señorita," he said, "it is very far. One needs food and a good motor. Mosquito net. There are no hotels. Someone has misled you. A bad person." He ran over me swiftly with his eyes. "The Ucayali is not for you."

"Señor," I said, "I must leave right now. In a boat with a motor. I will buy the boat. And I need a guide."

One of the men laughed.

I turned to him. "You? You have a boat?"

He looked away and shook his head.

The man with the gold tooth sighed. "It is impossible, Señorita. *Tigres,* boas, the Indians." The other man laughed again.

"Horsefeathers," I said—it is the same in Spanish—"nothing is impossible if this that I see is a river and those things over there are boats. If none of you can make such a trip, just tell me who can."

They stared at me now as if I were raving mad. I had finally gotten across that I meant what I said. A murmur of awe and amusement went around the group.

"Hermanito," one of the men said, and a couple of others nodded.

The man with the gold tooth broke into a smile. "Ah, *sí,*" he announced. "Hermanito. He is part *indio,* part *negro.* He is a *regatón,* a trader. Sometimes drunk. He has a boat."

The man laughed again at that. I didn't like his tone

of voice, but it looked as if there wasn't much choice. "Where does he live?"

They all pointed enthusiastically downstream. "There. The last house. The canoe with the old motor."

I thanked them and walked away. They didn't move but watched me all the way down the bank, until I was rapping on the wall of the tiny shack that was last in the row. Simultaneously I heard one more chorus of laughter from the dock and a thump inside the shack, as if someone had fallen to the floor. Then the dirty flour sacks that made the curtain hanging in the entrance were swept aside. I was looking down on a man with a head much too large for his body, a broad head framed in dense knots of soot-black hair. The nose was flat and wide, the lips thick, but his eyes were turned up at the corners, and he had the light-boned, bowlegged body of an Indian. His shirt was missing its sleeves and all its buttons, and his trousers had worn off at the knees.

"Hermanito?"

He leaned against the doorway, examining me with his brown, bloodshot eyes. An odor of old, sour drink came from the room. After a moment he nodded.

"*Sí*. You want the boat."

It wasn't a question. He stepped out into the full sun and blinked. "When?"

"Now."

He shook his head. "*Mañana.*" He turned and reached for the curtain.

"Today. Now. I will pay you twenty thousand soles."

He turned again and looked at me, not surprised but suspicious. "Why?"

"Because I must get to Pucallpa. In three days."

He grinned, a span of red gum where his front teeth should have been, bracketed by others white and perfect. "Very hard. No rest."

"I don't care."

He didn't answer but walked to the canoe that was drawn up by the house, listing on its side in the mud. It was a dugout, a narrow sharp-prowed craft hewn from a single great log, though a gunwale of six-inch plank had been nailed on to give it more draft. An ancient outboard motor was bolted to a plank across the stern, all its surfaces worn to bare, bright metal. There was nothing in the boat but an empty pisco bottle, a small chicken coop, and four five-gallon gas cans. Hermanito kicked the canoe speculatively with his bare toe, and it boomed like a drum.

"An old boat," he said. "The water is high this time of year."

"Twenty thousand soles."

"You have no food. No hat."

"Twenty thousand soles."

He threw back his big head, laughed, and flashed his red and white grin. "Okay, mister," he said, and extended his pink palm.

I dug out my wallet and gave him a five and five ones. He waited, and I grinned back at him. "In Pucallpa. Now let's go."

He moved with deceptive speed, and in twenty minutes we were launched, with the help of a couple of the dockhands. Hermanito had stowed a bunch of green bananas in the prow, two skinny roosters in the chicken coop, and a basket of cooked corn and yucca amidships. There were also a couple of mosquito nets and blankets rolled into a manta and a sack of odds and ends: matches, candles, rope, limes, a short machete, and a box of cartridges for the ancient single-barreled shotgun that Hermanito wedged beside the outboard. The gas cans were still empty, but Hermanito said we would be stopping around the bend at another dock to fill them.

I didn't take a full, deep breath until after we had the fuel aboard. It was delivered by a fat, voluble man who pumped it by hand out of his barge, which was merely a floating heap of hundred-gallon drums. The second dock was smaller than the first and deserted except for three men who were unloading what looked like sugarcane from a small scow. I hoped that it would be a day, or perhaps two, before the *capitán* figured out that I wasn't hiding in Tingo María. My luck depended a lot on the likes of the dock foreman and the fat gas merchant. If they chose to talk to the police, I had very little head start. But my best guess was that working people did not go out of their way to deal with people in uniforms and wouldn't help or hinder unless their own interests were involved.

In the meantime, everything depended on Herman-ito—the little brother—and his narrow boat. When we skated out over the bulges in the brown water, it rocked and an occasional bucketful of foam dashed in on us. Without being asked, I took the scoop made from an old plastic bottle and bailed from time to time. Otherwise, there was nothing to do but watch the green hills glide by. Scarves of mist hung about the tops of the higher peaks, but the sky was mostly a hot, even blue. The jungle grew to the river's edge and reached beyond, an over-hang of great limbs and looping vines. To avoid a rapid, we sometimes cut inside this green roof and drifted in a cool corridor of shade. There I saw a band of monkeys, skinny little dark brown fellows, and a toucan with a great banana beak sailed away with a screech.

After an hour or two Hermanito dug a few chunks of cold yucca from his sack and handed a portion to me on a bit of banana leaf. When we had finished this main course, he produced a huge, luscious orange, and I moved beside him to share its sections. Between bites we began a shouting conversation over the racket of the motor. I told him about myself, how I lived in a city called San Francisco in California. Ah, Hermanito sighed. Holly-wood. Actually, I said, Hollywood was not quite the same as California. He asked if I had an automobile of my own. I confessed that I did but could barely afford to keep it running. These odd combinations of fact mystified Her-manito, but they were no more marvelous than what he told me about himself.

His grandfather was probably descended from the Af-rican slaves in Barbados and had been brought by the

English to the Putamayo country in the years of the rubber boom. The Barbados blacks had been given the task
of enslaving the Indians along the rivers where the cau-
cho trees grew, herding them into camps, where they were
forced to harvest the black gold that went down the river
to the Atlantic and made vast fortunes for white traders.

After the market was ruined by cultivated crops in In-
dochina and Ceylon, most of the slave runners left the
country. Some, Hermanito said, were caught, cut, and
buried alive. A few like his grandfather made peace and
settled among the Indians. His father was thus—he
thought—half Conibo, and he had himself been reared
in a large village on the Pachitea, a polyglot community
of Indians, mestizos, and white renegades from the coast.
In such a place life was shifting, uncertain as the moods
of the river. His father died when he was a child, and his
mother ran off with a government surveyor. Then the
coffee plantations and cane fields brought settlers, roads,
and finally airstrips, so when he was grown, Hermanito
set out to make his fortune.

"Now you see," he said, and made a sweeping gesture
to encompass the boat, the motor, the shotgun, and the
miles of dense jungle, "what my fortune is. The same as
my grandfather's." He grinned. "I drink too much like
him, too."

"But to have all this," I said, repeating his gesture, "is
to be a rich man."

He nodded and grinned. "Why do you not, Señorita,
become rich this way yourself then?"

"My city is beautiful, too, in its way."

"Then why are you here now? Going to Pucallpa. Pucallpa!" He made a face.

I looked away, out over the broad brown river. It was
a simple, frank question. The same one I had been asking
myself for a month. The same one Frank asked me. And
Jack. And Stump. And Consuelo. But I seemed to get
farther from an answer each time. When I looked back,
Hermanito seemed to have forgotten the conversation. He

gazed up the river, a perfect blank serenity in his eyes. He knew exactly where he was going. He was taking a crazy *gringuita* to Pucallpa for twenty thousand soles.

I decided there was one direct, if superficial, answer. "Revenge," I said. "I am here for revenge. A man I liked very much—also an *indio* but from my country—was killed."

He woke up out of his blankness and looked at me with new interest. "Your man, what did he do?"

"He wanted to catch some men who were taking money for themselves. They killed a woman to keep this money."

"She was Peruvian?"

"Yes. She worked once for the convent at Tingo María. You know it?"

"Everyone knows it."

"What do they know?"

He looked carefully into my face. No longer bloodshot, his eyes were brown and deep. "Many things happen there that the good mother knows nothing of. An American comes, and then pretty soon there is a new generator or new clothes for the orphans. She does not ask why."

"Do others ask why? The police?"

Hermanito grinned and stuck his tongue out at me through the toothless gap in his gums. "You do not know our police. They work for the big *traficantes*. They do not bother us—the little ones, *regatones*—as long as we bring our coca from the jungle at cheap prices."

"You bring coca to Tingo María?"

"All the boats do, sometimes."

"What happens to it then?"

The corners of his mouth turned down, and his shoulders hunched. "Who knows? They make *pasta* out of it and send it away."

"*Pasta?*"

"Yes. The crude cocaine. A brown stuff. Very bad."

"But no one knows who does it? Or how it goes to Lima?"

He laughed a little at my eagerness. "It is strange. Usually everyone knows everything in the jungle. But these people do not talk. Yet they always seem to know when the coca is arriving and how much of it there will be. Very strange. The Americans appear sometimes just when the crop is ready."

No, they wouldn't need to talk, I thought. *They can read threads.* "But you do not know them?"

He thought for a moment, then nodded. "There is the *capitán* of police, of course. He has a big house and two cars and a woman from Lima. Then there is a fat little gringo without much hair. And another man, a mestizo with a mustache whose clothes and shoes are from America."

"He is one of the men who killed my friend."

"Ah." Hermanito was silent for a long moment. "You must be careful."

It was late afternoon now. The shadows of the trees reached over the water like long, inky fingers. I felt hypnotized by the steady, swift rush along the gunwales of the canoe. There was a tremendous temptation to forget everything and simply roll, forever, on the back of this great brown snake. A few scraps of thought did whirl by, and I held to them like a drowning woman.

My hunch that there was tension between Zwicky and Ferguson seemed to be accurate. Gutierez had been sent, obviously, to get rid of me or at least to take me out of action. It was a job he seemed to like. Whatever faction in the organization he represented—I figured he and Manuel were the executive arm—they didn't much like the idea of Zwicky chumming around with me. On the other hand, Zwicky didn't much like the idea of more corpses, especially corpses with prior associations to himself or his company. So he had tried to talk me into a limited partnership. Caswell tipped off his associates, and Gutierez came to break up the game.

If I had mailed him back with a lump on his head and his lungs full of water, they would be, I guessed, finally and thoroughly disenchanted. If Gutierez lived through

his swim, he would probably be anxious to do a number
of unpleasant things to me whatever his boss said. It occurred to me that he might delay any report from the
field until he had taken care of me and recovered the
shawls, since he wouldn't look very good at the moment.
Zwicky and Consuelo wouldn't know what to do—crying
for help would be an open admission of the failure of
their plan. I figured they would get back to Lima and put
a close watch on the airport, hoping to intercept me and
find out if I had the missing quipus.

Every time I glanced at my handbag and thought of
the fringes on the shawls, rows of particolored knots
bearing compact instructions, I got angry at my own stupidity. I had seen Consuelo fondling the goods at the
Cordilleras headquarters the first time I met her. Then
Alberto had told me of the ancient method of coding
messages into cloth. At the convent I had stood there
dumb as a post while the old Indian woman stroked her
work and passed it on to Consuelo, both of them laughing
at me in their own language.

Now I needed to know what the knots said because
there was still no real evidence. It would take the actual
bags of white crystalline powder to make the case. Stump
had been clear about that. We were dealing with a physical
presence—small, light, easily concealed—and we had to
know how it got from one place to another. Cordilleras
wasn't handling anything that could carry the stuff, except
a few pots. Alberto had thought that approach unlikely.
Consuelo could use her personal luggage, but that would
be risky. Stump claimed that the customs inspectors went
over traveling business people, especially importers, with
special care.

Something to mull over, I thought wryly, *as I forge deeper
into the trackless jungle.* We had rounded a shelf of rock
and entered a smooth stretch of river. I could see a break
in the green wall along the bank, then a couple of thatch
roof peaks and a flag of smoke. Hermanito cut the outboard back to idle, and we nosed toward the bank. When

we coasted up on the sand, there was already a little wel-
coming party of Indian children.

"We stay here tonight," Hermanito said, and tossed the
section of tough vine that served as a bowline to one of
the taller boys. He stepped out of the canoe and began
lifting out our gear, handing it to the children to carry.
He had to speak sharply, not because they were not eager
to help, but because they stared so hard at me that they
kept stumbling or forgetting to move their feet. Whenever
I stared back, they broke into ear-to-ear grins, their teeth
as dazzling and unexpected as snow.

"They are Amuesha," Hermanito observed. "They don't
know anything. They have never been to Tingo María or
even Oxapampa."

A small boy of perhaps six was struggling along beside
me up the riverbank, bearing the flour sack that held our
yucca and oranges. He kept his face upturned to me in
adoration.

"They know enough to stay away from such places," I
said. "I didn't."

Hermanito didn't hear or didn't respond. He met a man
at the top of the bank and began a conversation in some
kind of pidgin. The man wore a shirt that was once white,
castoff fatigue pants, a Mickey Mouse wristwatch, and
sunglasses. He must have been the village leader since
everyone else was dressed in a kind of handwoven cotton
sack. Some people had blue tattoo lines on their cheeks,
or smears of a bright orange paint. They squatted around
small fires in front of their huts and regarded us indiffer-
ently, waiting for their chief to decide matters.

After a time Hermanito turned and walked over to me.
"He wants to know what gifts you have brought."

I shrugged. "Not much. Let me see." I rummaged
around in the handbag, taking care not to flash the little
revolver. I came up with my compact and flipped it open
to reveal the mirror. The man in sunglasses grunted ap-
provingly.

"Good." Hermanito presented the gift, and another

long conversation ensued. We moved to the split bamboo floor of a large house, while the children piled our gear in a smaller dwelling next door. Because the buildings had no walls, I had an unobstructed view of the village as Hermanito and El Presidente, as he called himself, continued their discourse.

A few yards away, in the last bars of light that filtered through the trees at the edge of the clearing, two women were sorting through a heap of uprooted bushes, stripping off the leaves into a pile. In front of other dwellings I could see a few similar piles, some of them as high as my waist. Hermanito saw my look and threw me one word aside.

"Coca."

A woman came then with two gourd bowls full of a thick purplish liquid. *"Masato,"* she said with a toothless smile, and made the gesture of drinking. It was sour stuff, with bits of fibrous pulp floating about, and obviously heavily fermented. After half a bowl I felt giddy and drowsy.

The light was fleeing the earth into the sky, the streamers of cloud beginning to ignite in salmon-pinks and shades of peach. With a few long feathers bound together a woman began to fan the coals into snapping flame. Then she propped an aluminum pot on the logs over the fire and stirred it with a wooden handle.

I heard a squawk from one of the chickens in our coop, then the ring of a machete against the gunwale of the canoe and a tremendous feathery commotion. Moments later a young man appeared with the carcass, already nude, and dismembered it into the pot.

When the soup was steaming, two girls served us portions in cheap crockery bowls. It was thick, salty, and very nourishing. The fowl went well with boiled yucca and plantains. After two bowlfuls and another of the delicious oranges, I felt consciousness caving in on me. The red tongue of the fire grew bright as the night deepened around it, and a tremendous clamor of frogs, birds, and insects came from the darkness. The soft, musical speech from the huts in the clearing washed me inexorably toward sleep. One of the girls plucked at my blouse, then took my hand and led me to a mat in a corner of the hut where Hermanito had rigged one of the mosquito nets.

"Sleep," I heard him call from beyond the fire. "Tomorrow we must walk far."

Chapter XXVIII

By the time I was shaken awake, the woman had again fanned up the fire. The dark hills around us rose into a gray mist, and the trees dripped. Hermanito had already repacked our things and stood with two other men, eating smoking ears of corn. He nodded at me and gestured toward the fire.

"Eat," he said. "We must leave soon, before the sun."

The two men beside him I had not seen the evening before. They were dressed in the baggy cotton garment, with a touch of orange on their broad cheeks. Their straight black hair had been hacked off over the eyes, but a long hank of it fell over their shoulders. When I had slipped on my sandals and straightened my blouse, I went to the fire and took one of the ears of roasted corn from a flat rock. While I gnawed at it, the men stared at my hips and broke into excited whispers.

Hermanito saw my displeasure and grinned at me. "It is your *pantalones*," he said. "They have never seen such clothes, especially on a woman. This is Carlos, and this is Andrés."

Hearing their Spanish names, both broke into loud laughter, their teeth large and perfectly white, a wild light in their eyes.

"Señorita Stella," I said, and offered my hand. They seized it in turn, gave it a tremendous shake, and were convulsed with mirth. In a few moments El Presidente, his wife, the two daughters, and some hangers-on assembled to join in the fun, and I had to shake everybody's hand, each time to wild acclaim. I could see neighbors on their way to join what had become a reception line.

"What's this about?"

Hermanito looked away. "I told them you were from the cinema."

"I *what?*"

"From California." He seized the flour sack and shoved the basket containing our mosquito nets at one of the men. "Some of them have been to the cinema in Tingo María. They have seen Señor Travolta and Señor Wayne. They think you know them. We had better go. Carlos and Andrés will guide us."

I struggled along through the village, shaking as many of the outthrust hands as I could, like a head of state. The children were crazy with delight, and even after we had left the last house and were moving down the trail, they ran after us, whooping. I turned to wave before we rounded a bend, and the whole village seemed to be there, their hands fluttering like a field of brown leaves.

Good-bye anonymity, hello, Hollywood. Not that the chance of my passing through unadvertised was very great anyway. Hermanito avoided my look and began explaining that we had to abandon the canoe but carry the motor, which the men had unbolted from the mounts and slung from a pole by means of tough vines. We took also our little sack of food, Hermanito's shotgun, and a bow and a half dozen arrows which Carlos had brought and insisted on keeping.

We had reached the top of the first ridge when Andrés stopped abruptly and lifted his head, nostrils flared.

"*Avión!*"

We listened intently. I could hear nothing. Then Carlos nodded and stuck a finger at the sky to the west.

"*Sí,*" he said excitedly. At last I heard it, a faint mosquito whine.

Hermanito looked at me and grimaced. "We go," he said shortly.

Hastily he and Andrés shouldered the pole again. Carlos took the shotgun and bow and arrows. I slung my handbag and the food sack across my back. We set off on the trail, now fainter where the jungle frothed over its edges.

"I hope it is the missionaries," Hermanito said. He looked worried. "If it is not so, I have already told El Presidente to be very hospitable to anybody for as long as he can. Much *masato*. Maybe dancing."

The plane was thundering in the sky behind us. We turned and saw a flash of light from the wings as it banked steeply. An amphibian, dropping swiftly toward the great eddy.

"No," said Hermanito grimly. "Not the people of Jesus."

When the plane disappeared below the treetops, the sound of its motor diminished suddenly, muffled. A few seconds later it stopped altogether, and I was conscious again of the sounds along the trail: the men puffing and grunting under their load, the slap of bare feet on the damp leaves, distant screeches, and liquid burblings from the trees. Soon the path constricted, and I had to bat away creepers and gigantic dangling leaves. Even with the light load I was soaked in sweat. No air moved in the dim green tunnel where we walked, and the men kept up a smooth, unflagging stride that was deceptively swift.

At the end of two hours Carlos wordlessly relieved me of the food sack, but an hour after that I was near collapse. I was a good walker in my own territory, but there I didn't have to dodge hanging vines, tree trunks with needle spines, and columns of ants. My trailmates finally stopped at the bank of a small stream and indicated that we would rest for a few minutes.

The water was clear and fresh. I soaked a handkerchief and spread it on my brow. We had climbed enough to intercept a light breeze, and the green gloom of the forest was broken by scatters of dancing sunlight. I leaned my back against a tree trunk, removed my mud-caked sandals, and twiddled my aching toes in the cool water. Hermanito, watching me, smiled regretfully.

"We must go soon," he said.

I sighed and closed my eyes. I was not able to care

much whether we went on forever or stayed here forever. Or so I thought. Then we heard voices.

In an instant the men were on their feet, listening. The trees had effectively masked the sound until they were almost upon us. Carlos seized his bow and arrows and jerked me to my feet. Hermanito and Andrés started to lift up the pole, but Andrés, staring back down the trail, hissed a few words and shook his head. Carlos was pushing me down the trail ahead of him, and in a second or two we were out of sight in the trees. I was running as fast as the narrow trail permitted.

Behind I heard a cry, then two shots. The first was the dull boom of Hermanito's shotgun; the second sounded like a two- or three-round burst from a light automatic weapon. Neither of us looked back. I ran after Carlos, a vanishing wraith in a green dream. I could hear nothing then but the blood pounding in my head. Twice he darted away on side trails, mere cracks in the dense wall of jungle, where the ground rose more steeply and I had to claw with my hands at roots and shrubs to haul myself along.

There was a red haze before my eyes, and the breath tore in and out of my lungs like a knife. It was a second or two before I realized that we had halted. Carlos held my arm lightly and cocked his head, listening. When my breathing slowed a little and I stopped shuddering, he nudged aside the bushes along the trail and stepped between them. I followed. A few feet off the trail he knelt down before what first appeared to be a great clump of grass. Then I saw it was a kind of tiny hut made of saplings bent into a hoop and covered with bunches of tough grass.

"*Chozita*," he whispered, and lifted a few tufts of the grass to reveal a dark opening. He motioned me inside. I had to lie flat to wriggle through, and after Carlos had climbed in after me, we were kneeling together, shoulder to shoulder, in complete darkness. He smelled like woodsmoke and sweat. In a moment I felt his hand, like a great, light insect, climbing to my face. Without words, by the touch of his fingers on my eyes and lips, he made me understand that I must make no sound or movement.

He tugged aside a handful of the grass, and a patch of light appeared. Through the little window I could see a portion of the trail, an opening between two huge tree trunks. Carlos raised the bow then and planted one tip of it on the floor. He slid an arrow through the window, nocked it on the bowstring, and drew it back until the tip was just inside the fringe of the hut's wall. I fumbled in my bag for the revolver and eased off its safety.

We waited then for a long time, breathing sometimes in unison, sometimes out of phase. Once or twice in the faint light through the opening in the wall he looked at me and each time gave me the same splendid, gleeful grin, as if this were the most entertaining of games. I managed to generate some sort of wan grimace, but I was hoping fervently that we would not have to face any machine guns from this grass tomb.

Then I heard Carlos's breathing change. It became slow and shallow, almost inaudible. There was what may or may not have been a foot brushing leaves. Against my shoulder I felt the muscles in Carlos's arm grow solid, and the bow bent smoothly, silently. I watched the tip of the arrow, a spike of hard black wood with nasty little barbs, begin to tremble slightly with the strain. An arm and shoulder appeared in the gap between the tree trunks, then a head and torso. The head was swathed in a dirty bandage sprinkled with bits of leaf. It was Gutierez, for once not stylish, his boots mud-spattered and his shirt open at the throat and dark with sweat. One hand rested on the holster at his belt.

He paused, framed by the trees, and bent at the waist to examine the ground. He frowned. His eyes raked the trail ahead, found something. He straightened and turned, his glance probing the underbrush, until he faced us directly. The hand closed over the butt of the automatic.

There was a sudden hiss and a rattling of leaves as

something swift as a bat sped from our little window. The bow was thrumming, unflexed, in Carlos's grip. I saw the arrow sprout from Gutierez's chest. He looked at it dumbly. Then he assumed an expression of pettish anger and uttered a small, retching cough. He plucked at the shaft with the fingers of both hands, reeling a little, before he remembered his gun. He jerked at the flap of the holster, cursing and coughing at the same time. A pink froth dribbled from one corner of his mouth.

Carlos flashed me his insane grin and slid another arrow across the bow. In a single smooth motion he drew; the point did its tiny dance for a moment, and then the leaves shook again. A second deadly reed with its feather flower sprang from the base of the throat. Gagging, Gutierez let go of the gun butt, and the automatic tumbled into the grass. He fell to his knees and seized the shaft, jerking it back and forth. His mouth opened and emitted a burst of blood. Then he fell over on his side, and his legs thrashed in the undergrowth, as if he were trying to run horizontally.

We didn't move. At last the running became only a feeble pawing and then stopped altogether. I hadn't realized it took so long to die. The sounds of the forest came back: A bird whooped at a distance, a fly buzzed, and a branch creaked. Carlos waited. I noticed he had a third arrow hooked on the bowstring. He yawned. I tried to concentrate on telling my mind not to cramp at the images that had just been burned into it.

We heard a rustling, a few heavy footsteps, then a low exclamation. Another figure appeared in the hole in our wall, a soldier with a submachine gun. He was staring at the heap of Gutierez, his mouth slightly agape. I raised the revolver, but Carlos nudged me aside with his shoulder.

"Señor," the soldier whispered, "qué pasó?"

Inside the hut Carlos's arm contracted and the bow curved taut. I could see the soldier's throat pulse once as he tried to swallow. His eyes flitted back and forth between

Gutierez, the trail, the treetops, and his gun. I could hear the fly buzzing again, and the soldier lifted one hand from his weapon and batted at his ear. Then his eyes widened, and all at once he stepped back. We could hear his boots thumping rapidly down the trail the way he had come.

Carlos unflexed the bow gently and sighed. *"Vamos,"* he said, and pushed the grass away from the door.

I wriggled out the opening, gasping a little because I hadn't bothered to breathe for some time. It felt wonderful to be able to move freely again. And move we did. We left Gutierez to the ants and struck off up the trail. Now Carlos seldom looked back to check on my progress and went like a snake between and over trees. I plunged along grimly, striving to keep him in sight.

We crossed the ridge top, and for a moment the sea of undulating hills was visible all around. To the west they rose higher, turning dark blue in the distance, losing their heads in the clouds, but toward the east they smoothed and dropped, becoming finally only a smeared green line on the horizon. At the bottom of the ridge I caught sight of a bend or two of the small river. Carlos allowed himself a great deep laugh and one whoop, and then he began to bound down the hill.

Chapter XXIX

There was a village on the bank of the river at the end of our trail, and Carlos succeeded in securing the only canoe and guide available. Hermanito had evidently explained to him that I wanted to go to Pucallpa, and he intended to see that I got there. The obligation endured whether or not Hermanito was alive to enforce it.

We shared perhaps two dozen words in Spanish, so all I could do to express gratitude was to hand Carlos one of my remaining thousand-sole bills and point to his arrows, saying, *"Bueno, bueno."* He grinned hugely at both gestures and made a considerable speech to me in his own language. I gathered from the motions he made that the sight of me trying to progress through the jungle was one of the highest forms of entertainment he had ever experienced.

We shook hands, and I climbed in the canoe, smaller than Hermanito's but with a newer engine. An old man with a dour squirrel's face handled the tiller and his teenage son lay in the prow to keep an eye out for shallows or snags. They barely acknowledged my presence, and as soon as Carlos had pushed us off, they roared away full throttle without a backward look.

The Aguaytía was a narrow and often swift stream, very thinly populated. That suited me. And I never had to urge the pilot to hurry. Even through and around rapids we held to a fierce, unrelenting tempo. We stopped only once to take on fuel in army-issue five-gallon tins, near sundown, and we ate cold fish and mangos crouched in the driving canoe. In his broken Spanish the old man told me the river would soon widen and there would be half a moon for the night. We could continue if I wished.

So we set our backs to the sunset and bored down the river, now a sheet of hammered metal brighter than the sky it reflected. The banks drew farther away after a time, and the surface was calm as a pond when the moon rose. The hills had also vanished, and I could see only a rank of trees dark on the horizon. Riding the track of light that glittered on the water, I sighed and dreamed and dozed and mused, drinking relief from the cool wind, able for a few hours to lose track of where I was, who I was, what I had to do. A river seemed to offer the only haven, yet a river was forever moving, taking me somewhere, running out like the sand in an hourglass.

I thought I had been trapped inside glass, the sand pouring down, choking me, while Gutierez and Manuel and someone else I couldn't place laughed at me from outside the clear walls and thumped on them. But it was the sound of boats rubbing against a dock and the dust in the air. I was pulling myself groggily out of the bilge-water that soaked my blouse and jeans. The old man had been standing on the dock, rocking the boat with his foot to wake me.

"Señorita," he said, "Pucallpa."

On one side the river stretched away for miles, opaque as chocolate, with a fringe of trees on the horizon no thicker than a pencil line. On the other, on the muddy bank, staggered a loose line of shacks, derelict boats, and clearings heaped with coffee sacks, bananas, and crates. Platforms of weathered and rotten wood protruded into the water, docks where men swarmed. A road ran along the top of the bank and trucks, taxis, and jeeps thundered there, raising a fog of brown dust that drifted over the quay. The hubbub didn't seem to bother two vultures, enormous black hulks that perched on a half-submerged crate beside the canoe. When I moved, they flapped their dark wings in disgust and lifted away.

"Gracias," I said, and heaved myself to my feet. The teen-age boy handed me my bag. I groped inside and

verified that the important items were there: gun, passport, wallet, and five shawls. The old man and the boy gave me a final expressionless stare and turned their attention to the precious motor, now propped on the dock and partially dismantled.

I made my way up the bank, dodging the workers with their loads, to the edge of the road. I was getting a lot of stares, and when a truck paused for a turn, I got a glimpse of myself in its dusty window and saw why. Two days of jungle travel had left me stained and disheveled. It wasn't the face of a tourist anymore. I had the lines and tight lips of somebody who has seen too much.

I decided I would risk a hotel, take a bath, and have my clothes washed before I approached the problem of getting a message to Webster or finding transportation to Lima. A taxi swerved out of line and stopped for me. The driver nodded when I asked for a small place, not too expensive but with hot water. From the moment I settled onto the frayed back seat and the muffler rattled underneath me, I began to drift toward sleep. The dead brown earth of the streets, crowded with vehicles and people, blurred into my memory of the river, and the hotel was like a smaller and dingier version of the Turístico, as if time had done nothing but shrink and wear things.

I signed in, went to my room, stripped, showered, piled my dirty clothes in the hall for the maid, and put the shawls and the gun under my pillow. Then sleep came like a slammed door.

The door opened again at seven thirty in the morning. I had gone under for eighteen hours. My clothes were on a chair, fresh and folded, smelling of strong yellow soap. I climbed into them, dashed lukewarm water from the tap into my eyes, and brushed out my hair. In the mirror I looked sunburned and dazed, ten pounds underweight, and in need of a vacation. But I was already on vacation. Wasn't I? This vacation was killing me.

The problem was now simple. I had to get out of the country with the shawls. There was a chance that the *capitán* in Tingo María did not have a long enough arm to reach me here, and I could simply take the next plane. If, on the other hand, the police were waiting for me to show up, I would be trapped neatly at the airport. Perhaps it would be better to wire Webster in Huaraz—if he was still there—and depend on his embassy connections to get us out of any such trap. But that could take time. I decided I would try casing the airport first.

However, the solution to the problem was at the desk when I dropped off the key. This solution was a butter-blond young man with eyes like the sky over Nebraska and freckles everywhere.

"Well, howdy, howdy," he said. "Bet you're Amer'cun, right?"

He was checking out of his room, too, I could see by the flight bag in his hand. But he wasn't dressed like an ordinary tourist. He wore jeans and a crisp white shirt with sleeves rolled up, as if there were a Saturday night dance to go to.

"Right."

"California?"

"Right again."

"I knew it. Just knew it. California gals got a certain *look*." He ducked his head, shy at having made so bold a remark.

"So do missionaries."

He blushed between the freckles. "You got me dead to rights. Yes'm. I fly for God."

"I beg your pardon?"

He smiled with shy pride. "I'm a missionary pilot, ma'am."

The Summer Bible Institute of Linguistics had its own hangar and mechanics at the other end of the runway from the main airport, so there was no difficulty with police. By nine o'clock I was sitting in the copilot's seat while Mike flipped switches and gunned the engines. Jesus, in three colors, regarded me soulfully from above the windscreen.

"Ma'am!" Mike shouted above the roar of the feathering propellers. "You know any prayers?"

I shook my head. The plane eased into motion and began a slow jouncing over the runway.

"I shore need all the help I can get." The roar of motors began to climb in pitch. "We got a float valve in the starboard carburetor that's been mighty cranky. God's gotta put a shoulder under that wing! You join on in if you can." He closed his eyes while the plane paused at the end of the strip, rocking and straining at its brakes. His lips were moving fervently.

The plane looked old to me, and much used. There were dark streaks of oil fanning out of the cowling on the engines and an occasional flick of blue fire from the exhaust.

God, I thought, concentrating on the mysterious nest of wires and tubes that I knew was hidden behind the aluminum skin, *put your big shoulder under that wing. Bless our float valves. I'm sorry I never believed in you much.*

Mike released the brake, and the plane lumbered forward. Faster and faster the asphalt rushed beneath us. There was a heart-stopping hiccup from the starboard engine; then the whole frame shuddered, and I felt us lift. God raised us on his broad, invisible back, the rooftops and trees flashing by below.

"Whoopee!" Mike yelled, and gave me a wide grin. "His will be done!"

It was a fast trip, during which I heard about a tight end's fakes, the crime rate in Omaha, the childishness of the Indians, and God's designs. For myself I contrived an identity as a student of anthropology and showed Mike one of the shawls. There were some bad bumps climbing again over the white fangs of the Andes, but then we made the smooth drop to the coast in what Mike claimed was record time. A few minutes more over the wrinkled, dun moonscape of the western slopes, and the thin blue line of the Pacific came into view.

When we banked finally over the great, sprawling city,

I borrowed a handkerchief from Mike to blow my nose and wipe my eyes.

"Altitude?"

I nodded. It was a lie. It was sentiment. A decade seemed to have elapsed since I had first seen this city tilt through the window of a descending airplane. I still had to get out of the place, and it might not be easy to do, but I was a long step closer. The shawls were in my handbag, I had Alberto's address in my book, and I figured Webster would be checking regularly at the embassy for word of me.

Mike was surprised at the fervent gratitude in my otherwise ladylike embrace. He ducked his head, red-faced, and patted the old plane, still warm and giving off mysterious metallic groans.

"She's a mighty good old boat."

"Thank the float valves, and God, and, most of all, the pilot."

"Shucks," he said. He really did. "You get in touch if you need any help."

"I'll do that." I picked up my bag, stowed in it the scrap of paper with his address and number on it, and turned toward the terminal.

"Good luck in your researches," Mike called after me. "Hope you figure out them knots."

I waved over my shoulder. I hoped so too.

Chapter XXX

Alberto greeted me at the door of his house with kisses on each cheek. His mother gave me a decorous squeeze, and then the two of them stepped back to survey me closely. After a moment Mamacita clucked, shook her head, and said, *"Flaca, flaca."* She retreated to the kitchen, and I heard the bang of cabinet doors and the clang of pots.

Alberto also looked concerned. "You need weights."

"I need more than that." I walked to the table, pulled the shawls from my handbag, and spread them out. "Do you understand these?"

He pursed his mouth and bent to examine the fabric. "A little." After a moment he reached out to finger the knotted fringes. "Ah."

"You showed me that in your museum."

"Of course. But these quipus do not belong on a manta of this style." He shrugged. "It is like, perhaps like"—he blinked—"potatoes and champagne."

"Lechuga, you have a gift for words."

"You are an inspiration. Bringing such strange things. How do you say it—what has been up?"

"Maybe you can read the message there and tell me."

He shook his head. "It is a special art. I know the quipus are mostly for numbers, keeping accounts. But the colors and styles of knot also have significance. However, I have a friend. . . ."

I closed my eyes and expelled a long breath of relief.

"This is important?"

"Very."

"Tell me."

It was time for unburdening myself a little. I sketched in the situation for Alberto while Mamacita served us thick slices of torte and fresh coffee. The soup, she said with a disapproving look at my midsection, would be coming soon. The *traficantes* I was pursuing, I said, had perfected a system of passing information through the ancient method of knotted cords, which were attached as fringes to regular shipments of goods. I needed to have them deciphered, so I could take them back as evidence. There was still the problem of how the contraband was shipped, where it was hidden and who got it, but the messages in the cloth might provide some answers.

"Admirable." Alberto shook his head. "There cannot be more than three or four persons in your country who could begin to understand such matters. But Ramón may know who they are."

"Your friend is an archaeologist?"

Alberto laughed. "Ramón is many things. He was my teacher in medical school. Physiology. But he knows our country's peoples and their ways. Also, he has traveled everywhere, collected everything. When we have had our soup, I will call to him and arrange the meeting."

Ramón lived in a tiny flat on the edge of Miraflores, a den lined with jaguar hides, carved war clubs, and baskets. Books were scattered everywhere, and on a table I saw a small microscope and lamp. Ramón himself resembled a miniature rhinoceros. He was completely bald, and his mahogany bullet head grew into a thick neck set on a squat, powerful frame. He ushered us directly to the table with the microscope, apologizing somewhat gruffly for his informal attire—a velvet dressing gown and a cigarette in an ivory holder. He went over one of the shawls quickly with his fingers, jotting a few notes on a pad, and then examined one of the strands of knots under the glass.

Finally he looked up with a smile. "But, Alberto, you should be pouring us a drink. The Amaretto. Our friend from the United States will think we are barbarians." He shut off the light under the microscope, and both frowned and smiled at me at the same time.

"Madam, this is a curious piece of work, as Alberto promised. The fringes, the quipus, have nothing to do with the shawls. They are ordinary work. Quite new. The style of the quipus is a peculiar mixture of the modern and the old Inca."

"Like potatoes and champagne."

He laughed, and I bowed a little toward Alberto, who was pouring clear liqueur from a decanter into tiny yellowed glasses.

"Of course, my friend does make some interesting combinations of English words. I speak somewhat better. That is, duller. Now." He put his hands on his knees and tilted the dome of his skull toward me. "Alberto has explained that the matter is sensitive, so I ask you no questions. Certain things I already know. You found these pieces in Tingo María. By canoe you traveled, probably Pucallpa. The boatman was a coca dealer. Then you came by private plane to Lima."

I glanced at Alberto, who had put one of the tiny glasses in my hand, but he shook his head.

"I told him nothing."

"You are right about everything so far," I said. "Amazing. You know—"

"You are going to say I am Sherlock Holmes. No?"

I laughed. "Right again. I'm sure it's obvious. But all the fun is in telling poor Watson how it was done."

"It is very simple. Anyone who knows the market could spot these things from the María Magdalena Convent in Tingo. But you see how the bottom of your bag is stained with water? A canoe that leaks a little. Also, you are burned by the sun even under your chin—because the light is reflected from a river. Here on this shawl I found a flake of coca leaf—surely not your vice—so it must be a boat rented from a *regatón* who hauls the crop. Where would you be coming from? Pucallpa is the nearest large airport, and you must have flown because the water stains and the sunburn are very recent. But the companies have only two flights from Pucallpa each day, and the first had not even arrived when Alberto called me." He reached out with the glass and clinked it against mine. "Hence it was a private machine."

"Up the bottoms," said Alberto. We drank.

"That was remarkable," I said. "I wish I had time to discuss my whole situation with you. But if you can tell me about the quipus, it will be a tremendous help."

Ramón's eyelids lowered. He was holding the liqueur on his tongue, savoring it. He sighed. "A great misfortune. I call tell you the numbers, of course, because it is a perfect numerical system—readable by touch as well as by sight. But many of the other knots may be arbitrary in value. The Incas were not consistent in assigning meaning to certain combinations. Much depended on context."

"So?" I put down the glass.

His eyes snapped open again, and he smiled quickly at Alberto. "They are so direct, the Americans. Even the women."

"Sorry," I said. "I don't have a lot of time. I wish I did. But . . ."

"Of course." He went to the table quickly and spread out the shawls again. "But I do warn you that I can tell you only the numbers and the traditional significance of certain colors and patterns." He picked up his pencil and began making notes. From time to time he gave a grunt of interest or surprise. Alberto and I had a second drink, dawdled around the room examining Ramón's collections, flipped through some magazines from a stand. Finally Ramón folded up the shawls and sat studying the pad on his knee.

I cleared my throat, and he glanced at me. "Go ahead, think out loud. Maybe Watson can be of help."

He laughed. "You are smarter than old Watson, madam. Also more beautiful. So. Apparently these messages have an order. The first begins with salutations from the Inca—the king—to a vassal. Then there is an ac-

knowledgment of tribute received and what is I think a
date. The tribute is six of something and two of something
else. Six white threads, two of blue. Do you know what
these could be?"

I thought for a moment. "Let's call them snow and
horses."

"Horses?" Ramón and Alberto exchanged a startled
look.

"We have to call them something."

He shrugged and went on. "The date is 14–3–82. I assume that is according to our calendar. March fourteenth."

I nodded. "Reasonable."

"Then there is a number, by a new system, I believe.
The Incas seldom had need of amounts larger than a few
thousand, but the quipus are a decimal system and may
be manipulated to express much higher sums. We have
here a hundred twenty thousand, apparently as a gift from
the king to the vassal. The vassal's sign, curiously, is a war
club."

He paused, but I didn't want to intrude a guess yet. The
amount was too low to represent profit, but it could be
the crumbs that had to be thrown to the revolutionaries
by the "king."

"Then there is an indication of a certain lapse of days
and nights—alternate silver and black knots—and then a
cluster which means travel to the provinces."

"How much time?"

"Thirty-seven days."

"That would be . . . about April twenty-first." I got the
first little electric shock of recognition. It was the day our
party had flown from San Francisco. "Who was doing the
traveling?"

"That is interesting. It appears to be a petty chief. Or
his representative. A member of the Inca class. But after
this symbol is the knot that usually means 'beware' or
'watch and guard' and often accompanies a mission which
the king does not entirely trust."

Zwicky, I thought.

"Next there is a demand for new tribute. This time it is eight units of the snow." He smiled. "No horses."

I raised my hand to interrupt him and turned to Alberto. "Could you do something for me?"

"Of course. I try."

"A phone call. You must have a port authority—a commission in charge of regulating commercial sea traffic. Would you check it for arrivals of ships belonging to the TransPac-Orient Line during the last three months?"

The Owl rose swiftly with a flap and a blink and hooked the phone from a niche in the wall. As he dialed, I signaled Ramón to continue.

"Very quick as well as direct," he said. "Now again here is an interesting thing. The other two shawls are almost duplicates. After a greeting from the war club to the king, they repeat a confirmation of the demand for tribute, the eight snows, and promise to deliver it by April twenty-seventh. Then there is a sign for sending a messenger very far, out of the domain. The tribute goes with this messenger, who is apparently not a chief but a commoner."

"April twenty-seventh is tomorrow," I said. "When does this messenger go?"

"There is one black, one silver thread. The next evening I should estimate. Who is this commoner?"

I shook my head. "No idea. What else?"

"The number two, associated with the symbol for the llama, as the beast of burden, and a group, seven-one-four. I have it written here." He tore the sheet from his note pad and handed it to me. "Then the two become different. On one there is the knot signifying the royal seal, which usually ends a string and makes it authentic. It is the knot done by the king's agent in the provinces. There should be another date here, but it is missing. Then there is a cluster making another large number—one hundred seventy-five thousand—and all the threads are red, which declares that immediate vengeance will be taken if the price is not paid. All this is missing from the other shawl."

"I have made the call," Alberto interrupted. He consulted a slip of paper in his hand. "On February twenty-sixth the ship *Conquistador* docked in Lima with ironware from Taiwan. Another one, the *China Girl,* will arrive in a week, they believe. There is a berth reserved."

"Thank you," I said. Ramón and Alberto looked at each other, then at me. "I think it means there were no horses to send with the messenger. Horses come from the Far East."

Ramón smiled and frowned again. "Then you are beginning to understand?"

"A little, I think."

It seemed downright straightforward. The two identical shawls were a bookkeeping method, an original for confirming shipment of an order and demanding a "gift" for the growers and shippers and their guerrilla organization. A copy for the record, probably kept in Lima. Apparently the local suppliers were trying to squeeze out a bigger share, fifty-five thousand more. It wasn't much, if the units were kilograms of cocaine and heroin. I didn't have an expert's grasp of the market, but I could figure out from Stump's estimate that twenty pounds of coke were worth around a million on the street.

The problem was, as Ramón indicated, that the quipus had to be assigned a symbolic value. The dates and numbers might be suggestive, but they were useless without the hard evidence of contraband.

"You are troubled by complications?" Ramón had been watching my face carefully. He inserted a fresh cigarette in his holder and lit it. The smooth mahogany head sprouted a mushroom of smoke. "I do not wish to pry, but allow me to speculate."

"Do."

"You have intercepted a message. But you understand only part of it. The most important part is still dark."

"True." The dark portion was the identity of the messenger, the commoner, and the riddle of the numbers 2 and 714.

"So our problem is to throw light on this mystery."

"It is."

He smoked and mused. Alberto swiveled his owl's face from one to the other of us expectantly, and the jaguars on the walls regarded all of us with frozen grins.

"Well," I said finally, "intercepted messages don't mean everything until they arrive."

"Yes!" Ramón laughed aloud. "Very good. Now I am Watson. But how do you deliver them?"

"Not in person. They must believe their secret is safe, that no one knows of the messenger and his tribute."

"So we must have a plausible accident."

"That's how I see it. Somehow I lost them, and they are recovered by someone innocent."

Ramón puffed rapidly on the cigarette, his forehead gnarled in thought. "It is basically incredible that just these three mantas should be found."

"I took the precaution of mixing in two duds."

"Duds?" Alberto looked baffled.

"Placebos." Ramón smiled. "That was a remarkable bit of foresight."

"And since one of these is a copy, we can keep it."

"Excellent. Only two of four then. But how do you explain their appearance? This is a question of human psychology. Alberto, you should help us here. This is your field."

"You have come from the jungle," Alberto said. "And you say the shawls must be found by an innocent. There are many innocents in the jungle. But you need one who can fly. Here to Lima—where there are very few innocents—and he must know to take the things where you want them. So he must speak your language, no?"

"Difficult!" Ramón shook his head. "An English-speaking innocent from the jungle."

"Difficult," I said, "but not impossible."

They looked at me, detecting the relish in my voice.

"A man of God."

"Ah!" Ramón clapped his hands, and the report was sharp as a gunshot in the small room. "You flew with the missionaries, the *lingüistas*! Perfect. My dear, it is perfect."

"I will have to convince the pilot to tell a little lie for me."

Ramón gave me a level look. "You could convince a man of many things."

"That's nice of you to say. But a Nebraska missionary would be a great challenge even for Mata Hari."

"How will he have chanced across these shawls? That is the thing hard to believe."

"Suppose I gave them to him. It would be proof that I didn't know what the quipus were for."

"But why would you give them away?"

I shrugged. "It could be for a flight—to Pucallpa, say. From some village upriver."

"Very good. Probably if they checked closely, they would know you were in Pucallpa yesterday."

"It's worth a try." I nodded to Alberto, and we rose to go. "Thanks. A million thanks, as we say, but that isn't enough."

"My pleasure." Ramón handed me the shawls and bowed. "I regret only that I cannot see how your plan will bear fruit."

"I regret that I won't have Sherlock to give me advice."

He smiled. "I am not clear about who is the Sherlock."

He shook hands all around, and Alberto and I left.

Chapter XXXI

"He has bothered us a great deal," the woman said. Her receptionist's manner had worn through to petty irritation. "You are supposed to leave a number and he will reach you within two hours. He calls *us* every two hours."

"I prefer he waits there for my call," Alberto said fiercely. "One thirty. Remember it is about the silver fizzes at Sam's."

"But—"

"You are the American Embassy, is this so? Mr. Webster is an American, an important American. Give him my message." Alberto hung up with a crash.

"Excellent." I grinned at him. "You sounded more like a tiger than an owl."

He looked doubtful. "You are sure he will understand?"

"Very sure. Webster and I used to go sailing on his yacht and end up at Sam's in Sausalito, famous for its gin fizzes."

"What will he do then?"

"When you get him at the embassy, arrange to meet him in a place you know. Then you take him back here—without being followed."

Alberto nodded and blinked several times. "I like this. Am I now a spy?"

"Sort of. But don't worry. Webster is harmless. He may be crazy to find out what's happened to me, but he'll come quietly."

I picked up my new sunglasses and hat, walked to the hall mirror, and took a look. In a cheap dress Mamacita had lent me, with my sunburn fading, I didn't look so much like a tourist.

"Don't worry about me," I said to Alberto. "I'll be back as soon as I drop these off. Or plant them, as we say." I took the plain shopping bag full of mantas and eased out the door.

I was taking the four shawls to lovable Mike. He had been asleep when I called the mission center to tell him I desperately needed his assistance in a personal matter. "Shoot," he said. "You bet." The story I had concocted would strain the credibility of a five-year-old child, but I had noticed that in the presence of girls Mike could regress at least that far. The important thing was to swear him to secrecy. On the cross. If I managed that, I was safe. A Roman interrogation squad couldn't get it out of him.

At the Summer Bible Institute of Linguistics I was shown into a garden courtyard by an apple-cheeked matron who looked as if she had just stepped off the porch of a midwestern wheat farm and who told me pleasantly that she was completing her twenty-second year of service in the field. Mike was waiting in the courtyard and greeted me with a tremendous blush and a bone-crushing handshake. The matron looked curious and suspicious but finally dawdled out of the garden with the promise to return with tea before long.

"Gee," said Mike. "You look different."

"You too." He now wore a Hawaiian sport shirt and gabardine slacks.

"Well"—he gestured stiffly toward a couple of wicker chairs—"I sure want to help if I can."

I sat down and faced him with an expression of troubled earnestness. Blurting a little, I spun out the tale. I had acquired a few tapestries, somewhat illicitly, from a convent in Tingo María. I took them only to study them and make drawings and notes, and now I wanted to return them. They were a little water-stained and had picked up a few burs, but there was no serious damage. But if I were identified as the scholar who had taken these items, my career might be ruined. A young life blighted. Tears gathered in my eyes, and my lip trembled.

I wanted someone trustworthy to take the shawls to the office of a California import firm here in Lima. He could tell the people there that a peculiar young woman had given them to him for a flight to Pucallpa from some village on the Ucayali and that he had suspected they were stolen. A knowledgeable person informed him that goods from that area were handled by the California firm. Except for the changed flight plan and the omission of my name, the story was true. But no one must know that the young woman was now in Lima. The people in the office might be very curious about her whereabouts. He would have to insist that he had left her in Pucallpa.

Mike squirmed. "Golly Jehoshaphat," he said, addressing his feet. "I don't know. That's sort of fibbing."

"Only very little. You *did* see me in Pucallpa. And I *am* giving you the shawls."

"But if they ask me where you are right now?" He searched my face with his innocent sky-blue eyes.

"You can say you don't know because I won't tell you."

"Stella, are you in some kind of trouble?"

I looked away and bit my lip. "Please don't ask." There was a considerable pause.

"Gee. I dunno."

"Mike," I said, burying a little sob in the word and reaching to take his hand, "I'm trying to do right, to give something back that I shouldn't have taken. Wouldn't God want that?"

"If you could do it yourself, you'd feel better." He looked reproachful.

"No, I wouldn't. I won't do it at all then." I took my hand back and seized the shawls, making as if to go.

"That wouldn't be right!" There was agony in his voice. "All right. Okay. I guess there can be little lies that are better than stealing."

"Promise?"

He hesitated.

"On the Bible?"

He expelled a breath and gave a single sharp jerk of the head. "On the Bible."

"Oh, thank you!" I smothered him in an embrace. "Now I'm going, before you argue or try to convert me. The address of the office is on a slip inside the bag. Burn the slip after you know the number. I'll never forget you, Mike." I gave him another hug and fled, brushing by the matron, who was watching us, amazed, the steaming tea tray in her hand.

"Stella, Stella! I was crazy with worry!"

Webster was talking through my hair, where he had jammed his face. "I thought—I thought everything! You were lost or hurt or dead or—"

"I might get hurt if you don't let up. I hear ribs cracking." I worked my two hands up to his chest and managed to push him back a step. Alberto, standing to one side, coughed politely.

"Right. I'm sorry." Webster released his grip and ran a hand through his hair. He looked like a man who had not slept or shaved or bathed for days. An improvement, in my opinion. "But when Zwicky started dogging me, claiming you had stolen some sort of tapestry and run away, I didn't know where to start. Every guard station in the eastern jungle is looking for you, you know."

"I hope so. As long as they don't know I'm here, it's all right. You've got to keep up your act at the embassy now. Checking every two hours. Be frantic. Angry. And so forth."

"Why?" Webster was aggrieved. "What the hell is going on? You're through with Zwicky. Why can't we go to the Galápagos and why all the secrecy? The gin fizzes?"

"A lot of reasons, Web. But for the time being you've got to pretend you didn't find me. Especially right now. In an hour or two Zwicky won't care about me because he'll get his precious shawls back. Then, if we're lucky, they'll go back to business as usual."

"And send the messenger." Alberto cocked his head at me. "The commoner. Do you have an idea yet?"

"Not yet." I sank down in a chair. I was fresh out of ideas. Ideas depended on ifs. If Caswell bought Mike's tale, they would think I was out of commission, hundreds of kilometers away in Pucallpa, and they would think I had never understood the meaning of the quipus. If their code was safe, they might go through with the schedule, and on April 28 the mysterious commoner would join two beasts of burden to walk 714 leagues. Or 714 beasts of burden would walk 2 leagues, carrying one commoner apiece. Or none of the above.

"What's the matter?" Webster leaned over me, looking concerned.

"I'm exhausted. I can't think. Except for two things. Alberto can explain where we are at the moment and about the shawls. There are more of them at the Inter-American Business Institute, I suspect. Copies. Probably at Cordilleras in San Francisco, too. Alberto has an astute friend, Ramón. The three of you figure out a way to get those shawls." I closed my eyes.

"And the second thing?"

"Oh, yes. Get me a reservation on a flight to San Francisco tomorrow night."

"Tomorrow?"

"Yeah." My own voice sounded far away already. "I want to be there when he arrives."

"Who?"

"The messenger. The king's messenger."

Webster tried again, but I turned away, nuzzling into the chair. I was asleep before he got to the question mark.

Chapter XXXII

I woke to a bright morning coming through tatters of night fog. Someone had pushed me into the bedroom, and I had managed to undress and climb between the sheets. It was exquisite to stretch and yawn and peek out the window at the children playing under the trees in the park next door. The street was empty except for a few fruit vendors and a slow, grumbling bus. It was a pleasant neighborhood. A safe place, finally, on my last morning in Lima.

I was wrong about that.

After a hesitant tap on the door Mamacita came in with a tray of coffee and fresh, fragrant bananas. After I had propped myself up on pillows and worked my way through the first cup, Webster and Alberto peered around the doorway.

"We thought you might have a coma," Alberto said.

"No, I'm conscious. Come in."

They entered. Alberto took a chair, and Webster sat himself gingerly on the bed.

"We know how to get the shawls." Alberto looked immensely proud. He had combed the twin curls of gray hair that flanked his spectacles and had put on a suit and tie. "Ramón has contacts at the Ministry of Health. There is an ordinance that requires shipments of plant or animal substances to be inspected. This is usually for feathers and orchids and such affairs. But the dyes in the mantas are from plants. For a consideration"—he bowed respectfully toward Webster—"the people will impound everything in the office for inspection."

"Only five hundred dollars," Webster said wonderingly. "And the confiscation is good for thirty days. Is that enough?"

"Plenty." I smiled at them, feeling like the queen rewarding her courtiers. "That is very fine work, *lechuga*."

"When do you wish this to happen?" Alberto poised, ready to move for the door. "Your spy is prepared."

"In two days. I'll call you from San Francisco."

"Oh, yes." Webster dug in his pocket and produced an envelope. "Your reservation for tonight." He flipped open the envelopes and scanned the ticket.

"What time? I need to shop for a dress and a wig."

Webster and Alberto exchanged a look.

"A disguise. Not vanity."

"Eight forty-five. Braniff." He glanced again at the ticket. "Flight seven fourteen. We can get together after your shopping trip and talk over your plans. I'll take us to dinner."

He waited, but neither of us spoke. He looked quickly at me, then at Alberto. "Anything wrong?"

"So it was simple," Alberto said. "I was thinking it would be something very mysterious. Flight seven fourteen."

"Me too." I flung back the covers and swung my feet to the floor. "If you gentlemen will excuse me, I'm going to get dressed."

"What is so simple?" Webster stood up, his look beseeching.

"Numbers," I said. "Webster, change that reservation to tomorrow night, same time, same flight. It has to be the same. Seven-one-four. No other. Do what you have to to get me on it."

"But—"

Alberto took him by the arm. "I will explain," he said gently. "The commoner with the tribute is traveling on that plane tomorrow."

Webster backed through the door, his expression full of the pain of incomprehension.

* * *

April 28, 6:00 P.M. Jorge Chávez International Airport. Alberto and I sat in the small café on the mezzanine above the lobby, where I could see the Braniff counter. We looked, I hoped, like a couple. I balanced a blond wig and my sunglasses and kept a folded-out section of *El Comercio* in front of my face. Mamacita had laid down a dark powder base over my fading sunburn, so I might pass for a Latin at least from a distance. For the next two hours our task was to watch everyone who checked in for Flight 714 and ask ourselves if he or she or it was the messenger.

"Of course," Alberto said glumly, "we cannot see their faces from up here."

I took a sip of my soft drink. "It's possible when the shawls turned up, they suspected a trap and called off the whole thing."

"Possible? Perhaps you mean 'likely.' "

"I don't go that far. If the delivery was on time, they have nine kilos of cocaine around their necks and they will want to move it."

"Around their necks?"

"A metaphor."

"Ah." After a pause he said, "You think they believed your friend the missionary?"

"He would be easy to believe."

"Then you will be getting on this plane with the messenger and his cargo. If he spots you, it may be dangerous."

"It's already dangerous."

He looked even glummer and returned to his reading. I tried to make a game out of picking out suspects from the steady stream of people moving through the lobby. It was like all airport lobbies: cavernous, cold, with hard surfaces everywhere—hard counters and hard faces. Some Australian youths went by under their soiled backpacks. A woman with a child on a leash. Two mechanics in jump suit overalls. A couple of middle-aged American hippies decked out in turquoise and faded ponchos.

I sighed. No one looked likely. Or everyone did. The Australians might have it in their backpacks, disguised as sugar. The hippies might put it in guitar cases. It was all equally possible. Equally absurd.

"At least we will have the shawls." Alberto brightened a little. "It is nice that your friend has money. Here money can do almost anything."

"Without the messenger and his snow, the shawls won't be of much use." I saw his face fall and hurried to correct myself. "But if we can find the shipment, the shawls will be very important. You and Ramón have been wonderful. And Webster, too. Poor man."

"He was most unhappy that he could not come. But of course, the two of you would be conspicuous. With me you are quite ordinary."

I smiled, knowing he meant well.

The minutes crawled by. Finally the airline clerks in their matching saffron coats began to bustle behind the counter. A family got in line first. They were Americans: all fat, all with glasses, their bags of expensive leather covered with stickers from a dozen countries. I dismissed them. I also dismissed the two honeymooners who came next. And the five teen-age California surfers after that.

Alberto shook his head mournfully.

Then I heard a familiar voice. Loud, carrying through the lobby and up the stairs and across the balcony right to our table.

"Where you want me and the missus to stand? Over by that there window would be kinda nice, wouldn't it? We could hold up these whatchamajig award things."

Then a cluster of people came into view, two or three photographers and a man with a portable television camera strapped to his shoulder. They were turning various knobs and sighting through their viewfinders. What they aimed at appeared next. A spindly old man and his broad, stolid wife. The Chester Coopers, contest winners. Each held under one arm a large gold-plated animal mounted on a heavy wooden stand. In addition, Millie Cooper clutched a bouquet of white roses.

Porters swarmed after them with cartloads of baggage. To one side, smiling politely, walked a short, plump man with thinning hair and no chin. Like a shadow, a beautiful, impassive Peruvian woman moved close behind. Caswell and his receptionist Ada.

"Those things," Alberto said, and his voice fell to a hiss. "Those things under their arms. They are—"

"Llamas," I said. "Llamas. Two llamas. Beasts of burden. Alberto . . ."

The Coopers arranged themselves in front of the plate glass observation window, through which I could see a huge jet gliding slowly toward us, the thin scream of its engines now barely audible. They grinned happily for the folks back in Ainsworth, and Chester held his golden llama high over his head in a gesture of triumph.

"How's that?" I heard him call, and Caswell nodded encouragingly.

"Alberto, I am the dumbest, most idiotic, fluff-headed numskull on two continents. I am *stupid.*"

"No. Wait." He looked frantically from me to the scene on the lobby floor and then back to me.

"*Stupid. STUPID.*" People at an adjoining table stopped their conversation and turned toward us.

"We must be more quiet." Alberto gestured furtively toward the lobby. "They might see you. You are not stupid. You are beautiful."

"Shut up."

Now the group on the floor had reassembled, this time with Caswell and Ada lined up beside the Chester Coopers, and the flashguns went off again.

"I'm sorry." I patted Alberto's hand. He looked crestfallen and highly offended at the same time. "But I get tired of being beautiful. Some think the beautiful are dumb. Apparently they are right."

"But you could not have guessed—"

"Yes, I could. Oh, yes. I saw them at the Inter-American office. They even explained what they were for. Mementos for the contest winners. The TopTorts couple. Mr. and Mrs. Apple Pie. The Joneses. The people next door."

"Joneses? You know them?" Alberto looked surprised.

"The Coopers, actually. Yes, I met them. Didn't pay much attention because they were above suspicion. Exactly. Above suspicion. That should have made me suspicious. But I'm dumb."

"Please." Alberto winced. "Don't keep saying that. But how could they be above suspicion? If the cocaine is in the llamas—"

"They don't know that. That's the beauty of it. They'll brag about the damned llamas to the customs inspectors. Hold them right up to their noses."

"I see." Alberto allowed himself a small owl's hoot of respect. "They are very, very clever."

"Indeed."

We watched as the last photographs were taken. Caswell and Ada guided their charges to the check-in counter. People drew back, whispering and pointing at the odd-looking old couple with the awkward statuettes. The more publicity, the better. The more Mr. and Mrs. Cooper beamed and waved, the safer their million-dollar cargo was. As Alberto said, very, very clever.

"What do we do?"

I glanced at the clock on the wall. "It's still fifteen minutes before first call. Maybe the sendoff party will leave when these two go through the boarding pass check. Then we can dash for the end of the line."

"Okay. You must walk a little behind, like a Peruvian woman."

"It's against my principles. But maybe I deserve it now."

On the second call for boarding the Coopers shook hands and bear-hugged Caswell and Ada. Millie Cooper dabbed at her eyes with a lace handkerchief, and Chester Cooper's voice boomed through the lobby. "Wonderful country," he said. "By God, next to the good ol' U S of A this is the most wonderful country I ever seen." They moved toward the gate where a stewardess and a uniformed guard checked passes for Flight 714. They cradled the golden llamas like grandchildren and held them up for the stewardess and guard to see. With a polite, bored nod the stewardess fingered their tickets and gestured down the corridor. Chester turned to trumpet something about never forgetting, and his wife waved her white roses. Then they were through the gate, and Alberto and I were on our feet.

As we started down the stairs, I saw Caswell and Ada exchange an inquiring look. He shrugged and looked once around the lobby. She shrugged, too, and smiled. They began to walk to the exit, moving more briskly with each step, rid of the task of leading their docile beasts into harness. *They've done it before,* I thought, *it's routine. Unless the plane crashes, their cargo is in absolutely dependable hands. They could never trust each other, but they sure as hell can trust the Chester Coopers.*

Alberto took my ticket in hand and strode to the counter. He brushed past the clerk's outraged lecture on our failure to verify the reservations an hour before flight time and demanded that I sit as close as possible to my good friends, the American couple who had just checked in. The clerk looked at me with both contempt and curiosity. I could tell he supposed I was Alberto's mistress, but my name wasn't Spanish, and I must have looked like a shopworn Miraflores hooker. Alberto repeated his demand with a rap on the counter, and when he took his hand away, there was a five-hundred-sole bill tucked inside the ticket.

The clerk made the bill disappear somehow while he checked my passport. When he glanced from the photo to me, his mouth writhed in a mean smile, but he said nothing. With a jerk of his head he indicated the gate and uttered a toneless *"buen viaje."* Alberto took me by the elbow, and we moved toward the gate.

"They're gone," he said, glancing over his shoulder.

"Good. I should get rid of these sunglasses. I still have to go through immigration."

"This is Peru. They won't care, as long as you spent your money."

"I did. And Zwicky's money. And Webster's."

"No matter. Believe me, you are not stupid. The Owl knows." He smiled fondly at me and squeezed my arm. "Now go."

I slipped the dark glasses into my handbag and put my arms around his neck. "You are sweet." I kissed him. "I wish we had been able to visit more museums. Under different circumstances."

"I also. Next time. Now we say, 'See you later on, mastodon.' No?"

I laughed and shook my head. "You've got to get a more modern conversation book, *lechuga*. Take care of Webster. I'll be calling you in two days. The evening of the thirtieth. *Ciao.*"

Chapter XXXIII

A few minutes later I was pushing down the aisle of the plane past people removing coats and stowing bags. I found my seat and then located the Coopers ahead and across the aisle from me. They were well into an extended account of their miraculous experiences: how Millie had just decided at the last minute to send in an old recipe for persimmon cake, how the man from San Francisco had called long distance, when Chester was working on his balky tractor, how beautiful all the ruins were, and so old, too. The passengers surrounding them were properly awed and delighted.

"Lucky," a woman said. "Land, you were lucky. Just a recipe. Walt and I paid eleven hundred dollars apiece for our round trips."

"Damn lucky," a man said, shaking his head as if the Coopers had narrowly escaped a bad accident.

"Don't deny it," Chester said. "Damnedest thing ever happened to me."

I got up and moved into the aisle where listeners had gathered. "And do they take you clear back to Kansas?"

"Yes," said Chester.

"But we got to go to a big banquet in Frisco first," Millie admonished. "Don't forget that, Chester."

"That's terrific," I said. "A banquet—just for you folks?"

"Yep."

"Well, the company people will be there, of course. Mr. Caswell's company. It's an advertising company. And the people who make the TopTorts." Millie pressed her roses to her breast. "We had one banquet in Lima."

"Looks like you already got your awards." I nodded at the golden llama in Chester's lap. "*Two* of them."

"Yep. Funny." Chester looked at me for a moment, dubious. "Don't I know you from somewheres, ma'am?"

"I don't think so. I never won a contest in my life."

A couple of people laughed.

"Feller said it was equal rights now. Special award for the man, got to be one for the wife. Hell, she's wore the pants in our old shack right from the start."

"Chester, you're a liar." Millie put her hand on his arm and smiled. They were an honest, affectionate, hard-working, good-hearted couple. And between them they were packing about a million dollars' worth of cocaine.

"How do you tell them apart?" I asked. "Did they put your names on them?"

"Nope. Place for it, though." Chester's long, knotty finger traced out a little brass plate. TOPTORT WINNER 14 was stamped on the plate, with a blank space beneath. "They'll engrave the names in San Francisco."

"We get in at six in the morning. I hope they don't roust you out too soon for that," I said.

"Mr. Caswell said they'd send somebody to our hotel just after lunch," Millie said. "They've been so good to us. They think of everything."

"That's wonderful. Good accommodations too?"

"In Lima it was the Sheraton. My *land!*" Millie fluttered her eyelashes. "Fancy-pantsy."

"Didn't like it," Chester grumbled.

"In Frisco it's got to be the Saint Francis, right?" I said brightly.

"That's right." Millie looked at me inquiringly. "I hope it's not too fancy-pantsy."

"Not too."

The stewardess came down the aisle then, shooing us into our seats and checking belts, trays, and stowed baggage. The lights blinked on and off, and slowly, like a horizontal elevator, we began to move across the runway. I settled back and turned the pages of a magazine without seeing them. The stewardess was smiling like a robot as she dangled a little yellow mask from her manicured hand, while a bored voice on the intercom told us these masks would appear whenever for any reason all the air rushed out of the plane. As long as things are in their place, nobody worries. The little yellow masks were probably worthless, but as long as they showed them to us, we wouldn't worry about running into a mountain.

So it was with the Coopers. Everything was in the right place in their lives. The church socials, trips to town for the tractor parts, annual barbecues. All familiar, all expected, all aboveboard. Smiling in honest pride, they would haul their armloads of narcotics through customs and dump them in the laps of junkies and killers. Every time I glanced over a couple of rows and saw the snout of a golden llama protruding between two seats it gave me an eerie sensation.

But their simple straightforwardness also could make the doublecross very easy. I had until one o'clock tomorrow. The distribution apparatus was clearly so confident of its system that it could leave the goods with the Coopers for six hours without worry. I was sure it already had made up duplicate awards, complete with the engraved names, to substitute at the banquet. It would send a dependable man to the Saint Francis to pick up the llamas stuffed with dope. Then it would take them somewhere and decapitate them. And twenty pounds of very expensive powder would run out. But suppose the dependable man came an hour early? And was not so dependable? And was not even a man?

The flight was not long, or not long enough for me to work through the various threads of speculation that had been spun in my brain chambers during the last three days. The main tasks were clear enough. If I got my hands on the llamas and they were not fakes like the old Falcon, I could match them with the information in the mantas. An expert archaeologist would give credible testimony of their accuracy. That would link up Cordilleras, the producer and record keeper, with Ferguson's company, the wholesale handler. If Stump had done his homework on the Start Over program, we would also have the retail distributor and could put everything together. It would make quite a package. Ugarte and Drummond, assemblymen; Zwicky and Ferguson, respected businessmen and *bons vivants;* several heavyweight street hoods like Manuel and Gutierez.

But then what did I do with the package? Take it to the attorney general? To the press? To Frank? One thing I was sure of. I didn't want to hold on to it very long. I had no credentials as a crime buster, and as soon as Zwicky and Ferguson found out I was alive, they would try to find me and persuade me to return their shipment. Their persuasion would be very forceful. And if the lawmen caught me with twenty pounds of coke, I might have some trouble explaining that I was merely a curious bystander who took an interest in such things.

It was a murky and curious universe, crime was. I had operated for some time under the illusion that after I had unraveled various knots, the pattern would simplify, a villain would emerge, and once I had him, the whole structure would collapse. That's the way it happened in the books. The weapon was hidden in the coal chute; the killer dropped the countess's kerchief in the gazebo; the one o'clock train to Charing Cross does not run on the third Sunday of the month. Curses, foiled, twiddle-twiddle the lip hair.

This situation was very different. Things got less simple all the time. Consuelo and her guerrilla friends, for example, were struggling for noble causes—Mother Lefebre and her gentle nuns—but the overthrow of tyrants could become a deadly, dirty game. And maybe some kind of twisted political ideology motivated the pushers and killers on the street, though I suspected native American greed explained them well enough. It would be easy to see these violence addicts as the Big Badness. But were they? It could be argued that they only took advantage of schemes devised by men in tailored suits who placed family pictures on wide oak desks and stood forth as leaders among men—our best and finest.

These pillars of society always managed their minds in such a way that they could claim ignorance, or at worst an imperfect knowledge, of the consequences of their schemes. They didn't commit crimes; they just made errors of judgment. I could imagine them easily on the witness stand, sober and forthright, models of humble cooperation:

Why, no, Senator, we had no idea members of our staff were linked with prison gangs. Our wish was simply to aid former addicts become useful members of society.

At that point in time I asked Mr. Zwicky to help Assemblyman Drummond obtain a position on the board. Alvin was simply a friend helping a friend.

We did the advertising. Yes. Assemblyman Ugarte's campaign commercials. And the public service spots for muscular dystrophy. These were listed as a tax-deductible contribution from Cordilleras Imports. Simply a bookkeeping procedure and certainly not a "payoff."

That the TopTorts contest could be used to smuggle dangerous drugs—why, Mr. Prosecutor, it was more than shocking, it was incredible.

Unfortunately those records were in Lima, and Mr. Caswell took them before he disappeared.

I don't remember. The car was stolen before Mrs. Esposito failed to report for work. I don't remember when I reported it.

I don't recall.

Quipus? I'm afraid I'm not familiar with them.

But somebody knew it all, in some final, dank, foul corner of his heart. The king. Or kings. Perhaps three or four of them. Four kings was a strong hand. And soon he or they would also know that I knew. When that occurred, I would need a lot of hard, straight facts in order to deal with them. If I had the twenty-pound shipment and the company records for its handling, it was a very good start. If I moved fast tomorrow, put Alice to work in the library and Stump on the street, we might collect a few more items before the llamas were missed. It would be nice to have a look at the shawls in the Cordilleras warehouse and also the material Rosa had given to Billie Jo for safekeeping.

We were running from the sun, stretching out the night. Gray dawn held for a long time, and then, at last, the big, bright ball rolled up from the horizon and the plane tilted down and the robot voice over the intercom announced what we already knew: We were making our approach to San Francisco International. Across the aisle Chester Cooper stretched his long, thin arms, and I heard his wife mumble something sleepy and happy. Other conversations began, babies cried, and seat belts snicked shut. People craned to catch a glimpse of the city out the window. My heart swelled suddenly to a painful size. *San Francisco, here I come.*

But except for that quick glimpse through the scratched plastic window in the fuselage, none of us saw anything but corridors, stairs, and warning arrows for two hours. I stuck close to the Coopers during the long wait for our luggage. They sat on a bench, talking to anybody who would listen, their golden prizes on their laps. When finally they had assembled all their suitcases and stuffed baskets, they went to one of the counters where a customs officer waited to make his inspection. I got in behind them to watch.

The officer—Officer Turner by his name tag—went over each new subject with his quick, rodent eyes, dwelling an extra moment on the faces. He was a slender, precise man. No nonsense. So close-shaven that his cheeks shone, a uniform with creases you could cut a finger on.

"What do we have here, sir?" He reached for the llama under Chester's arm.

"This here is a replica of the yammer. They call it the camel of the Andes," Chester began, shoving the figurine firmly into Officer Turner's open hands. "We got these for winnin' a contest, my wife, Millie, did. She sent in a recipe, and goldang if we didn't win!"

Officer Turner tipped the golden beast and read the plaque. "It was just about the most amazing thing ever happened," Millie chimed in, and set her own llama on the counter. "I got one, too. They give us two whole weeks in Peru. Took us everywhere."

"Nice folks," Chester said. "Wonderful folks."

"We got a heap of stuff to lay out here," Millie prompted, and hoisted a basket onto the counter beside the llamas. "But we didn't go over our three hundred dollars' worth. We was real careful about that. But we could have spent just a *fortune.*"

Another officer looked over from the next counter. "We get 'em every month or so," he called. "The lucky couples." He smiled sourly at the Coopers.

Officer Turner put down the figurine and unzipped a bag. "Let's see the purchases," he said wearily.

And that was it. For the fourteenth time. Caswell picked them well, his beasts of burden. Stump had been right. The inspectors looked for the flinchers, the scratchers, those with the itch of secret paranoia. Honest folk like the Coopers never showed up on the officers' psychic radar. With great good cheer they must have packed between ten and twenty million dollars' worth of stuff over the border.

After a perfunctory poke at a couple of scarves and a raised eyebrow over an open box of cigars from Havana, which caused both Chester and Millie to blush furiously, Officer Turner stamped their declaration card and waved them on. Then he turned to me.

I opened my little handbag, looking around the inspector to follow the Coopers toward the exit.

"Nothing to declare."

"Ma'am?"

He was staring at my wig. I suppose Mamacita's makeup was beginning to deteriorate, too.

"May I see your passport?"

I had already been through this with the man at the immigration desk. I flipped open the little booklet to my photograph.

"It's me. I just wear a wig sometimes."

"Why is that, ma'am?" He was watching me watch the exit door swing open.

"What?"

"Why do you wear a wig?"

"I happen to think it improves my image. As an international smuggler," I said acidly.

"Really?" He gave a small smile totally without humor. His fingers were probing in the bag, like snakes going after a rat.

"Look, I'm a poor working girl who has just been through a vacation. I didn't bring back a dime's worth of goods. Spent it all in hotels and clubs. And I'm in a hurry."

"Are you?" Officer Turner had a maddening habit of asking rhetorical questions.

The exit door had slammed shut, and I had to repress an urge to bolt.

"What about this?"

It was the manta with the quipus.

"Oh, yeah. I forgot that. It's just a cheap shawl. Fifty bucks." I searched the wall for a clock.

"And this, ma'am? What is this?"

I glanced back at him, and he extended something in his hand. It was the barrel of the .32, no longer nestled inside the tampon case where I had put it.

There was a long pause.

"It appears to be a gun barrel," I said. "Or maybe it's a pumpkin."

He didn't smile. He touched a button under the counter, and I saw a red bulb light up at the other end of the room, where uniformed men lounged in a couple of offices.

Chapter XXXIV

"Just get me out of here," I said through my teeth into the phone. "You owe me that, Frank."

"Not until you tell me what the hell is going on."

"I won't tell you a damn thing until I get away from these creeps, take a shower, and grab a couple of hours' sleep. You're my lawyer. I have just one phone call."

"You show up from your insane Peruvian jaunt in a wig, carrying a gun and without your traveling companion. I'm very near being put in charge of this whole goddamned investigation. How would it look—"

"Frank," I said evenly, "you're not the special prosecutor yet. But if you get that appointment, you will want to hear what I have to say. Believe me. But I can't do it on the phone. Just get me out."

Officer Turner and his superior and the female agent who had put her hands all over me and in all my corners regarded me stonily from the other side of the counter. The various parts of the revolver, still disassembled, were spread out before them. A very large, silent man leaned in the doorway, blocking my view of the main room.

"When can I see you?"

"At three o'clock. The Jolly Roger."

"All right. Give me the man in charge there."

I turned toward the spectators' gallery. "He wants to talk to you," I said, extending the receiver.

It took another two hours to get extricated. Finally a man from the FBI called. A fingerprint check in Washington had cleared me. I was not a dangerous or fictitious person. The supervisor put the receiver back on the hook and looked at me sorrowfully. "You can leave," he said.

"The gun stays here. You done a dumb thing. Maybe you should see a doctor. You're real lucky your old man has some clout. You coulda been in jail."

I grabbed my bag and headed for the door. "You're right," I said. "Very dumb. Too late for doctors. I may have lost the golden camel, the persimmon cake, and the snow mountain."

It was almost eleven when I got to Alice's apartment and let myself in. Baudelaire didn't recognize me either and hid under the bed. I dumped the wig in the wastebasket, washed off the makeup, and slipped on a yellow blouse and a pearl choker. On the back porch I found two cardboard boxes, and in a drawer there was a roll of masking tape. These I threw in the back seat of the Porsche. When I turned the ignition key, the engine growled slowly. The battery was low after a week of idleness. I shut my eyes, remembering Mike in his cockpit, and murmured a fervent prayer. Maybe it helped. At the next twist of the key the engine roared to life. I needed a run of luck.

For the next twenty minutes I drove with cold, predatory concentration, and by eleven thirty I had passed the doorman at the Saint Francis, shouldering through the heavy glass door with the boxes under my arms. Before lunch, Millie Cooper had said. Twenty-seven minutes away. I had to talk fast. The desk clerk gave me room number 823. Eight floors on a slow elevator, with guests getting in and out on three, four, and seven, eyeing the bulky boxes with disgust. Then I turned the wrong way in the hallway and had to retrace my steps to 823, the next-to-last room in the corridor.

"Who is it?" Millie spoke near the door, her voice sharp and awake. They had probably been up for hours.

"Stella Pike—from Cordilleras Imports."

"Who?" I heard her rattling the lock; then the door opened a crack.

"Friend of Alvin Zwicky's? I met you in Lima."

"Oh, why, *yes.*" As the door opened, I glided forward and over the threshold. "Chester, it's Mr. Zwicky's . . .

friend. Miss Pike." She was looking over her shoulder, her voice raised. I could hear the plumbing thundering in the bathroom.

"What's she want?" Chester bellowed over the waterfall. He was a direct man.

"Don't mind him," Millie said, and smoothed her print dress and patted her hair. "We just got in this morning. How long have you folks been back?"

"Day or two ago. It's quite a trip, isn't it?"

"Oh, land!" She gestured with little bird flaps of her forearms.

"I'm here to pick up the awards, the llamas. For the engraving." I rattled my boxes.

"Oh?" She looked puzzled. "The man just called an hour ago and said he would come at one. With a van."

"I know." I laughed easily. "But as it turned out, I was planning to visit the office today, and when I called, they told me to swing by and save the delivery boys a trip."

"Makes sense." She smiled benevolently. "Let me help you wrap them."

We eased the llamas into the cartons, and I swiftly taped the tops.

"I don't know why they don't make those things just a little bit smaller, so they'd fit in a suitcase," Millie wondered.

"Ummm." I ripped the last bit of tape from the roll and plastered it on the box top. *Because they want you to flaunt them. Very, very clever.* I smiled, imagining what the deliveryman would think when the very, very clever idea was not quite clever enough this time.

Chester came out of the bathroom, hitching up his trousers. "Well, hello there," he said. "Back, eh? Mr. Zwicky, too?"

"Oh, yes. I'm just on the way to meet him at the office."

"What's this?" He eyed the boxes, glanced at the dresser where the llamas had reposed.

"I'm taking your prizes in for the engraving." I smiled brightly. "It's on my way."

"But that feller just called." He looked at his wife, then

back at me. His brow furrowed. "You know . . ." he began, and then stopped.

"What? What is it, Chester?"

He shook his head and peered at me again. "You got a sister? I coulda sworn—"

"I saw it, too." Millie nodded. "She's got a double. That woman we talked to on the plane. But I don't think she was on the respectable side."

"Only child," I said briskly, and bent to pick up a box. "Got to be going now. Lunch date."

"Here now." Chester stepped forward and seized the box. "Gimme that."

I fought panic, the impulse to grab and run. We tugged back and forth.

"That's a man's work, totin' and draggin'. You let me carry these. Where's your car?"

I closed my eyes, feeling faint. "In the lot."

"Let's go. Stack that other one on top."

Like a sleepwalker, I led him out the hall and into the elevator, then across the lobby and down the stairs to the parking lot. The two boxes filled my back seat, and Chester frowned.

"Damn little toys," he said. "You ought to get yourself a decent American automobile."

"Mr. Cooper, if things turn out all right, I may just do that. In your honor."

He looked hard at me again. "What do you mean, 'all right'?"

"Just all right."

I put out my hand, and he shook it. Then I climbed into the Porsche, and it started on the first try.

"Good-bye, and thanks, Mr. Cooper. You're a peach."

He waved absently, the little frown back on his forehead. Then he turned and stalked toward the hotel. He would probably be glad to get back to Kansas. People didn't confuse you so much there. But their trip wasn't over yet. The final banquet was coming up. They would have a lot to talk about with the folks back home, he and Millie. More than they bargained for.

Chapter XXXV

I called Alice from a Laundromat in a shopping center, where I could see the Porsche plainly through the big windows. It calmed me to hear her cool professional's voice and imagine her in the quiet, cavernous library. She wanted to know everything. Especially if there were fresh bodies. I said I couldn't give it all yet and asked if she had news. She did.

"Eric found out a few things. We didn't have a chance to tell you what he and Hand were cooking up before . . ." Her voice wobbled.

"It's all right. Go on."

"They had a plan for infiltration. Eric had done the part of a junkie in a couple of plays. He was good at it. So he didn't eat for two days, didn't shave, used a touch of makeup, and then started to hang around the Tenderloin. Somebody tipped him off to the rehabilitation center scam. Manuel is the honcho, all right. And the word is that a big shipment of stuff is due this week."

"Don't count on it."

"How come? You know something they don't?"

"The shipment got lost."

"Jesus, Stella. You didn't—"

"Didn't have to. Somebody did it for me. A very nice man from Kansas. But it's worth knowing that the word got through." So they believed Mike's story and sent the shawl air express or perhaps risked a cablegram. Very, very fast they were, as well as very, very clever.

"What word?"

"Ah, thereby hangs a tale. And there isn't time for it right now. I've got a couple of jobs for you."

"Shoot."

"Call Baker and Ferguson and get a list of the past winners of the TopTorts contest. There ought to be thirteen of them. Don't talk to anybody high up in the company. Then check your directories and get as many phone numbers as you can."

"Okay. Next?"

I had fumbled a card out of my wallet and managed to decipher the figures on it. "Call this guy, Harold Dryer, better known as Stump. A cop. Tell him to meet the lady who couldn't unlock her door in the rain at Eddie's Café, Seventh and Market, in an hour."

"That's all?"

"That's all."

I put the Porsche in a covered lot and walked the two blocks to Eddie's. Stump arrived early and slid into the booth opposite me. He didn't remove his coat or hat and didn't say anything, just folded his hands to wait.

"It was a lucky trip," I said. "Pure luck."

He was still waiting, not looking at me. The waitress started toward us, but he waved her off.

"You gave me some good advice. Watch for the records, you said."

He nodded.

"I know where they keep them. I think there is a complete set for every transaction. Dates. Amounts. Demand and delivery."

"That's good. If it's true. Where?"

"What do you mean if it's true? What's the silent treatment about?"

His muddy eyes stuck for an instant on my face, then drifted away again. He removed the hat, and his hand strayed into a pocket and came out with a black cigar.

"Heard about your ex." He bit off the end and spit it on the floor. It wasn't a question, so I waited for him to go on. "Movin' up in the world."

"What does that mean? The special prosecutor's job? That makes you nervous?"

He bludgeoned a match on the edge of the table and let the blossom of flame die back before he stabbed his cigar into it. "Depends."

"On what?"

"What he does with it. What you do with it."

"Ah, I see." I watched him build a cloud of smoke around himself, and then I reached up to fan a hole in it. "You think I'm his little helpmate. That's quite, quite wrong. But so what? He'll be involved in this sooner or later anyway, if he gets the appointment."

"Sooner. It looks like some people in town want him there. Some people on the force."

"The wrong people?"

"Not exactly. But not the right people either."

I shrugged. "Look, Stump, he's not my husband. Not my boss. I'm here, right? Not in his office. So do you want to trade horses or not?"

He puffed for a few moments. "Keep talkin'."

I dug the shawl from my handbag and spread it out between us. Then I told him about the quipus and my guess that the warehouse at Cordilleras would have similar records. The knots were a code no customs officer was likely to know, but matched with a shipment of narcotics, they were easy for an expert to interpret and provided all the usual information about who owed what to whom and when it was to be paid.

"So," I concluded, "can you get a warrant? As of thirty minutes ago they knew I'm back in town."

"I know one judge who might believe such a crazy god-damn story. But it takes time to prepare a warrant. Couple, three hours. And if the stuff ain't there, or you don't find it, you've tipped your hand and they'll turn it to ashes before you're out the door."

"Suppose we go without a warrant and bluff?"

He shifted the cigar from one side of his mouth to the other. "I could lose my job."

"So?"

He manufactured another cloud, and the eyes of mud

vanished in a squint. "It's all I know how to do. I got twenty-two years in."

"Sure, I understand." I dug into my handbag for change. "I'll handle it myself."

"Whoa." He put a hand on my wrist. "You said this knot business had to be connected with a shipment. Where's the shipment?"

"I can deliver it." I pushed coins for my coffee onto the counter and stood up.

"Okay, okay." He rubbed his bald head, covered it with the hat, and heaved himself to his feet. "You better."

When Darlene looked up from her muttering typewriter at Cordilleras Imports and saw us before her desk, she tried on several expressions in rapid succession: incredulity, disapproval, bewilderment, and then incredulity again.

"Well," I said, "the human pigeon is still pecking away. More inspection, you see. This time official."

Stump, behind me, said the usual officer-of-the-law things in monotone. His wallet flopped open, and he held it on her for a moment like a raygun. Her hand darted for the intercom, but I reached across the desk and stopped it.

"Ah-ah. No fair." I picked up the metal box and jerked. Wires popped.

"Jesus," Stump breathed. "There goes my job. Let's move."

We left her trying to get her mouth around words that kept evaporating into empty air and walked quickly through the outside office toward the storeroom in the back. The clerks gave us cursory glances, then went back to their papers. The door to Consuelo's cubbyhole was closed, and except for two men loading a forklift at the rear by the truck ramp, the place looked deserted.

I rattled the door handle. It was locked. But I heard movement within. Footsteps, a drawer grating open. I stepped back.

"Break and enter," I said.

Stump looked at me, at the door. "Jesus," he said. Then he gripped his wrist, bracing the elbow against his side, and charged. There was a sharp snap of metal, and the door whooshed open. Stump lost his footing and went down on one knee. Over his head I could see into the little room, see the open box, the stack of mantas, and Consuelo's drawn, dark face. She had a bottle upended in her hand, and a liquid was splashing out of it over the box and the shawls. A pungent odor of cleaning fluid filled the room.

Consuelo took two quick steps to a shelf, plunged her hand inside her purse, and withdrew a cigarette lighter. I shoved Stump aside with one hand and dove. I heard the wheel on flint, a tiny, abrasive noise, and a yellow spear of flame burst from the lighter. I clamped my hand over it and felt a sudden bite of pain in my palm. With the other hand I took her wrist and wrenched, and the lighter clattered to the floor. Then Stump lunged past me and pinned both her arms. I grabbed the bottle, still dribbling on the table, and righted it.

All at once Consuelo went limp, and Stump wheezed at the effort of holding her erect. I kicked a chair under her, and she dropped into it. For a while there was no sound but three people breathing fast and hard.

"Attempted arson," Stump said finally. "We can start with that."

"Consuelo," I said, "you travel fast."

She stared through me.

"What did you do? Charter a plane?" I snapped my fingers in front of her face. "Look. It's not what you think. You're loyal to the wrong people."

Her face convulsed, and all at once big tears overran it. "It's all over," she whispered. "We thought you were in Pucallpa. The mantas . . . You knew. You *knew*." She started a sob, then strangled it.

"No," I said. "You get off a sinking ship. Just in time. They'd betray you, you know. They don't care about your revolution."

"They gave us money. For guns."

"Only because they could use you."

"What the hell is this all about?" Stump pointed to the table. "Do we take this stuff and book her?"

"Take the stuff. Leave her alone."

Consuelo looked at me, dumbfounded.

"I know why you did what you did. I respect it. I'm giving you the chance to run. Or"—I nodded at the mantas—"you can read those for us. You'll get a break in court for that."

"What's the deal?" Stump squinted at me. "You're not going to let her go?"

"If she wants to go." I could see Consuelo thinking fast. "You might get a break for your husband, too. When this comes down, you know, they won't have much use for your services. In fact, you're a liability. Remember Rosa."

She bowed her head and after a long silence spoke softly. "Yes. I'll tell you."

"A very valuable witness," I said to Stump. "Can you find a safe place for her and the goods?"

He nodded. "My place. In Daly City. Where are you going?"

"I've got to meet somebody at three. The Jolly Roger on Clement. I ought to be through around five. I'll call you then."

Consuelo leaned forward and touched my hand. "I'm sorry I burned you. You must be careful. People are looking for you."

"I'll bet they are."

She gave the faintest of smiles. "You read the quipus? How?"

"A friend of a friend did."

"We believed that would never happen."

"Somebody famous and smart once said everything that can happen will." I grinned and showed the little red mark in my palm. "And I have the stigmata to prove it."

Chapter XXXVI

The Jolly Roger was down to its skeleton crew. A couple of hard hats were nursing beers and watching television, an old-timer was taking all the time he needed to drink his way through a pension check, and a table of young women were chattering over gin and tonics. Danny came out of his parade rest and moved to the liquor shelf to find the Chivas.

"Hey, sweetheart. Long time no see. What you got there?"

"Listen, Danny, have you got space in your stockroom for these packages?"

"Sure." He uncorked the bottle. "If you promise to slow down and lemme flirt with you. Frank's gonna be late anyway. He already called. Important meeting."

"Oh?" I felt a small pang of something close to jealousy. What I carried in the two battered and hastily taped cartons should have been the very highest priority, I thought, for the aspiring young prosecutor. But of course, Frank didn't know what I had. Who did know? I wondered. *People are looking for you,* Consuelo had said. Looking hard, I figured.

"I'll show you where to stash those," Danny said. He poured my drink and then beckoned me behind the bar. He opened a door with a key from the ring on his belt and led me into a stockroom. The walls were lined with cases of bottles, boxes of napkins and straws, and rows of glasses. In one corner beside a double iron sink were a large broom and mop closet and, beside that, a worktable with a rack of tools above it.

"In here okay?" He opened the broom closet.

"Fine."

We stacked the boxes inside, then went back to the bar. I took a stool and sipped my Scotch. Danny didn't ask any direct questions. He waited, his face sagging into its familiar expression of stoic commiseration, but I didn't say anything.

"You been in the sun," he observed finally. "Lost weight, too. You been goin' too hard again."

"What is this, a health club or a bar?"

"A person that looks like you should take care of themselves."

"That's sweet of you, Danny."

"Don't gimme that sweet line. I mean it. You look"— he considered me mournfully—"you look like . . . *haggard*. Yeah, haggard. Is somethin' happenin' between you and your ex?"

"Nothing but business. And that's the way it ought to be."

"Yeah, in the paper a couple days ago I read that the attorney general is gonna nominate him to run a special investigation. A real hot spot."

"Frank will love it. He wants to be important more than anything."

"So you're still helping him get there."

"I don't know. I may be an immense liability. Exes have a way of becoming that, even without wanting to."

"You couldn't be no liability to any guy who was worth a damn."

"Danny, you are tremendously good for my self-image. It leads me to ask you a favor."

He drew himself up like an old cavalry horse that hears a distant bugle.

"Don't mention those packages to anyone."

He was downcast. "I thought somebody might be botherin' you." He massaged his egg-sized knuckles. "I'd—" The door swung open and let in a sharp white square of afternoon and then three black cutouts of people.

The two men with Frank were older and very well dressed. He spotted me, nodded, and then all three of them walked quickly to a table at the back of the bar. I picked up my drink and slid off the stool.

"Yeah," I heard Danny mutter behind me. "Big shots. Be careful, sweetheart."

They stood, wearing perfunctory smiles, until I arrived at the table. The taller of the two was a well-preserved sixty, with fashionably styled gray hair and no sign of softness around the middle. The other man looked like a high school football coach who drank too much: thick neck, crew cut, tufts of coarse black hair on his knuckles, and a nose netted with tiny red veins.

"Stella, how are you?" Frank took me formally by the shoulders and brushed my cheek with his mouth. "I'm late because of some highly unusual developments. We're here to discuss them with you. I'd like you to meet Clarence Ferguson. You know his agency, of course."

The tall man extended his hand and smiled swiftly when I hesitated an instant before shaking it. "I believe we have friends in common," he said.

"Do we?"

Frank went on smoothly. "And this is Assemblyman Hugh Drummond."

The football coach jerked his head, and like a light going on, his face became affable, open, warm. "Hello there. A pleasure, always a pleasure to meet a beautiful woman." He moved a chair from the table, and I settled into it.

I took a good slug of my drink, mostly as an excuse to close my eyes for a moment and make some sort of wild guess about what was going on.

"There are some things I had better explain about how this can be handled," Frank said. I opened my eyes again and watched him as he continued to talk, his voice strong and well modulated but not audible beyond our table, his hands folded over a note pad he had taken from his pocket. It was the manner he used on a difficult witness, or a dull judge, or—I remembered well enough—an irate woman.

"We are in a very sensitive area. There are investigations in progress. Indictments will surely follow. The chances are very good that my status will change in the next day or two and I will be a public employee charged with the duty of collecting evidence preparing those indictments. I cannot therefore guarantee that this conversation will be in confidence, and I must make clear to all of you—and to myself—the boundaries of this discussion. Otherwise, there is a risk of conspiracy to commit a crime."

There was a pause. I had an uncontrollable urge to laugh. Drummond looked very serious and concerned, nodding his head vigorously at all of us. Ferguson may have been listening very carefully or not at all. His face was as composed as an undertaker's when the relatives file by the casket, and what transpired in the chamber behind his eyes I could not divine.

"It is an unorthodox procedure for a potential prosecutor to discuss an investigation with potential witnesses, but we have a highly unusual case before us. Mr. Ferguson has come to me with what may be an opportunity to break the largest single drug distribution system in the history of the state of California."

Frank paused, and I realized all at once that he was rehearsing the moment when he would be making this dramatic announcement before the cameras or before a gallery in committee chambers, where the gasps of spectators and the flash of camera lights would provide punctuation.

"And Assemblyman Drummond has been very forthcoming in offering to supply information that he may have mistakenly withheld earlier. But you gentlemen can summarize your positions better than I can." He gestured slightly toward Ferguson.

"I can explain it very simply, Mrs. Pike. We—"

"Stella."

"Of course, Stella." His smile was a twitch. "Assemblyman Drummond and I are, of course, both aware that an investigation has been going on, an investigation that involves the Start Over program, which is a rehabilitation program whereby convicts and the relatives of convicts are given priority in certain supervised jobs, especially counseling jobs dealing with narcotics—"

"I'm familiar with the program," I said.

"Certainly. Forgive me for repeating the obvious. Now we have been active in supporting these programs, so we were very disturbed at the possibility that they had been corrupted by elements of organized crime."

"I was outraged." Drummond pointed his stubby finger at an imaginary reporter.

"Oh, dear," I said, and picked up my Scotch again. "I'll bet you were."

There was the barest of pauses, and then Ferguson went on. "Mr. Drummond and I began to compare notes and put a few things together. A man named John Caswell who worked for Assemblyman Ugarte joined my firm three years ago, and other personnel recommended to us by Ugarte's staff worked for me and for an acquaintance of mine, Alvin Zwicky. Who I believe is also a friend—a close friend—of Stella's."

"Not that close," I said evenly. I hadn't liked the slight shift of intonation he had given the word.

"Oh?" Ferguson looked at Frank, and his mouth twitched again. "I see. At any rate it appears possible that these employees have been engaged in a smuggling operation—utilizing the facilities of my firm and Mr. Zwicky's import company."

"No! You don't say so!" I did an ingenue's version of shocked surprise—eyebrows high, fingertips over open mouth. A very faint tinge of color appeared in Ferguson's cheeks.

Assemblyman Drummond looked stern. "Clarence and I woke up one fine day to find ourselves—in a manner of speaking—compromised. The reputations of a lifetime on the line. The efforts—immense efforts—we funneled into these programs may have boomeranged. Stella, these men—and just how far up the ladder in Ugarte's machine the buck goes we cannot at this point in time say—"

Assemblyman," Ferguson broke in with a warning glance, "we must be careful about allegations."

"Of course, I meant—"

"Oh, one little allegation would be all right, wouldn't it?" I looked around at them, eager and wide-eyed. "Assemblyman Ugarte surely can stand a *little* one. If we can get away with a funneled boomerang."

"Stella." Frank spoke in the deadly tone I remembered from our last confrontations.

"Sorry, Mr. Drummond. Please go on. Tell me about your campaign commercials."

"My what?" Assemblyman Drummond looked startled. Then he frowned, and his neck bulged so that he seemed to be trying to withdraw inside the soft silk collar of his shirt, like a turtle.

"These cute commercials that Clarence does for you. With the money from the campaign funds that he and his acquaintance Zwicky drum up."

He glanced at Ferguson, then at Frank, and opened his mouth, but nothing came out.

"You know, the commercials. How are they different from the ones he does for Assemblyman Ugarte, and do they cost the same for both of you? Peter and Judas get the same rate?"

"Stella. That's enough. We're not here for that—"

"Stella does not seem very interested in background," Ferguson said with an easy little laugh. "I feel perhaps we should come to the point." He leaned across the table, his two long, pale hands spread on the surface palms down. "We believe that you have proof of this drug-smuggling operation and have even intercepted an illegal shipment. Working entirely on your own. It is a remarkable achievement, and we are deeply grateful that the rot in what we thought were beneficial social reforms has been uncovered. However . . . but I think perhaps Frank can best outline the plans for your discovery."

Frank inclined his head slightly and then turned to me with his rueful, boyish mask on. "My former wife," he said huskily, "does not care for what she once called this legal buzzard shit. All right, Stella. Here it is. If you let the shipment go through, and we are set up to track it, we can catch them all—the little fish and some big ones, too. Manuel Esposito, Caswell, Consuelo Palacios—and every major street pusher in the city. In one swoop."

"It would look very good." I picked up my glass and drained the last of the Scotch. "Very good. Start Over becomes All Finished. Hardly are you appointed prosecutor and—presto!—you lock up the meanies and call in the press to tell the public how you did it. That's terrific. It calls for a drink. Anybody mind if I have another?" I waved over my shoulder, and Danny went into action behind the bar. He had been watching me from the corner of his eye, I knew.

"I'm not doing this to look good, Stella." Frank put all his earnestness into a long look. "I would be the first to acknowledge that you broke this case wide open. You'll get due credit. But the point is we have got to nail the responsible parties, or as many of them as we can, right now. Once we have them in custody and begin questioning, there is a good chance we can find out who killed Rosa, who set up the Start Over network, who runs the prison gang."

"So let the last shipment connect. Put out the poisoned bait. See who comes to feast."

"You've got it." Frank's eyes shone like polished metal.

Chapter XXXVII

Danny set down my drink with a crack of glass against the tabletop.

"You gentlemen want anything?" he asked. There was an obscure implication that they had better not want the wrong things.

"Martini," Assemblyman Drummond said automatically. "No olive." He looked at me and brightened. "They're real bad for you. Can't say that in front of my constituents, though—they grow 'em!" He guffawed and then stopped short, seeing Ferguson's curt gesture.

"You are probably wondering how we know about this shipment and how delivery of it could be made credible," Ferguson said quietly.

"It crossed my mind."

"I had grown curious about the contests we were running for TopTorts. And today our pickup man reported that the awards for the most recent winners had been stolen. Two young men in my office were extremely upset, and under questioning they confessed finally that the figurines—a pair of llamas—might contain contraband. They had been paid off to switch these awards for duplicates and turn them over to a man they knew only as Juan. Since this contest is a promotional venture for Zwicky's company, I called him. He had just returned from Peru, where I gather he and Stella traveled together?"

"That's right. We traveled together for a while, then separated." I took another belt of Scotch. "And he was disturbed, right? Outraged?"

"Quite so. Alvin also is convinced that you grasped the nature of the smuggling operation and were interested in actually—I'm sorry if this offends you—taking it over. He thought you were working independently and hoping to extort money for keeping quiet."

"Amazing," Frank said with an amused chuckle.

"My God," Drummond trumpeted. "This lovely creature?"

"But our thinking is this," Ferguson said with a glance around the table to include all of us. "If the drug ring believes that Stella is not connected with the law, is in fact an independent operator, they might either buy back their shipment or steal it—if they were given an opportunity." He smiled encouragingly at me. "Precautions would of course be taken."

"Of course."

"You see, Stella," Frank broke in, "time is crucial. You took the llamas only four or five hours ago. If we can get the stuff back to them by tonight, or tomorrow at the latest, they might fall for the idea."

"Yeah, I suppose they might." There was a silence while Danny approached with the assemblyman's martini. I winked at him as he turned back to the bar. The silence lengthened. They were waiting for me to give them what they wanted.

"If I had the llamas."

The bit of color that had touched Ferguson's cheeks was suddenly gone. "You don't have them?" He leaned across the table towards me.

"Just kidding." I swirled the remains of my drink around the glass and finished it. "But they've gotten expensive, those llamas."

"What? What do you mean?" Drummond looked baffled again and uncomfortable. The collar of his silk shirt was damp.

"Well, Mr. Drummond, you know how it is. The cost of transporting them, a week's work lost, the mental strain of responsibility. Most of all, the bother of having to lie about them. You know how it is." I wrinkled my nose at him.

"Ah—yes. I perfectly agree with you. Expenses. I'm sure—" Drummond's small eyes, shrewd with fear, flicked to Frank.

"Shut up," Ferguson said softly.

"I hope you are still kidding, Stella." Frank's voice was quiet and cold. "I warned you about conspiracy charges. You are in possession of stolen property as well. You—"

"I have the goods. The coke. And you want it. These gentlemen want it. If buying it is out, you move on to threats. Go ahead, Frank. Lock me up. The ex-wife of the leading candidate for prosecutor. Dope smuggler. How would that look? You'd never get to prosecute anybody, would you, Frank?"

He only looked at me, his eyes a blaze of ice.

"And if you aren't the prosecutor, this little deal falls right through, doesn't it? The little game I guess we can call 'Get the Spic.' Ugarte did all the dirty work anyway. Fought off the investigation, bought off the cops and the junkies, hired the killers. All the rest of you had to do was look the other way, stay dumb, and take the juice."

Ferguson stood up, his face white. "I've tried to give you an opportunity, Frank. I hope you haven't abused it. I hope you haven't brought us here to be berated by your ex-wife, who I believe has had a little too much to drink—"

"Like hell I have." I stood up too, and Drummond, looking stricken and outraged at the same time, moved the chair aside for me. "You're not handing out any opportunities. You're trying to save your hides. How's that for a little allegation? Here's another. You want to sell out your partners. Maybe if you and Mr. Drummond are the first to cooperate—or rat—you can dump Ugarte and maybe Zwicky, too, and get off with a minimum of damage—influence peddling or misuse of funds—but nothing so ugly as dope and murder."

"Come on, Drummond." Ferguson strode for the door.

He paused a moment and matter-of-factly spoke to Frank over his shoulder. "She's ruining you as prosecutor. You've got to reason with her."

"We've got to rethink our thinking on this," Assemblyman Drummond shouted at Frank. "I remind you that an appointment as prosecutor must go before the Judiciary Committee, of which I am—"

"Hugh," Ferguson said sharply from the doorway, "shut up and come on."

Frank had been sitting like a man carved from marble, his eyes closed, his lips and nostrils pinched. All at once he rose from the table, his movements stiff and sudden like those of a marionette.

"You crazy bitch," he whispered. "You let them get away. Everything I've worked for. For months. Years. The opportunity of my life." He took a jerky step toward me. "We have a chance, you goddamned little idiot, a chance to get at least most of them—"

"Most!" I laughed. "Most isn't good enough. Not nearly good enough. I want the kings, Frank. The bastards who always buy and lie their way out of it. The people who *let it happen.* Not Manuel or Gutierez or Consuelo. I'm getting downright sympathetic to the plight of the common criminal."

"You've gone crazy. Like a religious fanatic. You think you're in charge of judgment for the human race."

"I know what I'm in charge of," I said, and laughed from far down inside myself. "I'm in charge of twenty pounds of coke and the company records."

"I don't think that will last long. Ugarte's men will see to that. You think about it awhile. We have about twenty-four hours." He drew his mouth into a hard line and turned to go. His walk was still stiff and awkward.

"You're one of them, Frank. You belong with them. One of the big boys now!" He pulled open the door without looking back. "You buzzard shit!" I picked up the glass and threw it, a little low, but it would have caught him in the small of the back if the door hadn't closed in time. It shattered, spraying ice and splinters of glass on the floor.

The room was very still. Nothing but the canned laughter from the television set and the traffic noise from the street outside. Danny was staring at the door where Frank had been a moment before; his hands played with the cutoff pool cue he kept under the bar. The two hard hats had swiveled around in their stools, leaving the television and their beers untended.

"Jay-zus," I heard one of them breathe, "that broad is mad."

The pensioner seemed only mildly interested in the scene he found himself in, so I made my way to the bar and sat beside him. He focused on me, nodded, and lifted his glass an inch or two off the counter in a restrained salute.

"It's a tough one," he said.

"It sure is." I smiled. "And getting tougher."

Danny put the pool cue away and sidled toward me. "Sweetheart," he said, "I told you. You're goin' too fast."

I looked at myself in the mirror behind the bar. Flushed. Hair out of place. Face twitching a little. All at once I thought of Rosa, and the chill that went through me turned the twitch into a tremble.

"You're right, Danny." I prodded at the stray hairs and then gave it up. "Listen, give me the broom. I'll clean that up. I'm sorry. Really sorry."

"No, sir!" Danny fumbled out his key, unlocked the door behind the bar, and brought out the broom and pan. "You don't move a finger. He had it comin'. I'm sorry you missed." He began gingerly sweeping up the glittering fragments of ice and glass. "Listen, whatever I can do—"

"It's all right, Danny. I'm making it." I was staring through the doorway into the stockroom, thinking about the two packages in the broom closet. *Ugarte's men will see to that.* I felt a sudden heaviness, a dread in the middle of my being. I recognized it, loathed myself. *Think about it,* Frank had instructed, and I was thinking about it. I was realizing that without him and his prosecutor's power I

might not make it. Might not nail anybody. Might get
nailed myself. So maybe I needed him and his new associates. That notion made me sick to my stomach.

What would the final pitch have been? I wondered. Star
witness first, perhaps. Media exposure. GIRL CRACKS CASE.
REDHEAD STEALS 1 MILLION IN DRUGS. BEAUTIFUL PRIVATE
EYE SCORES. Then my own business. Loans easily arranged.
A fashionable office in North Beach. Plenty of accounts.
Why not? It had worked on Frank.

Ferguson had sized him up rightly. Catching an assemblyman and an assorted bag of criminals, destroying the
Start Over program, and revealing a clever smuggling
system—that would make Frank's reputation in California
politics. He could skip a lot of steps, aim for the attorney
general's slot, and be in the running for United States
senator or governor before he was forty. Ferguson's advertising and promotional skill would be at his disposal;
so would the Zwicky fortune unless they sacrificed him
along with Ugarte.

And the price was cheap. Frank had only to believe
that Ferguson and Drummond were "forthcoming," that
although injudicious and tardy, they now were rushing
nobly forward to confess their suspicions about certain of
their "employees" or "professional acquaintances." During the confession I gathered they had managed to mention that Frank's appointment still had to pass a committee
where Drummond had some influence and that his ex-
wife had meddled in the matter in a dangerously unpre-
dictable way.

So they hurried over to convince me to let them strike
their little bargain. After all, the bad brown people who
did the killing would be rounded up and caged, and we
could cast ourselves as white knights, upright citizens,
fearless defenders of the public weal.

Probably they were startled when I didn't find their offer
attractive. Maybe I was a misfit. A fury like a lava flow
was still inching through me, as strong as the dread. I
knew that I had to have relief from one or the other, or

I might find myself immobilized between two terrific forces, unable to think, and make a mistake from which I wouldn't recover.

Danny came back to the bar with his broom and a pan full of broken glass. He dumped the fragments in the trash and headed toward the stockroom.

"Do you have a hacksaw in there, Danny, and some good glue?"

He stopped and regarded me quizzically. "Yeah. What for?"

"Just let me borrow them." I came off the stool and followed him into the room.

He stowed away the broom and jerked a thumb at the worktable. "There on the hook to the right. New blades in the top drawer left. Glue in the center cupboard. You wanna work here?"

I nodded, and he shrugged, regarded me for a moment speculatively, and then turned away.

Chapter XXXVIII

The metal shells of the llamas were not hard and not very thick. The alloy was tough rather than brittle, so the figurine could be dented without rupturing. I sawed the heads off just in back of the ear, taking care not to mar the edge of the cut any more than was necessary. The metal teeth pulled out shreds of clear plastic bag and a dribble of white, crystalline powder. I picked up a few grains on the end of my finger and dabbed them on my tongue. They left a bitter taste, not sugar and not salt, and in a few seconds the tip of my tongue was numb.

I looked around for wrapping materials and came across a week-old issue of the *Chronicle*. I opened it to an inside section, spread out two pages and emptied the contents of the llamas there. I covered up a column by Herb Caen, last of the silk-scarf bohemian journalists, wondering what he would think of being buried in ten pounds of cocaine. Probably he would think it was groovy. The other ten pounds I dumped on the financial page. After I had wrapped up the powder, I packed it in a green plastic garbage bag from one of the supply boxes, and with tape and a marking pen I sealed it and wrote "NOT FOR DISPOSAL" on the sides.

In a can in the broom closet I found enough dry floor detergent to fill up the figurines again. After touching up the edge of the cuts carefully with a file, I glued the heads back in place. In poor light, or from a couple of paces away, the new seam was not noticeable. After half an hour of reading week-old news while the glue set, I carefully replaced the llamas in their boxes and placed the garbage bag on a shelf in the broom closet.

Danny helped me load the boxes in my car and repeated his instructions carefully after me.

"If you ain't back in two days, I call this guy Dryer and tell him to come and get the sack you got stashed back there. And I don't answer no questions about you. To nobody."

"That's it, Danny."

"You sure you don't need no other help?" He appeared disappointed.

"I'm sure. I owe you already."

"I told you to fergit it. I meant it."

"Okay. Maybe I'll see you tomorrow."

"I sure as hell hope so." He ambled away, disconsolate as a circus bear on his way from the ring to his cage.

Alice's Fiat was in the driveway, and the hood was still warm. She met me at the door, very pale underneath her makeup. Behind her I could see books mounded on the floor and a scatter of goose feathers.

"Oh, Stella," she said in a very small voice, and hiccuped on a sob. "They shot Baudelaire."

I stood on the bare floor, for the rug had been thrown to one side, and surveyed the apartment. Drawers hung open, their contents scattered. Pictures had been ripped from the walls. The cushions on the couch had been slashed.

"They took an ivory and gold carving set and some jewelry. Nothing worth much except to me. The color TV and the hi-fi weren't touched. I guess they didn't find what they wanted." Alice turned away and her shoulders hunched and shook. "But Baudelaire. He wouldn't have hurt anybody—"

"The bastards." My voice sounded far away and very tired. "The chickenshit bastards."

"Stella, Stella." Alice sat down suddenly on the eviscerated couch. "I don't know. Maybe you ought to turn it over to somebody. What happened to that woman and to Jack Hand . . ." She trailed off, staring at me, not with reproach but with an agonizing querulousness that gave me a sharp spasm in the heart.

"Where is he?"

"On the back porch."

I walked through the mess in the kitchen—pans and cereal boxes and broken bottles—to the porch. Baudelaire had shrunk in death and wore an unpleasant grin. He had been shot behind the ear with a small-caliber slug, and one leg was at an odd angle. *They kicked him,* I thought, *and shot him when he wouldn't stop howling. Nice people.* Probably they used a silencer.

When I returned to the living room, Alice was on her feet, picking up things and looking dully at them.

"Have you called anybody?"

"Eric's on his way. That's all."

I nodded. "Good girl. Bright girl." I felt things giving away inside and reached for her. "Poor girl." We held each other for a long minute or two.

"But what about you?" Alice stepped back, keeping her hands on my shoulders. "Where can you go now?"

"The library?" We laughed together, more than the poor joke warranted. "I don't know. Not here. I can't bring this kind of grief on my friends."

"Hush. We can keep a twenty-four-hour watch if we have to. Eric's not working right now. Don't you have a—" She pointed her index finger and wiggled her thumb.

"They took it away from me. The customs inspectors. For my safety."

"God." She examined my face. "You look terrible. Get in the tub, and I'll make us a chicken sandwich. They didn't destroy everything."

"I want to make a call first. Then I'll take that advice."

I sat on the bare bed frame, my feet on the ripped mattress, and dialed Frank's apartment. On the third ring he answered.

"Hello?"

"Frank? Stella."

There was a considerable pause.

"I've thought about it, as you recommended. My thoughts have been prompted by a little visit somebody paid to Alice's apartment."

"I told you Ugarte's people were not patient or pleasant."

"That's an understatement. So I gather my options are limited. You want to help Ferguson and Drummond save their skins. I suppose they're making it worth your while. In turn they deliver what it takes to bust up the coalition between the radical prison gangs and the Start Over bunch."

"Grossly oversimplified."

"Because we leave out Drummond's part in getting rid of the Chrysler? And the minor fact that Ferguson has been on the take from the beginning?"

"You can't prove that."

"I could come close."

Frank sighed audibly. "You can't seem to grasp a very simple principle, Stella. Those two men went very far out on a limb. They want something in return."

"Like immunity."

"I can't grant them that. I have to review the evidence that's available. Nothing more. And you get evidence by paying for it."

"It stinks, Frank."

"I'm not interested in another brawl." Frank's voice had dropped suddenly in temperature. "I thought you had something to propose."

"All right. Cancel that. I'll bring to you what it is those gentlemen, as you call them, want. I've had it. You work out your little deal. Make yourself important. But if they name you prosecutor and you don't move on Ugarte, I'll go to the state attorney and tell him you withheld evidence."

"Of course I'll move on them. That's what this is all about."

"It's only part of what it's about. But let it go. Where do we meet?"

"You have the llamas with you?"

"That's right."

"The house on Muir Beach. You remember?"

"Sure." It had been a favorite retreat. A secluded bay not far from the city, where redwoods brooded over the sea cliffs.

"How soon can you make it?"

"A little after sundown. Say eight o'clock."

"Fine. And . . . thanks, Stella. You know this is—"

"Save it. I'll see you there."

I hung up and dialed Stump's number. No answer. I let the ring go on and on. The dread reappeared in the pit of my stomach. I was counting on buying a little time. I had hoped to have an ally, some protection, for the next few hours, until I could find a place to hole up and work on the quipus with Consuelo and check out previous TopTorts contest winners. When I had a solid body of evidence, I could make my play. But all that depended on my staying alive.

Eric arrived while I lolled in a tub of steaming water, which for once was not generating any insights, though it soaked away some of my anxiety. His footsteps passed through the kitchen onto the porch, then out the back door. After the garage door had slid shut, I heard the clink of the shovel at work.

He finished burying Baudelaire while I rubbed down and changed into a pair of white painter's pants and a black silk shirt. We met in the living room, now restored to a semblance of normality, and sat down on the rug to sandwiches and cold milk.

"You still look like a junkie," I told Eric. He took it as a cue, hollowing his cheeks and making his eyes furtive. "Very good."

"You look like a nun assigned to a spaceship."

"That's pretty good, too. I only wish I could change galaxies for a few hours."

"Yeah. This is getting serious."

We glanced around the room and fell silent, eating mechanically, almost like prisoners. It had occurred to us that the apartment was probably watched, but none of us felt like bringing it up. I asked Eric about his snooping in the Tenderloin, and he told me frankly that he had stayed only until he got scared.

"I heard Esposito's name a time or two, but nobody trusted me far enough to give any more than a vague outline of the system. Then a couple of guys showed up on each side of me and told me in two or three sentences that I could take a little walk with them to visit somebody special, or I could take a longer walk right out of the district and not come back."

"Monopoly capitalism," I said, and remembered the girl in the old house in Berkeley, who had also been frightened away.

"So now what?" Alice interrupted. She had regained some of her usual impertinence. "You want the numbers for the TopTorts winners?"

"How many did you get?"

"Eight out of thirteen."

"Fantastic. That's going to be a help."

"So what do I do?"

"Call them up. Invent a story for yourself—follow-up study, ad campaign, whatever. Find out, first, if they all came back from Peru to San Francisco; and second, if they all turned over their gift awards to the company for engraving and got them back later at a banquet."

"All right." Alice was jotting notes on her telephone pad. "And now?"

"Now I disappear for a while." I pushed back my plate and glass. "I have some errands."

"Hey, come on." Alice put forth a hand to pull me back to the floor. "You've got to tell us what's going on."

"I don't think that would be smart."

"For God's sake, Stella!" Alice frowned fiercely and tried to rise, but Eric stopped her.

"She's right." He gave me a shrewd look. "You do understand that we'll do whatever you tell us to do?" I nodded.

Alice opened her mouth to protest, and he put a hand

gently over it. "Look, love, those guys on the street had a look at me. If they connect me and you and both of us with Stella, they just might feel they have to get rid of all three." He took his hand away, and Alice closed her mouth. She had the baffled agony in her eyes again.

"That's about it," I said. "We've got to split up for a while. But don't worry. In a couple of hours I think I'll unload several pounds of trouble and earn a breather. I'll get a room in a good safe hotel for the night and call you at the library tomorrow." I went to the closet and took my coat. At the door I hesitated, and Eric got swiftly to his feet.

"I'll cover you," he said quietly. Having stepped to the window, he pulled the blind aside a few inches.

"See you." I gave them the best smile I had and went out into the street, now a canyon of deep shadow below the last flecks of gold light in the topmost windows of concrete cliffs.

Chapter XXXIX

I crossed Golden Gate Park on Arboretum Drive so that I could scan the lighter traffic for any car that might be tailing me. After a sharp turn on the far side of a grove of trees I swung into a side road and doused the engine and lights. For ten minutes only an occasional car passed, and none of them looked like a hunter, so I eased back onto the main road and followed it to Highway 101. From there it was a straight shot across the bridge to the Coast Highway turnoff in Mill Valley.

There was enough light in the sky to etch sharply the great pylons and graceful swoop of the suspension cables. One part of my mind drifted over memories: hiking on the walkway Sunday mornings, the glittering bay far below, ruffled by a boisterous wind. Or driving toward the city for an evening, when a dazzling sea of fog swirled just below the deck.

Perfect days, I had once thought. Glory in the flower, splendor in the grass. Laughter, sun, wine, love. We hadn't believed those old poets who warned that every bloom withers; we'd thought it would go on forever. Forever turned out to be twenty-seven months and fourteen days.

The other part of my mind was trying to deal with the dread, now tinged with self-disgust. I clearly had had a severe case of bad judgment, possibly a fatal case. It had been very stupid to try smuggling the .32 through customs. Maybe it was equally stupid to rely on Stump. Where had he gone? Perhaps to take Consuelo to the station and book her. That would be another clear example of bad judgment. And I had gone back to the old habit of depending on Frank, then discovering I couldn't stand it and had to lie to him or to myself.

Here I was, on the same road to the beach house, stringing him along in order to buy a little time, enough to get a really good grip on the rug before I jerked. Tough realism could sometimes appear as craven duplicity. The eye of the beholder. I wondered how an objective observer would size it up. *This grim lady driving down a dark lane toward a lonely beach house with twenty pounds of floor detergent strapped to her tail is (a) a coward, (b) crazy, (c) stupid, or (d) a thrill seeker.* You have thirty seconds to answer.

Frank's Mercedes was tucked into the carport, and there was a yellow square of light in the house. I noticed the patio was mounded with dead needles from the trees. He hadn't been using the retreat much. There were three acres of hillside around the house, and I hadn't seen any lights from nearby cottages on my way down the lane.

I climbed out of the Porsche, leaving its door ajar. For a few moments I listened to the whine of cars passing on the highway, that sound fading in and out of the soft crash of surf below. Then, as I wrestled the two packages from the back seat, a crack of light widened suddenly in the dark wall of the house. "Stella?" Frank's silhouette brought up an arm to shade his eyes.

"Here." I came up the walk, and he hurried to meet me and take one of the packages.

We set them on the floor in the middle of the room. I opened one quickly and held up the llama, one hand around the neck. The gold body shone dully in the lamplight.

"Well." Frank's face took on a look I knew very well, a mingling of triumph and renewed voracity. "Well. So." He took two paces, turned and came back, ran a finger over the metal surfaces. "It isn't a very big package for a million, is it?"

"It worked."

"Indeed. I find it brilliant."

"Who was the brilliant one, Frank? The couple of punks new to the firm?" I slid the figurine back in its box and flipped down the lid.

A shadow passed over his face and was gone. "We'll find out," he said firmly.

"We already know. What I haven't figured out is how you expect to get this stuff back on the street." I shrugged off my coat and threw it on one of the leather cushions before the fireplace.

"Let's not talk shop all night." He moved to the three-foot redwood plank that served as a bar. "I'll mix you a drink. A little celebration."

"I'm not in the mood." I walked to the glass doors opening onto the deck that hung over the sea. A few stars pinpricked the sky. I heard him go on with the ice and glasses anyway.

"Stella, you have a very persistent temperament. It's an advantage. A tremendous advantage. But you can over-look some things that way."

"What have I overlooked?" I watched his ghost in the door, moving toward me through the stars. When I turned, he put the glass in my hand and patted my arm lightly.

"Part of cracking a case like this is maintaining a ne-gotiable position. I don't like the idea of collaborating with Ferguson, but it will allow us to trap the worst elements in this business—the real scum—in one lightning maneu-ver."

"Well. A lightning maneuver. You have the language down, I see. The reporters will be able to take it verba-tim."

His companionable smile began to erode. "You think it's just the old egotism, eh?"

"That's right." I walked to the fireplace and placed the drink on the mantel. "And I'm still curious about how this stuff gets from me to the distributors without arousing suspicion."

"You called up Zwicky, tried to arrange a blackmail.

He pretended to go along and tricked you to recover the goods. Then it gets complicated. He—"

"Let me guess. Badly shaken, still protecting the family name, he turns to the very employees whom he has begun to suspect of manipulating him, asks them to take the awful dope off his hands. They are delighted. To the state attorney you say that Zwicky came to you first, then faked his panic to put the goods back into circulation and set the trap."

Frank sipped his drink. "More or less."

"Which is the true version, Frank?"

He grimaced in irritation. "That's not even clear. What does it matter, Stella? Zwicky is a very devious man. Unfortunately not very strong. But at this point he is cooperating."

"When did you talk to him last?"

"This afternoon about one o'clock."

A little less than an hour before we invaded the warehouse and took the mantas. I smiled. "Some of those treacherous employees may be more treacherous than he counted on."

Frank's glass stopped on its way to his mouth. "What do you mean?"

"You know what a quipus is?"

He shook his head.

I reached for my bag and took out the shawl I had brought from Lima. "This—" I began.

"Oh, that." Frank smiled. "Ferguson asked me about that. I didn't know he was a collector. I told him the customs inspectors caught you with a gun and some sort of tapestry, but—"

"He called?" I dropped the shawl. "When?"

"Right after you did. I let him know you had begun to talk sensibly and would—"

"Would meet you here tonight to deliver the big golden prizes. And might have the shawl, too, since he couldn't find it at Alice's. Oh, Frank!" Even as I reached for my coat, I heard the tires crunching on gravel. They had switched off their lights and killed the engine in order to coast silently down the driveway.

"What—"

I heard the car doors clunk shut and then quick footsteps on the walkway. I glanced around the room, but I already knew the only other exit led to the deck jutting over a sixty-foot drop to the ocean.

Frank lunged for the front door, but it had opened by the time he got there. He stopped and then took a step backward. Manuel filled the entrance. In his hand was an automatic with a long, ventilated snout. Behind him was a sallow-faced young man dressed in the light green coveralls of a mechanic or furniture mover.

"See here—" Frank raised one hand in a gesture of restraint. Manuel slapped him on the jaw with the barrel of the automatic. It wasn't a hard blow, but it left an ugly welt.

"Shut your fuckin' mouth and lie down. On your face. Now." He drew back the gun again, and Frank went down, first to his knees and then full length. Manuel stepped swiftly across the room to the cardboard boxes and flipped open the lids.

"Yeah," he breathed, and then laughed. "Yeah. They're here." He saw the shawl then and scooped it up. "Everything."

He walked back to Frank and prodded him in the back. "Keys. Car keys. Move real slow."

Frank's hand edged along the rug, crept into his pocket, and came out with a key ring. Manuel snatched it and tossed it and the shawl to the other man. "In the trunk." The man in coveralls picked up the boxes and trudged out with them. He looked like any workman at his job, except for his junkie's pallor.

Manuel turned his mad goat's eyes on me, grinning. "Well, well, well." He stepped closer. He was quick on his feet, almost mincing. "The survey lady. How you doin', survey lady? You still goin' around pokin' your nose in things, I see. That's too bad. A foxy thing like you got in a lotta trouble. Oh-h-h, man." He giggled, and with the snout of the silencer he traced along my collarbone to an earlobe. The metal was like a tiny, racing chill, and I could smell oil and burned powder. "But you done us a big favor, and we're gonna reward you. Take you on a little ride. In the country." His pupils were huge black pits in the yellowed eyeballs. "How about that?"

"No, thanks. I've been feeling poorly." I moved around him and reached for my coat on the couch.

"Ah-ah." He rapped the silencer across my knuckles lightly. "Now now."

"You've got what you came for. What's the problem?" I did my best to generate a look of honest amazement. "So we lose. You win. So?"

Manuel laughed, his mouth a very wide pink cave fenced with white teeth. "You crack me up, survey lady. Full of shit, but you crack me up. You got one thing right. We win. And we gonna drink to that." He went to the bar, picked up the bottle of Scotch, and took the cap off with his teeth. Then he walked to where Frank lay on the rug and jabbed a toe into his ribs.

"All right. Up."

Frank rolled over and got to his knees. With his foot Manuel shoved him back to a sitting position.

"That's far enough. Now drink." He tilted the bottle, and a little of the whiskey dribbled out over Frank's head and shoulders. *"Drink."* He nudged with his toe, and Frank lifted his head and opened his mouth. The whiskey came in spurts with a loud gurgle, splashing down his face. Frank tried to say something and gagged. *"Drink,* motherfucker." The toe shot out again, and Frank grunted; then his throat convulsed, and he swallowed until the whiskey welled over his lips and soaked the front of his shirt. Manuel righted the bottle just enough to cut off the stream.

"I . . . can't . . ." Frank choked, rubbing at his face with his wrists.

Manuel kicked him hard under the arm, and Frank

retched. A trickle of fluid ran from one corner of his mouth.

"You drink, or I jam this whole fifth down your throat." Manuel held out the bottle, and Frank took it and swallowed once. "More." He managed two more gulps and then jerked away, his lips compressed to keep the stuff from coming back up.

"That's better." Manuel returned to the bar and picked up a glass, which he slid over the snout of the gun. Then he came to me, picking the bottle out of Frank's grasp with his free hand.

"The survey lady gets a glass," he said. The tone was soft, intimate, menacing. The other man had come back into the room and leaned now against the bar.

"Come on, man," he said. "Let's not fuck around."

"We got time. Ain't we got time, survey lady?" He waved the gun in front of my face, the glass clinking on it. "Have a drink. You ain't gonna refuse one, like your old man there, are you?"

"Stella," I said. "My name is Stella, and that isn't my old man." I picked off the glass and held it ready, keeping my eyes on his leering face, bisected by the line of the gun barrel.

"You hear that, Buddy? We got time." He laughed and poured. "Time for Stella. Too bad you picked this fuckoff, Stella. You got on the wrong end of this deal. Drink up."

He waited, fingers locked around the bottle, rising a little on his toes. I could see the tip of tongue edging between his teeth. Anticipation. He wanted me to refuse.

"Cheers." I tossed off the Scotch, and tried to keep the raw heat of it from flaring into my face.

"*Yeah.*" Manuel filled the glass again. "One for the win, two for the show. Hit it."

The second shot went down more easily.

"Hey, hey." Manuel dashed the glass full to overflowing. The whiskey ran along the back of my hand, and I saw him smile.

I drank most of it, then poured the rest on my pants

at the thigh. "That ought to do it. If there's anything left, they'll think we were drinking. Blood samples will confirm it." I felt as if a blast furnace were going under my ribs, the alcohol turning my insides to liquid fire. "Though someone might remember what happened to Rosa. They might get curious."

"You're real smart. Too smart. That's your trouble." He moved close to me again, his smile gone, his breathing more rapid. "I'd like to—"

"Man, come *on!*" Buddy came away from the bar and knotted a fist into one sleeve of Frank's shirt.

"Where are you taking us?" Frank gasped. "Wha's this all about?" His eyes rolled slowly in his head, back at the man behind him, then across the room to us. He focused on me, and a frown congealed on his face. "Stella. Stella, how did they—"

"Ferguson changed his mind," I said. The room rocked slightly under me, and I widened my stance a little. "You shouldn't have let him know until you had the stuff safe. Now here we are all together—the witness, the prosecutor, and the evidence—and that negotiable position you talked about—"

"What you mean, 'changed his mind'?" Manuel stepped between us.

"You didn't know? One of your bossmen was going to sell you out. Blow Ugarte and Start Over right out of the game."

Manuel's eyes widened, then narrowed. "Bullshit."

Buddy jerked Frank to one knee. "Yeah, bullshit," he said. "They just thought it up between themselves."

"He's too drunk to think. How do you suppose Ferguson knew we were meeting here tonight?"

Manuel grinned, confident again. "Little old bird told him."

"Zwicky, you mean." It was my turn to laugh.

"What's so funny about that?" Manuel's eyes were yellow slits again, with a chip of flint in the middle.

"Maybe you're too dumb. That's your problem."

"You—" He had drawn back the automatic, but after a moment he lowered it again. "It's gonna be fun with you," he said. The tongue tip protruded again. "Real fun."

"It could have been real fun for me," I said, fighting to keep the room from tilting. "Ferguson and Drummond were all set to squeal, until they found out that we would both be here tonight and that their records had been stolen. So they concocted the story that I tried to blackmail Zwicky, and he played along, agreeing to meet me here. You were going to show up instead and take care of me and the goods."

There was a pause. Manuel and Buddy traded a look. Then Manuel made a nasty noise with his lips. "Too smart. It's gotta be bullshit. Why they gonna sell us out? That's crazy."

"Crazy like a fox. They protected themselves all the way through. Zwicky could play dumb, say he never knew what was going on. And he really didn't know about the shawls. Caswell was in Peru and ready to slip over the border anytime. Ferguson planned to lay the rap on a couple of guys in his company, maybe giving them the chance to turn state's evidence, too. The deal was to let you rip off the coke from us, then bust you for selling it. All the way up to Ugarte."

"Ugarte, shit." Manuel sneered. "All the way up to *me.*"

Darkness was moving in at the edge of my vision. I made an effort to grasp Manuel's meaning. The puppets and the puppeteers changed places.

Chapter XL

"So it's you," I said. "You."

"That's right, baby. Me." Manuel grinned wide again and did his crouching, obscene dance. "And nobody is gonna bust me. Especially no chick."

"Like Rosa?"

"Yeah, like Rosa."

"We take a drive. All full of whiskey. Like Rosa."

"You got it, baby. This time I get to watch."

Buddy pulled Frank to his feet and steered him toward the door. "Come on, goddamn it! Let's move!"

Manuel put the end of the gun behind my ear and nudged. "You heard the man."

"Listen," I whispered, "I did you a favor. It's true Ferguson and Drummond tried to double-cross you. They—"

"Bullshit."

The silencer tapped, ringing against my skull. I walked in front of him, weaving now as the floor rose and fell like the deck of a ship beneath me. "No. Not bullshit. Not bullshit." The words felt thick and huge in my mouth. I stopped, and the gun muzzle jabbed into my ribs.

"Hey, I need somebody." I giggled and lurched into the gun. "He's no good. He's a punk." I made a motion like swatting a fly toward Frank, who was staggering beside Buddy down the walkway. "C'mon, *amigo. Por favor.*"

Manuel laughed and snaked an arm around me. He slid his fingers inside the band of my pants and with the tip of the silencer tilted up my chin. "Too bad you got on the wrong side. Too bad. Nice piece of white meat like you." The hand left my pants and hooked up under my breast.

I moaned a little. He caught the nipple between his thumb and forefinger and rubbed, then pinched. I moaned louder, gave a sob, and nuzzled at his neck.

Buddy waited at the wheel of the Mercedes, both doors open. Frank was slumped on the seat beside him. "Man, we been here too long. Let's do the deal and get the fuck out." He turned the key, and the engine ground, then caught.

"Cool it. We got all the time we need. Don't we, baby?" He pulled me to him and jammed his wide, hard mouth over mine. Then he shoved me into the back seat, climbed in beside me, and swung the door closed.

"Shit, man, this makes me nervous. This ain't no time to—"

"I said, cool it, motherfucker."

"Hey," I said. "You lef' me. 'nother punk. Whassa matter with you?" I fell over on the seat and dredged up some more sobs. Manuel jerked me erect again. The automatic was still in his hand.

Buddy laughed. "She's loaded, man. And he's fuckin' out cold. This is gonna be tube city."

"Hey," I said. "Be nice. Nice guy. You're not kinna guy hurt me, are you?" I leaned across the front seat and blew in his ear.

"Sure, baby."

"It's you. You you you. Yo-o-u y-o-o-u yo-o-u, 'm in love 'th yo-o-u yo-o-u yo-o-u . . ." I put my arms around Manuel's neck.

Manuel laughed. His hand went back down inside the pants. We were climbing, swaying on curves, the tires yelping. A car passed in a flash of headlights. The Coast Highway, north toward Bodega Bay, winding above sheer cliffs.

"We're close," Buddy said softly. "The other car's at the next turnout. But we got somebody behind us."

I put my tongue in Manuel's ear. His breathing changed.

"You want it, baby. You want it one more time, yeah?" he crooned. I could feel the cold ingot of the automatic on my back.

"Oh, yeah, you you you . . ."

The Mercedes slowed, then swerved. Manuel cursed softly. I heard gravel under the wheels, then the crank of the emergency brake. The car tilted all at once downward and stopped.

Buddy shut off the motor, and for a moment I could hear the dull pound and sigh of the surf over rocks.

"All right, man. She's set. She'll coast right off from here. Let's get the shit out of the back and go, for Christ's sake." I heard Buddy's door open.

"Hold it, man. I got some business first."

"Jesus, Manuel. I ain't gonna—"

"I told you once, motherfucker, to cool it." His voice had a tremor of danger in it.

"Hey, whassa deal? You mus' be a punk, too."

He opened the door and jerked me outside. The black sky yawned overhead, scattered with stars. We were at a turnout on the highway where a dirt road dipped sharply down, cutting across an almost sheer bluff. The Mercedes was parked on a slant, pointing across the dirt road toward its outside shoulder. Far below that shoulder were the rocks and the sea.

"Cut the lights," Manuel said. Behind us, partially screening us from the highway, was Gutierez's Mustang. "What happened to the car you said was following?"

"Must have turned off." Buddy sounded anxious. He snapped off the headlights. "Make it quick, man."

Manuel pulled me to the rear of the car. His fingers digging under my collarbone sent hot wires of pain through me. His face was only a clot of darkness in a greater darkness, but I knew his mood had changed. His breathing came fast and through his teeth.

"You call me a punk, bitch?"

The fingers tightened, and I cried out.

"You want it now, don't you? Right now. Before you burn."

The wires glowed white, all of them leading to an explosion of agony in my brain. He jammed downward, and I dropped to my knees against the car bumper.

"Get down on it, bitch," he snarled, and laid the silencer across my cheek. "You want it."

"You you you," I whispered. Looming above me, he threw back his head and laughed until I could see a faint sheen of starlight on his brow and wet lips. I fumbled at his zipper, giving it a half turn and pulling on one side until it jammed.

"I can't. It's stuck," I moaned.

He did what a man has to do with a jammed fly in an urgent situation. He cursed, and then, in order to hold his waistband with one hand while he jiggled the zipper with the other, he put the gun aside on the fender.

The fly came open, and I felt both his hands knot in my hair. He tilted his head, eyes closed. A low laugh started from his belly and then stopped in his throat.

The mouth he felt on his manhood was very cold and very small. His eyes opened, widened suddenly, and he made an odd sound, like a waking baby. His hand flopped like a beached fish across the bare fender.

"Step back—quietly—and don't say anything more, or I'll blow it right off. The pun is intended." I kept the gun trained on him as he swayed and bent a little at the waist, moving like a crab.

"Hey, Manuel." I heard Buddy's door open. "Listen, man, we got to get out of here. This bastard is coming to."

I gestured with the gun, and Manuel spoke, his voice skating up a scale of terror. "Don't, don't get out. Man, stay there. . . ."

"What is this?" I saw a silhouette rise above the car door, and Buddy peered toward us.

"Nothin', man. Go back. *Go back!*"

"What the hell—where's the chick?" He was moving now, feet squeaking on the gravel. "What's she—" He saw me and then the gun swinging around. He froze, except for one hand that scuttled over his hip and into a pocket. Before the hand could emerge again, I pulled the trigger and there was a sound, not loud but definite: *Thwop.*

Buddy took another step, but something went wrong with it, and he sat down, legs splayed. His hand was out, gripping a stubby revolver.

Thwop. The legs kicked, and he appeared to twist suddenly, as if struck on the back by some practical joker. His revolver started going off in loud, echoing blasts. I dropped to the ground and rolled. A foot smashed into my side, and I gasped. Manuel was over me, swinging clawed hands to grab at the gun. The blasts went on. I heard glass exploding, gravel spraying against the hubcaps, then a solid thump. Manuel stumbled over me. He didn't get up but began to crawl toward Buddy. They were not more than four feet apart.

"Mother . . ." Manuel began, but the revolver flicked a tongue of fire, and the explosion drowned him out. Manuel stretched out, slowly and almost luxuriously, on his stomach. Buddy fell over on his back and fired once more into the starry heaven above him.

In the tremendous silence that followed I lay motionless on the gravel. I was aware of the sound of my own breathing, the sea thudding on the cliff, and Frank's moaning and murmuring. Then I heard footsteps, someone sprinting along the shoulder of the highway. I pushed myself to one knee and swung up the gun, the long barrel wobbling like a compass needle.

"Drop it!" Over the roof of the Mustang I saw a head and an arm. The head was round, itself like a bullet. I heard the click of small metal parts falling into position. "Drop the gun."

I lowered the barrel slowly. "Stump?"

"Right. Now put down the gun."

I placed it on the ground and stood up. My body still felt rubbery with the liquor, but my head was clear and empty as the night. I watched the squat figure detach itself from the shadow of the car and approach. A few feet away from me he stopped, the black chunk of metal still in his hand.

"You're not very friendly. But I'm glad to see you."

"You were pretty friendly to these guys, before you blew them away."

"Just one. Manuel got it from his buddy there. How did you get here?"

"I've been tagging you around, since you left the Jolly Roger. Real interesting."

I thought for a moment, then laughed. It wasn't my usual laugh, but something like ice breaking. "Yeah. You saw us meet these guys, carry out the goods, and drive off merrily into the evening. Well, you could get the wrong idea."

"Could I?"

"Definitely. They brought us here to drive us off this cliff. They forced liquor down us so we'd have alcohol in the blood. If any blood was left."

"You looked pretty chummy on your way out."

"I'm not proud of it. I had to do something to get close to the gun. They roughed us up. Go look at Frank's face."

He walked over to Manuel and Buddy, probed under their clothes with one hand, feeling for vital signs. Manuel emitted a wet hiccup.

"Somebody got roughed up, for damn sure." Stump went around to the passenger door, opened it, and glanced at Frank.

"Where are we?" Frank swung his feet out onto the gravel. "Stella? Where's Stella?"

"I'm here, Frank."

"Heard shots. Somebody . . . who's here? Who're you?" He stared at the gun in Stump's hand and groaned.

"Police." Stump thought a moment, then turned to me. "What were you gonna do next? With the coke."

"There isn't any coke. It's floor detergent."

He didn't say anything, only reached across Frank and took the keys from the ignition. He threw them to me.

"Open it."

I raised the trunk lid and removed one of the boxes. When I had the llama in my hands, I beckoned to Stump.

"You didn't trust me? Even after I delivered Consuelo?"

"Nope. You said you could make the delivery. I wasn't gonna let you think about a million bucks' worth of snow all afternoon. I took the chick home and left her with my wife."

"How come nobody answered the phone?"

"I told them not to. Unless it rang a certain number of times. In case I had to reach them. So what is this thing?" He tapped the llama with his gun barrel.

"It's what they use to ship the stuff. It's an award they present to nice old couples who win the TopTorts contest. Nice old couples always win—they send in their pictures as part of the competition—and they always go to Peru. They always come back with something they don't know they have. Like you told me, an inspector can't tune into them because they don't know they're carrying the stuff."

"So what's in there?"

I rapped the figurine sharply on the bumper, and the head snapped off neatly at the cut. I tilted the headless beast, and the coarse, oily grains ran out. Stump caught a few in his palm and sniffed.

"Floor detergent, like I said."

"Goddamn." Stump shoved the revolver in his coat pocket. He laughed, almost a growl. "The dumb bastards. They got blown away for nothing. Where's the real thing?"

"At the Jolly Roger. What time is it?"

Stump frowned at his watch in the starlight, but before he could answer, I heard a siren wailing around a curve, then fading behind a hill. "I called 'em," Stump said matter-of-factly. "There's an all-points out on this car. It's nine thirty."

"We could perhaps make the final speeches at a banquet in the city."

Stump didn't speak. He waited. He was getting to know me.

"You know who Clarence Ferguson is?"

"Yeah. A big fish in city politics. Your ex-old man's been playing around with him. What's the deal?"

"He and Drummond and Ugarte and Zwicky—Consuelo's boss—are all part of this thing. But Ferguson is the big shark. He's handing out duplicates of these awards to a couple from Kansas tonight at the Saint Francis. He thinks I've been taken care of. I'd like to show up—with you—to ask him a few questions. After we go by Danny's bar and pick up the coke."

"You think we've got enough on him?"

"We?"

I couldn't see him smile, but I could hear it in his voice. "Yeah. We. I was wrong. Sorry."

"It's all right. If you hadn't been the suspicious type, I'd be fish food right now."

"What about . . . me?" Frank was leaning against the Mercedes, one hand on his head. The siren was loud now, and I could see the winking red roof lights, a string of them snaking toward us. "Stella, we can't be here. The police . . ."

"Too late, Frank. You're going to have to go back to being a lawyer. And your first job will be explaining yourself. I don't envy you the job."

"Christ. Oh, Christ." Frank staggered along the car. "Stella, *Stella!*"

"So shall we go?" I saw the first patrol car come around the curve, the siren swallowing itself in a sudden gulp.

"Yeah. I'll line things out for the sergeant quick. They can shovel these bastards up and start taking their measurements. And get him sober. Oh, yeah. You're in my custody. The car's parked about two hundred yards over the rise. It's gonna be a long night."

"I could use a stroll. I'll wait for you in the car."

"*Stella!*"

"Stay put, friend." Stump's voice was edged with distaste.

I walked away, along the edge of the highway. Behind me I heard the cars skidding in the gravel, doors snapping open, and the sharp clatter of metal. The breeze was fresh and salty. I drank it in and looked into the vast sky full of glittering needles.

"STELLA-A-A-A!"

I smiled, tightly and to myself. *Even if you were Marlon Brando I wouldn't go back.* My legs stretched, strengthening against the rising earth. It was good, so good, to walk away.